The Seven Stars
Book I of The SenZar Evolution
Todd King
(Revision 1.04 – September 23, 2021)

I0639569

PREFACE

I created the original version of *The Saga of the Seven Stars* in the early 1990s as a seven book series. It went through my literary agent, then a large publishing house, then through a bartering process in which the first three novels were condensed into a single novel to please the publishers, because they had recently lost a six-figure advance on another unknown author whose first book of a proposed seven book series had bombed. I then discovered what happens when an author's original seven book series gets whittled down to some fraction of its original number and the agent makes less money: The agent prioritizes his stable of established authors to bankroll his business, demotes the neophyte to the lowest tier of his business totem, and slow-walks anything dealing with the unpublished author.

Thus, with no hard feelings, I decided to shape my fate myself. The Brüne, Joseph Giacone, and I formed Nova Eth Publishing, Inc., and it was there that we published the condensed version of *The Saga of the Seven Stars*, which was called *The Seven Stars, Book I of the Saga of the Seven Stars*. Nova Eth simultaneously published the *SenZar* role-playing game and its ancillary products, in multiple trade paperbacks, electronic format books, and CD-ROMs, selling them in 14 countries. The *SenZar* role-playing game system provided not only a vehicle for us to share our unique game with everyone, but also as a way for us to define the characters and worlds in my novels. The *VoidSpawn* novel soon followed. But we never expanded the single, condensed book back into its original three-book format, or seven book series, because we had focused our energy upon the game itself, continually expanding it into a true game world.

Now that David Newton and I have joined forces to create Anshadar LLC, and have written and published two books in *The EarthZero Evolution*–*The Lightbringer's Sigil* and *The Anshadar Effect*– it seemed to be a good time to resurrect my older, original novels, expand them to their original states, and publish the entire series.

We decided, after reviewing the source material, that we would maintain its Terran Timeline, which is set in the pre-Millennium, early 1990s. No smart phones, no true Internet to speak of, and a return to what, even now in 2021, most of us would call "retro" times. So, in that respect, it's a bit refreshing to cast one's imagination and memory back into those days.

David and I implemented this new Anshadar LLC story arc as *The SenZar Evolution*. *The Seven Stars – Book I of The SenZar Evolution* is first up. Then, the remainder of the original, unpublished series will come to life. Because both share the same Metaverse, *The SenZar Evolution* will parallel, and sometimes interact with, *The EarthZero Evolution*. This synergy affords us a unique opportunity to cross creative streams, and then bind them together in new and unexpected ways.

And, yes, if you're of the discerning sort, you'll pick up on some themes, characters, and scenarios that we created in *SenZar* which have made it into the public domain, pop culture, and Zeitgeist since the early 1990s. We did not edit out, augment, or bring up-to-date the original content, and you might be shocked to see what we have shaped on Terra. In the preface of the *SenZar* sourcebook, we predicted that we were going to shape the face of gaming, and we certainly did. Both on the tabletop, and in the virtual world. And, yes, the Trump comment in Book II is original, from the early 1990s. Prescient, as always.

In this first book of *The SenZar Evolution*, we witness the death and rebirth of the Seven Stars, the legendary heroes of SenZar who selflessly served the Cause. We witness their struggle to defeat an ancient evil from SenZar who now threatens the world of their second birth, Earth, while they wrestle with synergizing their old lives with their new ones. We witness the birth of new, immortal Anshadar to counter the menace of the Shadar, as the Dragon's Game begins anew. And, ultimately, we shall witness the shockwaves that arise and resonate throughout the Metaverse when the heroes inflict their immortal wrath upon those who threaten their worlds.

Enjoy the trip, my fellow travelers. It's a doozy.

INTRODUCTION
WHO ARE THE SEVEN STARS?

Mad Sam Sprunge, Luckster, Master Rogue, and living creation of Maelstromm the Mad. Tal'N Hawkwind, Master of Shy'R, and Prince of Petra. Rhiannazaar, the four-armed Azaar warrior, bearer of Tark. Guthal Dirge, proud Khazak and forsaken heir to the throne of the Kaza-Ka. Silverdancer, daughter of the Thin Man, Mistress of Assassins, wielder of the Soulsword. Sigil Talisman, Archimage of Krystallmyst and loyal servant of the Dragon. Tatternorn VoidSpawn, Spellsinger and living embodiment of the Pact of the Impossible Blade, Skurge.

The greatest champions of SenZar who do what they do best: Kill in the name of the Cause. In final battle with Lord Valthrustra on SenZar, they die while in the midst of *The Dragon's Breath*, only to have their screaming souls blasted through the Dream Barrier to be reborn on Terra at behest of the Dragon. In this new world they must integrate their new Terran souls with their SenZar souls in order to become realized as Anshadar, and thus to seek out and destroy Lord Valthrustra, who has designs of conquering the magick-blind world of Terra and its sleeping Dragon in order to achieve his ultimate destiny of becoming All That All Which Is, and All That All Which Binds.

Too bad the Stars aren't exactly the "heroes" that the legends of SenZar described. They've grown not only in power, but also in hatred as well. The Dragon's Game will never be the same again. Death can do that to a soul.

"A little while, a moment of rest upon the wind, and another woman shall bear me. Farewell to you and the youth I have spent with you. It was but yesterday we met in a dream. You have sung to me in my aloneness, and I of your longings have built a tower in the sky. But now our sleep has fled and our dream is over, and it is no longer dawn."

Kahlil Gibran —"The Prophet"

PROLOGUE

Howling like a blood-crazed dire wolf, Tatternorn VoidSpawn grasped the Impossible Blade, Skurge, in two hands and flicked it to within a gnat's hair of Sigil Talisman's slender neck. Writhing fractal runes marked its vile Shadar steel length, pulsing like a hateful heartbeat. Around, between, and among the two and their five companions, the spent esoteric energies of Talisman's hastily woven *Space Warp* flickered through the blackened gloom surrounding them, tickling their senses with garbled perception.

"Smirking Starin fool!" Tatternorn growled, his furious gaze fully focused on the tall Starin, who leaned heavily into his purple Krystallstaff. Tatternorn's leather boots crunched improbably into the basalt floor beneath them as he snarled, "Once again, you steal my kills and deprive me of my rightful glory!"

An ethereal silver blade lightly touched the terminus of Skurge, and Samantha Silverdancer eased herself between the two.

"Tat," she said, seeking his eyes, "get yourself together. Your other is in ascendence. We need *you*, not *him*."

Sigil continued staring at Tatternorn, his purple, almond-shaped eyes unblinking. Around them, the rest of the Seven Stars shifted uneasily. They wondered, yet again, if they were going to have to act to defend the Starin wizard against the increasingly hostile aggressions of their possessed, and thrice-damned, friend. Skurge, the ancient Shadar Lord who possessed his soul through the Pact of the Impossible Blade, had indeed been in ascendence as of late, as duly noted by the Silverdancer. The evil of Lord Valthrustra was now rampant over SenZar. Most certainly, this magnified the VoidSpawn's terrible burden even moreso than ever before. Here, now, so close to the End.

Rhiannazaar, the towering four-armed Azaar, added the mass of his mojo-mazumba, Tark, to Silverdancer's Soulsword, where it touched Skurge.

"Yo, mon," Rhiannazaar rumbled, his sharply accented Zengaran lilting, "be cool. C'mon back, Tat. We need you here, now."

"Aww, come on, Tat!" Mad Sam Sprunge, Master Rogue of the Forever City, Zengara, pleaded. "Stop being a dolt. We got what we needed, and Sigil got us out of the temple just in time. There's no way we could have stayed in one piece with all those mortogolems that Lord Valthrustra ported on top of us!"

"*I* could have stayed in one piece, prattling little half-man!" Tatternorn replied, his gaze still locked on Sigil. "I could have destroyed them all! The might of the Shadar Lords flows through my soul!"

Guthal Dirge, the Khazak heir to the throne of the Kaza-Ka, and Tal'N Hawkwind, outcast Prince of Petra, the remainder of the Seven Stars, chose to hold their silence. Yet, the Axe of Thrumble rested lightly in Guthal's armored gauntlets, even as the twin katanas, Warhawk's Avenging Talons, rested in Tal'N's own unarmored hands.

"Tatternorn?" Sigil finally said, breaking his silence while rising to his full height. "The Temple of Skardesh Par Pak gave us the final clue we needed in order to find Lord Valthrustra. Even though you ended the High Priest Marthramalax before we could extract the information from him, the warp woven by Valthrustra afforded me the opportunity to divine its origin. There was no need to engage in combat after that point."

"Yeah, dummy!" Mad Sam teased, looking up at Tatternorn, who was now shaking his head from side to side. "Don't you remember anything? You been smokin' more of Zaar's lotus when no one was looking?" At this, Rhiannazaar grunted something choice and nasty in his native Azaar.

"He's still going blank when Skurge arises," Silverdancer said evenly, banishing her ethereal blade, returning its material hilt to her over-the-shoulder black moonlight scabbard. She gave Zaar a quick nod. The massively thewed Azaar returned his blade to a rest position before him. Tark's warmly glowing, fiery runes cast an eerie sheen upon his deep blue skin. Guthal and Tal'N, satisfied, assumed a tight forward and a slightly looser flank group configuration, respectively.

Tat stopped shaking his head. His bright blue eyes softly shimmered now with eldritch, electric blue sparks.

"He's back," Mad Sam said. "Good. Glad you're back. Loon!" he tittered, abruptly and most deftly back-pedaling behind Zaar.

"What happened?" Tat asked, his voice again his own, mellifluous and charming. Lowering Skurge, its wicked Shadar steel length now not quite so energetic, he looked sheepishly at Sigil. "Sorry about that," he apologized, to which the taciturn Starin politely nodded. "Where are we now? Where's Lord V? We've got to hurry, or he's... he's..." he finished, not quite remembering what Lord Valthrustra was supposed to be doing.

We are going to fulfill the Pact of the Impossible Blade! Skurge brayed like a mad jackass in Tatternorn's psyche. *All of your accursed souls will then be enslaved to empower his soul batteries. The world of SenZar he shall first annihilate, then forge anew! That's what he's going to do, you preening, out of tune bard!*

"Tatternorn!" Silverdancer urged him. "We're in DruusDome. That's where Sigil warped us after he traced the incoming warp. Lord Valthrustra is here. He's going to try to merge himself with the Dragon, in order to end everything, then create it again in his own twisted image. The Shadar will rule the cosmos once again. That's what we're here for, Tat. To stop him from performing such an abhorrent abomination. To stop him from ending our world. This is it, Tat. It is truly, one way or another, the End of All Things."

His mind returning, Tat breathed deeply, nodded twice, then said, "Okay. I'm back. Thanks, guys." He paused for three seconds, gazing swiftly to and fro. The clinging, shadowy darkness limited normal mortal visibility to just a matter of a few strides. However, being soulbound to an ancient immortal did have its benefits, one of which was immortal-level perception. He inclined his head to the left. "And that's where the dome itself is. A few hundred strides yonder," he motioned with Skurge as he began to rapidly walk across the cold basalt, his companions falling in around him in a tactical group configuration, "and we'll hit the dome, inside which is the Black Point Pool, or, as the Shadar used to call it in Druus, '*Dhakvhülsh-Zhyl'zz*,' or 'Dark Fountain of Souls.' Commonly known as the gateway to the Dark Earth Mother, Chthon. The Dark Womb, for real."

"Yep, the scholarly scribe is back," Guthal snorted, his thick Khazak accent rolling the phonemes of the words around. "Silly, spellsinging bard. You do recall that my people were here, in this very same place, thousands of years before the Shadar, right? Don't pay us short shrift."

"Wouldn't dream of it, my friend," Tat admitted truthfully. "Yep, the Khazaks were here first. Most of the city of DruusDome itself was crafted by your ancient ancestors. If it weren't so unusually foggy down here right now, I could show you a few of their original structures. But, speaking of both short and shrift, take point and War Tank, Guthal. You're best armored, you have gloom sight, so you can see better than most of us down here, and you're probably the most skilled among us in this underground environment."

"Correct, and got it," Guthal replied gruffly, his squat armored legs pumping as he sped up to assume point. Simultaneously, Tal'N and Silverdancer tightened their flank stances, moving a step closer to the group, which remained in a tight configuration.

As they neared the fantastic dome, the entrapped and eternally doomed souls bound to DruusDome began to sibilantly whisper to them, a polyglottal babble of many tongues. Blacker-than-black shapes slid at sharp angles across the floor, which once was a grand square hewn out of the basalt so prevalent in this hollowed out underground monstrosity.

"Aww, shaddup!" Mad Sam wheedled, mocking the spirits who dared to assail him. "I'm already insane. You can't do anything to me! *Hee-hee-hee!*"

"Shut it, Sammy!" Zaar whispered harshly, his mighty blade held at arm's length in an effort to physically distance himself from the ambient spirits.

"Quiet, both of you," Tal'N bade them. "Your lack of combat discipline still continues to amaze me."

"We don't need any of your Shy'R martial arts combat discipline," Mad Sam said *sotto voce*, knowing fully well that Tal'N could hear him anyway, "because we're so good at what we do, we kill everything we fight before we can even get into combat."

Guthal chuckled. "Maelstromm the Mad might have made you unusually intelligent, Sammy, but he totally failed you when he chose not to grant you the knowledge of Logic."

"But you know I'm right, right?" Sammy taunted him. "We plow through entire legions and don't even break a sweat. Don't need no logic to see that we're pretty damn badass."

"Pride will invite Downfall, Sammy," Tal'N reminded him. "Don't need no logic to see that," he concluded as Sammy pretended to zip his own mouth shut.

Try as they might, everyone, even those armed with superior senses, had difficulty seeing more than an arm's length before them. Such was the oppressive nature of the dark fog that creeped around them.

"Stay tight," Mad Sam whispered after a few more steps. "My magick monocle just informed me that this is magickal fog. No wonder it feels like ants are crawling all over me."

Halting abruptly, Guthal shifted his two-handed axe into his left hand, and held his right hand up just above his broad shoulders, fist clenched. Everyone froze. He pointed down with his right index finger, then, raising it up again, made three quick counterclockwise circles in the air. As he finished, all of the seven prepared for immediate combat, their weapons at the ready.

Then, in the span of a single, wicked heartbeat, the magickal fog retreated, revealing the towering dome above them.

"All That All Which Is
All That All Which Binds
The Beginning of All Things I Bind..."

Lord Valthrustra, Overlord of the Shadar, the Dark One, and foul progenitor of a thousand other black-hearted epithets, hovered some ninety or so feet above the Black Point Pool. The pool dominated the central area of the massive dome. The Nine Black Stairs stretched forth from his feet, flowing down toward the pool beneath; each stair aflame with soul-sucking Void energies that danced like demonic dervishes.

Behind the towering Shadar fiend, the Runic Wall pulsed and throbbed in dreadful syncopation with the very pulse of the Dark Earth Mother herself. The wall grew and expanded in all of its dimensions with each new pulsating heartbeat as Lord Valthrustra channeled a portion of *The Dragon's Breath* itself into its spidery, rune-covered essence. Valthrustra himself was awash with baleful bubbles, strands, and webs of interconnecting multicolored and multiphased energies that lit the air around him like a thousand simultaneous strokes of lightning. His triple-braids of white hair were standing on end, transfused with divine static from the bioelectrical field of the Dragon itself.

A torus of vibrating black spokes of power bloomed from about Valthrustra, even as the echoes of his first words threatened to shatter the sanity of the Seven Stars and smash them physically to the ground. The torus-shaped energy blossom expanded in less than a second until it completely filled the space between Lord Valthrustra and the inner walls of the dome. Only the counterinfluence of Sigil's Krystallstaff held the blackness at bay, defining a ten foot radius of purple force from it that spared them the brunt of Valthrustra's opening attack. As it was, all save for Sigil and Tatternorn were blown to the rear of the force sphere by the few whispers of blackness that pierced the sphere in a few places. All save for the Archimage of Krystallmyst and the VoidSpawn felt their brains and spines spastically attempt to tear themselves away from their host bodies. Yet, even as screams of pain and tears of rage ripped from them, the darkness died out, replaced by an absolute stillness and the sensation that Time itself was somehow holding its breath in anticipation.

Somehow, they had weathered the first wave.

Lord Valthrustra looked down at them, where they huddled within Sigil's force sphere at the northern end of the dome. He smiled a pointy, fanged smile, then his left index finger twitched. With a sudden cold implosion of air, a veritable army of destruction appeared on the floor of the dome before the seven. Defining a rough giant triangle of Mokarr shock troops and dark forces, it stretched from the other side of the floor, coming to a point some ten paces from their protective sphere. Nearest them stood a cadre of nine Mokarr warriors decked out in heavy Shadar steel battle armor. Each wielded venomous vermix two-handed blades which were a fusion of katana and flamberge. They bore on their breastplates the sign of the Dark Earth, the Thon: a counterclockwise-deviced triskelion. They were dark knights, or Sentinels, of Chthon. They sported nearly impregnable armor, awesome venomous blades, and hellish spellcasting skills. Behind them stood nine platoons of Mokarr Death Squads. Three companies of lightly armored Shadow Hawk Battlemages, who were already in the midst of some insanely powerful group spell, stood to the rear and flanks of the death squads.

Accompanying them was a battalion-strength horde of Mokarr assassins and a reinforced platoon of drooling Servitor trolls. The trolls were interspersed throughout the assassin's ranks, where they could be more readily "driven" by their remote-linked "slave visors," which cybernetically linked them to a "driver" who directed and guided their formidable destructive fury. Hundreds of giant black scorps, massive human-sized Midnight Realm scorpions, clattered onto the floor of the dome from dark recesses, their mashing mandibles and clacking claws anxious for the feast. To the rear of the battlemages were thirteen mortogolems. To their rear were some thirty or more of their "lesser" kin, Shadar steel battle golems. They were festooned with armor-smashing spikes, and programmed with lethal Black Wyrm martial arts abilities.

There was silence for a stillborn second. Then, a massive war cry issued from Lord Valthrustra's troops:

"For His glory we all shall die!"

"Indeed!" Sigil sneered, sweeping his staff in front of him like some cosmic broom. Even though no one was yet in range for a physical strike, the Krystallstaff bent the rules of spacetime, striking everything within a one-hundred-and-twenty-degree arc before it. At once, apple-sized gashes of purple flames opened on every being within the arc of destruction all the way to the opposite side of the dome's floor, arcing even upon the units that were not yet on the floor itself.

The golems took this first assault fairly well and continued to churn relentlessly in their direction. The dark knights, in their Shadar steel battle armor, reeled, yet none went down. Many of the remainder, however, went down in a thousand different piles of purple ashes.

"Not bad, old man!" Mad Sam chortled as he whirled away into Shadow, reappearing almost instantaneously on the first of the Nine Black Stairs. Again, almost instantaneously, black flames rose from the first stair and encircled him up to his waist. He went down at once.

"Damn!" Tatternorn yelled as the first of the dark knights charged forward to hack at Sigil's force sphere. Chunks of scattered scarlet light flew at Tat's face from the force of the knight's blows. Sigil's sphere would not last long. Neither would Sammy.

"Everybody grab on!" Tatternorn shouted, willing the first few tones of the *Song of Transport*. Everyone but Sigil found a piece of him to grab.

"C'mon, Sigil!" Tal'N implored him as the rest of the knights fell upon the sphere.

"I cannot set foot 'pon the stairs," Sigil said. He leveled his staff and blew one of the knight's heads completely off, the knight's nearly impregnable Shadar steel armor not quite up to the task of warding him versus Archimage-level personal blasts.

"Why not?" Guthal roared, taking a hasty swipe with his axe at one of the knights.

"Lord V's in the middle of the Breath, and he'd suck Sigil's soul out if he touched one of his personal toys," Silverdancer said, cleaving one of the knights with her Soulsword, which passed through his mighty armor without leaving a trace. No trace, that is, save for the sudden snuffing of his soul and awkward collapse of his body to the dome's cold floor.

"Then go, mon!" Zaar shouted.

"Move it! Move it! Move it!" Tal'N ordered furiously.

Catching the proper tone, Tatternorn projected the five of them through what seemed like nine different clutching webs of hardest magickal diamond until, at last, they appeared on the first stair at Mad Sam's side. At once, black flames rose from the dull onyx-looking stair and coursed up their legs to about the height of their knees. There was no pain. There was only a coldness that began at once to seep into the very being of their essence. But with six of them up here now to divide its power, the cold, cloying flames released Mad Sam somewhat, and Zaar scooped him up with one of his arms and steadied him.

All perception of sight and of sound at that moment seemed to flip-flop and become another entirely new set of sensations altogether. Sight became a grey, foggy mirage of images; each ripple of motion became a palette of grey tracers and black-tinged white outlines. Their voices—even their breathing—became the trip hammer pounding of crashing thunder mixed with the absurd faint tinkling of silver faerie bells and wormwood wind chimes.

The perception-warping effects of the Nine Black Stairs had begun.

"Clossh YOUR iiii..." Tatternorn felt himself bellow.

Stumbling forward, Tatternorn felt his waist bump into the edge of the second stair. Reaching forward, he used his forearms and elbows to haul himself up and over the lip of the second stair. His senses returned immediately, but more black flames raced through him upon contact with the second stair. Being the first one upon it, he got the full effect for himself, too. Intense heat seemed to bathe him where the black flames crackled over his body. He could smell his own flesh roasting. A tiny sliver of fear threatened to explode within his mind and overwhelm him at that point. And, at that point, he quite vividly recalled the lore of the second stair and the lie which it whispers: Fear.

With knowledge came power. Now that he knew what he faced, Tatternorn easily broke its hold upon him, then shook himself free of the black flames and hauled himself up to his feet. Already, his five friends were hauling themselves up to the second stair, more than ready to match their wills with the hellish lying thing. Looking up, he saw Lord Valthrustra give him a quick, cold glare. Then the Shadar fiend drew himself up to his full height, threw his head back, and cackled with insane glee.

"Breath of Dragon
Charm of Death and Life
Thy Song of Making..."

Hot, black acrid fog rolled forth from Lord Valthrustra's eyes, nose, and mouth. It sizzled and turned to seething acidic black droplets as it touched the topmost stair, then this precipitation began flooding toward those on the stairs. Behind him, the Runic Wall grew such that it blocked out all sight of the dome. The runes etched in soul's fire upon its face began to dance, whirl, and writhe like a nest of mating black vipers, each one calling out the name of the Dark One as Lord Above All. Dazzling indigo strobe lights flashed about his head. The image of a titanic draconic eye began to form about him, congealing from the nexus of power with which he was now interfacing. Lord Valthrustra looked into the Eye of the Dragon, and he did not despair. In another few moments, he would be plucking forth that very same eye and devouring it like the big black crow that he was, and ultimate power would be his.

"We're not gonna make it in time!" Tal'N cried out, startling Tatternorn.

"Seven more stairs for the Seven Stars!" Mad Sam tittered insanely as he bounced up to the third stair, danced a short jig, then went straight on up to the fourth one.

"Stair of Insanity," Guthal snorted as he pulled himself up to the third stair and went over.

Sigil, somehow pacted not to come close to Valthrustra while in the midst of summoning the Dragon, was mopping up things down below, judging by the awesome blasts of power that were rocking the floor of the dome. The remaining forces—even the dreaded golems—were simply no match for his true, unfettered power. He could cut loose when others were not in his vicinity. Mad Sam was already starting to pull himself up to the fifth stair, again somehow ignoring the blackish-blue static that clung to his legs. Guthal, Tal'N, and Silverdancer were already fighting the third stair's effects and moving along quite rapidly. Zaar was shaking away the lies of fear from the second stair and preparing to mount the third. Tatternorn grabbed him by the arm and, surprisingly, turned him around to face him quite against his will.

"This is too slow!" Tatternorn told him. "So..." he said fervently, clutching at straws in their final moment, "...so throw me up the damned stairs, Zaar!"

"You'll take seven at once, Tat! No way!"

"Do it!"

Zaar stared hard at Tatternorn as ultraviolet lights flitted past them. Suddenly, his decision made, he grabbed Tatternorn with both of his lower arms, shouted an Azaar war cry, and hurled him straight at Lord Valthrustra's face. Reality exploded around Tatternorn as he endured the combined onslaught of the seven remaining stairs at once. Every little creeping, nagging childhood fear raced back on spidery legs to scrabble over his mind. Every single bad dream that he had ever experienced crashed back into his conscious mind simultaneously. Every emotion that he had ever experienced, from the purest love to the most pristine hate, crucified his soul.

Doubt assailed him; hope escaped him: Zaar breaks him in half like a helpless child and then spits upon his non-regenerating carcass; Guthal laughs while driving vermix nails into his forehead; Tal'N mocks him while inscribing an inverted Phoenix Crest upon his

chest with the tip of his solara blade; Sammy betrays him to Lord
Valthrustra for thirty pieces of silver; Silverdancer takes his soul from
within while they make love in a shady faerie glade. And then...

And then he was there, on his hands and knees, breathing deeply
with eyes wild and wide, at the top of the stairs, some ten paces
away from Lord Valthrustra. Tatternorn's hair stood on end from
the magickal static that suffused the air around him. Instinctively
he knew that no spellsinging would work in this place. The
concentration of deadly forces pulsing and throbbing around him
would drain it or pulse it away even as it left his lips. Lord Valthrustra
would claim the raw energy as his own, sucking it into his waiting
soul collector like some magick-hungry Shadar steel vampire bat.

Tatternorn rose to his feet. His companions would never make
the top of the stairs in time. The Eye of the Dragon was nearly
material now. Now it came down to the two of them, as it was always
meant to be.

Slowly, deliberately, Tatternorn raised Skurge. Slowly,
deliberately, Lord Valthrustra smiled a rictus smile, then turned to
regard him through the transparent Eye of the Dragon. There was
total ecstasy in his eyes.

"All That All Which Is
All That All Which Binds
The End of All Things I Unbind..."
"NOOO!"

The world shook as Tatternorn began a slow-motion charge.
With utterance of those final words, *The Dragon's Breath* was
complete. With those words, the Dragon is summoned to what
mortals and fools call "Reality." With those words, the Dragon is
compelled to obey the commands of the summoner until dawn,
when it can at last return to its lair in the heart of the world. The
Dragon grants wishes and alters realities. It has the power. It *is* the
Power Magick.

And now so did Lord Valthrustra become the Power Magick, for he now held the Dragon in thrall.

"Strike him, Tatternorn!" Sigil cried from below, his voice thick with rare emotion. All reality was changing around them. New rules of existence were being called into play even as the old ones were being cast out. Soon, all reality would be lost; recast in the eye of the Dark One.

Lord Valthrustra glowed in neon black as the eye locked upon him, then vanished. The Shadar steel walls of the dome throbbed foully as they fought to contain the essence of the Dragon.

"Kill him, mon!" Zaar bellowed, his voice a strange echo-flange.

Rapt with power, Lord Valthrustra's eyes rolled back in his head as he made contact with everything. The perception of relative time slowed to a near-infinite crawl as he became All That All Which Is, All That All Which Binds.

"Get 'em, Tat!" Three words, three more strides, three seconds seeming like three hours.

The dome's Shadar steel walls began to creak and groan as the forces of the infinite touched them and began to infuse them with power beyond mortal comprehension. The collective essence of all living things on the world of SenZar began to scream in a trillion different voices at once.

As Tatternorn trudged forward in a slower-than-slow motion shower of black sparks, he looked down at the blade in his cold, clammy hands. It became his entire reality; his entire *raison d'etre*. It—and his infinite hatred for Valthrustra—kept him going when nothing else possibly could.

"*Slay Him, maggot!*" Skurge raged in Tatternorn's psyche, steeping his soul in fiery Shadar hatred. "*Take His soul and fulfill the pact! Do it! Strike, 'ere He doth become everything!*"

"Liar!" Tatternorn replied, his jaw clenched in pain.

Tatternorn tore his attention from the hateful blade. Gouts of black sparks were pouring up his chest, stabbing into his eyes. He felt his boot hit ground. Another step, another seeming hour... another piece of his shattered soul slipped away. And now, after all the effort, all the pain, he could see that he was no closer to Lord Valthrustra than when he had begun his charge seemingly hours before.

"No!" Tatternorn gritted as total rage filled his being, burning into his soul like a pulsating black Void star.

Nothing would keep him from his destiny. Nothing. Not Skurge. Not Lord Valthrustra. Not even the Dragon. He was VoidSpawn. His was the power of will. Reality itself might indeed be against him, but he would be thrice-damned again before he gave in without the Fight of Fights.

Lord Valthrustra, Master of Reality, looked down from his place at the center of everything and noticed Tatternorn's inexorable, ant-like progress toward him. He smiled like a black ice glacier.

"Yes, Tatternorn! Do it! Strike me—if you can!" Lord Valthrustra hissed like a cosmos-eating black hole.

He threw his arms wide. Radiant spokes of black lightning raced from his fingertips and flew off toward the ceiling, gouging living runes of power upon the Shadar steel. His eyes burned into Tatternorn's.

"See if your puny soul can touch the infinite power that is mine!"

A single black bolt flew from the center of his forehead and raced to the floor of the dome. A harsh crackle of purple light sizzled from down below, followed by the scream of a thousand souls being shredded into slivers at once. In the next instant, Sigil Talisman was pinned to the face of the Runic Wall, his Krystallstaff the single spike that held him fast, piercing both his heart and his soul.

Shouts came from behind Tatternorn. His friends had reached the top of the stairs.

"Too late! I AM EVERYTHING!" Lord Valthrustra howled obscenely in the voice of the Dragon.

Five new black bolts of lightning roared from the fingers of his left hand and raced over Tatternorn's head. Five soul-screams howled as one from behind him. An instant later, his five friends appeared on the face of the Runic Wall, each one of them crucified upside-down with Shadar steel nails. As one, they began to writhe in absolute, helpless agony as the wall began to leach them of their very souls, and more.

Cold tears filled Tatternorn's eyes. They were all dead now. All of their plans were for naught now. They had failed.

This world would die now, screaming, and all would be lost. The End of All Things was calling from beyond the Void. Tatternorn heeded her siren call. The Dark One would have his way after all. Raising Skurge high overhead, he prepared to end it all.

Valthrustra began to croak with black laughter as a cone of absolute darkness stabbed down from the ceiling and enveloped him. Somehow, his form still glowed in glory from within the all-consuming darkness.

"Come, child," he whispered, his arms thrown wide. "The Great Wheel has gone round at long last. The Cycle of the Ages is now complete. The pact must be fulfilled. Strike me. It is time."

Like a zombie Tatternorn shuffled toward him, the screams of his companions and the screams of SenZar's collective souls ringing hollowly in his ears. Lord Valthrustra looked down upon him as if he were a father welcoming home the long-lost prodigal son. There was the spark of something, perhaps even something as alien as love—or the fulfillment of an ancient, aeons-spanning hate—written upon his features. Tatternorn gazed upon him, and met his soul-blasting eyes. Then, Tatternorn's gaze shifted slightly, falling upon the image of the Eye of the Dragon, which was now hovering silently, unblinking, above Lord Valthrustra.

Fighting soul-shattering pain, Tatternorn drew himself up to fully stand, unsteadily, Skurge in his hands. Slowly, he raised the great Shadar steel blade above his head, preparing for a mighty head cut on the eerily passive form of Lord Valthrustra.

"Do it," Lord Valthrustra told him coldly.

Torquing himself into striking position, Tatternorn cut hard with Skurge. The massive blade whizzed just past Lord Valthrustra's triple-braided white hair, cutting not the Shadar fiend but instead cutting the Eye of the Dragon itself.

As Time itself once more stood still, Tatternorn stared hard into Lord Valthrustra's sepia eyes: "You will *never* win, even if I have to destroy *everything* to defeat you!"

"No!" Lord Valthrustra uncharacteristically screamed, the ghostly echo of Fear itself dancing awkwardly in his eyes for all to witness.

Lord Valthrustra immediately began working his hands, silently moving his lips, even as the Eye of the Dragon issued forth a halo of primal energies, Source and Void combined. A writhing wall of brilliant white magickal energies zigzagged by pulsating slats of darkness materialized, separating Lord Valthrustra from Tatternorn. The Eye widened, then crackled with cosmos-shattering power.

Tatternorn stood tall, staring into the Eye of the Dragon. "I am only what you have made me," he told it, his words searing. "I am the Godslayer. The End of All Things. I am VoidSpawn."

Bitter, his soul forever marked by his actions, Tatternorn VoidSpawn drew his head back and spit into the Eye of the Dragon.

All souls yet alive in DruusDome screamed as one, then grew silent as the Eye of the Dragon judged all present, and found them all lacking.

The Eye of the Dragon blinked, and they were no more.

CHAPTER 1: If I Die Before I Wake

"Tatternorn!"

Who?

"Move it! Move it! Get your ass in gear!"

Me, move? But I'm comfortable and warm and—

"Go!"

Race of six amber flies, buzzing by.

Who the hell are those guys?

Black shadow-fog... cloying, grasping.

Wait a minute... How can I go if I can't feel my feet?

"Go!"

Screw you... This is a dream... I'm dreaming... This is only a dr—

"Tatternorn! Look out!"

I'm not—

Blast of molten blackness. Heat, vibration. Sensation.

Holy... I felt that...

"Tatternorn!"

Her cry chills ... It chills...

"He's okay, Silverdancer! It'll take more'n that to bring *him* down!"

Thanks for the vote of confidence, Sammy... Sammy? What the hell are you doing here... This is my *dream...*

Nervous laughter, hard to pick out over the dull roar in my ears.

"Dream? Did that magma blast fry your brain or something, Tat? This is *real*..."

No.

"C'mon, mon! We gotta go kill the Bad Guys!"

Luther? You're here, too? But why?

Cold shock, so warm, as the black fog breaks for one pale moment. And I see:

He's got four arms! He's got blue skin! What the hell?

I laugh, despite the growing sense of all-damning horror in my soul. Luther Gates is not blue. Luther Gates does not have four arms. He plays drums like he's got four, but he doesn't have four arms.

Now, I know it's only a dream. Now, I can control it. I can control—

At the edge of the blackness, something draws my attention: a flash of purest silver. I turn to face it in the frustration of dream-time slow motion, and I see her.

Samantha?

Not you, too?

Samantha Teale, covered in noxious black blood; a predatory, feral light gleaming wickedly in her green eyes. At her feet sprawls the shriveled form of an ornately armored jet-black warrior, whose dead eyes shine with a pale silver light.

This is only a dream. Only a dream.

The sudden flash of a wicked smile, and I know her for who she truly is.

Silverdancer?

"Silverdancer..." her voice sings in my head before she bounds away to claim more souls.

No. This is no dream. This is real.

The black curtain descends again, but not before the horror, the truth, of the moment stains itself irrevocably into my soul. And with that horrific stain of truth comes the damning realization that this is how we died.

That this is how I damned us all.

God, no.

Shouts... echoes... sibilant hisses of hatred.

"All That All Which Is
All That All Which Binds
The Beginning of All Things I Bind..."

No.

Death in D Minor. Sympathetic pulse inside my soul.

What the hell is in my hands? Don't look.

Skurge.

Hate/Pain/Death-Brother!

Fly-spawn mind-burrow. *Mindtouch.*

"Tatternorn! The Void calls!"

Sword/blade talk?

"Yes. As never before."

Resistance—no avail. Here, in DruusDome, in the deepest bowels of the Midnight Realm, there is no such thing as resistance. Here, the Shadar rule supreme. Here, for the glory of the Dark One, we all shall die.

"Time to die, Tatternorn!"

Fuck you and fuck that!

"See me and see *yourself,* VoidSpawn."

Words of hate in hell-tongue.

Vision: Death-blade raised to eyes... purple runic rows twisting, pulsing in time to heartbeat, three beats to one.

Realization: Hate/Pain/Death-Brother. The Pact of the Impossible Blade!

Oh my god this is real wake up wake up wake up!

Rush: mad, rampant death horde; a sea of black Shadar steel in
danse macabre, weaving the counterpoint to the D Minor thrum of
Death.

"Don't just stand there, Tat! Kill him!"

"C'mon, Tatternorn!"

"Do it, mon!"

"Too many of them to—"

My friends... My god...

Mocking denial *Mindtouch* as I am forcefully reminded of the
truth.

No, no gods anymore. There never were.

"Fulfill the pact, maggot! Face him! Face the only *god* that *you*
know!"

Damn you, Skurge!

Lurch-lunge-stumble-curse up the nine stairs of blackest
obsidian to face the Lord of the Dark, Lord Valthrustra: the demon
god of the Shadar, absolute King of Hate!

Madness beckons with skeletal claws. His dead eyes gleam, my
soul mirrored within. Recognition. And with it, sardonic rictus
sneer.

Heknowsheknowsheknows...

"Kill him now, Tatternorn! Spill his black blood with Skurge
before he completes *The Dragon's Breath*!"

Who said that?

Death-smile from the fiend.

Heknows...

Urge. Hate. Fulfillment. Strike and kill the Dark One.

But he knows!

He smiles and whisper-screams: "Heed my thrice-damned
brother's last words, VoidSpawn. Strike me! Discover for yourself
his betrayal. Set the wheels in motion and learn the price of
immortality."

Liar!

"There is but one truth! Strike me now, or be forever denied it!"

I hate you.

"You hate yourself, VoidSpawn."

No.

"Strike me, false soul!"

No.

"Face me!"

No! Deny Him three times.

Mindtouch. Skurge mock-laugh directly into my own mind.

He does not give us a choice, Tatternorn!

Screams. Time: wounded by mortal blow. Space: ripped apart by power-not-meant-to-be. Mind-scream.

"Where are you now, Silverdancer?"

Down, down, down... into the Electric Angel of the Void.

...into the Void.

CHAPTER 2: Pray The Lord My Soul To Take

"*Where are you now, Silverdancer?*"

Soul-scream. Then, the lying silence of cold rain drizzling outside.

"Samantha?" I finally managed to choke out. But my lady, my love, was far away, and my silken sheets were cold with my own sweat, not hers. An occurrence most common as of late.

To sleep, perchance to have nightmares that scare the hell outta you and whoever's in bed with you.

If only Ol' Bill would have known the current irony of his words, he would have gone swimming in the Thames with a ton of bricks. "Perchance to dream" my ass!

Cursing the benefits of my so-called college education, I took a peek over at the nightstand, hoping that I wouldn't see what I thought I'd see. Alas—thanks, Ol' Bill—my vintage Rocky and Bullwinkle alarm clock betrayed me. Its baleful red LED glow read 4:44 AM, the precise time of my previous nightmares.

Et tu, Bullwinkle? Well, at least I was consistent in my madness. Three nights in a row now. Same time, same Bat Channel.

As quietly as I could manage, I got out of bed, then staggered over the hardwood floor until I made it to the bathroom. Once there, I closed the door, hit the lights—which I instantly loathed—and stared at myself in the mirror. A faint twinge of something blue arced across my eyes, a bloom of electric blue light. This subtle threat to my even more subtle sense of sanity caused me to look away.

For a brief, terrifying moment, I was totally alone. Then, my soul shaking, I was back in the here and now, and I was forced to consider what had only so recently seemed to become my focus of existence.

One hell of a nightmare. Again. Three nights in a row, the same damn dream. That did not bode well. Superstitions and Old Wives' Tales speak of horrible fates for such poor, doomed fools.

Superstitions? Dreams? Omens?

Sure, *let* it be an "Omen." Damien Thorne—Antichrist or not—didn't scare me one bit. I'd happily shove all Seven Knives of Megiddo into him and not even bat an eye while doing it. But that reject from *Creature Feature*—Lord... Valthrustra, was it?—now *that* was an entirely different matter.

Just *thinking* about that name made me shudder all the way down to the small of my back.

I rubbed my temples, trying my futile best to rid myself of another migraine. I noticed that the throbbing in my head was in perfect synchronization with the crash and bang of the approaching thunderstorm, which had begun to announce itself with gathering ferocity. Leave it to a musician's habit: always in time, no matter how bad things around became. I thought about taking out my contacts, which had been in for about a week, but I quickly decided against anything that had to do with looking into my own eyes. I'd just as soon let them rot out—contacts *and* eyes—before I was forced to cross *that* electric bridge again.

Besides, a handful of Ibuprofen from my convenient economy-sized bottle of generically labeled "Ibuprofen" would knock the pain out about as well as a Quaalude. Sort of.

However, since Luther wasn't here at the moment, I was stuck with taking the generic over-the-counter "Good-Good."

Hmmm...

"Good-Good." That's what Luther Gates, Rastamon Supreme, called all species of reality-blurring substances, legal or not. Too bad this candy-assed version of the "Good-Good" *was* legal. What I really needed was some prescription-strength medication. And the "prescription" part didn't matter as much as the "strength" part did. I knew Luther would forgive me this one slip, though. Considering the day's possibly supernatural circumstances, it would be the least that he could do. Besides offer me some *real* "Good-Good," that is.

"C'mon, mon! We gotta go kill the Bad Guys!"

"What? Luth—"

I did a double take. Avoiding eye contact with the mirror, I gave the bathroom a thorough look-see. No Luther. Nothing. No one. Feeling totally paranoid, and now somewhat silly, I laughed once, nervously. Hollowly. Possibilities stumbled through my mind. It had definitely been Luther's voice that I had heard. Definitely. But Luther wasn't here. No way you could hide a seven-one monster like that in my little bathroom—even from an idiot like me. Luther definitely wasn't here. But Sammy?

Had it been only Sammy, messing around with me or something? Some tape recording, or digitized sample of Luther's voice, channeled into the bathroom in some lunatic Sammy-engineered way—say, perhaps, like through the toilet bowl? No, not even a Total Loon like Sammy would have—

Hmmm...

Maybe it *had* been Sammy. After all, Sammy *was* enough of an instigator to rub some salt into my wounds, and he definitely *could* imitate Zaar's voice fairly well, and... and...

Who the hell is "Zaar?"

Distant thunder crashed. An invisible rat seemed to tap-claw-dance up my spine. Something, some alien, searing force, seemed to suck my face toward the mirror.

"No way," I mumbled, shaking my head spastically from side to side like Eddie Vedder at the end of the "Jeremy" video. "I'm *not* gonna look," I promised myself as I turned away from the waiting mirror by sheer force of will. "At least," I snorted, feeling ridiculous, "I'm not gonna look till it's time to see the hate in my eyes give me away."

Too damned much for one day. And too damned many song lyrics floating around up in that oatmeal brain of mine.

I laughed nervously. A sound like a muffled cough issued from my throat. Poor Sammy. I wondered how loudly I had screamed *this* time. Bad enough that my nightmares were jeopardizing my relationship with Samantha, but my roommate Sammy didn't have anywhere else to go to avoid the noise.

Quickly tying off a handy black silk kimono around my waist, I crept out of the bathroom, flicking off the light in afterthought. Then, I made my way to the bedroom door, and carefully opened it. Another dose of Reality vs. Surreality: I turned, suddenly staring into the half-light of the creepy old hallway, and red light filled my left eye.

heknowsheknowsheknows...

"Shit!" I yelped in instant, paranoid disbelief. Then I blinked, despite my wide-eyed fear response, as the laser light from Sammy's Glock nine mike-mike filled my left eye. And probably burned a hole in my contact lens, too, in the process of blinding me.

"Shit and double-shit!" Sammy squeaked right back at me in his best Curly Howard voice. It was *very* good, for it was *entirely* natural. Total Loon. "What are ya tryin' to do, Logan?" Sammy whispered excitedly. "Scare me to an Edgar Allen Poe premature burial or something?"

Sammy, my dull brain noted. At least it wasn't Curly, for Chrissakes.

The red haze left my eye as Sammy Joseph—all four foot, some-odd inches of him—rattled his Glock in his hand with a nervous-sounding *snik-snik-snik*. Then he cleared his throat.

"Another one, huh?" he stated flatly. "As if Tuesday morning and Wednesday morning weren't enough. Now you've added Thursday morning into the mix. I can almost hear The Mamas and the Papas playing your theme music: 'Thursday, Thursday—blah-blah, blah-blah-blah-blah.'"

Sammy's voice, normally lively and lilting, sounded like the canned, tinny music from an AM radio to my dream-blasted ears. There were, however, no deranged farm animal noises from him, which was a welcome relief. A tense moment followed as we eyed each other through the gloom, the pale half-light of the creepy hallway our only source of illumination now that his laser sighting was out of my eye. Maybe I wouldn't get glaucoma after all.

"Yep," I gritted, still happy as sin. "You got it, Sammy. And this time I got a couple of new names, not just shadows and weird noises. They—whoever the hell 'They' are—obviously aren't content to leave it at just shadowy figures and gruff voices," *or at calling me 'VoidSpawn,' which was just wicked enough to sound cool by me,* I didn't say aloud. No need to blow Sammy's mind any more than necessary. At least, not like this. "This time somebody called me 'Tatternorn,'" I admitted, the very name itself sounding too *familiar* to keep at bay any longer. "And that scares the living hell out of me."

Sammy smiled at this, his teeth flickering in the dim light. I heard a soft *thunk* from the floor as he lowered the tip of what had to be his katana in order to holster his pistol in his shoulder rig. Damn scary and damn ambidextrous he was. If not a bullet, then a blade. I almost snickered at his extreme preparations until I realized that, if the situation were reversed, I probably would have done the same damn thing. There is no such thing as paranoia, after all. Still, with the Glock out of the way, I breathed a little easier for the first time today.

"I think I see a pattern starting to develop, Logan," Sammy blurted as he moved past me and flicked on the lights, much to my dismay. As I softly cursed this new enemy called "Light," Sammy cleared his throat like a used car salesman about to make his sales pitch and leaned against the doorframe. There was a wide grin spread on his cherubic face.

"A pattern? What kind of pattern?" I asked.

"Well," Sammy laughed, "I think I see you sharing a nice little patterned padded cell with me in the Loony Bin!"

Sammy tittered at his own pun—one of his most annoying habits—then howled like a demented hyena, lending credence to at least one part of his statement.

"Yeah, right," I countered glibly. "And I'm sure our little padded room will have a bunkbed so that you can roll off of it and fall onto me in the middle of the night, you little shit."

Sammy stopped his hyena noise to show me the back of his middle finger, then he scrambled out of the room, tittering softly to himself. He really hated to be reminded of that long ago, highly embarrassing summer camp incident. So I rubbed it in whenever the opportunity presented itself, like now. And like how.

I laughed at my own mean streak—one of my annoying habits—walked back into my room, then looked out through my skylight. I regarded the silver sliver face of the waning Moon with no small feeling of apprehension.

"What are you trying to tell me, you liar?" I asked of its ancient, fickle wisdom, not entirely expecting an answer.

My mind lied to me as I heard the whisper of an echo speak to me in ancient, unknown tongue:

"Where are you now, Silverdancer?"

Jesus, I thought numbly as I consciously tried to avoid any more eye contact with the Moon, *Sammy might be a little closer to the truth than he realizes.*

After that blatantly foreshadowing episode, I exited my room and followed the familiar trail of Sammy's merry humming, negotiating the creaky old hardwood floor of the Pad like an automaton. I was like that, at times. Wake with a start, then zone off for the next hour or so. I was never the morning type of person who could jump out of bed, shove some coffee down his throat, then commute to a shiny happy job, all smiles and hugs. I probably never would be, especially not after these hellish nightmares left me feeling as if I had just run a mental marathon. And it had been that way since I was a kid, constantly, slowly iterating from bare shadows to what I was seeing now. Almost every single night. How could anyone be sane after all of that persistent psychic punishment?

Well, maybe I'm not sane, after all, I thought. *But, in the Words of St. James, "Fuck it all and fucking no regrets." Right?*

My state of sanity settled, I shuffled along, content in my discontent, still following the sound of Sammy's eager beaver humming. I barely noticed as the hallway gave way to the den, then the den to the kitchen. Focus returned, however, as soon as I saw Sammy perched upon a small stepladder in front of the sink. He was combating a small army of filthy dishes with a Brillo pad in either hand, a neon green apron his most curious battle fatigues.

Praying that he was too busy to notice a stumbling zombie out of the corner of his eye, I turned sharply around and scooted back down the hall, then into the den at double-zombie speed, wondering if his notorious all-seeing eyes could have seen me. I *hoped* not. I hated doing the dishes with a passion.

Thinking as fast as I could in my zombie-state, I shuffled over to the holy shrine of the "Cathode God"—Sammy's pet name for his big-screen television set—and frantically began searching the hazardous den area for the remote control. I thought that if I could get the TV up and running in time, I could actually fool him into believing that I had walked in *here* first and not the kitchen, where doom in the shape of plates and glasses sat waiting. *At least, that was my plan, if I could find the damned remote thingie!*

"It's underneath the *Penthouse* on the coffee table," Sammy blared over the noise of running water and furious scrubbing. His all-seeing eyes never blinked.

"Uh, thanks!" I replied, at last finding the blasted thing with Sammy's clairvoyant directions. "Fucker. Uh," I quickly added over his muffled laughter, "do you need any help with those abominations?" Even though he had "busted" me, I'd be damned if I'd go willingly into Dish Hell.

"Nope!" came my salvation, and that was that. Now he knew that I knew that I owed *him*, in the Way of Slovenly Men. Or something inane like that.

Relieved, I sank into the plush, heavy pseudo-leather couch—the holy shrine of the Cathode God, that is—and flicked on the tube with the remote, deciding to zombie-out with the latest ram-it-down-your-throat CNN newscast. Such was my habitual, vicarious absolution. My personal demons were *nothing* compared to those of the news. Seriously: How could a nightmare, no matter how insane, compare to a terrorist bombing, an earthquake, or even the latest Third World Bus Plunge? I was already starting to chomp at the bit and foam at the mouth as I considered the insane shit that the Talking Heads on the tube were about to tell me with their hilariously straight faces and their preprogrammed Disneyworld Animatronic movements.

Much to my disgust, though, once the Cathode God roared to life, I got nothing but static. Jittery, creepy-crawly white ant-static. Not good, that. Feeling disconnected from my cable-umbilical cord, I scanned the channels, only to get more and more and *more* static.

Dammit, Sammy! I fumed, wondering how close the Kremlin was to red alert because of his latest mad scientist experiment.

"What in the hell's wrong with the TV, Sammy?" I complained loudly over the hissing static. "Have you been down in your 'lab' again?"

"Innocent on all accounts, whatever they be!" was his instant, snappy reply.

"But there's nothing but static on every channel!"

"Still innocent, boyo! I haven't caused any electromagnetic pulses lately!" Sammy's hyena laughter denied his denials. But, before I could get my zombie-self in gear to get up and give him a swift kick in the ass, he added, "But knowing our cable company, Logan, I'd bet that whatever it is isn't just an isolated occurrence. Hell. Most of southern Louisiana is probably disconnected even as we speak. If they weren't already disconnected before, that is."

I considered that no-brainer for about half a second, even as the little lunatic started belting out the raunchy lyrics to the Fear song, "Disconnected." Right as rain he was. Those crazy cable guys. They never could get it right, whatever "it" was. Knowing how they operated their brainless monopoly, those cable bozos were probably using their satellite dishes for woks even as we spoke.

Hmmm...

Wheels turned in my mind as I considered this ridiculous notion. Woks to Chinese food; Chinese food to martial arts; martial arts to my old sparring partner, Michael Reese. Funny how those wheels turned in that oatmeal mush that I called a mind.

Michael was coming home today, if good fortune prevailed, which it rarely had lately. He was up for some leave from the Navy for a couple of weeks according to our phone conversation last week. And, according to our tight-knit little group's infamous Mardi Gras custom, he was going to spend *most* of it getting as toasted as he could with his best friends, in the finest of naval traditions.

Ahh, I considered, already tasting the Southern Comfort, *good friends reuniting and old drinking ways renewed.* And if David had somehow managed to get his long overdue vacation from his slave-driving superiors at China Lake, then we were gonna have one helluva Brüe Crüe reunion. One that no one would *ever* forget!

I *heh-heh'd* at that prospect. Had to. Mardi Gras, you know? Besides, our band, Electric Bard, was finally in position to showcase its collective weirdness/talent before the electric eyes of the world, with a hootin'-hollerin' hometown crowd to boost our appeal.

The Place: the French Quarter, at that infamous watering hole known as *Bad Streets.* The Time: 11:00 PM next Tuesday night, which just happened to be Mardi Gras night as well. We had "confirmation" from three labels' representatives, who had supposedly fallen over backwards and foamed at the mouth after hearing our self-produced EP, that they would be in attendance at the gig. We also had "assurances" that an MTV crew would be there to broadcast periodically, as they always do from the French Quarter during Mardi Gras. To top this line of hokum off, we also had "promises" that Electric Bard would be featured for at least a couple of seconds during the live MTV telecast.

Our turf, our crowd!

And, if only *one* of those "possibilities" came through, we were as good as signed. If the bigwigs could even catch a *glimpse* of us, we were signed. Hell, how many three-member bands in the world could boast a *seven foot, one inch* Jamaican-born drummer/octopoid percussionist from hell/vocalist who had a *white mohawk* instead of the traditional dreds; a stunning green-eyed and *naturally* white-haired *goddess-virtuoso* with Juilliard training on both bass *and* keys (*and* vocals); and a maniacal demon-guitarist/vocalist with an *eight octave* vocal range to run the show? Not to mention a Total Loon by the name of Sammy Joseph running the computerized sound and light shows for us, too! Electric Bard *couldn't* lose, if only because of our sheer shock value! We all sang. We all wrote. We all contributed. We were *tight*!

And here I am, dreaming of being a star.

Then, the wheels turning again, I muttered an expletive about not getting my MTV and turned the volume down to nil. Those little creepy-crawlies parading across the face of the Cathode God had just inspired me to try something. I got up off the couch and, after working a kink out of my left knee, sat down before the mute god. I crossed my legs, tucking them into each other, assuming the "lotus position," which Luther, in his decidedly Rastafarian way, was always trying to get me to teach him. I guess he thought that he could get more of a buzz from his ganja if he smoked it while meditating. Nirvana, ascending from the lotus petal.

I allowed myself to sink into a state of concentration, in the same fashion that Michael had taught me so many years before. There was no humming of mantras, or any of that hokey stuff. There was only a calming of thought, then a concentration upon a single line of thought. Next, the idea was to get the single line of thought down to a single word, then get that single word down to a single infinitesimal point which could then be focused fully upon, with no waste of energy. Finally, from this point, the adept could draw upon inner reserves of mental energy called *ki* or *chi*, the name depending on if you studied Japanese or Chinese martial arts, respectively. Still, they amounted to basically the same thing: concentration.

Soon, I was flowing along, destructuralizing the components of the things that confounded me, slipping deeper and deeper into my concentration state.

Down, down. ...*down into the Void!*

"Whoa!" I started, shivering and blinking furiously, as if that would really help.

What in the hell is wrong with me?

The chills reintroduced themselves to my vertebrae. That feeling of everlasting damnation from my nightmare returned to my conscious thoughts, leaving a foul taste in its wake. Suddenly, I had the feeling as if someone were tap dancing on my grave. Turning my head quickly to the side, I could almost see... *something?*... moving at the edge of my peripheral vision. But it was gone before I could decide that it had even been there. *Geez.*

Wheels turning, twisting, burning.

My alleged "mental training" was a joke! Not even those years of one-on-one hardass martial arts training with Michael had prepared me for the onslaught of my recent nightmares. Nor had nearly two years of postgraduate training in psychoanalysis and dream interpretation with some of the best instructors in the south. True, Ol' Jung had never dealt with horrors like "Lord Valthrustra."

Or, at least, he had never *written* about it. He would have been *crucified*!

What was most frustrating, though, was the fact that I was, as a rule, a "lucid" dreamer—someone who could *realize* a dream for what it was and *control* it. But this latest series of nightmares had me licked. I felt like one of my case studies, dazed and confused by the horrid, unconquerable fiends of the nightmare world. And, to further confuse things, I kept smelling the aroma of Sammy's Southern Fried Breakfast, which was sizzling and popping ninety-to-nothing in the kitchen. I should have never started thinking about those damn woks!

Michael would kick my ass for this.

Well, never one to give up the ship, I decided to accept the fact that my mind was a bowl of mush and get on with the main problem, besides hunger, that was plaguing me: the name "Tatternorn."

My name is Christopher Hathorne Logan, not "Tatternorn." My first name was given to me by my mother, who just happened to like the little boy from A.K. Milne's *Winnie the Pooh* books. Given the possibilities, I guess "Christopher" was better than "Eeyore" or "Piglet." And it was fitting, no doubt, that both Christopher Robin and yours truly had trouble separating fiction from reality. Except, of course, that he had stuffed animals and I had Lord Valthrustra, Skurge, and something really nasty called *"The Dragon's Breath."* Hell, if they made a Saturday morning cartoon about *my* imaginary friends, it would scare the absolute pee-pee out of the little kiddies! *And* their parents, too!

My middle name, with its unusual derivation of "Hawthorne," came from a not-so-distant uncle on my father's side. After a lengthy genealogical tracking, it turned out that this not-so-distant uncle of mine was in fact some sort of faith healer, one of mixed Native American blood who claimed relation with not only the Choctaw Nation, but also with the Cherokee and Hopi Nations as well. Guess he got around quite a bit. And I guess it was from that side of the family that I got my high cheekbones and long, straight black hair—not to mention my own penchant for getting around and seeing the world. Playing in a constantly gigging traveling band can work wonders for that wanderlust, dig?

My surname, as custom permits, was from my father's side of the family, passed down from some long ago mountaineer ancestor. I preferred my surname in conversation; and, as such my friends knew me. Besides, "Logan" made a better stage name than "Christopher," which I refused to shorten to "Chris," which was androgynous; or to "Christ," which was, at the very least, offensive to about half of the world. Not to mention, a bit presumptuous. Well, maybe *just* a bit.

So, to make a long story short, my friends called me "Logan," not "Tatternorn."

Still, it seemed so... so *familiar*, so *right*. Tatternorn. *Shit*!

Names! Damned names!

"Frailty, thy name is," I paused, unsure how to continue. *What is thy name, cruel Frailty?*

Tatternorn? Right. And the only "Skurge" I'd ever heard of before was a cat-o'nine-tails.

I exhaled a long breath and rose to my feet. The static on the tube was still going strong, sharply accented by the sound and fury of frying bacon, which sizzled and popped like nothing else in the world. My stomach growled immediately, so I moved into the kitchen, an invisible noose of bacon smoke pulling me onwards to my cholesterol doom. Sammy had toast going, bacon cooking, scrambled eggs frying, and a full pot of black chicory coffee brewing. I felt as if I had walked into heaven, although I had trouble imagining Sammy as anything but a misplaced imp looking to stir up some fast trouble.

Sammy Joseph.

Sammy always looked like he had a secret to tell. There was always that Cheshire Cat smile that slid open just wide enough for you to see the tips of his canines. His big brown eyes held an inner mirth that was reflected in almost everything he did. He was always whistling or humming some old song, always busy with some task or another. Sammy could make the sun shine on a cloudy day, whether by personal magnetism or by electromagnetism.

There weren't many people who would be so happy in his shoes, however, because Sammy's shoes were very small. Sammy was only an elbow taller than a yardstick. He was an adult by age but not by physical development, looking for all intents and purposes like a very young, albeit well-built, eight year old boy.

Good Ol' Smilin' Sammy.

Throughout the many years of pricking and prodding by the best medical specialists in the country, he always kept a tune on his lips and a smile on his face. They subjected him to tests that were as hellish as Nazi war atrocities, and still the eggheads were baffled. He was neither suffering from achondroplasty—a sanitized name for dwarfism—nor from a defective pituitary gland. He was neither dwarf nor midget, as the eloquent eggheads would bleat, slamming their textbooks in rage.

Except for a couple of his DNA bases being garbled—forming, in some very interesting places, a third helical strip between the two "normal" DNA strands—they could find *nothing* to explain his condition.

Right. Even the Blind Man could see the word "mutant" glaring in billboard-sized neon green letters at this point. But none of the eggheads could, or did. Strange, that. Or totally incompetent, take your pick.

Although Sammy seemed frozen in time as a child, his strength was deceptive for his size. Moreover, his physical coordination was simply astonishing for *any* size, and his reaction time was simply amazing. His brain-melting high scores on video games were testimony enough of that.

Sammy the Enigma. And not just physically. Sammy Joseph was a living, breathing hypergenius, more intellectually capable than any of the "specialists" who had studied him. His IQ alone made Einstein look like a retarded wombat, if one placed such emphasis on such a flimsy standard alone. Of my five best friends—the members, including myself, of the illustrious Brüe Crüe: Luther Gates, Sammy, David Miller, Michael Reese, and Samantha Teale—Sammy was the most brilliant by far, surpassing even David, a genius in his own right, who was one of the hottest R&D men out at China Lake. Hell, Sammy was the first person from our small town to ace both his ACT and his SAT— before he got into high school. Probably one of the first people *ever* to do that. Well, at age seven, of course. He had attempted to take them both at age four, but no one wanted to proctor such an abomination of common sense and goodwill toward men. For fear of being made to look like a microcephalic, of course. But he probably could have done it. Old soul kinda thing, like he had been born with a magick mind.

And, best of all, the little shit fooled the living hell out of the starry-eyed teaching establishment that sought to exploit him as the latest prodigy. Sammy Joseph played the perfect rogue, smiling that teacher's pet grin of his while he turned our small town into his personal playground, stirring up a ruckus that no one ever pinned on him, or on me. He sold crib sheets to all of the jocks, who made him rich for it. He forged hall passes so well that the school board offered a citywide reward for the busting of the "professional" who was corrupting their young students' minds. No one ever turned in Little Robbin' Hood though, because he threw the best keg parties that money could buy. There was even that one, beautiful moment right after graduation when he electronically overrode the local bank's scrolling sign and made it say, in an endless scrolling loop: "This is what it sounds like, when ducks quack! Quack-quack-quack-quack! Quack-quack-quack-quack!"

Really. He did that to a Prince song, the blasphemer!

Anyway, Sammy Joseph could have used his genius to change the world. He could have gone to MIT or Cal-Tech or anywhere else in the world for free, but he chose to stay with his buddies and go to LSU, to raise hell and to have as much fun as possible. Personally, I believe that the *real* reason was that he was too lazy to have to work hard for his degree. At least, that was *my* reason.

"Dinnah is soived!" Sammy rollicked in his best Curly voice, jumping down from the small stepladder in front of the stove, all the while somehow deftly balancing two heaping platters of breakfast goodies in his outstretched hands. The coffee, though, would be for me to serve. After all, fair is fair. Realizing this, I brought the entire pot to the table, along with two large tourist-looking naval mugs that Michael had sent us from Coronado a couple of years ago.

As we ate, Sammy hummed a merry tune that sounded remarkably similar to the song that always played at the beginning of "The Three Stooges" shows. He smacked loudly, crucifying Emily

Post, while he used his fork to move pieces of his scrambled eggs into the huge pool of ketchup that dominated one half of his plate. He was definitely hyperactive for someone who had just recently gotten out of bed. That was, however, typical Sammy behavior. Unfortunately.

"So, Logan," Sammy began with no preamble, "the Dream Police are calling you 'Tatternorn,' are they?"

Eerily enough, as he spoke, his eyes fixed calculatingly on a horribly mangled piece of egg that was slowly sinking in the pool of ketchup.

"Yep," I said, feeling a strange sense of dread creep upon me. I knew that he was about to spring a "funny" on me in typical Sammy fashion, but that name—coming from someone else's lips—bit deeper than hot nails.

"Tatternorn, huh?" Sammy commented without looking up from his plate. "You know, I'm beginning to wonder if you haven't subconsciously been considering switching Electric Bard's song format to something along the lines of one of those weirdo fantasy novels. Wouldn't that be a kick?"

"Well, we're pretty close to that already, Sammy."

"Yeah, I guess you're right about that," Sammy admitted. "So maybe it isn't some warped subconscious projection on your part. Maybe it's because you're just too involved with all this upcoming gig stuff and you're not getting enough time to clear your thoughts before you zoom off to
La La Land."

"Could be," I replied, taking a sip of strong, paint-peeling coffee. The Psych grad in me had
already considered that possibility, along with a host of other less savory ones.

"Still, the word 'Tatternorn' sounds familiar to me," Sammy said bluntly, his eyes still fixed upon the sinking piece of egg. My breath caught in my throat at his mention of that damning word, *familiar*. "It's etymology refers to Norse Fates and rags. Tit for Tat; *quid pro quo*. Tatterdemalion. Pieces of cloth and wild, woolly Fate. It could very well mean that you're fated to become a..." He looked up, the corners of his mouth twitching, fighting back a smile.

"A what?" I asked, urging him on.

"...a bum!" Sammy's laughter was like Woody Woodpecker's. Only worse.

"I guess that's why your eyes are so brown, Sammy," I said between bites, trying to disguise my relief, "'cause you're so full of shit."

"Ha. Anyway," he continued, trying not to smile, "I got confirmation via BBS that David and Michael are both coming in today. Michael's gonna be flyin' in, and Samantha and Luther are gonna pick him up at the airport around three or so this afternoon. David should be pullin' in around four or five—if his crappy old Nova can make it, that is! Looks like the legendary Brüe Crüe is finally gonna make its long-awaited Mardi Gras rendezvous! We can be there in less than an hour from here in Baton Rouge, of course, because I drive like a total pro. And I can squelch any band of radar set against us. But you know that already, don't you?"

"Hell yeah!" I exclaimed, a fist in the air, ignoring his talk of "squelch" and such nonsense. Even though I realized it as a verbatim truth. Sammy was Sammy, after all.

We *would* be together again! All of us! This was the first piece of good news that I had gotten today, and it felt pretty damn good. Far within, I tittered with glee as I considered unique methods of group inebriation.

"Sammy," I finally managed to gibber, "In just a few hours the Brüe Crüe will be together again for the first time in a *long* time! Tonight, after practice of course, we're gonna lose ourselves in the madness that is the French Quarter at Mardi Gras! The Brüe Crüe, along with about a million of our closest friends! Oh, the horror! The horror!"

"Horror..." Sammy said, doing his best Colonel Kurtz, "and moral terror... are your friends."

We both started laughing then, spirits high in shared amusement; Sammy's high-pitched, lilting *hee-hee-hee!* laughter temporarily banishing from my mind the evil thoughts of Lord Valthrustra, Skurge, and other such fantastic nightmare nonsense.

Right.

CHAPTER 3: Psych!

S chool crawled by like a crippled turtle.

Thursday was always like that. I had three classes on Thursday, each a little more difficult than the last. I loathed grad school—especially the program here at LSU. Not that it was bad. It wasn't. As a matter of fact, it was one of the best in the country. At least that's what the programs said. In any event, too much energy was spent refuting the knowledge that was learned during the undergrad years, and not enough energy was spent preparing for "The Real World", infested as it was with its indifference, cold shoulders, and sightless eyes. At least that's what *my* program said.

Anyway, diatribe aside, of the twelve grad students in my Advanced Psychoanalysis class, four were going into social work, three were going to teach at the secondary level, two were going to pursue doctorates, two were going to flunk, and one long haired rebel type was going to sign a record deal within the week. Or so I fervently wished.

This class is so freakin' boring! I struggled inside my mind. *C'mon, let's go! I'm going to be a star soon, and this slow-ass shit is a drag!*

Groaning, I slumped my head down onto my notebook with a *whump.*

Silence. Then the prick of stares on the back of my neck.

"Mister Logan!" Dr. Passman lisped icily in his practiced, clinical tone. "Are you so well versed in Jungian dream interpretation that you may practice it while in my class?"

Dr. Anthony Passman was one of the big brains on campus. He was a highly regarded, if somewhat overpaid, local psychiatrist who could get on an academic high horse that could trample a Mack truck if necessary. One trip to his letters- and awards-decorated office would drive that point home even for the dullest first year undergrad. Dr. Passman's constant needling of his students was, at least in his own erudite opinion, necessary to prepare them for his own puritanical version of "The Real World"—a version which just didn't happen to agree with my own slightly cockeyed one. I wasn't in the mood for any of Dr. Passman's antiquated, uptight "Real World" shit right now, though, considering recent events, and he had just hit a very sore spot in my soul with his words. Normally, mind you, I would have just laughed along with him and the other sheep in the class. After all, a joke is a joke. And you humor the guy who's handing out the grades. But, right now, that laughing, good-natured "me" seemed like someone else from long ago.

And I just hadn't been myself lately.

"Well, Mr.—or, should I say, *Dr.*—Logan?" Dr. Passman inquired again, a faint smile tugging at his waxy lips as the rest of the class began to laugh along with his needling. "Might you have any illuminating observations on dream interpretation to—"

I... *snarled?*... and lifted my head, fixing Dr. Passman with my eyes, willing him to feel but the smallest measure of the splinter of the nightmare that kept hounding me. The classroom suddenly grew still, as silent as a tomb. Then, as Dr. Passman and I stared at one another—neither giving an inch, each to his own reasons—a deep, boiling well of pure, alien hate filled me and I spoke:

"Go fuck yourself, you overblown, blind, pompous asshole!"

Sharp intakes of air, "oohs" in chorus.

Some hateful force seemed to compel me, forcing me to my feet, forcing me to advance toward the shocked Dr. Passman like some stalking carnivore. Anger filled me, bathing me in hot, salty urine stench. The lights overhead began to flicker, throbbing in time to my pulse. The sensation of spiders racing up my back to the base of my neck felt *good*. Their nestling there in a web of potential energy felt familiar somehow, a welcome thing to the prisoner in my soul. Dr. Passman/human/maggot must have felt it, too. His hands began to tremble, and his chalk dropped to the floor. He stumbled backwards, his protruding rear brushing against the blackboard. Our eyes remained locked, a psychic Gordian Knot.

So close were we now that I could smell the sweat on his neck. I wanted to rip it apart, to tear into the soft human flesh and gorge upon his life blood. Animal passion consumed me. I was lost in myself, and the prisoner within was free. My mental voice was jibber-jabbering like some holy man speaking in tongues. Electricity exploded in my mind, crackling like a bolt from the thunder god himself. I could feel my hands reaching for his pathetic, double-chinned neck.

"Die! You squirming human maggot!"

Crash. *Shatter-pop-pop-pop-clink-clink.* Screams. Sheep bleats.

My mind numbed with the detached fascination of terror, I regarded the slow motion dance of my fellow students as they made their stumbling, screaming way from the classroom. Shards of fine glass covered the entirety of the room, along with the metallic skeletons of a few smoldering light frames. Dark, foul smoke began belching from one of the fused wires overhead. It all seemed so distant.

Scurrying of mind rats. Mocking, hideous laughter.

Nausea. Sick gut wrench.

Bending double, I vomited out Sammy's awesome breakfast on the side of the teacher's desk. After the second dry heave, I collapsed, leaning against the bile-streaked desk for support. Excited inquiries, which still sounded like harsh sheep bleats to me, came from the hall outside. A whimpering issued from beneath the desk, jolting me back into the here and now.

"Dr. Passman?" I asked, the name a strange thing to utter. Sobs answered me. His behind was jutting out from under the desk, shaking like a parody of Saint Nick's jolly old belly. One of his Gucci loafers was upside-down on the floor between his ankles, covered in glassine shards. I stood up—too quickly, as my head argued angrily—and moved over to him. Squatting quickly, I rested my arm on the side of the desk to regain my balance. I reached out to him and placed a hand on the back of his leg, the only thing that I could reach. The muscles bunched at my touch.

"W-what?" Dr. Passman exploded, a whump resounding from the underside of the desk as he raised his head too far.

"C'mon, we have to get out of here," I pleaded as I began to coax him out from under the desk. The smoke was really billowing now. Far away, on the threshold of hearing, a fire bell began to chirp. That seemed to do it for him. With some help, he extricated himself from beneath the desk, then he quickly began brushing the glass from his clothes. I helped him find his loafer, then, as he knelt to slip it on, he looked up at me and asked, strangely enough:

"What language was that?"

Dr. Passman coughed once, then plucked a shard of glass from his hair. Meanwhile, I went to the Bahamas.

"Uhh, what do you mean, 'What language was that?'" I bent down closer to him, avoiding the thick, burnt plastic smoke.

"That snarling, rasping, guttural phrase that you spewed forth, right before the lights blew out!" Dr. Passman slipped on his loafer, then stared at me point-blank. His face was flushed with anger. Or fear. "I am fluent in nine languages, Mr. Logan! I have letters from five universities! I am more regarded in certain circles than... than... Agghh!"

Dr. Passman clutched his temples in pain as a streamer of drool oozed from the corner of his mouth. A pit opened in the bottom of my stomach as I saw the fire of humanity dim within his eyes.

"What language was that? What language?" He recoiled from me, pointing at me with an accusing finger. "Your eyes! You're not human! That wasn't human!"

All that I could do was stare at him, gape-mouthed.

"What language? What language? *Whaaalaangggg...*"

Dr. Anthony Passman lost it then, in a big, bad way. He grabbed my hands in his and stared at me hard, his eyes lost in a gale of inhumanity.

"We have to get out of here, Doc!" I screamed, feeling that familiar nausea creep through my bowels. I began to back out of the smoke-filled classroom, his hands still locked in a death grip on mine.

"Whatlanguagewhatlanguagewhaggglllggg..."

Dr. Anthony Passman's pathetic gibbering trailed off then, melting into the chaos that burned its profane image into my soul.

CHAPTER 4: You're Next! You're Next!

T he police report went well.

It had to. No one remembered anything. No one except me, that is.

And I wasn't talking.

From what I gathered, though, the "official report" would read that the antiquated fuses in the classroom had blown, producing a power surge, and causing the resultant five-alarm fire. This five-alarm fire, the "official report" would read, was, of course, the cause of the subsequent "panic" which had sent all but one member of the graduate-level Psychology class in which the fire had started to the infirmary for "treatment." The only good news to come from this "unfortunate incident," as the "official report" would call it, was that classes for Friday would be rescheduled for the post-Mardi Gras holiday period.

Right. As if we'd all live that long.

Numb, I picked my way through the last few rows of curious rubberneckers—who stared at my dazed zombie-self only a little too long—and felt my way to the parking lot, where my temporary salvation from the hordes of bleating sheep rested in the form of another variety of farm animal: my Hog. A pair of cheap sunglasses and an even cheaper helmet later, danger in the form of a Harley 750 rolled out of the Stadium lot, guided by a madman.

Mad thoughts roiled through my head.

How could no one recall what had happened? Were they that jaded? Or did the lesson of Kitty Genovese just fly over everyone's heads? And Dr. Passman, my daydream adversary? Had he paid the ultimate price—the price of madness—merely for the sake of... of...

Of what? What the hell was it? Mass hypnosis? Shock? Mass hysteria?

Things just didn't make sense. Didn't make sense at all. There seemed to be no logical explanation for what had just happened. But I had to try to make sense of it anyway, try to wrest some semblance of reality from the shards of chaos gouging out my grey matter. Had to.

Was it all just another bizarre example of some paranormal phenomenon? Some heretofore unknown power of mine to produce psychokinetic effects? Some ghost in my machine? Or did I really hate class *that* much? Had too much Heavy Metal finally made me a slave of Satan? Would I soon see my face staring right back at Satan's cloud face on the cover of the *National Enquirer*? Or was I just... hell, I don't know... possessed?

Possessed? Hell, I can't even think straight! Why would something wanna possess me?

I considered that last line of logic deeply, trying not to gibber and foam. Maybe Sammy and I would share that nice padded cell somewhere soon. And maybe they'd even let us move in next to Dr. Passman, the poor bastard.

At this, I harrumphed, and, feeling mindlessly aggressive, down-shifted, then raced past a school bus full of kids, ignoring the red octagons that flapped forth from its yellow, metal neck.

'Scuze me... the evil Kurgan in me laughed.

And laughed. And—

Geez...

Realizing that I was acting like a total asshole, I skidded onto the nearest side road, making for the boonies. All I needed right now was to screw up some little kid's life by being a self-possessed, inconsiderate fool. That would really top things off.

Soon enough Mr. Un-Easy Rider hit River Road, its gnarled trees and burnt-out ruins his sole comfort of the day. I cruised, thoughts lost in highway hypnosis mode. The storm clouds running in off of the mighty Mississippi River didn't faze me. The biting drizzle that ricocheted off my visor didn't touch me. The eerie mid-afternoon darkness was lost on me. After all, I had on my sunglasses—even though my visor was tinted. I didn't even consider the absurd events of the day. Or the redundant way in which I shaded and visored my eyes from the light of day. Then, yet another wave of bizarre thoughts broke in my mind, despite my unwillingness to meet them, and I kept getting lost on the dilapidated houses that lined River Road. Somehow, the ruined antebellum structures were familiar. Somehow, somewhen. The polished chrome of my bike, the dull black tarmac of the road... these were strange things.

A good steed could make way like this, if properly motivated. But this... this... steel horse?

Ahh, Samantha, I'm really out of touch with it all.

A moment later, I was miles away, pulling into the driveway of the Pad.

What the?

I idled the Hog, rain my pitter-pat focus. Then, still expecting the hidden cameras to reveal themselves, I keyed the garage door remote and removed myself from my musings. Wet leather and hot oil greeted me as I killed the engine. I looked over at the great wall of blackened Visqueen that separated my half of the garage from Sammy's. The blurred, ill-lit silhouette of Sammy's van greeted me from within. From the smell of things, Sammy had been busy with his Mad Scientist Kit while I was at school. Fresh welds always smelled the same. So did fresh solder. So did everything that he ever tinkered with.

What a reality check.

Sammy had probably just installed some kind of "death ray" or something equally insane in his van, his madcap version of Mardi Gras crowd control. Whatever the case, I didn't really want to know what he'd been tinkering with. Better for my sanity that way.

Shaking my head again, I hopped off my "steel horse," checked the kickstand to make sure that it wouldn't fall over—'cause that would really piss me off—then made for the door. As I keyed in the proper code for the burglar alarm—5150, Sammy's idea of a joke—I felt the promise of another good thunderstorm to come rumble under my feet. I realized I had only driven ahead of this latest one, but I still felt for a moment like Bad Luck Schleprock, with my own personal storm cloud following me overhead.

That wild and woolly Louisiana weather was predictable in its unpredictability. By that, I mean that if you were smart enough to take a look outside, you could predict what the weather was going to be for the day, which was more often than not the exact opposite of what had been forecast for the day. I often wondered why those weather people just didn't do the same damn thing. Maybe the NWA had a prohibition on such common sense.

By NWA, I refer, of course, to the National Weather Association, not the rap group. That would seriously be bizarre. *Fuck the Forecast!*

Almost as bizarre as stepping out of the shower stall a few minutes later, only to find that I still had my socks on. Disgusted, I bent down and pulled them off one at a time, hurling their limp, soggy forms into the bathtub. They could dry rot there for all that I cared. Stupid socks.

"Christ!" I half laughed as I saw them form the outline of a cross amidst the draining suds and water. Divine inspiration at last! But via footwear accessories? Bad karma, if you ask me.

As I rubbed my temples, trying my futile best to rid myself of another migraine, I noticed that the throbbing in my head was in perfect synchronization with the crash and bang of the thunderstorm, which had begun to announce itself with a gathering ferocity. Leave it to musician's habit: Always in time, no matter how bad things around became.

Satisfied—but with what, I really didn't know—I stumbled out of the hell bathroom and down the hall to my room, where I went through the motions of shedding my towel and slipping into some clean, glass-free clothes. Perhaps being stark naked had made me feel defenseless, and I had just imagined the whole thing. Or perhaps I was slowly being driven insane. If the latter were the case, though, I just had to get some clothes on. Couldn't let them come to take me away while I was parading around in my birthday suit. Even Total Loons can be modest, you know?

With that thought lingering in my muddled oatmeal brain, I made for Sammy's room, eager to begin the festivities a bit early with my barley product-swilling roomie. Much to my instant dismay, though, the door to his room was closed, which meant that to disturb him was to court Death itself. The door's various artwork, if such you could name it, reinforced this concept, promising swift, cruel disembowelment to any and all transgressors of his sanctum sanctorum, his "Hidey-Hole."

For a moment I considered going in anyway, in defiance of his wishes. After all, I was his roomie and his bestest of buddies. But, remembering his childhood experiments involving copper wire, electricity, and doorknobs, I left well enough alone. *He's just gonna have to drink more later on tonight to catch up,* I fiendishly rationalized.

Denied my drinking buddy, I "walked on down the hall," as Jim Morrison would have said it, and waltzed into the kitchen, determined to start the party off right, even if it meant that I had to do it alone. The fact that Samantha, Michael, Luther, and David were probably doing the same thing right now was not a factor in my decision, mind you.

Ignoring the numerous weird newspaper clippings stuck to the face of the fridge—one of our shared insanities; Sammy and I both took morbid pleasure in reminding ourselves of such things as "Mean Mildred the Moose" and "Goat Hurling," or the ubiquitous "Bus Plunges" that plagued society—I opened the door to behold a box of Bigg Mixx cereal—Sammy's all-time favorite sugar high—shoved neatly into the space between the Albertson's quasi-generic chocolate milk and the not so generic twelve-pack of Coors. Despite my barley fervor, however, I had to pause and stare. The horribly amalgamated animal features of the Lovecraftian chimera oh so happily displayed on the cereal box made me snicker with fits of unadulterated contempt. Maybe the Madison Avenue ad executives could pull the wool over little Billy and Suzy's Muzak-blinded eyes, but I could see the 666s gleaming in its hellish, malformed visage! They couldn't fool me.

I laughed at my own foolishness, wondering when Wilford Brimley was going to do an oatmeal commercial with my brain starring as the oatmeal. Then I grabbed a Coors in honor of the Bandit and, with a bit of luck, managed to grab a pack of Graham Crackers from the fridge door before it closed. Sure, Sammy would bitch later, but he was the one who had put them there in the first place so that my thieving hands could get to them easier than if they were in some normal place, like in a cabinet or in a bank vault.

With brew and munchies in tow, I strolled into the living room, hoping that neither the approaching storm nor Sammy's infernal tinkering would knock out the TV once more. In light of this, I decided that the safest bet would be a video tape rather than the normally unreliable cable service. So I perused our videotape carousel until I found what I was looking for: Sammy's collection of

Pee Wee's Playhouse, my favorite answer for a rainy day. Personally, I didn't give a rat's ass about the media-led puritan witch hunt that had branded him a "pervert." They were all full of shit, the vultures. Hell, the city in which Sammy and I lived had tolerated its own masturbating hypocrite "Miracle Man" for years. To us—and perhaps we were too cynical to really give a shit—such a thing wasn't worth losing any sleep over. Spend one night in the French Quarter and you'll probably feel the same way. We could deal with the guy that we laughed *with*. We just couldn't deal with the guy we laughed *at*. We could see the horns holding up his halo. Why couldn't anyone else?

Besides, Pee Wee's stuff was insanely funny; not funny, insanely. Watching Pee Wee was like eating a bushel of mescaline and chasing it with a barrel of Everclear, except that there was no hangover, or death, afterwards. Today, though, much to Luther's regret again, I would substitute Coors and Graham Crackers for the hardcore stuff and pass away this gap of time.

"Thanks, Mandragora," I said, sipping on my Coors as I selected the tape marked "Loon" and popped it into the VCR. Next, after properly slouching out on the couch, I keyed the remote, striking infrared paydirt, and the Cathode God roared to life.

Pee Wee's bizarre house filled the picture, complete with all of his bizarre creations flitting this way and that, a gaggle of schizoid amalgamations. As the opening credits filed past, led by a smiling Pee Wee of course, I heard the distinctive crack of a thunderbolt ominously nearby outside. I crossed my fingers and prayed that the power wouldn't kick off before I got my fix. Such was the inevitable in Louisiana: The power would always go out during a thunderstorm if you were depending on electricity to do something for you. It was the vengeance of the gods, who were still ticked off that we had stumbled onto their holy secret. If I ever got a chance to talk to Benjamin Franklin, I would quietly suggest to him to make the appropriate sacrifices to the powers that be before flying his Promethean kite.

As the thunder boomed, I sank deep into the "plot" of the day. It seemed that Pee Wee wanted for someone to come over and play with him—no pun intended—but all of his friends had to work. They all had to *work*! Imagine that! No one could come over to Pee Wee's because he had to work! By this time—about five minutes into the show—I was well into my Coors and feeling no pain, laughing my ass off at Pee Wee's unique insanity.

The word for the day was "thing," a definite salute to Groucho, who was just as bizarre as Pee Wee in his heyday, and all of his little household friends kept on saying it, bringing about choruses of demented laughter. My sides were hurting, each laugh shortening my life span. The day's events were fading away into memory, which could always be edited, aided, and abetted by Pee Wee's contrived insanity. It made me feel better to know that, for a moment, there was someone else to identify with in my insanity, no matter how crazy things became in my "real" world. Someone else besides Sammy, that is.

Suddenly, a large crash of thunder shook the room, causing a short brownout as the breakers in the neighborhood tried to deal with the surge. I crushed my beer can in a rage, thinking that the power was about to go out. But the lines held, miraculously. The tape kept rolling and I smiled. Seeing as how my beer was now gone, I weighed the age old choice of whether or not to uproot myself to go get another, or to wait until the show was over. Since there were no commercial breaks in Sammy's edited tapes, I made the red-blooded, god-fearin' choice: I stabbed the pause button on the remote and went in search of cold brew.

As I rummaged around in the fridge for a fresh brew, a huge bolt of lightning crashed nearby, lighting up the grey green sky and shaking the entire house. Shaking, as in the Richter Scale kind of shaking, too. Dishes rattled around in the sink from the concussion. I shook my head in mute awe, wondering if they were kicking old Ben's ass in the Great Upstairs, then started back into the den. *Oh, well. I just knew he had it coming. Anyone who'd fly a kite in a thunderstorm...*

Rounding the corner of the kitchen, I stopped in my tracks.

A misty, green haze filled the den like a fog in the moors. Flashes of green, blue, and purple darted across the room under cover of the fog, looking like evil corpse lights. A deep, basso hum sounded from all around as the big screen flickered from pause into motion. Like one of George Romero's infamous zombies, I stepped forward to the screen, my mangled beer can slipping from numbed hands, gushing foam and fury on the hardwood floor.

There, on the screen, leering like some mad ghoul, "Pee Wee" taunted me with blazing green eyes as he plunged a horrible black sword—*Skurge?*—over and over again into a flaming, screaming Chairry. A foul wind wafted in from the big screen, chilling my soul with its putrescence. "Pee Wee's" pals, transformed now into leering, cavorting corpses, began a horrible, droning chorus, chanting "Die, Tatternorn! Die! Die! Die!"

The demonic Pee Wee thing hefted his mammoth black sword from Chairry's flaming ruins, licking forth from the blade a viscous ichor. As his "friends" began to weave a dancing circle around him, his hell blade began to rise and fall like a mad hammer, smashing their laughing little deformed skulls into bloody pulp. His demonic face twisted into a mocking sneer as he held the blade at arm's length toward me.

"You're next, Tatternorn! You're next!" he cackled, the words burning in my ears.

Then, as that horrid blade vanished into a jet-black figure eight of webbed energy, the Pee Wee thing let out one of those patented nerdy laughs of his that shook the windows in their frames. My heart skipped several beats as he faded away into a similar web of energy, his laughter still rumbling like a calving iceberg.

As the laughter died, the wind rose once more—if, indeed, it had ever died away—punctuating my horror. Nausea racked me as my mind began to realize the familiar.

I knew that voice.

I knew that throat-twisting tongue, that soul-burning language that I had blasted poor, mind-blasted Dr. Passman with.

It was the Dark Speech: the damned, gut-wrenching high tongue of the Shadar, the Spawn of the Dark Earth. Or, as I—Tatternorn?—knew it, Druus.

And the voice was Lord Valthrustra's!

heknowsheknowsheknows...

The world went dark at that moment. The ground shook hard beneath my feet, so hard that I fell to my knees. I couldn't fight it. I never could. We never could.

"Shit!" Distant, behind some door.

Sammy?

Hail skittering, rebounding outside.

Outside?

Pitter-pat of icy cat feet. Gale force howl of wind. Banshee moan. *It was like this the day we left Zengara, hell bound on our final mission.*

Knees. I am on my knees in the middle of my den in front of—

We died! We died. Oh, Rel help us all, we died down there in DruusDome, down there in the deepest blackened bowels of the Midnight Realm.

I am vomiting on my floor, on my knees. I am real. Vomit is real.

Tiny bugs with pointy teeth tearing at my spine. Electric tingle. Static charge at base of back, flitting there like dark moths drawn to soul's light. Pulse throb, circulation hinged on terror. Small soul nova gone haywire.

Far within myself, I listened and remembered.

Alien words. Expressions. Formulae. Magick—

"Hey man, why is it so dark in—"

Scream/double scream.

"Sammy!" The name—"name" was a lie—was torn from my lips, along with my frayed sanity.

Sammy fell against the corner of the big screen TV, his arms raised to his eyes in horror. Tremors rocking me, I gained my footing and swayed toward him. Sammy recoiled in absolute horror at my shambling approach, screaming again at the top of his lungs. Blue fire enveloped my field of vision as I fell against the screen of the television. Electric soul ants crawled behind my eyes, blinding me. Through thick lips I tried Sammy's name again. He screamed in response, his hand trembling as he pointed at me. Or at something behind me. I screamed again, too, as I turned around to seek the fiend of my nightmares.

Then, through static clouded eyes, I caught an image of crystal blue damnation flaming on the other side of the room. It was covered from top to bottom in a cocoon of writhing, pulsing electricity. And it was staring straight into my soul!

The single, burning thought in my wounded mind was to face it, to meet it and destroy it, before it did the same to me!

An oath on my lips, I charged my nemesis, death my promise.

Again, the world betrayed me. Gravity checked momentum, and then the coffee table checked my back.

Struggling to free myself from the debris—I had yet to face my nemesis—I kicked out blindly, launching the heavy couch across the den into the far wall. Something then fell into my right hand, something hard and... metallic? I crushed it in contempt, my rage splintering whatever it had been into a thousand pieces that rained down onto the floor. Steadying myself, I raised my head and snarled at my... reflection?

The splash of this morning's tepid coffee across my face froze me in disbelief. A blinding, stabbing light played across my eyes as Sammy inspected me with his flashlight.

"Holy shit, Christopher!" Sammy finally managed to say, ignoring my prohibition on that name. The light began to strobe across my eyes like some bad acid trip. His hands were shaking uncontrollably. "What... *what in the hell just*... happened? What the hell was that, huh? *What the hell was that*?"

Not even Sammy's word salad could feed my mental hunger. My ears tickled from coffee drip. I felt like a six foot, one inch pile of shit. I could see my reflection in the wall mirror, a slightly dull but otherwise normal sight. Besides those few sensory images, I was a blank. My mind was swimming with the bright tropical fishies off the Great Barrier Reef. Boy, was that water warm.

Great Barrier Reefer brain then discovered that he had a voice:

"C'mon, Sammy, ditch the light." The storms inside and outside of my mind died away as I spoke, much to my here and now relief.

After a slight pause which crawled by on broken legs, Sammy flicked the flashlight off, plunging the room into a twilight state. Then, as we stared at one another in the dim half-light of the receding storm, he looked at me with a strange mixture of fear and something wild eyed that I can only call, upon looking back at it, exhilaration.

"So," he began, clearing his throat, "I guess we're both in the dark now, huh, Logan?" Sammy split a slow grin that revealed his big, perfect teeth, which, for a moment, made him look like the Big Bad Wolf's little brother.

"Very punny. Ha. Ha. Ha." I got up on landlubber's legs and staggered for a little while, looking for some convenient object to wipe the coffee and the vomit from my face. One of Sammy's stuffed animals was nearby, so I grabbed it and did the dirty work. I silently noted to myself that it felt good to use a stuffed llama this way.

Sammy's grin melted away like the proverbial Cheshire Cat's. He had maimed guys twice his size for desecrating his "pets" on more than one occasion. Only the current madness—and, perhaps, Sammy's own insatiable curiosity—prevented him from maiming me.

"What did you see, Sammy? And spare me the bullshit, please."

"Well," he began, his hand stroking his chin, "...uh, since you dealt me that particular hand, you card shark, you, I'll tell the once in a lifetime Sammy Joseph truth. From what my 'inquiring eyes' saw, you were covered with some kind of highly excited blue plasma, kind of like what you might see at the topmast of a ship during a wild storm. Ya know, St. Elmo's Fire? Moby Dick? The Pequod? Captain Ahab and all that Melville stuff?" Sammy's eyes flashed as he shifted into Total BS mode. "Say, you haven't baptized any harpoons lately, have you?"

"Stow it, Starbuck!" I commanded. Two could play at this game.

"Aye aye, Cap'n Bligh!" Sammy saluted, stiffly. The little shit was still the Boss of the Game, no matter what the game was.

I let out a weak laugh, despite myself.

"Now," he continued, satisfied that his "funny" had been recognized, "that was Sammy the Scientist talking, mind you. And if Sammy the Scientist were to begin to calculate the foot-pounds involved in your little couch-punting stunt, or the PSI involved in your remote-crushing Robocop demonstration, he would probably have to fudge a bit, if only to avoid the Loony Bin, if you catch my drift."

"...uhh, did you say 'remote?'" I dimly recalled how easily the reinforced plastic casing had snapped in my angry grasp. Then I remembered how much the damned things cost.

"Yes. My remote. But let us not digress! Screw Sammy the Scientist! To tell you the god's honest, strange, Ripley's Believe It or Die truth, it really looked like those mondo special effects at the end of *Highlander*. I was half expecting you to say, 'There can be only one!'"

"Sammy, I just saw Pee Wee Herman turn into a total lunatic, drag out a nasty black sword, and hack everything in his playhouse to pieces! And then, to top it all off, his face twisted into this horrible expression and he told me, no shit, 'You're next, Tatternorn! You're next!' But it was the voice of that maniac from my nightmare, that Lord Vulva-Thruster or whatever. And then all the fireworks began, and all I could do was freeze up and sit there like some little chickenshit kid. All those years of training in martial arts with Michael and I still couldn't move. I've never felt so helpless in my life!"

"You're joking! Pee Wee? *Hee-hee-hee*!" Sammy doubled over, clutching his sides. Before I could get to him and kick his teeth in, though, he stopped laughing and got very serious.

"Just kidding, man. You know how I worship His Lunacy." Sammy bowed three times, arms out wide. "But you're damn right about that being scary. I think I peed my kilt! Look..." he said in a thick Scots burr, indicating his underwear, which I could see was unstained. Sammy was still in *Highlander* mode, which meant that for the next few hours all that he would say would somehow have bits and pieces of that classic movie woven into it, a perverted Mosaic From Hell, so to speak.

"No, really, Logan," Sammy continued, exhaling slowly. "This is pretty weird. First those dreams, now this special effects stuff that I can see, too. The dreams were bad enough, but they were that and only that—dreams. But when your dreams lapse over into the real world, boyo, that's when things get a little scary."

Sammy pivoted quickly, then flicked on his flashlight as he walked on down the hall—thanks, Jim—heading for his room. I followed him, not wanting to be alone at this moment.

The hardwood floor creaked ever so slightly underneath us. Usually, both of us could negotiate it quietly; Sammy pretending to be a ninja, I myself actually using Ninjutsu. Or, at least, using what Michael had taught me a couple of years ago and had *said* was Ninjutsu. But right now we lumbered on down the hall like two rutting hippos, because it seemed more expedient to conserve time and get the lights back into working order.

We passed my room and came to his door, which faced my door at roughly a forty-five degree angle, both doors forming a rough cul de sac at the end of the hallway. Whatever madman had designed this place must have had a degree in non-Euclidean geometry from Miskatonic U, since both of our bedrooms qualified as "lofts" according to the agent who had leased the place to us, even though they were both landed on the first floor of the Pad. A step or two ahead of me, Sammy bent to the floor in front of the door, his ridiculous whistling starting up once more. I heard the sound of a floorboard being pried open, followed by a dull metallic click. As Sammy had his back to me, obscuring the view, I could only guess what was going on. More wood creaked as Sammy fitted the floorboard back into place. The lock on his door clicked and the door swung soundlessly inward, revealing a laboratory that would put Dr. Frankenstein's to shame.

Running on what he mockingly called "emergency" power, Sammy's private little hideaway seemed unscathed by the loss of outside electricity. On all four sides of the huge loft there were banks of electronic equipment, one entire wall being devoted solely to a massive computer station that probably had a database bigger than the NSA's. Reams of printer paper were scattered around the floor, each little piece crumpled into a ball or shredded into countless strips of white. Old cans of Barq's Creme Soda were jutting from an extra-large purple K&B trash can, which appeared to be ground zero for some sort of atomic dump. Posters from almost every cool movie ever made occupied every square inch of his walls—including one of Pee Wee's, which I tried to avoid staring at too long. Vulgarly displayed in a row of department store glass display cases were several different collections of Star Wars toys—many of them still in their original packages—tons of Star Trek memorabilia—including several autographed props from the original TV series—Dungeons & Dragons books, modules, and miniatures, and god knows what else that my mortal eyes would never be able to discern. Stack upon stack of hoary, mylar-wrapped comic books filled the corners and the spaces beneath the long equipment tables. Countless thousands of them, ranging from Golden Age classics to the most recent issues of some runs. Complete runs of the series, too. Complete, as in totally complete. All issues of several of his favorite titles: Batman, Conan, Crow, Flaming Carrot, Predator, Punisher, Ralph Snart, Spawn, Spider-Man, Superman, Terminator, Watchmen, Weird Science, X-Men, and just about everything else in the world that was cool were prominently displayed. Multiple copies of some of them, too. In "pristine mint" condition, and with some choice issues even signed by the artist or writer. Sammy's "loft" was stocked like the ultimate comic book convention. And it was all his, if you know what I mean. If Sammy the Hoarder ever flipped out and sold off even a portion of his hoardings, which he would never do, mind you, he could probably finance a small war, or even a small Third World country, with the profits.

As if all of that wasn't enough, even the ceiling wasn't immune from Sammy's lunacy. No, it too was cluttered beyond belief—but cluttered with a multitude of naughty, tasteless girly girl centerfolds. How the little lunatic ever got them all up there, I'd never understand, as the upper reaches of the loft were unscalable and out of his reach, even by ladder. To complete the hoarding madness, in a conveniently cluttered corner of the loft there were guns of every known caliber—and some of unknown Sammy caliber—resting within an immense antique display case, whose glass doors were slightly ajar. Enough firepower that, should Sammy actually flip out and sell his stuff to finance a war, he would be more than armed enough to carry it out all by himself.

Needless to say, even though I had witnessed the Hoard Show millions of times before, it still threw me for a loop. That's why it took me an extra second or two to catch on to the fact that Sammy was standing stock still, barely breathing. His left index finger stabbed toward the opposite side of the loft as if into the heart of Hell itself.

Mr. Perception, who could feel another round of chills begin to nestle along his spine, stared across the cluttered sanctum and saw... and saw... nothing?

"What is it, Sammy?" I whispered, ready for fight or flight.

"Ehhhnnn..." Sammy foamed back, a still-pointing, gibbering statue.

Mr. Perception took another, harder look. There, directly across the loft from where we stood, precisely where Sammy was still pointing like some lunatic version of a Manic Retriever, was... *Huh? Why is he gibbering at his computer like that?*

There, in plain sight—as it had been all the time, only Mr. Perception couldn't make his Save vs. Perception—was Sammy's comfortable-looking if somewhat worn high-backed black leather chair. As always, it sat in front of the converted HDTV big screen television that Sammy used for his main computer monitor. And this was what Sammy had been gibbering and foaming about the whole damned time! Silly me! No more fiends with demon blades, at least.

Mr. Perception took another, harder look.

Hmmm...

Normally, the converted HDTV screen would be a crisp blue color, filled with some arcane computer language that Sammy had been tampering with. Or filled with more dazzling images of his several gigabytes of hardcore computer porn. I really couldn't tell. But now the heinously expensive and sorely abused HDTV screen was spewing meaningless garbage across its face at a tremendous rate. And this, of course, was what had captured Sammy's full Manic Retriever attention the moment that he walked into the room.

"Holy Snart!" Sammy loudly exclaimed, the spell now broken. Bolting across the loft so fast that I could barely follow, Sammy virtually levitated up to his waiting chair, sinking into its large, custom-fit confines as if he were some wayward Alien returning to its brood egg.

"Sammy!" I called out, just pulling up to side of the chair, breathless. "What's—"

"Shhhh!" he clipped back instantly. "Access One Ring, priority override Vulcan Zulu! Vulcan Zulu!"

For a long, confused moment, I thought that he had been talking to me. Then, just as I was about to babble back a response, Sammy's manic little hands started to finger dance across a small army of raised buttons which were recessed in the arms of the old black dreadnought. Sammy was desperately trying to regain control of the screen, which was still pouring forth gibberish.

"Can I—"

"Quiet, Spock!" he waved me aside with a quick gesture.

Tatternorn, now Spock! No wonder I'm going mad!

"I'll have to go to manual now! Voice recognition is shot!"

At this baneful pronouncement, Sammy blurred into action and pulled a spare keyboard out of the main drawer of the computer hutch worktable in front of him. Shining and gleaming under the digital glow of the huge screen, the keyboard looked like a slick acrylic butcher's block with many rows of multicolored lights playing about its face—a keyboard that was only in existence on some of the more imaginative space shows on TV. *If that was manual...*

Feverishly, at a speed that the best court stenographers could only dream of approaching, Sammy went to work, tiny fingers virtually dancing a blur across the slick keyboard. Even though I had seen him do it many times before, it was still a humbling experience to witness his genius—especially his computer genius—at work. And, with that thought stirring the oatmeal in my brain, off I went to Tangent World.

If there was one thing that Sammy was ever serious about, it was computers. As a teen, he had used them in his constant search for knowledge, eventually contacting via modem other enthusiasts, who had no way of knowing that Sammy wasn't a "normal" kid. There was no way for them to upset his precariously balanced ego by insulting him. It was friendship by proxy, a friendship that drove him to master the machine and improve upon the vehicle that made him "normal" in the unseeing eyes of the computer world. It drove him to major in CompSci/EE at LSU, where he commanded the highest honors that a student could command; sometimes politely pointing out to the professors how some current fad computer language was grossly inadequate, then proving how it could be done better. Sammy already had his Master's—in both CompSci and EE—unlike your favorite struggling Psych dude. To top this, Sammy also had not one, but nearly a dozen patents to his name, with several dozen more waiting in the wings. Computer Nerd type patents, too. Not patents that the rest of us mere mortals could easily understand, mind you, like patents for "safety pins," "paper clips," and "Chia Pets." No, more like computer babble-ese things with descriptions reading like the fine print soldered onto the insides of your personal computer's motherboard. Unwholesome things. Bad things.

And Sammy the Hoarder, as one might expect, used the income from their licensing to hoard everything he could, to tamper with everything he could, and even to finance my band. Which was, by far, at least to me and my bandmates, the coolest of the lot. Sammy had even "splurged" and bought himself an old, boxy '81 Ford van recently, which he had immediately christened "The Van." Why? Well, if you mean "why" as in "Why did he name it something so unoriginal like 'The Van?'" then I can't help you. But if you mean "why" as in "Why did a computer whiz buy an old, boxy '81 Ford van?" then I could at least bluff enough of a response and say that Sammy planned to customize the damned old boxy thing in some outer space style known only to himself. I could even go so far as to admit that, when prodded as to "why" he had bought the damned thing, Sammy would mumble something about "lasers" or "jacuzzi". But don't expect me to make sense of that. I'm only a graduate Psych student, not friggin' Dr. Fraud. I can't define "Loon!"

Be that as it may, I had to admit that I really didn't want to know. As a general rule, I never peeked into Sammy's side of the garage. Safety considerations, as it were. And sanity considerations, too. Remember? One could never know what one might find behind "Curtain Number Three," as Sammy not so jokingly called it. More like Hangar 18.

Hmmm... Back to "Reality"...

And right now, if my wild, rambling, tangential guess was correct, Mr. Computer Whiz was engaged in some inane pirate hacker war with a very heavy duty system. A hacker war which Mr. Computer Whiz looked like he was... losing?

"Shit! Double-shit! NYAA! Crab foam!" Sammy blurted, his manic hands at last coming to a halt as the screen turned a nasty shade of red. Next, disgustingly enough, a large, flashing "Morthon SatLink Module A1 01A—Disconnecting" began to flash in hand-sized red letters at the top of the converted HDTV big screen. At this point, the hacker war now was another one for the history books, Sammy tossed the slick keyboard back onto the worktable in front of him and sat back in the deep chair. He was smoldering like a pint-sized Atomic Bomb.

An awkward silence reigned for the span of a dozen seconds. Then:

"Damn it all to hell!" Sammy suddenly exploded, his voice strangely deepened by the walls of the chair. For a weird moment, I thought "Darth", then just cut it off right there. I had to hear his excuse. "I just lost a hacker war! I never lose!" he cried out, striking his hands on the sides of the chair. "I shouldn't have gotten distracted by that... by that lightning," he continued, temper abating as he blatantly lied. "It sounded like it struck right outside, and I had to see if it... if it did any damage, you know? Yeah, that's it!" he said with a bit more enthusiasm. "Had to go check up on the damage that the lightning did! And since all of my windows are welded shut, I had to go check outside."

Welded shut?

"All of the house lights were out, though," Sammy continued, warming to the occasion. "But that's just about par for our power company. Anyway, so, figuring that a cruel combination of Mother Nature and Mother you-know-what-ers were the probable cause, I thought I should get back to my work. Just when I was about to return to my sanctum, though, I suddenly heard some... something that shouldn't have been, I guess. Nasty laughter. It kinda distracted me, I guess. So, I went to check why I heard all this nasty laughter coming from the den. Thought maybe it was coming from the Cathode God or something, and this made me kinda wonder how you were watching television if the power was all out." Sammy paused, drawing a deep breath. "Hmmph! Little did I know that you'd be going mad, and that you'd be lit up like a Christmas tree in neon blue! I should've just stayed put and let my curiosity suffer. Now I'm nuts, too."

"Look, Sammy," I said, still contemplating the welds on the windows, and considering the pros and cons of that in regards to our electric bill, "I'm sorry that you saw what you did, too. I'm sorry that

I saw it." I walked up to the chair, resting my arm gently on the top of its hulking frame. It reminded me of how I tried to comfort Dr. Passman. But I pushed that from my mind. It was as easy as stirring hot oatmeal. "But I'm glad that you were there when it counted," I confided, "'cause without you, I really don't know how we would have finished off the rest of the morning's coffee."

Gotcha!

Sammy slowly turned his head around to look me, teeth bared. He hated to be "got", especially at a time like this. Had to do it, though. What better way to fight the madness than to invoke the contagious spirit of laughter? Maybe invoke the spirit of Southern Comfort?

The flicker of the computer screen drew my eyes from his. A giant, evil-looking Pac Man ran across the screen, clearing the screen in front of it with a large broom, sweeping the strangely foreboding words "Morthon Industries—Access Terminated" into a gaping Miss Piggy mouth.

What the hell?

While I pondered Sammy's deranged Muppet fixations, the converted HDTV computer screen mercifully went blank, then flashed back to its normal blue. All was "normal" once more.

Right. As if that would ever be the case again.

Sammy, though, never one to let a "Gotcha!" go to rest, swiveled around the chair to face me, then smiled that evil little Cheshire Cat smile of his.

"Pee Wee Herman, huh? I fucked him!" Sammy leered in his best Andrew Dice Clay impersonation.

CHAPTER 5: The Gathering

We made relatively good time from Baton Rouge to New Orleans in Sammy's customized '81 Ford van, a Star Trek phaser-looking radar detector our state trooper watchdog. Sammy claimed that not even laser radar could touch us. I didn't bother to ask how, or why. I just accepted it as another "Sammyism": something that not everyone could understand, only accept. Add to that a gaggle of other not so noticeable, or pronounceable, electronic "surprises" set into the van's futuristic, ergonomically efficient dashboard, and you begin to get the proper, warped picture.

Loud, raunchy music was blaring from Sammy's Crest-powered audio system at what was approaching the threshold of pain, insistently imploring us: "Let's have a war, so you can go die!" Brilliant punk rock lyrics from the early eighties, if you believe in total catharsis by means of temporary insanity. Or by means of Fear. To tell the truth, though, it was somehow fitting music for traveling I-10 at 95 miles per hour in "The Van." Lawrence Welk just wouldn't have been appropriate.

The sodium vapor streetlights were just kicking in around the New Orleans metro area as we left the interstate, the lights illuminating the dark void with a sickly yellow orange glow. Strangely enough, the sickly yellow orange glow was reminiscent of the color of the cheap double-stick popsicles I'd sometimes share with Sammy. Bad karma, first through footwear, and now through foodstuffs. I considered for a moment what the final member of that "F" triad would be, and I had to shut down that line of thought quick, fast, and in a hurry.

After a while, I had to close my eyes behind my Oakleys—not because of Sammy's demonic driving, though, for I was used to that. I had to close my eyes because, somehow deep inside, I suddenly realized that this was all a lie. It was all a terrible lie; another nightmare from which I could never wake, for I was living this nightmare as my life.

As we drove down St. Charles, Sammy turned down the blaring music and looked over at me, an inquisitive air about him. Still considering the possibly frightful karma of the situation, I did not like this at all, and my body language all but blared this. Sammy, of course, didn't give a shit about bad karma or bad body language.

"Still thinking about it, huh?" Spidey Sam said, one eye on the road and three or four more inquiring eyes on me.

"Hell yeah," I said, looking out the polarized window, trying to avoid his too-perceptive gaze. Since that was not in the realm of possibility, and since he'd keep on asking me until he got the answer he wanted, I continued, "I can't stop thinking about it, Sammy. First of all, three very real dreams—three nights in a row at exactly the same time every night, too—with each dream going a bit farther toward some... some... I don't know? Toward some fantastic conclusion, I guess." I stopped for a moment, and Sammy was cool enough, for once, to let me gather my thoughts. Totally unlike Mr. Motor Mouth, strangely enough. "And, if those stupid dreams weren't enough, there's those damned names, Sammy! I mean, get real! 'Tatternorn?' Who calls somebody a 'Tatternorn?' But... but they—the dreams, I mean—were so real that I could feel myself in them, almost as if I had lived them out before, somewhere else... No, make that *somewhen* else."

Unbidden, another rat horde of cold chills scampered up the small of my back. I turned to look at Sammy as we stopped for a red light. Time to get it all out.

"And, Sammy, I... uhh... and...?" The world stopped, and a pit opened in my stomach.

No, not yet, Common Sense seemed to whisper to me. At last, the silent bastard.

I couldn't tell Sammy about Dr. Passman yet, no matter how hard I tried. It would have to wait until we were much less sober, when such things could be properly laughed at. And then promptly forgotten.

Right. As if.

"And!" I recovered triumphantly, if not too smoothly. "And—silly conjunctions—unless I'm suffering some very severe schizophrenia, which I hope I'm not, 'Pee Wee' spoke to me in the same voice as 'Lord Valthrustra' did in my dream. How's that for weird and vaguely surreal?"

"Violent Lucidity, eh?" Sammy said, eyeing me up and down. "Not to mention the vaguely surreal blue sparks that you shot out all over the place too, huh? Well, who knows?" Sammy temporized with a sneer. "There might be too much lead in the pipes, or too much Rodan gas creeping up from the foundation of Monster Island. Or maybe we shared a hallucination. You know, mass hypnosis and the whole mind trip bit? Or maybe there's still too much Poppa Luther's Purple Haze still creeping about in our systems, and it just triggered our brains into a shared flashback!"

"Right."

"Anyway, I'm just saying that that's what it might be, Logan. Maybe. Probably. Because, from what I remember of my Psych readings, I really don't think that schizophrenia can be contagious. Besides," Sammy giggled, "I'm already loony! I'd definitely be immune to any sort of mind games!"

Sammy's hyena laugh would have gotten him committed anywhere, immediately.

Nevertheless, the Mad One eased the van into the tight traffic of the narrow boulevard with a contemptuous ease. Inwardly I agreed with Sammy—as contradictory as it seemed, he really was too loony to be schizoid. And from what I knew about schizophrenia, we were both in the category of "safe" from its effects. Poppa Luther's Purple Haze, though, was an entirely different matter.

Still, I was uneasy with the conclusion that was drawn from this data. I couldn't even share with my best friend what had happened at school. Bad karma, that.

Turning around in my seat, wishing my frailties upon someone else, I stretched my seatbelt to its limit as I peered around into the dark, forbidding interior of the van. Straining to see in the shadows of light that filtered through the tinted, black curtained windows, I could barely make out that my guitar cases were nestled safely in the rear, along with my four foot tall effects rack, which was securely resting between the van's two rearmost rows of seats. As always, in times of stress, I looked first to the safety of my instruments, sometimes even at the expense of my own well-being. After all, without my music, I was just another fool in the rain.

Right. Singin' I'm deranged. Gene Kelly would have loved it, and he had danced with cartoons.

Noting that everything seemed proper despite the demands of the city traffic, I turned once more to regard Sammy, whose little fingers were beating a staccato drum beat on the top of the leather-wrapped steering wheel.

"Well," I said, releasing a long sigh, "do you think we should bother the rest of the gang with this? With all of the upcoming big events and all of the pressure on 'em, do you think they'd even want to hear about it at all?"

"I think they would, Logan." Sammy said, feeling somewhat more at ease now. "But I think that you should wait until all the Mardi Gras stuff is done. Why spoil everyone's fifteen minutes in the spotlight with something that couldn't possibly make sense to them, something that might even make them all think that we were dropping acid or getting seriously inebriated? After all, you wouldn't want everybody to feel as if they had been left out, would you? Especially Luther!"

I chuckled and murmured an affirmative, picturing the look on Luther's wide-eyed, disbelieving face if he were to think, even for a second, that we had indulged in some grey sin without him. His mohawk would probably fall off.

Thinking about this, I turned to look out the tinted side window at all of the partying people. St. Charles was just starting to come alive with the Thursday night crowd. Most of the college kids were walking up and down the grassy boulevard, drinks in hand, shouting at passing motorists, drunken grins on their faces. Obviously, there was a parade going on somewhere nearby, judging from the hordes of people moving about. Traffic was crawling to a stop up ahead, as a few police officers were rerouting the crawling St. Charles traffic over to Magazine St., which roughly parallels St. Charles into downtown. Since our destination was Samantha's uptown St. Charles pad, the venerable Teale House,

this was contrary to our plans. And contrary to the ever-contrary whims of Sammy the Demon Driver.

As the officers began waving us on, Sammy rolled down his window and eased the van out of the queue. He drove right up to one of the startled traffic cops.

"What the hell do you think you're doing?" the officer yelled abruptly, waving his flashlight frantically toward the line of cars, hoping that the van would miraculously turn on its axles and move off. Little did he know that, once upon a time, the van could have done just that. But Sammy had shelved that Bucky Fuller idea long ago in favor of wider wheel wells for bigger and better tires for bigger and better traction, or something to that effect.

"Good sir," Sammy implored, his voice tinged with a slightly English accent, "my destination is but three blocks ahead. If I were to detour I would certainly miss it, and mum would be very upset with me."

"Who do you think you're kidding?" the exasperated officer yelled back, walking up to the van. "Get back in line and be a good boy before I bust you for being underage!"

As Sammy's face began to turn red, I put my hands over my own face to hide my smile, silently intoning a prayer that Sammy wouldn't go Loon on me and get us both arrested.

"Did you say 'underage,' sir?" Sammy blurted, his accent mysteriously vanishing.

"Yeah, I did, kid. Now get your ass back in line! You're holding up traffic."

"And you're holding up my balls with your mouth, *you idiot!*"

The officer did a double take, mouth dropping open as if to accommodate Sammy's accusation. I shook my head, wondering if we would be waived our one phone call from jail.

"You're in a lot of trouble, kid," the officer said, tucking his flashlight into his belt and reaching for his walkie talkie. "Step out of that van, slowly, with your hands where I can see them!"

"Aww, shaddup!" Sammy leered, his right hand reaching for his futuristic dashboard. With a deft flick of his wrist, he flipped a tiny green lever, one of many incongruously set into the face of his Star Trek cabin. At that moment, the officer's walkie talkie shrieked a static scream that began to build in intensity with each passing second. The surprised officer began to frantically turn the squelch knob, which only made the howl worse. Stomping on the brake,

Sammy began to rev the engine, a demonic look on his face. Unfortunately, I knew exactly what he was about to do.

"See ya!" Sammy yelled as he floored the van and hit the middle ground, tires gouging out furrows of soil like some mad double plowshare.

"Sammy! What the hell are you doing!"

Tittering like a fiend, Sammy ignored my frantic protests, gunning the vehicle's custom engine to its limits. I was pinned into my seat like an Apollo astronaut, unable to do anything except scream, which I did freely, and at the top of my lungs.

Driving right down the trolley tracks, Sammy covered three blocks in what seemed like seven seconds of hell, dodging construction work and startled pedestrians with but inches to spare. Jerking the wheel sharply to the left, he made a turn into a narrow, car-choked side street, missing a brand new Mercedes convertible by a coat of paint. I closed my eyes and gritted my teeth, certain that I was going to miss not only my gig but also the rest of my life.

After several blocks and two more rapid, sharp right turns and the tortured squealing of brakes, all motion ceased. The engine idled like some massive beast as Sammy hummed some insane tune to himself. I barely heard some sort of whirring noise outside, the distinctive sound of a garage door being opened. The vehicle eased forward into what I knew, even without opening my eyes, to be the Teale House's garage. My hands fell from my face as I leaned my head heavily onto the dash. As the engine died, I felt Sammy staring at me. Opening my eyes slowly, I fixed him with the most dispassionate glare that I could muster.

He just smiled that impish grin of his.

"I'm going to crucify you, you stunted shithead."

"Who, me?" he replied innocently. "Gonna need a junior-sized cross for that, boyo!"

"We're going to go to jail! We're going to miss the gig! We're going to go to jail!"

Sammy began whistling and popped his door open. Seeing that I was frozen in place, he called up to me.

"Aren't you coming?"

Arms frozen with post-adrenaline letdown, I unfastened my seatbelt and popped my door. Then I shuffled like a zombie around the van to where Sammy stood smiling, bumping into Samantha's midnight black 1987 Buick GNX, which shared the roomy two car garage, as I did so. Sammy was parading about, inspecting the side panels of the van, and caressing its glossy black hull with his agile little hands.

"Nary a scratch on her, if I may say so!" he laughed, looking at me with a used car salesman's eager gleam.

"Sammy, you can't outrun the law. They have radios nowadays, in case you've forgotten that in your mania. Cars have license plates! People tend to notice things like huge boxy vans running amok!" I could feel my control slipping away. "What in the hell have you done? I'm gonna miss my chance to get signed!"

Not batting an eye, Sammy pointed at the rear of the van with a supremely confident look. I stared at him like a hungry wolf, but he shook his head and continued pointing. I sighed, knowing that I had to play by his rules, and walked to the back of his van.

It took a full two seconds to realize that something was missing from its usual exterior.

The license plate was gone!

I kneeled down to get a closer look, an extreme stupidity clouding my features. The license plate well was covered with what appeared to be an extension of the van's black exterior, neatly flushed and, for all intents and purposes, indistinguishable from the rest of the vehicle. Sammy snickered when I looked lamely up at him.

"But, they had... radios..."

"Squelched," he noted matter-of-factly, as if "squelched" were the most natural thing in the world for him. "As were all of the broadcast electronics in a one hundred foot radius of my van."

"How in the world did you manage that James Bond stunt?"

"Moi? Am I not an electronics whiz and all-around genius?" Sammy bowed deeply, smiling like a master magician who wouldn't share a trade secret with a novice.

The little fink had me and he knew it. It would take an extreme run of bad luck for someone to actually trace the van here, and Sammy was the Master of Insane Luck, the Drawer of Inside Straits, the Disappearing Cheshire Cat. No, no one would report a berserk van in New Orleans during Mardi Gras. Hell, that sort of driving was typical for New Orleans.

I mumbled some deleted expletives and played out the long string of wordy-dirds just as Luther Gates walked into the garage. The big gangsta mon was stooping slightly forward to ease his seven foot, one inch form through the interior garage door so that he would not whack the lintel with his head. Or whack the ceiling with his dyed, white mohawk.

"It 'bout time you boys got here," Luther growled in his musical Jamaican patois. He crossed his thick, ebony arms and leaned heavily against Sammy's van. Gleaming like polished onyx, Luther's mohawked head reflected the golden gleam from the gold gangsta chains about his neck like some sort of new wave/modern art deco. It was the Sun King all over again, except this time in black and gold. His black muscle shirt with the neon green "Gold's Gym" letters on it looked as if it were about to rip apart from the strain of keeping in his over-huge chest as he breathed. Luther Gates—island-born, city-bred drummer supreme; big, bad, black, and dangerous—looked like an artist's Cubist impression of Mr. Clean meets Mr. T, with a good dash of growth hormone thrown in to boot. Despite his habitual put-on displays to the contrary, he was maintaining a rock-steady 4.0 at UNO just a semester away from his MBA. With his combination of brains, brawn, and musical talent, Mr. Luther Gates truly was one dangerous dude.

Barely half Luther's height, Sammy brazenly walked right up to the towering Mr. Gates and stabbed a finger at him. Or, more precisely, up in his general direction.

"How many times do I have to tell you, you big silly illegal alien!" Sammy wailed. "Contractions! Use contractions, you Maroon! It's not *it 'bout time*, it's *it's about time*, you big burnt Jamaican plantain! IT! IS! ABOUT! Speak American or die!"

Luther smiled wickedly down at him, a look that would have sent starving bears fleeing back into the deep woods. "Make me, lil' boy," the extremely dangerous Mr. Gates said coldly.

Once, not quite so long ago, I had seen a gang of pissed-off, drunken bikers get the hell out of Dodge at that tone of voice from Luther Gates. Sammy, though, idiot that he was, charged forward, swinging wildly. Luther shook off Sammy's love taps like a summer sprinkle and scooped him up in his massive arms, holding him at arm's length like a deranged kitten. Then, of course, the two of them began to laugh like idiots at their typical game.

"Boy, you're light! Go on a diet recently, mon?"

"Put me down, you big Grape Ape!"

Luther tossed him onto the van's slightly sloping roof like a ten pound sack of potatoes. "You drink your milk, son! You grow up big mon like Poppa Luther."

Sammy got to his feet, preparing to spring. But he started to snicker as Luther stuck his thick tongue out at him and waggled it. Sammy knelt down on the roof, clutching his sides, his annoying *hee-hee-hee!* laugh clanging around the garage. I laughed in spite of myself, right at home with the rest of the Loons.

"Where's Samantha?" I asked, wanting very much to see my one, sole reality.

Luther, not taking his eyes off of the treacherous Sammy for a second, waved an arm toward the door. I took this opportunity to purge myself of their lunacy and stalked off toward the inner door.

As I walked into the vast interior of Samantha's kitchen, the scent of patchouli and something else that I couldn't quite place hit me like a subtle sledgehammer. The one constant in the Teale House was the fact that Samantha always had incense burning, no matter what time of day, or for what occasion. Maybe that's why the Teale House always reminded me of an ancient Egyptian temple, like the ones in the old Cecil B. DeMille movies. Not that Samantha would have looked out of place in one, either. Except for her absolutely white hair, and the fact that she was taller than most ancient Egyptian males.

Clearing the kitchen, I came at once into the dining room, which proved to be empty except for two silver censers that were pouring forth thick, oily incense smoke. I stopped for a second to grab an apple from the crystal centerpiece, a proverbial cornucopia that probably could have fed a good-sized family of fourteen or so for a week. Doting on that salient fact for a second, I didn't hear Samantha pad softly up behind me.

"Don't spoil your appetite just yet," she purred as her lithe arms coiled around my waist. I was certain that she felt me jump out of my boots. My nerves were a little beyond shot. "I've ordered some Thai take-out for us," she added, her crystal clear, lilting laugh at once disarming me. Although I had heard Samantha laugh more than a thousand times before, in many different circumstances, this time it pierced my fragile senses like a bolt of diamond sharpness with its strange, out-of-place familiarity. It reminded me of what some castaway might hear after a lifetime of loneliness on a deserted isle, such was its foreign-yet-familiar quality.

"You don't have to worry about *my* appetite," I laughed, regaining my composure as I leaned back into her, the scent of patchouli ensnaring me. My free hand snaked backwards, grabbing her about her own firm dancer's waist.

It was typical for us: an inverted embrace, no Kama Sutra necessary. Not that two extremely creative people would ever need instructions to do what just came naturally. Or unnaturally.

"Kiss me, you fool!" Ms. Samantha Teale drawled sensually over my shoulder in her best make-believe Southern Belle accent.

With a nod to Adam, I tossed the apple back into the bowl and pulled her squarely to me. It reminded me of kissing her that long ago first time back on the Moonwalk, when we were both a little too young and too inexperienced to realize what we were getting into.

After a brief but passionate reintroduction, Samantha and I made our way into the den, which was the only concession in the Teale House to the modern world. As in the style of the Victorian manor, the Teale House gave ample space to each and every room, especially to what was now called the "den." The ceilings were steepled, at least fifteen feet high, with thick, oaken crossbeams crisscrossing each other about three feet below the slanted ceiling. While not typically Victorian, the crossbeams gave the den a timeless look, somehow ancient yet somehow modern.

Or at least that's what Samantha's great-great grandfather had thought when he had built it: Three levels of architectural juxtaposition, drawing from cultures and times as diverse as feudal Japan and golden age Babylon. And with an atrium that would knock your socks off.

Because Samantha's parents were spending the year in Sarawak on an archeological dig, we had taken the liberty of converting the den into our practice room. We had carefully moved most of the valuables into the connecting dining room and rearranged the non-antique furniture into a bizarre gallery that favored the "stage" and the Teale's entertainment center. It was a concession that Sammy had insisted on, even though he didn't live here. It was an "improvement" which no doubt would have greatly pleased the eccentric Professor Teale and her equally erudite husband.

Or so we hoped like hell, if they happened to drop in unexpectedly.

Our other "improvement" was the greenery, which occupied every nook and cranny of the converted den that wasn't *already* occupied by musical gear, speakers, or miscellaneous electronic equipment. What had begun as a ploy to "confuse" Samantha's parents lest they return too soon had grown into a new hobby for Samantha, who embraced it now with two maniacal green thumbs. She was certain that we had at last proven beyond shadow of doubt that the old, worn out theory that plants thrived on music was, indeed, no longer a theory.

But, skeptic though I was, I had to admit that the flora had thrived in the few months since we had begun our acoustic-botanical experiment, urged along, of course, by Samantha's budding interest in things green. And, skeptic though I was, even I had to admit that most of the "things green" looked pretty cool. Especially Luther's towering "experimental" plant. *Heh.*

"Where are David and Michael?" I asked eagerly, plopping down onto a very incongruous, very ancient bean bag. Several steps away, Samantha knelt before a large video carousel and began to search for a video tape.

"They decided to get festivities off to a good start by raiding the nearest liquor store," she replied eagerly, still searching for a tape.

"Figures. I would have done the same thing."

"*That* I know all too well!" Samantha remarked with a short, knowing chuckle. She knew it "all too well" because *she* was often the one who instigated such debauchery. "They were really excited about seeing you and Sammy again. Well, I mean, seeing everyone. It's only been about three or four years since we were *all* together, you know?

And you know them. I mean, us. The Brüe Crüe! We just couldn't wait to get going!"

"I'm already starting to feel a major hangover."

"Oh, no! Not yet, you fish!" she warned, chucking me on the knee with a swiftly hurled tape.

How she always managed to hit me without turning around and looking always rolled me. It was almost as if we were so connected that she always knew where I was, even if I was behind her. And she could *always* pull it off, much to my regret. "We've still got to perfect our set for the gig," she added casually, noting with a playful smirk as she turned to face me that she had, once again, been right on the mark.

"It's as good as it's gonna get until we play it live," I protested, rubbing my knee, knowing fully well that she was right. But I just couldn't shake the party attitude, despite all of today's stranger-than-strange happenings. After all, it had been half of forever since all of us had been together, and we certainly deserved to celebrate our impending signing with a major record label.

Confidence, I reminded myself.

"Get *Highlander*!" Sammy yelled as he suddenly bolted into the den, Luther right behind him with a vicious-looking banana in each hand.

Sammy, mere steps ahead of a banana-possessed Luther, ran right for me, a wide grin on his face. I didn't even have time to cringe. All I could do was watch, in not-so-veiled horror as "Reality" took another 180-degree turn into "Loon."

My jaw dropped as Sammy expertly cartwheeled across the den's slick hardwood floor and vaulted *over* me *and* my beanbag, and then onto the nearby three-sectioned sofa. Instantly, using his forward momentum to propel him upwards some ten or more feet to the lowest level of crossbeams, Sammy expertly mounted the beams like some miniature uneven bar virtuoso. A collective gasp sounded from those gathered as Sammy made an improbable revolution about the beam's girth and landed a perfect round-out dismount from ten feet up onto the hard, wooden floor. Luther, arms limp at his side, dropped his bananas from numbed hands. Samantha, crouched down before the video carousel, dropped a handful of tapes onto the floor. If it would have been possible, I would have fallen out of my bean bag.

We stared. First at Sammy, and then at one another. Then, of course, right back at Sammy.

That same wild look of exhilaration was etched upon Sammy's broad, smiling face. After three ticks from the big grandfather clock in the far corner of the den, Sammy made an elaborate flourish and bowed deeply.

"I *meant* to do that," he lied.

Right. Somewhere or somewhen else, maybe.

"Sammy," I began, words sticking in my throat like cotton candy at the absurd *familiarity* of the scene, "how in the world did you do that! I mean, that was *at least* Olympic caliber." *Not to mention slightly impossible*, I almost added.

"Yeah, Sammy!" Samantha added, regaining her composure. "How long have you been practicing on uneven ceiling beams? Have you been seeing Mary Lou Retton lately, or what?"

Sammy smiled nervously, something he only did when he didn't have a readily available response. Or when he was caught red-handed in the proverbial cookie jar.

"Uhh... gee, guys, are we interrupting something?" came a duet of familiar voices. Much to Sammy's delight, mind you.

Heads swiveled round, and Sammy smiled to himself. He was off the hook. For now.

David Miller and Michael Reese stood in the doorway, their arms filled with various deadly devices of intoxication. Curious, expectant looks were etched upon their faces. David Miller, bearded, hirsute and stocky, had a bizarre, quizzical look on his bespectacled face. He stood in the doorway of the den, slightly leaning against its frame to counter the weight of the several cases of Abita Turbo Dog that he bore. I could almost feel his powerful engineer's mind calculating the odds that Sammy could have pulled off his virtuoso stunt. Michael Reese, LT USN, stood at David's side, filling the rest of the doorway with his powerful, deeply tanned frame. Michael's corded arms were bent against the weight of a case of Boone's Farm Wild Mountain wine, a couple of fifths of Southern Comfort, and, of course, the ubiquitous Black Label Jack.

Although the weather was far from typical, humid Louisiana fare, David, as usual, wore short sleeves, his usual uncaring response to cold weather. Michael, as usual, wore the old, worn flight jacket that his father had given him when he had graduated from high school and won his appointment to Annapolis. It had been several years since last we had all been together, and all of our faces showed it. Not to mention our collective shock.

"All right!" Sammy yelled as he ran across the room and careened into a surprised David, who nearly dropped his beer cases. "Dave! Mike! It's been half of forever! I never thought I'd see you guys again!" Sammy chattered excitedly, hugging both of them about their waists, little arms stretched to their limits.

"Yep, it's been a while, big guy!" David replied, his red whiskers apparently waving of their own volition. "The modem lines just don't cut it, you know!" David laughed as he set the cases down on the nearest table and bear-hugged Sammy.

Tussling Sammy's hair for a friendly moment, Michael smiled a curt smile toward me as he set his own goodies down and strode over to where I sat, looking down at me with an appraising grin.

"Still kickin' ass, Logan?"

Bearing a mock grimace, I slowly stood up, fixing him with a riveting glare. As we locked eyes, I noticed that the corners of

Michael's mouth were twitching slightly, as if he were trying to stifle a laugh.

"Them's fightin' words where ah come from, podnuh!" I began to reach for imaginary six shooters at my side, arms held wide like a swaggering badman. Michael backed a step away, his own arms mirroring mine. I could see Samantha and Luther begin to giggle.

"Ten dollars on the marshal mon!" Luther called.

"I'll cover ya, and raise ya twenty on the longhair!" Samantha responded, getting to her feet.

Michael looked at me with a long face. "Well, longhair, looks like the pretty lady is tippin' her hand a little too soon. It's gonna be a cold day for you on Boot Hill before I'm done with you, you polecat!"

By this time, Sammy and David were also watching, whispering mischief to one another. From the corner of my eye, I saw Sammy run to where Luther's bananas had fallen, scooping them up in his hands. With a swift motion of his wrists, the wicked Chiquitas flew toward the middle space between Michael and me. With an equally swift motion, they were in our hands before they hit the floor. After a quick, understanding glance, both of us sheathed the bananas in the front of our jeans, slinging them in the best spirit of the old gunfighters. Thus armed, the tension immediately began to build as Michael and I grimaced and leered at each other; a comical, western/samurai standoff.

"But," Sammy blurted suddenly just as the tension came to a head, "what if he comes at you with a pointed stick!"

All of us, including Sammy, bent double with laughter. The twice-deadly bananas hit the floor, twisting slightly around as if they, too, were laughing. Sammy probably could have saved a lot of lives in the old West, if only Monty Python's Flying Circus had existed in the nineteenth century.

After the laughter, I grabbed Michael and exchanged consociative accolades, as William

Harper Littlejohn of Doc Savage fame would have put it. Well, sort of.

"Michael, you fuck! It's certainly been a while!"

"Well, Logan, you know how time flies when you're having sand!"

"That's the Persian Gulf for you, man. How are the SEALs doing?"

Silence, as if I had just slapped him in the face.

Now, every single one of us knew that Michael was a SEAL. Hell, *I* knew beyond shadow of a doubt that he was a SEAL, probably on Team 6, too, knowing his reputation as a soldier. But LT Michael Reese, USN, would *never* admit it to any of us, though. Not in a million years. Not even if we could figure it out for ourselves, which all of us had by now. And not even if the old "need to know" goatfuck *had* sent me and Sammy a couple of souvenirs from Coronado and Norfolk, two places where SEALs were more common than at Sea World. For a long second, Michael looked away, embarrassed. For a second, I thought that he wasn't going to say anything. For a second, I wished that I could have taken it back when I saw the thousand yard stare in his eyes.

Then, hesitantly, LT Michael Reese, USN, my martial arts/ Southern Comfort guru, spoke in subdued tones:

"Well, to tell you the truth, man, *we've* been pretty busy with all of this bullshit that you've no doubt seen on CNN lately."

Ah-ha! An admission! He was *a SEAL! Not like we didn't already know, but...*

"I mean, it's been nonstop for the last four or five months," Michael continued. "No rest for the wicked, as they say," he said with an ironic grin, the stare at last fading from his eyes.

"At least you've got one helluva tan," I said, noting how dark he had become. He looked as if someone had dipped him in a pool of bronze. "I'd kill for that Coppertone one that you've got, Michael."

"It's kinda funny that you said that!" Michael blurted, which was a rare thing for him to do. Usually, even though he could be just as silly as Sammy if the situation called for it, Michael always had his brain in gear before his mouth went to work.

"What do you mean?" I pushed, more than a tad curious.

"Well, it's a little weird, but since you brought it up, I—"

"C'mon, Michael," Luther interjected as he began to tear into the cardboard Boone's Farm crate, "tell us 'bout your crazy tan. You're almost dark as the gangsta mon himself!"

"Yeah, right!" Michael snorted, flipping Luther the bird, which would have brought the Death Penalty to any outsider who had tried it. But Luther was as dark as chicory coffee *sans lait*, and he knew it. It was just Luther's way of trying to egg Michael on to some serious partying, perhaps even a drinking match or two to settle who was "darker" than who. Or something inane along that Faustian mode of thought. Tonight, it seemed, we had a room full of "instigators."

"It's a little bizarre, Logan," Michael began, ignoring Luther's long, teasing tug on a bottle of Boone's, that distant look surfacing again on his teenage idol face. "My team was getting some much-deserved rest at a forward base. I was minding my own business, working out with a couple of Delts—you know, the guys who don't exist?—exchanging some bullshit karate moves and some old war stories, waiting for my leave to come up. I was my normal old crazy self, pretty good tan, considering most of my duty was nighttime-op." The stare disappeared from his face as he seemed to relive one of his missions. From the half-subdued grin on his face, she must have been pretty interesting. "Well, one night, after a smuggled bottle of Jack—you know how they are over there—and a shitty poker game, I cruised off to La La Land. The only problem was, I didn't have my typical dream of stateside babe-hunting and all-night fun in the Quarter." His eyes once again clouded over as some powerful memory weighed upon him. "Now, this is really weird, especially for me, but—and I swear to God on this—I had the most insane dream that I've ever had."

Michael paused, inhaling deeply, seeming to take my own breath away with this somehow familiar preamble. "Now this may sound like I was eating some of that native hash..."

"Way to go, mon!" Luther bellowed, tearing off a fresh Boone's bottlecap and draining a very large portion of its contents in one huge swig.

"No, you head, I'm serious!" Michael exploded, his usual ease gone. "I dreamed that I was this total badass martial artist guy! Better than Lee and Norris put together! I had two awesome katanas—golden ones, I think, 'cause they shone like sunlight—and each one was like an extension of my own arm." He held up his arms to show us how they would have looked. Bizarrely enough, Michael's confident form struck some distant bell of memory in my oatmeal brain.

Then, before the blasted cobwebs could clear, he continued: "I was standing before this huge, black wall that had squirming, writhing, neon green writing on it that I couldn't read, but that I knew was wrong. Really wrong." My mind began to retreat into a dark corner of itself. "The script reminded me of Arabic, not exactly right-to-left, though. More like up-and-down, with a little sideways thrown in. It all flowed together wrong. Backwards, almost, like mating snakes or something. There was a thick mist all around me, a blackish-grey mist that I couldn't see through. But I knew that there were other people with me there, because I *felt* them there, like a sixth sense or something very Zen. The feeling of dread was *real*, I'd swear it."

Real?

"And then there was this big, black *being*—some *thing*—in front of the wall, that I knew I had to kill. No, make that *obliterate*. I had to *obliterate* it, or I knew that I wouldn't wake up again. But, as I began to charge it, I saw another guy run in front of me. And he reminded me of somebody, mind you," Michael seared in my direction. For whatever reason, though, this seemed to affect my friends more than it did me.

"This *guy*," he pressed on, "had a big black sword in his hands—a sword like nothing I've *ever* seen before. Scary. Big, bad, black, and scary. Kind of like you, Luther."

Luther spewed some wine from his nose, acknowledging Michael's off-the-wall "Gotcha!"

"Then, the guy with that *thing*—I can't really bring myself to call it a *sword*, you know?—he struck the big black being before I could get to it, and the world screamed. The whole world *screamed*, man, like Hiroshima and then some. Nuke city. Endgame." Michael shook his head slowly trying to banish the thought of it all. "The next thing I knew," he forged on, his will too strong to bend, "I was bolt upright in my bunk, screaming at the top of my lungs. My CO was there in front of me, slapping my face, probably thinking 'combat stress' or some shit like that. I remember giving him a grin and telling him that I was okay; that I had dreamed of a giant camel spider that was trying to latch onto my ass, which was a total lie. But, you know? Camel spiders? Even SpecOps are scared of those things. Apparently, so was my CO, because he bought it. Then, I went to take a shower to calm down."

Now, I could *feel* Michael's pain. All of us could. It was a tangible thing. It was a *familiar* thing.

"Man," he exhaled slowly, winding down from the pain of memory, "when that shitty desalinated water hit me, it felt like heaven." Michael smiled an ironic smile then, one that reminded me of someone else, somewhen else. "Imagine my surprise when I looked down and saw *this...*"

Michael pulled off his flight jacket and set it down on the bean bag. Next, he pulled off his tee-shirt, revealing something so mind-numbing, so familiarly horrible, that I gasped despite my best effort not to do so.

Inscribed upon his strangely golden-hued chest was the solid black tattoo of a hawk, its talons rampant, clutching within them a seven-pointed star.

The room seemed to grow distant. The sounds of labored breathing and the rush of adrenaline shook my heart to the core. That numbing sense of foreboding ran headlong into my brain like a runaway train. I began to hear—no, make that *feel*—that sense of hopelessness that had plagued me in my own nightmares.

For a damning, soul-wrenching split-second I knew *who* I was, *what* I was. A distant, sepulchral voice called my name:

"*Tatternorn!*"

When "Reality" had once more anchored me, I was aware that all of us were in front of Michael, staring stupidly like cows at his strange tattoo.

No, his... Honor Crest?

I distantly felt Samantha press against me, an urgency in her being. Sammy's eyes were boring into me. It was then that I felt Luther's bottle against my chest. Luther, the Mediator of Madness.

"Hey, mon, have a sip of elixir. Calm you down."

It was not a request.

Never one to argue with a seven foot, one inch drummer's logic, I gulped down a quarter of the bottle's sweet, Kool-Aid-tasting contents and passed it along to Michael, who finished it off eagerly. Now, we stood in silence, looking everywhere but into each other's eyes. Even the irrepressible Sammy was quiet for once.

I took a chance and looked into Michael's wavering gaze.

Here was someone that I had known for years, a brave man whom I respected in many ways. Michael had taught me more about how the real world works than anyone else ever had. He had tutored me in martial arts for years—needing a punching bag at first to practice on, then later a partner to practice *with*—teaching me first to heal and then to hurt. He was a brilliant source of motivation, of achievement, of winning. Anything he set his mind to do, he did. He had followed in his father's footsteps, entering Annapolis to pursue a career in the Navy. He was a full lieutenant in the USN and poised to soon be a Lieutenant Commander —an unusual accomplishment for someone his age—a decorated veteran, and a SEAL in addition to that. Nothing could ever get under his skin, or so it had always seemed. And I knew, without ever asking, that Michael had killed other men in the line of duty; seen things that would probably drive lesser men insane.

But now the mask was gone.

I saw in his wild green eyes the same nagging doubts, the same unanswered questions that plagued me, the inescapable feeling of certain, impending doom. And from the grim faces of my friends, I was suddenly certain that it was a feeling which all of us in the room now shared.

CHAPTER 6: Electric Blue

Shuddering inside, I started as the Teale's ominous doorbell bonged once, then twice.

"Uhh, Samantha?" I asked her, edging slightly backwards as I imagined Death himself knocking on the Teale's door, a wicked smile on his skeletal, worm-eaten face.

"Oh, hell!" Samantha nervously laughed. "The Thai food. I'd forgotten."

"Here, let me—" I recovered, reaching chivalrously into my back pocket for my wallet. To mask my former retreat, that is.

"Since when do *you* have any money?" Samantha pointed out to the slow grins of my friends.

"But—"

"It's my treat, and that's that!" she said with a finality that only a Teale could manage.

As Mommy Warbucks melted away to the door, tensions eased. Males that we were, just seeing her walk away made us all smile with appreciation.

After she was out of earshot, Michael smiled at me, a curious grin on his face as he donned his tee-shirt. He was back with us, wherever "back" was. Wherever "we" were.

"You're one lucky son of a gun, Logan. She's perfect."

"If you only knew," I replied.

We laughed then, quite fatalistically; thumbing our noses at strange dreams and sinister snake-walls as the spicy aroma of Thai food hit our reality-starved senses.

After several minutes of silently pigging out in front of the TV, David cursed loudly and snapped his chopsticks in a fit of fury.

"Samantha, could I *please* get a fork?" he asked plaintively, his bearded lips pursed in some hairy state that resembled anxiety. "I'm through with these stupid pieces of wood!"

Calmly, Samantha picked through the massive pile of square, white boxes of Thai food on the table and tossed him one of the several plastic-wrapped packets of Caucasian cutlery toward him. Sammy began to snicker to himself as he looked up from his personal box of Bigg Mixx, which he always mixed with any Asian food that he ate, supposedly to "aid in digestion."

"What are you laughing at, shrimp?" David asked, tearing open the plastic packet with an impatience that was almost comical to the extreme.

"You, O Bearded One," Sammy leered between gulps of the spicy Thai food and handfuls of sugar-loaded cereal. "You've only eaten with chopsticks about a hundred-dozen times, and you still use 'em like you've got arthritis! Don't you have the hang of it yet?"

"I'm an American, dammit, and I'll use *American* utensils when I eat, no matter *what* I eat, not some stupid balsa wood airplane model sticks!" To emphasize his point, David stabbed a plastic fork into the box nearest him and began tormenting some noodles.

"But don't you know that you're robbing yourself of an interesting cultural experience, David?" Sammy chided.

"Sure I am, Mr. Bigg Mixx cereal eater!" David snorted, still struggling with the slippery, elusive noodles. "Think of all of those poor saps over in Thailand who just *wish* that they could use forks, instead of two sticks from some jungle tree to eat their rice and fish with. You know, I bet if they used a goddamn fork once in a while, there wouldn't be so many starving people over there!"

"David," Samantha said, "that's mean!"

"No," Luther interjected, struggling to talk with a mouthful of noodles, "that's pretty funny!"

David continued to stare indignantly at a grinning Sammy as the rest of us, including Samantha, let out some much-needed laughter. While it wasn't funny to laugh about starving people, there was a twisted logic in what David had said. Until I had mastered it myself, I'd *always* wondered how anyone could get *anything* into their mouths, especially rice, with two thin pieces of wood.

Still, I wasn't about to lecture David on the proven superiority of the Thais when it came to kickboxing, all supposedly on a diet of rice and fish. David, an avid sports fanatic, already knew that. He was just being a dick.

Oh, well, the ancient Egyptians were supposed to have eaten with their fingers, and they still managed to build those pyramids. I think.

"So," I began, changing the subject and initiating the small talk, "how have things been at China Lake, David?"

"Pretty good, Logan," David replied, at last getting a load of steaming noodles on his plastic fork. His look of triumph evoked a snooty laugh from Sammy, who was going ninety-to-nothing with his chopsticks in one hand and his cereal box in the other, consuming mass quantities like a Conehead on speed.

"What do you mean, 'pretty good?'" I asked him, waving my chopsticks like a conductor to elicit some lengthy, tell-all reply.

"Well, you know," David replied slowly as he munched on his hard-won noodles, "my R&D team is working on some pretty cool shit right now, and I'm getting a bit more leeway with my individual designs. Especially the new SpecOps stuff." David's eyes lit up with anticipation as he sought Michael's eyes, seeking some confirmation on the results of his work. All he got for his blatant efforts was a masked smile and a slow nod from the secretive Michael, who could not confirm, even to his gathered friends, that he had some connection to David and his weapons-designing buddies out at the Lake. As if we didn't know by now.

China Lake—or the Naval Weapons Research Center as it was officially designated—developed many of the new high tech gizmos and "black" thingies that the elite forces, such as Michael's SEALs, employed in the field. David Miller, who had graduated *summa cum laude* from Tulane University with a degree in Biomedical Engineering, had shopped his prodigious talents around to the highest bidder until he had at last settled upon China Lake. Although it had not offered a truly competitive salary for someone of his talents, the Lake had landed him because of its more than competitive environment of academic competition, along with a fair package of patent-sharing incentives. Sammy nearly had the rest of us convinced that the clean desert air and the twenty-four hour workdays were what had finally convinced David Miller to leave his friends and his spartan Covington roots behind.

Now, the fact was that David was a notorious homebody, almost as bad as Sammy, mind you. But, in reality, most of us realized that it had been the promise of all the techno-toys that he could *ever* hope to play with that had *finally* turned the trick and convinced the old homebody to spread his wings and fly away.

One *could* almost imagine that Sammy was a bit peeved that his computer buddy and techno wizard

friend had actually gone so far as to *leave* his friends and Louisiana behind. But the true fact of the matter was that Sammy was happy to see his mental sparring partner do so well for himself, although Sammy would probably never mention it aloud to anyone except for David himself to hear. Then again, even I could be proven a schmuck by that ever undefinable quantity known as "Sammy."

"Glad to see you're doing so well, Dave," Sammy suddenly said, much to everyone's relative surprise—mine even more than David's.

David smiled broadly, his red beard defining the outlines of his heartfelt gratitude. "Well, thank you, Sam," he said, acknowledging Sammy's out of character compliment. Knowing Sammy as well as he did, he took the rare "compliment" at face value, forgetting in his haste that Sammy never gave any compliment for free.

Sammy, smiling sagely, set down his chopsticks along with his box of Bigg Mixx. Then, with a wolfish smile, he uttered a loud, vomitous, glass-shattering belch.

Another "Gotcha!" We shared another group laughing spell, a few more moments of pigging out, a few more comments on how spicy the Thai food was, then: "Is there something going on that I don't know about?" Samantha asked, setting her Turbo Dog bottle down on the table with a piercing *thud*.

As her emerald eyes shot accusing glances around the table, I turned toward her and half-whispered, "What in the world are you talking about?"

Samantha gave me a curious glare, one which promised a bombshell of things to come. "I don't mean to sound like a bitch, Logan," she said evenly, her agile fingers combing back a lock of white hair that had fallen across her eyes, "but there's something in the air, something that's eating away at every one of you guys. I mean, here we are, at long last reunited as the Brüe Crüe, it's Mardi Gras season and almost Mardi Gras day itself, we're about to do our biggest gig as a band, and we're sitting here half-in and half-out of focus! Doesn't that strike you as more than a little funny, Logan? Guys?"

Sammy nudged my foot under the table as my mouth opened for a reply to Samantha's strange yet timely inquiry. Biting back my reply, I looked at my masculine counterparts to see who would take the floor to rebuke Samantha's seemingly paranoid remark.

Paranoid my ass... I thought as I recalled the day's bizarre events.

The expressions on the faces of my friends was a collectively haunting thing. Sammy was hiding his grim face behind a long swig of wine from one of the Boone's bottles that was circulating around the table. Luther was pretending to stuff his face with the remnants of a box of chicken and curried peppers. Both Michael and David were sitting with dull, vapid expressions on their faces. And I was left awash with the soul-damning possibility that maybe things were already far too gone to salvage with any sense of normalcy. Or "Reality."

"What in the world do you mean, Samantha?" I asked slowly, fending-off Sammy's desperate under-the-table kicks with a shove of my boot that sent him sprawling backwards, much to no one's delight.

"I mean *that*!" Samantha cried, leveling a finger at Sammy, who was giving me a "go to hell" look as he pulled himself back up to the table. "What in the hell are you two trying to pull?"

Well, with that, at least the others were off the hook. Now the blame rested solely on the shoulders of me and Sammy, whatever that blame might be. The need to insulate and protect the innocent from what had transpired earlier—my own blatant psychosis, Sammy's gravity-defying acrobatics, and Michael's dream-tattoo-thing—kicked into overdrive. If there were some way to protect Luther, David, and Samantha from this brewing madness, then I would willingly do anything in my power to see that such would come to pass.

Therefore, I lied.

"Nothing is 'going on,' Samantha," I assured her, giving her a confident grin. "Sammy's a klutz, that's all. He's just getting a rush from all of the MSG in the food."

"You promised you wouldn't tell, Black Bart!" Sammy yelled, taking my cue as he hurled a box of half-eaten noodles over his left shoulder and halfway across the Teale's den. The box flew straight into the wicker planting pot of one of Samantha's big and leafy philodendrons.

"Dammit!" Samantha yelled in disbelief as the relief of laughter once more filled the room. "That's gonna cost you, you little imitation Bilbo Baggins!"

With that most profane pronouncement, Samantha rose to her feet and took a swipe at Sammy's bobbing, giggling head. And, with the sound of a coconut being hit with a ball-peen hammer, she connected.

Now, normally, she would have had a snowball's chance in hell of tagging Sammy with a "nuggie," as catlike as his reflexes were. But tonight was very special indeed, for Samantha tagged him so hard that he made a complete revolution to his left and wound up three feet from the table. He listed to his left with a look of absolute shock on his cherubic features.

"Ouch!" was all that Sammy could mumble as he cradled his head in his hands, rocking slowly in place.

Samantha, not pausing a moment to witness the incredible results of her Babe Ruth swing, was already leaning over her prized philodendron. She retrieved the take-out box from the confines of the wicker planting pot with a grimace of contempt on her face.

"Holy shit!" Luther whispered carefully, not wanting Samantha to suddenly stalk over and take a swipe at him, too. "She tagged Sam-I-Am!" Luther's wide, expressive features were drawn up into a dark mask of absolute shock. He would have made a perfect double for that illustrious radio commentator who had described so eloquently the ill-fated destruction of the Hindenburg. Except

Luther would've eventually marred the gravity of the scene by laughing heinously at all the cool fire.

David was already over at Sammy's side, hoisting him up to a sitting position while Michael and I exchanged blank looks.

"You okay Sammy?" David asked, bending down to examine his computer buddy.

"Ouch!" was all that Sammy could say, still rubbing his head.

"Samantha," I asked her more calmly than I ever thought that I could, "do you realize that you just nailed Sammy for a loop?"

"The little asshole deserves it!" she rejoined, turning around, and tossing the slightly bent box onto the tabletop. The sticky contents spilled forth into a pool of runny, brown sauce. Placing her hands on her hips in righteous indignation, Samantha fixed us with the Cold Glare of Good Housekeeping and bade us, in not so many words, to "Clean this shit up!"

Never one to deny the request of a lady—especially if the lady were about to bury her foot in my groin—I at once bent to the task of clearing the table of white take-out boxes and the various empties that crowded the perimeter. Following my silent example, my friends did the same, cleansing

their respective places of any and all debris. David took the stunned Sammy's slack, picking up after him, even down to the point of using some elbow grease to wipe up the pool of runny brown sauce. I picked up after Samantha, who was busy dealing with the Thai food contamination of her precious greenery. The remains of our meal now filled the cardboard delivery boxes in which it had been delivered, precariously balanced in several stacks of four or five boxes apiece. All the while, bruised male egos were trying to sort out what had just happened. Quietly, mind you.

"What the hell is eating her?" David asked me tightly.

"Nothing, so far as I know," I admitted, stacking the empties in the center of the table. They would, of course, remain behind, a trophy collection of sorts; an unwitting offer to Dionysus for a hopefully cheerful celebration to come.

"Maybe that's the problem," Michael said snidely under his breath, earning himself a frog in the arm. Curiously, the frog didn't croak. Instead, the impact just thudded dully, and Michael, surprised, laughed directly in my face. "She done wimped you out, didn't she, hoss?"

"And maybe we're all just a little thatched, me buckos," Sammy chuckled, finally overcoming the noggin-thumping that Samantha had delivered to him. "And the solution for that is Fear!"

"'Brain damage, but it's only permanent!'" David cheered lustily, waving a fist in the air as he quoted lyrics from his and Sammy's favorite punk rock band.

So, now that the mood was set, Sammy at once got up and ran over to the soundboard and threw a few switches, one of which caused the compact, yet extremely *loud* PA system to roar to life. Giving a thumbs up, Sammy, looking for all the world like a demented Mr. Scott trying to beam the entire lot of us to Venus or someplace equally hazardous to our health, cued the CD carousel that surmounted one of his effects racks. And the... Fear... began.

The hair on my arms started to blow in the stiff breeze that followed. David ambled over to Sammy's soundboard, a bottle of suddenly conjured Bass Ale in his hand and a contented smile on his face. Between sips of wine, Luther sang along at the top of his lungs, drowning out the music in a small radius about him. Michael took his cue and produced the Southern Comfort, which he dangled before the goggling eyes of Luther. More than likely, he was trying to bribe him with the "Good-Good" to shut up and get down to some good old fashioned, down home, shit-kickin' partyin'. It did the trick, too.

Through all of this, Samantha kept staring at us, roving us with her eyes, shaking her head back and forth as if to disbelieve and thereby dispel the entire scene. Finally, realizing that nothing could be done once the booze and the music were in effect, she shrugged her shoulders and gave me a conciliatory grin.

"C'mere," I mouthed to her, motioning her toward me.

Then, time did a funny thing. In slow motion Samantha approached, every step a fresh, new line of freeform poetry. She was, to my muddled brain, a white furred tigress stalking her prey; a personification of the silver Moon in its ever-changing yet constant phases; an ice dancer in calculated, provocative pose.

In that moment I knew that I had seen her somewhere else, somewhen else, before.

"Silverdancer?" I found myself thinking aloud.

And then she was before me, a question in her eyes.

"What?" Samantha asked, her voice barely audible over the crashing power chords of the music.

I could almost feel Sammy kicking me in the leg again as a wave of cold washed over my head, snapping me out of my confused reverie.

"Nothing," I lied, adding a half-smile and a wink to cover my tracks.

Accepting it with another shrug, Samantha pointed to the table at the boxes of Thai food. Realizing that a trip to the kitchen was in order, I hauled up an armful of debris, careful not to stain my sleeves with duck sauce. Samantha tended to the rest. We made our way into the kitchen, tossing the paper and plastic into the garbage bin and scraping the few edible scraps that remained into the "doggie bowl," as Samantha liltingly called it—all for her "puppy," Lobo. He was, as the name implied, half-something big, furry, and mean. And something half-wolf.

While I waited for Samantha to deliver the goods to Lobo, who was enjoying the cold weather out in the Teale's spacious back yard, I chanced to see my reflection in the polished black surface of the towering economy-sized fridge. For the fraction of the second that it took me to look away, I could plainly see a blue nimbus of light around my eyes, centered mainly upon the iris of each eye.

"Screw this!"

I really wanted to take a look, as horrible as that may seem. The Spirit of Perversity was whispering into my ears, saying "Do it! Do it!" while the Spirit of Preservation was begging "No! No! No!" Such was my state of mind that I *almost* took another look, if only to conquer my fears. But Samantha's return quickly killed that particular notion.

"C'mon, Logan," Samantha urged playfully from the doorway, fog breath curling from her lips. "Come on out and get a load of this! Lobo's having one heckuva time with those hot noodles!"

"No, I don't think so," I said, laughing weakly. The very image of Lobo having fun eating *anything* was a bit beyond me at the moment.

"Aww, c'mon!" she pouted, poking me with her index finger. "Lobo misses you. C'mon out and see him."

"Not while he's eating."

"Don't be silly. He knows you, Logan."

"He damn well better know me! I was the one who found him!"

"I know. I was there, too. Don't you remember?"

"Yep. Last Christmas, up in Seattle. Don't think I'm so brain damaged as not to remember our little group promo 'skiing trip.' And don't forget what Sammy and Luther said about finding the dismembered sheep carcasses, either."

"Those idiots! Lobo didn't do that! He's just a puppy!"

"Just a wolf, you mean."

"Like you, huh?" Samantha breathed as she moved into the kitchen like the Queen of the Pack herself, stalking me with a strange light in her twinkling green eyes.

"Maybe. Maybe not."

I let her back me into the nearest corner, then, as she was about to pounce, I lunged forward and caught her, backing her up against the fridge. Fortunately, she was tall enough to block any view of my reflection. And, fortunately, she was more than eager to allow me my "way" with her. She was also sneaky enough to maneuver us over to the wall, so that she could kill the lights. And, for a while, things were right.

Soon, as we both came to the same disappointing conclusion that this was neither the time nor the place to continue—after all, we still had rehearsal to labor through—we reluctantly broke our embrace and started off arm in arm down the long hallway to the den.

As we made our half-inebriated way back toward the den, the sound of Sammy's blaring punk rock music once more dulled our ears, leaving nothing but the soft, shared sensation of our sashay and the libido-teasing scent of Samantha's patchouli.

But before we made it to the den, something tugged at me, deep within—something about Samantha, about *us*; something so distant, yet so damned hauntingly *familiar*. So, there, in the still of the darkened hall, I stopped Samantha, out of earshot of the others. I *had* to know, whether or not it would damn me—or all of us—straight to hell. Thus did my pride doom us all, as it did once so long ago before we knew this world.

"A penny for your dreams, my dear."

Samantha regarded me for a moment, in silence. Tension stalked between us, weaving an invisible yet tangible wall of suspicion in its wake. Her green cat-eyes were distant, almost clouded in the semi-darkness of the hall. Still, they were guarded, and both of us knew it.

Then, a flicker of something flashed across her eyes.

"I didn't—" she began defensively.

"Yes, you did!" I cut her off. "I *know* you did." I nearly had myself convinced that Michael and I were not unique in our nightmares. The voices in my head were starting to whisper an unholy chorus, compelling me to take the leading role in this Passion Play. It was a schizophrenic, inexplicable feeling. But it was a feeling that was so sudden, so strong, so powerful, that it felt as if *I* had suddenly lapsed into another nightmare myself.

Samantha drew in her breath, then crossed her arms, pulling slightly away from me. She looked as if she were debating whether to talk to me, or whether to knock me silly.

"Since you *seem* to know something you're not saying," she said, shaking her head slowly, her eyes downcast, "I'll go ahead and tell you, as crazy as it sounds. I... I *saw* you last night, in a very disturbing, very vivid dream." She paused for a second too long, then bit back a clipped laugh. "You're gonna think I was partying with Luther."

We both chuckled at that. Some of Luther's parties, as hardcore and far out as they were, *could* influence your dreams. Sometimes for many weeks afterwards. Remembering some of those wild after-gig times, we both bit back hedonistic grins. It was a full ten seconds before Samantha could regroup and continue.

"Well—and I *was* straight last night, by the way—you..." Samantha trailed off, hands animated in her frustration. "I only say *you* because whoever it was just *seemed* like you. You know how it is in dreams? Assimilate the familiar, etc.?"

I nodded an affirmative. I knew only *too* well about that lately.

"Well," she continued, her eyes fixed on the memory of her dream, "*you* were dressed in black, a cloak on your shoulders that the wind was tossing about. A hell-wind, worse than a hurricane could possibly be. But, somehow, there was a mist that defied the wind, grey and forbidding, like a storm cloud. And it clutched at us with invisible, skeletal hands."

"Us?" I interrupted.

"Yes, *us*, dammit!" From the glare that she gave me, I decided not to interrupt her again, in spite of what the erudite practicing shrinks had taught us budding psychoanalysts. "I was there,"

Samantha continued, "dressed in a jet-black outfit with silver fringe that felt like aerobic workout stuff. It was like a second skin, but it was really tough—tough like a bulletproof vest. Don't ask me how I knew that. I just *did*. Next, there was a throbbing, a pulsing, all around us, like we were caught in the heart of some giant beast. I noticed that both of us had swords. Mine was a silver katana, curved like the crescent Moon, as light as a baton. It was horrible, the way that it pulsed. Almost as if it were alive, or something. But yours... yours *was* alive. Alive, and scary. *Scary,* Logan."

She shivered for a second before continuing.

"It wasn't that it was so horrible to look at it. It was actually quite beautiful, in a... I guess, *sadistic* sort of way. I just got the chills knowing that it was yours."

Mine? Hate/Pain/Death-Brother!

"And, just like Michael said, I got the distinct impression of others being there with us. They were shadowy, hidden in the mists, but I'm certain that I knew them, shared their fear. And like all dreams, everyone else was there, too, in some sort of unconscious fashion—you know, dream assimilation stuff? Luther and Sammy were definitely there. I heard both of them cussing up a storm. I think David and Michael were, too, even though I couldn't hear them. And, like Michael said about his dream, I knew that we had to stop something bad from happening. I think that's where that weird guy started saying things about some dragon or something."

Dragon?

"But before I could do anything, you ran past us, that black blade in your hands, and you slashed at a huge, shadowy figure who screamed. He sounded like a dragon, too. Or at least what a dragon's *supposed* to sound like, if you believe the movies. Still, it was hard to pick his scream out over everyone else's. Especially mine."

I saw Samantha's eyes cloud over with a thin mist. Reaching out, I pulled her to me, crushing her to me with a surprising fierceness. I felt her chest heave slowly as she fought back tears.

"We *died*, Logan!" Samantha cried, her eyes brimming with hot tears as she relived the pain of her nightmare. "We died, and there was nothing we could do about it! *Nothing*!"

As I stroked her long white hair, my hand trembled uncontrollably. Things were already out of hand and getting steadily worse. I'd heard of shared dreams, collective Jungian unconsciousness, group psychoses, and the whole nine yards. But this? This was too much, too close to home to ignore. I'd bet my eyeteeth that David, Luther, and Sammy had dreamed the same dreams, but just weren't ready to say anything about it. David would never admit to something like that unless backed into the proverbial corner and confronted with it. Luther would gladly laugh about it and dismiss it—if he were high enough. Sammy, well, he *knew*. I don't know how I knew that he did, but I did. Hell, I *knew* that he knew. That little acrobatic stunt of his was enough to make anyone question sanity. And now, Samantha.

Even in the face of such evidence, I had to ask myself—as a supposedly rational, late-twentieth century man who had seen disco come and go on its evil way only to have even suckier music come and take its place—if we were all going stark, raving mad. The voices started taunting me again, beckoning me to follow them down the Roads to Madness.

"You know, Samantha," I said, my voice calm, guided by my mind, a million miles away, "I'm really starting to feel as if I'm slowly becoming lucid in the face of damnation." My next words came out on their own, unbidden. "But before we all hit the padded room, I really want to show you something."

I raised her head to look into her eyes. Instead of green, I saw blue. Electric blue.

Blue sparkling light arced between us with unbridled, lightning fury. My brain caught fire as brilliant, unfettered essence poured out of my being, a numbing fear combining with purest ecstasy. I saw Samantha's eyes grow wider and wider as she held my gaze, my communion.

"I... *I know you!*" she whispered, strange realization filling her. The sparks flew as she spoke, kindled by our embrace of their maddening, electric ways.

Purity, her essence flowed into me, a warmth that I freely accepted. "I" knew now who "I" was. It was only now, with the union of our being, that I realized how empty my soul had been.

"*And I know you, Silverdancer,*" I said, not speaking in words of this world. Her eyes became the world; her soul, eternity. "*We made it, Silverdancer,*" I whispered, pulling her to me for a kiss for which I'd waited a lifetime.

My Silverdancer screamed then, shattering my selfish illusions.

As the sparks began to fade rapidly away, I realized that Samantha was standing still, her hand over her mouth, a glazed look in her eyes. I saw the terror written plainly on her face. She slipped out of my grasp, edging backwards to the wall until she was pressed firmly against it.

"Saman—"

"*Shut up!*" she hissed, turning her head away.

I began to move to her, palms upwards, trying to calm her down.

"Stay the hell away from me!" Samantha groaned through gritted teeth. She began edging further down the hall, still pressed against the wall.

"Look, it's okay! Try to understand it, go with it! If you fight it, you're just denying yourself—

who you really are!"

"What the hell do *you* know?" she accused. "Huh? How in the hell can you explain something like that? We all had the same dream, didn't we? *All* of us, including *you*! That can't happen in real life! That just can't happen! And look at what happened to Michael's chest! He's wearing a tattoo from his *dream*, Logan! *His dream!*"

Samantha was almost hysterical now, tears pouring down her face as she fought for breath between sobs. If I could've just gotten a grip on things myself, instead of standing around, mired in slow motion platitudes, I could've helped her. But I was feeling that sickening nausea again. The temporary euphoria had faded away, leaving behind that same mind-numbing doubt and the urge to retch my guts out. I wanted to shake her. Make her understand and accept it. But I was lost, just like her.

Samantha collapsed into herself, sobbing. She slowly folded up against the wall and sat there cross-legged like a confused, hurt little girl who'd just lost her favorite puppy. Or her soul.

"Is she okay, Logan?" Michael asked softly as he appeared from nowhere.

I was too numb to be embarrassed by his seeing us like this. I hadn't even noticed him in the hallway, not that I would have if he didn't want me to. Not that I *could* have with all of those blue sparks jumping around between me and Samantha. Michael padded over to me, making no noticeable sound on the old hardwood floor, although he was wearing cowboy boots.

"Logan?"

"No, she's not," I said under my breath as Samantha clumsily began to wipe the tears away, reminding me once more of the sad little girl. "None of us is, Michael. Not anymore."

"I didn't mean to interrupt," Michael said a little louder, "but I thought that I heard you... uh, ask for some help with the mess. It was pretty hard to hear over Sammy's loud ass music, you know." LT Reese fidgeted awkwardly for a second like a nervous schoolboy, torn between concern and good manners. Then he looked over at me, a sheepish look on his deeply tanned face. "I had to check it out, you know?" he confided. "Training! *We've taught them not to feel...* or so the song says. I've been in the goddamn sandbox too long!"

Michael turned away from the bad scene and walked on down the hall, looking like a great golden tiger in the dark.

Sammy's music began to blare loudly, pounding the walls of the Teale House like a giant snare drum. Only now, after all of the fireworks, did I realize how loud it truly was. Good. Maybe only Michael had heard us, I wished to myself.

"Logan?" Samantha whispered, her voice choked with emotion.

"Yes, love?"

"Hold me. Please? Just hold me for a little while. Let me know that you're real."

If the eyes were really the windows to the soul, then she had just had hers torn apart. And I had been the one who had torn it.

"Everything's gonna be okay," I soothed as I pulled her up into my arms, assuring her that everything *was* going to be okay. "I promise," I lied, knowing in my heart-of-hearts that nothing between us was ever going to be the same again.

CHAPTER 7: Electric Bard

R ehearsal.

A word in the same perpetually hated league as "taxes," "death," and "condom." Words that we hate to hear, let alone abide, if only because we *have* to for some stupid reason or another. We hate taxes. We don't understand death, so we hate it, too. And the last... well, suffice to say that we *especially* hate that one.

Rehearsal, on the other hand, we could *almost* tolerate, if only because we got to polish and hone our varied musical talents and have a good time while doing it. One could argue that a good time could be had while obeying hated thing number three above, but we'd be laughing at them too hard to hear them say anything.

Electric Bard was starting to hit a groove by the second song, despite the heavy duty shit that we'd all been through today. Samantha was still refusing to look at me directly, using her keyboards and her bass like Perseus using his shield to keep away the gaze of the dread Medusa. Luther, who was already working up a good sweat where he sat encaged behind us on his great throne of drums, seemed to be unaffected by what he had seen tonight. It had been limited to Sammy's improbable acrobatic stunt. I think. Whatever the case, Luther still showed no inclination to share his dreams with us. And no one here was going to press him to do so if he really did not want to. None of us was that crazy.

And I... I was glad to have my guitar in my hands, a mic in front of me, and a song on my lips. Already the adrenaline was flowing, along with the sweat, washing away my iniquities and cleansing my sin. We were ripping into our eclectic set of songs, careless and carefree to those who looked upon us, but not quite feeling the same way inside. To me, that was the most awesome aspect of making music: The mood- and mind-altering effect it always conveyed. Especially to those who listened to it with open ears and open hearts, through any and all such distractions of the soul. Such things merely added fuel to the all-consuming magickal fire of music. And, tonight, we were burning.

Things always seemed a little bit more concrete when the three of us, along with the manic sound master Sammy, were burning together, jamming together, and feeling the music as if it were a living thing. Things seemed a little bit more *real*.

Almost familiar! I taunted myself as I crunched down hard on an ascending octave solo run, mimicking note-for-note a bar from Jimi Hendrix's badass solo on "All Along The Watchtower," warping it into the segue of an off-kilter harmonic minor sixty-fourth note assault. A wide grin bloomed on Luther's face as he caught himself laughing into his headset mike. Shaking his head in utter disbelief that I could have blasphemed "The Master" in such a heinous way, he added a whacked out cowbell paradiddle as we headed back into the refrain that totally caught me off-guard. I stumbled back into my microphone stand like a spastic child.

This brought the smallest of flickers to Samantha's eyes, which made me feel so damn good inside that I just broke into a spontaneous version of Steppenwolf's classic tune, "Born To Be Wild," to which I substituted the lyrics of "Petticoat Junction." And, surprisingly, it fit.

Yes, there was no longer any doubt from the demented looks on the faces of the Loons in the room: We were determined to make ourselves "number one with a bullet" on the Loony Tunes Hit Parade.

Luther, our rhythm anchor, was, as always, right on time, despite the laughter; driving us along whether or not we wanted to go. That was his main gift: consistency. Luther was like a human metronome, an octopus with a rhythmic brain. His drum kit—a cyclopean hodgepodge set pieced together from several different smaller kits—was like a great cage around him, from which it seemed that he was trying to pound his way out. As big as he was, it was difficult to see him behind the fifteen Zildjian cymbals that surmounted his double-bass kit, not to mention the double bell trees, chimes, crotales, and a row of synthesizer-slaved trip pads for those really bizarre electronic percussive effects. Behind him there were also two sets of congas and a well-worn set of steel drums, which he could grab in a second and swivel around in front of his drum throne. Sammy had conveniently mounted the entire kit on a Lazy Susan construction that could revolve 360 degrees like Neil Peart's, if necessary.

Samantha, recovering from her hallway shock, was taking out her frustrations on her Hamer bass (the 12-string one, too; not her normal 4-string beauty), shredding with an intensity that surprised everyone in the room. Not that we *should* have been surprised: Samantha had transcribed over two hundred pieces of *extreme* music ranging from Bach's *Toccata and Fugue in D-minor* to Paganini's *Caprices* to Billy Sheehan's and Paul David Harbour's most insane metal bass solos. Two terms as a child prodigy at Juilliard *did* have its advantages. In her "spare" time, which was mainly during the intros and the breaks of our songs, she manned a rack of Yamaha, Oberheim, and other Sammy-warped synthesizers that nearly hid her when she stepped behind them. Samantha performed both bass and keys with equal skill, if not with equal playing time. After all, her piano ability was what had landed her the Juilliard gig in the first place.

The guitars were all mine. My personal hoardings were a host of weird stringed things that included an ESP 6/12-string double-neck, an Alvarez classical guitar, an Ibanez 7-string adorned with one helluva psychedelic airbrush job, a smooth-backed Ovation 12-string acoustic, and my pride and joy: an all-original, mint condition '64 Strat. Strung upside-down like Jimi's, of course. Add to that one eerie-looking lute, which I had crafted myself one crazed summer from a twisted piece of driftwood that I had found off Grand Isle, and you get the picture.

In addition to the stringed things, there was also an ancient set of Taurus bass pedals, which were slaved to one of Samantha's synthesizer sequencers for an array of bizarre foot-triggered special effects that ranged from Star Wars-sounding laser blasts to contrabass choruses that doubled and enriched our own three-part harmonies.

Together, the three of us made enough music for an orchestra, although no sane person would ever draw such a lofty comparison, even if highly bribed.

Sammy's keyboard sequencing and creative use of background video "enhancement"—we had two separate video-imaging screens for the psychedelic fills and thrills that were synched to follow our show in real time—rounded out the technical end of our little traveling medicine show. Call all of the techno stuff "cheating" if you will, but at least give us the credit for writing our own stuff and singing it in three-part harmony. We would never be accused of being Milli Vanilli. Never.

Halfway through our set, we had begun to work up a healthy sweat, sinking deeper into the rambling, rumbling groove of things, the night's earlier events lost somewhere in time. Sammy was working like a madman to coordinate the sound and light boards, running them both from a single, decked-out system that he had customized from the guts of eight—count 'em—*eight* other boards and a Synclavier, the Cadillac of computerized digital systems. David was playing Igor to Sammy's Baron Frankenstein, assisting him with the more trivial things while goggling over all of the shiny lights and pretty electric thingies, some of which I'm sure he had probably worked with at China Lake. Michael slouched happily on the couch, a little to the side of our mega-powerful Crest-amplified PA system, with a bottle of Black Label Jack curled up in his hands and a wide grin on his face as he sang along with us.

It was magick as we rolled like an out-of-control Mongol Horde into our finale, the one song that WCKW was rotating heavily on its "Homegrown Hour," our kicking, rhythm-driven iconoclastic "love song," "Now That You're Gone":

"I see your eyes in every star...
I call your name a thousand times
I hear your voice softly fall like rain...
Long ago I was your lover
Now see my eyes, I am
Another long lost soul, lonely in the night
Now I call your name
But the faces all have changed
I'm crying in the rain...
Now that you're gone
You've made believe our love was wrong
Now that you're gone
All the good times shared
Can't be shared alone...
Shattered mirror, broken shards
Each a dream no more
I walk the night, alone
Now I call your name

Only memories remain
You're crying in the rain...
Does it matter?
Do you feel the same?
Do you feel at all?
...I see your eyes in every star..."

Sweating, smiling, and exhausted, Samantha, Luther, and I held out the last rousing chords of our finale, exchanging triumphant smiles as we imagined the stunned, slack-jawed faces of all of the music execs who would be chomping at the bit to sign us Mardi Gras night. The three eager pairs of clapping hands, however, brought us back to reality, if only for a little while.

"That's a wrap, guys," Sammy announced over the talk-back mike at the board. And that was that.

See ya, re-whore-sal!

Feeling very satisfied, for once, I shot Samantha a smile and unslung my guitar, tossing my pick over my shoulder, our signal to exit stage left for the nonce. She gave me a grin and a thumbs up—it made me feel warm to see her eyes alive again—then stepped out from behind her synthesizer rack, a bottle of Guinness Stout already in her hands.

Suddenly, a double-bass kick-drum rumble threatened to knock us all to the floor as Luther cut loose like a total maniac.

"Party! Party! Party!" Rastamon bellowed through his headset mike like the Delta House version of John Belushi. Sammy took the cue and, with a flick of the switch, blared "Low Rider" through the PA, peaking the meters. For the duration of three repetitions of our favorite party tune, we formed an impromptu conga line and cavorted about the den, acting like a den of fools, singing at the top of our lungs, spilling cheap wine on priceless antiques. And having fun.

After our "low ride," we decided that it was in the best interest of the Teale House to move our party elsewhere; preferably the French Quarter, where our lewd behavior would fit right in with everyone else's. Sammy suggested "The Van." Figuring that the police would probably have better things to do than harass a van stuffed with a drunk midget lunatic and his twice-drunk band of fellow Loons, I reluctantly acquiesced to Sammy's nagging. Besides, if it did come down to it, we could always claim that we were a Mardi Gras float or something, considering how weird we looked as a group.

Gathering up the last of our goodies, Luther took the last of the Boone's Farm while Sammy and David shut off all the lights. Because Samantha was going to be out of the scene for a time while she showered and changed clothes, Michael and I hatched a plot. Under my direction and without Samantha's approval, Michael stealthily made his way to the Teale's well-stocked wine cellar like the highly trained SEAL that he was and procured a bottle of '66 Dom Perignon, securing it in his flight jacket. I made it my highly untrained, un-SEAL-like duty to procure a corkscrew. Champagne for the celebration of the Lizard King. We would spring our surprise later on the rest of the unsuspecting Brüe Crüe, and pray that Samantha wouldn't take it out on our heads.

At least, that was our plan.

Therefore, we tried to get to the van before Samantha, or, for that matter, before anyone else did. As fate would have it, though, Luther, always the first one at any party, spied us giggling like the total idiots that we were as we entered the garage.

"What's so funny?" Luther asked, eyeing us both like some gargantuan hawk.

"Uh, nothing, you big drummer, you!" Michael said without breaking up. Almost.

As we both began to guffaw at being "busted" by someone more corrupt than any DEA double-agent could ever *hope* to be, Luther, smiling craftily, reached forward and grabbed both of us by the shoulders. He clutched us both to him conspiratorially.

"You got the Good-Good, huh?" Luther's wine-breath hit us like a Mack truck, dulling our senses for a second. A second which he used to frisk us both down for the "Good-Good."

"Hey! I don't do that on the first date!" Michael laughed as he tried to keep his jacket closed over the bottle. But it was too late for him, because Luther already had one of his economy-sized hands around the Dom Perignon bottle.

"Ahh-ha!" Luther shouted triumphantly, drawing the bottle out and holding it high over his head. "The Good-Good!" he shouted as he began a weaving, drunken dance around the garage.

Instantly, Michael and I were in hot pursuit of the runaway Rastamon.

"Luther, stop!" I shouted, reaching for the bottle.

"No way, mon!" he teased, holding the bottle *waaay* up out of reach. "You boys give the tribute to the king, and that's *moi*!"

I looked over at Michael, who gave me a desperate look right back. There was no getting it wrong: We would much rather take the chance of getting thrashed by a seven foot tall version of King Kong than take our chances with a pissed-off Samantha Teale. So we both jumped him, securing his arms in double elbow locks.

Silly us.

Now you have to realize something here: Between me and Michael, we had the equivalent of seven black belts in various martial arts styles, not to mention some four hundred pounds-plus mass on our side. While it should be noted that the slim majority of the mass and the overwhelming majority of the belts were Michael's, though, *neither* one of us was your average schoolyard pushover, mind you.

But Luther just shrugged us off like fleas, hurling both of us a full ten feet in either direction with a casual flex of his arms, dancing all the while. I was lucky and hit the side panel of the van with my backside. Michael, however, flew head over heels across the garage and thumped into the garage door with a loud clang. And this was what finally snapped Luther out of his mad version of the *Tarantella*.

"Wow!" Sammy shouted from the doorway. "Did you see *that*, David?"

"Yep," David said slowly, thoughtfully stroking his beard, "but I'm still not sure that I believe it."

Rubbing my shoulder, I turned to see Sammy and David standing at the door, arms at their sides, mouths agape. Luther, startled for once, turned to face them, the bottle still held high over his head.

"What's up, bros?" he asked, his eyebrows arching up to his mohawk. "You don't like the dance?"

"Have you been smoking steroids, Luther?" Michael said as he dusted himself off and walked over to Luther's side. Thankfully, Michael was not wounded in the least. Had it been me, I would probably now be in traction. But, like I said, the majority of those belts *did* belong to Michael.

Sammy and David walked over, exchanging sidelong glances with each other as they did.

"Yeah, Luther!" David cajoled. "What have you been smoking? Testosterone or something?"

"You know I smoke only the ganja, now, mon! No impurity for I, you know?"

The tone with which Luther delivered his statement of personal Rasta opinion left no room for doubt, either.

"You realize you just tossed off those two like you did me earlier, Luther," Sammy said, his

tone even and analytical.

"But you're just a lil' boy, Sam-I-Am," Luther said, a smile creasing his wide face. He loved to taunt Sammy with an endless onslaught of obscure Dr. Seuss references. And to Sammy Joseph, genius nonpareil, Dr. Seuss was *sacred*.

"I know *that*, you big idiot!" Sammy said sharply, slugging Luther futilely on the leg. "But those two together at least quadruple my mass, and you tossed them off of you like insects. No offense, guys."

"None taken, Grasshopper," I said, smiling at Michael.

"Not to mention that both of them together—*marital* artists that they are—should have been more than enough to hold even you, big guy," David added, rubbing his hands together as he sought to ignore the looks of disdain from both Michael and me. Like Sammy, David was probably calculating the vector forces involved in Luther's action and reaching some fairly high foot-poundage. Yes, they were both *that* good. And they weren't allowed to be on the same team when we played *Trivial Pursuit*.

"I've got an idea," Sammy said quickly, his hand at his temple in concentration.

"Oh, no!" Luther moaned, backing away from Sammy, the Dom Perignon bottle held out to ward off Sammy's evil thoughts.

"Oh, yes!" Sammy said, reaching out in a blur, grabbing the bottle from Luther. I breathed a sigh of relief as Sammy slipped me the ill-gained bottle. Michael wiped his brow in not-so-mock relief, then took the much-abused bottle and secured it again within his flight jacket. Meanwhile, Sammy was busy dragging a pleading Luther to the side of his van while David was calling out specs on the size, estimated mass, and something that sounded like "moo-static potential" of the van. Sammy only corrected his guesses once, on the mass of "The Van," adjusting it upwards by a cool four hundred pounds while smiling a knowing smile to David, who just shook his head and mumbled something unintelligible. Sometimes, I just felt like an idiot around those two Monsters of Math.

"Okay, Rastamon," Sammy said as he placed Luther's hands under the frame of the van, "lift it up, and I'll make you some of my special Rastamon brownies."

"Hey!" Luther foamed, his eyes lighting up.

"Now that's what I'd call proper motivation, Sammy!" David said, shaking with laughter.

"You lie, runt," Luther said, rising up and folding his arms.

"That's for me to know and you to find out," Sammy said evenly. "But you'll never know unless you do it."

Luther grumbled, muttering some choice French gutter-words under his breath as he bent to his task. "Lift the goddamn van, he says, just like I'm some big beast! If I lift the van, runt, I'm gonna throw it on you!"

Reluctantly, Luther bent down, grabbing the frame of the van with his massive hands. As he set himself and took in a series of short breaths, I once again felt that strange feeling of displacement. As if I were someone else watching this, somewhere else. There was no doubt in my rational mind that he was going to give himself a double hernia trying to lift a two ton van, all for Sammy's cruelly promised reward. I started to feel sorry for Luther, whom Sammy always took for a ride, but that pity was replaced by the more pressing concern that my drummer was going to get ruptured before our big gig.

"C'mon, Luther," I said, "Sammy's only teasing. Don't hurt yourself."

"Screw you! I want some brownies!" Luther spat through clenched teeth, his habitual patois mysteriously disappearing in his stress.

"Yeah, screw you!" Sammy mocked, shushing me.

The van was rocking slightly as Luther exerted himself. I shook my head, picturing a gig without a drummer. When the van rose a half-foot off of the garage floor, though, my heart skipped a beat.

That feeling returned, hitting me like a runaway freight train. This was too much for one day.

My vision blurred, my legs felt weak as the voices started calling again. Not even the shell of alcohol I had submerged myself within could protect me this time as Luther hoisted the protesting van up to his chest, his arms bulging like twin anacondas.

"I don't believe it!" Michael exploded, echoing the very thoughts that each of us held.

"You better believe it, Mikey," Luther gasped as he began to straighten his arms, "'cause I'm the Mon!"

"Wait!" Sammy started screaming. "Stop, or you'll crush the GNX!"

"You gonna pay up, then?" Luther said wickedly, balancing the van on its tortured wheels.

"Yes! Yes! Yes!" Sammy pleaded. "Now, set it down, *gently*. Please, big guy? We all know you're the Man... I mean, the Mon... now!"

Satisfied that he was, indeed, "The Mon," Luther set the van down gently, the shocks only bouncing slightly. David let out a cheer, then started dancing a little jig with a smiling Luther. Without missing a beat, Luther, who probably somehow knew he could do the impossible all along, or so my paranoid mind screamed at me, plucked an exhilarated Sammy right off of the floor and set him upon his broad shoulders.

"Incredible," Michael said to me, shaking his head in disbelief. "No wonder he tossed us off like little kids. He's as strong as the Hulk!"

"Michael," I asked, taking him aside, my voice sounding just a little bit hollow, "what's happening to us? What's going on? Are we all going crazy?"

"I've been wondering about that one myself for the past few days," he said, looking me straight in the eyes with that eerie, calm, green-eyed stare of his. "But, I've already made up my mind to go along with whatever *is* going on. To comprehend it. Then, to conquer it. The best thing that you can do, Logan, old buddy, is to focus yourself. Get a grip on this new reality. Of all of us—even me—only you have the internal strength to pull us through this."

Michael Reese, my old martial arts guru and drinking buddy, placed his deeply tanned hand on my shoulder and gave it a squeeze.

"But how do you..."

"Don't ask," he interrupted. "Just accept it. I *know*. It's that simple, yet that complex."

"And that's the Zen of it, then?" I stated flatly, not allowing my discontent to enter my voice.

"You could say that," Michael said with a haunting, secret smile.

I considered this deeply. For all of three seconds, then:

"Okay, I'm ready guys," Samantha said cheerfully as she entered the garage. She took one look around at all of the idiots, then put on a slightly confused face. "Did I miss something?"

"Only this," I announced, holding up the corkscrew only after the lunatic laughter had died down to a small roar. *Did I miss something?*

The sign given, Michael produced the champagne from his jacket and passed me the bottle, which I quickly opened despite the glare I got from Samantha. "A toast!" I proclaimed, holding up the bottle. Eager cheers greeted my announcement, so, warming to the occasion, I stood front and center, then paused a moment to consider how best to put into words the thoughts that were roiling through my mind. "Well, like Jim says," I offered, raising the bottle high in tribute to the Lizard King, "'Try to run, try to hide...'" I began.

"'Break on through to the other side!'" we finished together.

Then, as one, their eyes lit up with something just a shade beyond what most would call anticipation as the irony of my toast struck home. In the curious silence that followed, we passed the bottle around and all but chugged the expensive bubbly. Judging by the knowing glint in their eyes, it appeared that the doors of perception had indeed been opened.

CHAPTER 8: Remembrance Of Things Past

Finding a parking place was—to put it in terms that someone unfamiliar with parking in the French Quarter at *any* time during Mardi Gras might understand—hell.

Fortunately, we were able, due to Sammy's *Death Race*-influenced demonic driving, to cut off several less-demonic motorists and find our way into the parking lot between the Moonwalk and the Vieux Carre Riverview, before the Fuzz could get us.

But let me point out the fine print here: Getting into the parking lot and finding a parking place were two entirely different arts. The lot was jam-packed, with cars illegally parked on the small median beneath the Moonwalk, not to mention the motor homes and RVs that were hogging more than their share of the lot. It was enough to make a sane person mad. Consider that, then recall the fact that Sammy was driving.

While the twenty or more cars that sat in line like cattle waited patiently for a spot to open, Sammy gunned his engine obnoxiously and blared some really cool Soundgarden as loud as his system would allow, which was somewhere in the neighborhood of a Concorde taking off. Add to that the fact that Luther was shaking the entire van with his air-drumming, his foot-stomping, and his uncanny reproduction of Chris Cornell's I'm-so-pissed-off-it-that-it-hurts voice, and you could see that we made quite a sight.

Reaching up to where David sat in the passenger seat, I grabbed his bulky shoulder and motioned for him to turn down the stereo for a minute. Smiling, he complied, turning it down to slightly-less-than-earbleed level. Earbleed abating, I reached over the back of Sammy's seat and grabbed him by the shoulder. Then, I shouted into his ears. Loudly.

"Samantha says she saw a car pull out of a spot behind us! It'll be a tight fit, but—"

"What?" Sammy yelled insanely, his Monty Python accent once again creeping into his voice. "A spot! Why didn't you say so, man?"

With that, Sammy gunned the engine and pulled out of the line of cars, nearly smashing the rear fender of a white Bronco as he did so. Hanging onto the rear of his seat for dear life, I had the inestimable pleasure once again of experiencing Sammy's *Death Race* as he hit forty miles per hour in a very, very short clip. Then, slammed into a controlled power slide, right into the vacant space between a rather nice Ford Taurus and a rather silly Yugo. Now safe once more in his imaginary Bat Cave, Sammy revved his engine to the redline once, then twice, then thrice, then let it idle like the gas-hungry thing that it was.

As Sammy killed the engine, however, a very irate, clean-cut young man and his conservative-looking group of male friends with matching Polo shirts piled out of the rather nice Ford Taurus next to us and walked up to Sammy's window. Their faces were flushed with rage.

"You asshole!" barked the clean-cut young man as his knuckles rapped on the tinted window. "Get out of that dope wagon so I can teach you how to drive like a human being!" His buddies, five more just like him, were starting to bow-up and catcall as they paraded around Sammy's van, shaking it from side to side.

I could understand their reaction at having almost been killed. What I did not like was the fact that, due to Sammy's heavily tinted windows, they were assuming that only Sammy and David were inside, easy pickings for the six of them. Those were hardly fair odds.

And I just hated bullies, especially stupid ones.

Remarkably, Sammy just sat there, shaking his head a few times before finally reaching over and killing the music. Their outraged shouts were really starting to get imaginative. Luther was hooting and hollering like a wild man, waiting for the word to be given. David was trying not to laugh. Sammy was strangely quiet, which I didn't like at all.

"C'mon, Sammy," Samantha said calmly, "just let them get it out of their systems, then they'll go on their way."

"Yeah, Sammy," Michael reasoned, "we don't need to get into any police trouble here, especially with a bunch of drunken daddy's boys."

"Well, okay," Sammy said, a tense edge in his voice, "but—and I mean this—if they fuck with my van, I'll kill them."

For a split-second, I believed every word he said. So did everyone else in the van.

Everyone except for a certain Mr. Gates, that is.

"Dead by dawn! Dead by dawn!" Luther suddenly taunted, egging Sammy on with that horrible line from that horribly cool movie. Instantly, Luther earned himself a van-full of "shush's" for his efforts. Damned instigator. And he knew it, too.

The Polo Gang, apparently having their fill of fun, began to file back into their car. But just as they were getting situated, the driver of the car, the guy who had first got out, suddenly jumped back out and ran around to Sammy's window once more. There was a large deer-knife in his hands.

Oh, no...

As Sammy calmly looked on, the clean-cut Davie Crockett brandished his knife, then plunged it into the driver's side door with a grinding metal-on-metal sound.

"What do you think about that, you asshole?" the clean-cut guy demanded, bearing his teeth like a fiend.

"NYAAA!" Sammy growled as he shoved his door open and leaped for the guy's throat.

A chorus of expletives went out from both vehicles as both sides started to pour out, ready for action. Following Sammy out of the door, I was the second one out of the van. Hitting the tarmac of the parking lot, I landed on the two of them, trying to isolate the knife so that no one would regret the night's fun. But I got nothing except a squirming Sammy. I pulled him off of the screaming guy just as the first and second of his buddies reached me, arms pumping like crazy.

"Back off, and we can just forget about this whole thing!" I offered as knife-boy got up and took a wide slice at Sammy, who wasn't helping things by wiggling like a greased otter in my arms.

"Get that son of a bitch and his midget friend!" Knife-guy screamed to his swinging buddies.

They missed their first swings, but one managed to catch Sammy Spastic with a left hook that jarred

his hard head into my chin.

"Fuck this!" I shouted, blood welling from the underside of my chin. They had just crossed that thin, red line. And now they would pay for their sins.

I threw Sammy's wiggling form at the nearest Polo guy, catching him at the waist and knocking him backwards into the Taurus.

Yeah, I know. Dwarf-tossing. And you go fuck yourself for even thinking that dwarf-tossing was illegal in combat. Combat slobs. I'd throw you, your momma, and your entire toothless, maggot-infested, rat-bastard family at an enemy if it gave me even a nanosecond of advantage in combat. Win at all costs. Even if you have toss a dwarf at a crippled nun.

The second Polo guy took a bull charge at me, hoping like hell to knock me into the van with his slovenly, beer-bellied, two hundred twenty-plus-pound mass. Once tonight was enough in my book, so his bull charge suddenly ended with a *Dragon's Fist* to the collarbone, which, gratifyingly enough, snapped exactly like Michael had promised a collarbone was supposed to snap. I cleared my stance, regaining my *chi*, then stared at knife-boy and his other four Polo boys.

Something gleamed in reflection from their eyes. Something brief, but something blue.

Needless to say, they stopped in their tracks, staring in open, drunken wonder at me. So I took this fraction of a second to take in the scene. Sammy was rolling on the tarmac with the guy that I had thrown him into, which made the odds just fine in my book, knife-guy still standing in front of me or not. And I could hear the mad scramble of my friends as they approached. Fine. Were these bozos in for a rude awakening.

"What are you waiting for? Show him some fists!" knife-boy screamed. Panicking, he waved his knife around his head as if swatting gnats. "Get him!"

So eloquently urged on, the four Polo Guys broke from their trances, then broke into two groups: one group circling around to the front of the car; the other group coming straight on from the rear. Just like sheep to the Big Bad Wolf, the fools.

The two racing around to the front never quite made it. Michael, rounding the front of the van, nearly decapitated one of them with a flashy, spinning back-fist that dropped Joe Polo in his tracks like a sack of wet sand. David, his glasses off, rushed around Michael and bulled into the other one. David slammed him down hard onto the tarmac and pinning him face-down, much the same as he used to do when he was an undefeated light-heavyweight wrestler his senior year at St. Paul's High School. Such was the same for the two racing from the rear of the car. They met Luther, who introduced them to Pain.

Now, the tables turned in the space of three seconds, knife-boy was suddenly very much alone. And pissed off to the max.

"What the fuck are you people, freaks or something?" he asked. His voice cracked and his eyes grew wide as he looked first at Sammy, who was busy kicking the curled-up form of his fallen foe, then to the towering Luther, who smiled and cracked his gnarled knuckles with a sound like railroad ties being driven.

"You don't scare me, you freaks! I've still got a kn—"

The metallic *che-clak* of a semi-automatic's slide drawing back carried in the murky night air like the toll of doom. Samantha, a Sig-Sauer 9mm in her hands, held a dead bead on knife-boy's heart from her perch on the van's roof.

"Lose the knife, or lose your life. You make the call," she said coldly.

Knife-boy's face turned a sickly shade of green as he finally realized the stakes of the game. Then, like the good little boy that he was, he dropped the knife from his nerveless hands and bolted to his car. Those of his friends who could still function dragged those who couldn't back to the car, and they beat one of the fastest retreats I'd ever seen. They left ten feet of burnt rubber behind them as they sped off.

"Pussies!" Sammy said as they sped off. He flew the finger the whole time.

"They met the Mon and his homies tonight!" Luther said loudly, ruffling Sammy's hair as he did so. And, hopefully, defusing the eight mile long fuse of vengeance that burned in Sammy's mind. Good Ol' Luther. He could bring you back as well as take you there, the old instigator.

Slowly, my scrambled senses seemed to return to what passed for normal. Now, with the hue and cry gone, I could hear... laughter? It was David, who was laughing about something with Michael. Slowly, I turned to look at the two of them. Both of them smiled at me, then pointed up at Samantha. I gave in, and swung around to look up at her. For a very dangerous moment, Samantha stared back down at us, a feral green light flickering in her eyes. Then, with a contemptuous sneer, she raised the Sig-Sauer over her head, released the mag and caught it in her free hand. She pulled the trigger, which clicked on an empty chamber.

"You trickster! Your mag was empty," I said admiringly as I helped her down from the van's slick metal roof.

"Well, *he* didn't know that, now did he?" Samantha countered with a hollow smile. Try to hide it as she might, though, I could still feel her muscles tense at my touch.

"Don't ever load an empty mag. Always load a full mag. And always keep one in the chamber, Samantha," Michael muttered, shaking his head at her. "Even during EDC. Even if it's not technically 'legal'. Better to be judged by 12, than—"

"I know, I know," she replied tersely. "—than carried by six. I remember your lessons. Just slipped my mind earlier today after I cleaned it. I loaded an empty mag. I think at one point I even put my shoes in the freezer. Damn. Too much going on."

Exhaling sharply, Michael conceded the point silently. Even pro operators might have been spooked enough by recent events to have done the same. Doubtful, of course, but his friends were still civilians.

For as long as that's going to last... Michael thought ruefully, sensing what was just over the horizon, looming, waiting to pounce upon them like a devouring dragon.

"My van..." Sammy sighed sadly as he inspected the four inch gash in his door panel. It was obviously going to take some repair work.

"Looks like it's time to move up to Kevlar, Sammy," David said matter-of-factly, examining the panel with Sammy.

"Hey..." Sammy's eyes lit up like little red coals.

"Guys, let's go party, okay?" I said, trying to downplay what had just happened.

Nothing.

"Okay?"

That did it. At least the slow shuffles and the halfhearted mumbles said so.

"Goddamn Crawfish Circuit all over again!" Sammy grumbled as we gathered round in a loose circle.

How right Sammy was. Playing the so-called "Crawfish Circuit" could lead to things like that. Things like fights. In Electric Bard, we had seen more than our share of them down here in southern Louisiana, where many of your average patrons weren't so much interested in enjoying the music as in getting ripped and starting drunken fights with "the longhairs." Remember that old philosophical bullshit line about "no one ever wins a fight"? Well, it's just that: Bullshit. You see, in our band's unique situation, at least while playing the "Crawfish Circuit," it was sometimes essential for us to "win" our fights just to get *paid* for the night. Sad, but true. And let's just say that we never went home empty-handed, either. For some strange reason, it seemed that no one, no gang, no random collection of adversaries, could beat us. Perhaps we had always just been a bit lucky when it came down to fighting. But I doubt it, given recent events, and recent revelations.

But now, despite the apparent similarities, the circumstances were just a tad bit different.

Sure they were. Just like then, we won. And nothing else matters.

We retrieved our requisite bottled goodies out of the van, locked it up, then headed for the nearby Moonwalk. All the while, Sammy and David held a whispering, highly technical conversation, maniacally discussing things like "proximity mines," "implanted armors," and "composite resins."

"They're up to no good," Luther grumbled. He was probably wondering if Sammy was hatching something to weasel his way out of their bet.

"Don't let it get to ya, Luth," Michael said, lighting up a foul-smelling cheroot with an old Zippo lighter. "That kinda technobabble just causes the women to ignore *them*, and *that* just leaves more women for us. So just have a smoke and play it cool, big guy. No composite in *these* resins."

"Yo, mon!" Luther said with gusto as Michael passed him a gnarled, dried-up cigar.

"Hey, Michael," I said, looking over at a grimacing Samantha, "why don't you pass me one, too?"

"Since when did you start smoking, homeboy?" Michael asked, giving me a daddy-scolds-the-
bad-kid look.

"I haven't, really. At least not until you pass me one of those cancer sticks."

"No, Logan," Luther said, inhaling deeply from the cheroot, "these aren't 'cancer sticks!' These are just tem-po-rary smokes, if you know what's goin' on."

There was no arguing *that* logic. Or at least no understanding it.

Michael, a slick grin on his face, passed me one of the mangled-looking cigars, offering his Zippo right along behind it. As I held my hands around it to ward off the river wind, I noticed that there was a peculiar insignia on it, some sort of triangle with a sword running through its center. Michael saw my eyes light up along with my cheroot.

"Team 6 it is, then!" I cheered, almost dropping the cigar from my blabbing mouth. I recognized the SpecOps insignia from some of Sammy's more bizarre underground war literature. "That's fuckin' awesome, man! Why didn't you tell me, Michael?"

"Well, you know, if I told you, I'd have to kill you," he said, quoting that overused spook line.

"You mean you'd have to *try*!" I said shoving him on ahead of me.

After a quick drag on the cigar, though, I concluded that he wouldn't have to do it himself. Now I knew why Clint Eastwood was always squinting in those old westerns.

When we reached the top of the Moonwalk—which was really nothing more than a fifty-by-fifty foot square of stone with a couple of benches and a few small, raised enclaves that held some fairly scraggly trees—we stopped at the edge overlooking Jackson Square, lost in the moment. The view was commanding. If you overlooked the bumper-to-bumper traffic that clogged Decatur Street, you could almost imagine yourself in another time, almost another place.

...a *familiar* place?

I quieted that nagging thought immediately, blowing out a thin spear of smoke, wishing that my thoughts would go along with it.

Calmer, if not more rational, I allowed myself to view the scene as if it were my first time. Between the towering spires of the St. Louis Cathedral, which dominated the scene, and the Pontalba buildings which lined the edge of Jackson Square, you could almost figure yourself to be in eighteenth century... Paris, perhaps? I always got the Spanish and the French architecture confused, unlike David, who could quote volumes about it. Or Sammy, who knew just about every unimportant piece of trivia in the world. But they were still in Monsters of Math mode, and I wasn't about to interrupt them. At least, not as long as I could lose myself in this juxtaposed, almost otherworldly view.

You could lose yourself looking for vampires here. I know, because Samantha and I had tried our best to find some ever since we had been coming here together, hoping for a glance, or a smiling figure in the shadows. Perhaps even finding Lestat, that awesome fiend of fiends. But now, for the first time that I could remember, that wishful fantasy was gone. Hell's own spawn? Blood and moonlight? That would be easy. I had the grim, foreboding sense that what we were now facing—whatever game we were unknowingly playing—would be impossible for mere mortals to play, and win.

"I give you, my friends," Luther suddenly said, extending his arms in a kingly gesture, "The City That Time Forgot!"

Holding Samantha close to me, a chill running up my spine, I felt intense *déjà-vu* as my mind wandered in some darkened, long-forgotten corridor of memory. I felt like something was at the tip of my tongue, ready to come forth, and, with a single word, blast my fragile reality to smithereens.

Where are you now, Silverdancer?

"Did you say something, Logan?" Samantha asked softly. The world of cars, electricity, and neon lights came back, piece-by-antsy-piece, like a nitrous oxide buzz in reverse.

"No," I lied, wondering if she had somehow heard my thoughts, "I didn't say anything. Nothing at all, Samantha Teale."

Samantha smiled at the way I said her name, stretching the syllables like some preschool child who was just learning how to talk. What she couldn't know was that it now felt like her name was a foreign thing to me, vague and unconnected nouns with nothing to give them meaning. It was like suddenly waking up one day from a deep Rip Van Winkle sleep, pointing up to the familiar Sun, and calling it "doorknob."

"Cheer up," "Samantha Teale" whispered, giving me a peck on the cheek. Then, strangely, she gave me a stare. Noticing the cut on the underside of my chin, she dabbed her finger to her tongue and began to clean it up.

"Cut it out!" I exclaimed, macho male ego upset by her playing mommy.

"Well, what do you know," she said, holding my chin in her hands as she inspected the underside of my chin. "The blood's already dried up. Looks like it was only a little nick."

"A little nick?" I barked, incredulous. "More like Old Nick! Sammy's *head* hit my chin! You know how hard that noggin is, Samantha! I could feel the blood pouring down my throat, and now you're saying that it's only a nick?"

"C'mon, you two lovebirds," Michael said, before "Dr. Teale" could rebuff me, "let's get going before we freeze to death."

Before I could even think about how the obvious cut on my chin had mysteriously "healed," we were on the move. The six of us walked down one of the long, inclined walkways, which were crawling with tourists. Crossing Decatur was easy, considering the fact that none of the cars was moving. We took St. Peter, a cool little thoroughfare that was cobblestoned, for an entire block. Given the time of night, I was surprised to find a couple of painters still going strong, portable lights and all. There were also several groups of promsters, decked out in their rented best, who were desperately trying to enjoy walking around the Quarter in their ill-fitting, rented shoes. Normally, I wouldn't have even looked twice at prom goers. You could see them every weekend walking around with big, wide eyes, sharing an "illegally" gained Hurricane between the three or four of them. But tonight their stares were just a second too long. I really thought that my stage experience and my walking around with Luther, Sammy, and Samantha all these years had prepared me a bit more for all of the attention. I was wrong.

Tonight was just different. It was almost as if they were staring right through me, seeing something that was hidden inside that I couldn't see myself. It bothered the living hell out of me.

Strolling on down St. Peter, we soon passed in front of the ever-crowded Pat O'Brien's. The lines to get in stretched all the way down the block, three or four people deep. The sweat-and-piss reek of the streets combined with the cacophony of several competing bar bands and booming car systems to create an intoxicating morass of sensory overload. It was crowded, rude, filthy, dirty. And we loved it!

"Luther, my main man," I said as I slapped him on the back, a sudden joy filling my heart, "I thank you profusely, from the bottom of my black soul, for your gift of the City That Time Forgot!"

Luther Gates turned around then, a smug, all-wise, benevolent look on his face, and gave me a big Fonzie-style thumb-up. Michael, taking a swig from one of Luther's many hidden bottles, sent a spray of cheap wine onto a passing taxi. The passengers in the back of the cab, who were definitely tourists, started laughing. The taxi driver, fortunately for all of us, hadn't seen it, or he probably would have flipped down his secret *Death Race* lever, which all taxi drivers have, and run us down like street scum, scoring ridiculous amounts of points in the process.

Soon enough, we hit the infamous stretch of asphalt that was Bourbon Street. The street party was in full force here. There was barely enough room to squeeze through the wall-to-wall crowd of screaming, stupid-drunk people. Fortunately, Luther took the lead and made good headway against the insane throng. However, just as we shoved past a group of some twenty or so intensely chanting fraternity brothers, who were vehemently requesting a mammary display from any and all passing females, one of them did a double take and started bellowing at the top of his already hoarse voice, "Look! Shaq's got a mohawk! Shaq's got a mohawk!" The group of guys turned as one, "wow's" and "no way's" escaping with reverential awe.

I could hear Luther start to laugh in a wholly unwholesome manner as he quickened his pace through the crowd. He was always being mistaken for one basketball star or another, much to his displeasure. Over the past few years, though, especially with the emergence of Shaquille O'Neal at LSU and his subsequent rise to NBA superstardom, it had gotten considerably worse. Now, they were both seven-footers. That much was true. But anyone could tell, at least at second glance, that while Shaq was right around three hundred pounds and huge in his own right, Luther Gates had him by an easy fifty and a pound of gold. Really. It was just another glaring example of Orwellian *groupthink*.

Seek... locate... assimilate.

Luther was still grumbling when we hit Toulouse. "Silly boys think I'm Mr. Hoop Mon!"

"C'mon, man," Michael said, "how many seven foot tall brothers do you see out partying around here? Take it as a compli—"

"But I *never* shoot hoop, Michael!" Luther complained, throwing his arms up in total indignation. It went without saying that many local basketball coaches bemoaned this fact. But Luther would have been banned from the game after his first in-your-face dismemberment. "So why they always gotta say the same damn thing?"

"Well, Luther, at least they don't think you're Larry Bird!" I teased.

"Hell," Michael said, stifling a grin, "they just wish they were in your shoes, my friend. Everybody wants to be a star. When they see you, it just reminds them of how close it all is."

"'A key to a door so wide open,'" Samantha added, quoting from Sting, catching Luther's hand in her own. She then fixed him with a green eyed stare and batted her long eyelashes.

"T'ank you, Miss Sting!" Poppa Luther said in his thickest patois, accepting her arm and continuing down the street. The Island King and his Exotic Queen, just strolling along without a care in the world, flanked by Tattoo, Yosemite Sam, Mr. Coppertone Tan, and The Foole. What a scene we made.

The crowds had thinned out somewhat here on the side streets, although they were still what anyone would call *crowded*. If the crowds held out in this number, I could only imagine how tight things would become in a few more days, when the madness that is Mardi Gras Night would officially transform this place into a scene reminiscent of a painting by Hieronymus Bosch. A gust of wind kicked up, rustling trash and forcing us to bundle up for a second as it passed. *Bad Streets* loomed ahead, half a block down Toulouse from Bourbon, brilliant in its neon glory. There were the typical wannabees milling about outside, desperately wishing that fate would have given them a jumpstart in the birthday department. Longhairs, punkers, and shaggy weirdoes mixed casually with Madonna imitators and Go-Go girls. Truly, it was one of the strangest melting pots in the City of Melting Pots, with the best—or worst—of both downtown and suburbia.

As we moved into the queue, I pointed out with some glee that our promo posters were pasted everywhere. It was good to know that a couple of Lincolns along with a good word or two from Luther had done the work. As we came to a relative halt, Luther motioned up to the marquis and smiled that kingly smile of his again.

"Top billing, mon!"

Yep. "Electric Bard" was at the head of the class, the topmost name on the glowing marquis. *That* was a relief. In a world in which every little thing mattered, that fact alone could be what made the difference in a "yes" or a "no" from the record execs. The fickle bastards. As we finally made it to the door, we noticed that there was a cover charge to get in.

"Don't worry, guys," I said, stepping forward confidently past Luther, who was just about to fish out his wallet and pay for all of us. "I know the doorman. He might just give us a break on the cover if I can sweet talk him into it."

"This I gotta see, Logan," Michael sarcastically muttered.

Ignoring him, I stepped smoothly up to the counter, a bright smile on my face. The doorman, a guy I knew from a couple of the after-gig parties that we had thrown, was busy stamping wrists with a glow-in-the-dark rubber stamp. After stamping a scarcely dressed girl an additional time between her breasts, he sat back with a satisfied smile, then noticed that I was there.

"Logan! How's it been, man?" Kurt "The Friendly" Doorman asked, extending his hand. And yes, that was his real name. Kurt Doorman was one of those rare souls who had a job which precisely suited him. Even precisely suited his name, too. Kinda like "Schitmann the Plumber."

"Not bad, Kurt," I amiably replied, shaking his hand. He winced. Curling an eyebrow, I pretended to give the departing girl a quick glance. "I just wish *my* job had that kind of fringe benefits."

"Yeah, right! And *you* have to settle for Samantha!" Before Samantha could even get a sneer out, Kurt added between quick gulps from a Dixie longneck, "Nice skirt, that chick I just stamped. Too bad Luther's already been out with her."

"You know it, mon," Luther leered.

We all had a laugh, even though Luther had probably never seen the girl before tonight. Then, Kurt leaned closer to be heard over the house music. Besides the pungent aroma of the Dixie, I also could smell the remnants of the muffuletta that he had for supper. Too much salami, but, then again, that was Kurt.

"The cover's five bucks tonight," he explained, wiping his mouth on his jacket sleeve. "That's 'cause of the half-price pitchers and the too-numerous-to-mention drink specials. Especially Dixie. It's like

Dixie Night tonight, or something. I think their rep cut some special deal with Big J to do some promo thing here tonight. Who knows? It's all half-price or less tonight." Our eyes lit up at that good piece of news. "And the band that's headlining is a real heavy thrash band, not like you progressive band dudes at all. They're called Kill 'Em All! You know, like the Metallica album? Can you dig it?"

"Sure, man. Aggressive death," I said, knowing deep in my heart that at least Sammy and David, metalheads that they were, were going to have an extra-good time tonight once they thawed out from their ignore-the-world conversation. It wasn't that *I* wasn't, mind you. It was simply that, to me, that name was *blasphemy*! It was like using the Lord's name in vain, and stuff like that. *They'd better be* damn *good to use* that *name,* I promised myself.

"I was kinda wondering, Kurt," I continued, using my left leg to keep a curious Luther behind me, "if Big J had put us 'band dudes' on the guest list for tonight? Can you check and see?"

Always eager to help out a "band dude," as he called each and every member of each and every band that he had ever seen or heard of, Kurt nodded quickly, then looked over a crumpled sheet of paper. A foul, crumpled sheet of paper that had the most illegible chicken scratch on it that I had ever seen. I doubted that even Sammy could decipher it.

"Uhh, I don't see..." Kurt began to fumble around behind the counter for something else, dashing our hopes to get in for free.

"Then we must be on the *other* sheet, Kurt!" I said quickly, smiling again, hoping to at least bullshit him a bit. I had meant for my voice to carry a little bit; to carry over the house music, which was blaring away. But what came out instead was a mellifluous, echoing ringing that sounded as if someone had added a heavy flange effect to it.

Suddenly, Kurt stiffened, then turned back to face me, a vapid expression on his face. "You're right, man," he said in a dopey monotone, "they must be... on the *other* sheet."

With this ludicrous statement, Kurt reached forward, grabbed my left hand, and stamped it. Not being one to question Divine Providence, I waltzed on in; a giggling Luther, a disbelieving Michael, a stunned Samantha, and two blathering techno-lunatics lagging somewhat behind me.

Heading straight for the bar, I flagged down the nearest bartender. A curiously intact twenty my calling card, I ordered a round of cold, cold, cold Dixie Blackened Voodoo for all of us. Still in a state of shock, I left Mr. Jackson's remains as a tip.

"All right, Mr. Charming," Michael asked finally as he and the rest of our group settled into the bar stools around me, "just how did you manage that little feat?"

"Yeah," Samantha said skeptically, her eyes lighting up with curiosity, "did you slip Kurt a dead president while we weren't looking?"

"You heard what I said," I said innocently. "I just told him the truth. The truth according to Scarface, that is. I always tell the truth, even when I lie!" I took a long pull from my bottle and looked away, not wanting them to see the strange flicker I'm sure my eyes held.

"I didn't see a thing," Luther said, lighting another of Michael's cheroots. "And I was standing right behind him the whole time! No Babylon biz from Logan, y'all." He blew out a plume of foul smoke, then added, with a grin: "He's simply the Mon. Irie, Irie!"

"C'mon, Logan," Michael said, offering me another cheroot, which I accepted, much to Samantha's disgust, "you can tell *me*! Did you slip him a bill, or give him a quickie?"

"Oh, you know me," I said, raising the bottle up to my lips and poking my tongue around in my mouth, causing my cheeks to undulate. Samantha hid her head behind her bottle while the rest of us laughed like dirty schoolboys. The weird mood passed as quickly as it had begun, much to my relief.

Over the next two bottles of brew, we spent a few minutes chit-chatting and analyzing the neo-modern art decor of the place. The first floor was nothing more than a U-shaped terrace, with booths lining the top half with a pit in front of the stage, which actually wound up on level with the terrace. There were pictures of racing cars, dragsters, and everything else that burned high octane hanging from every nook and cranny of the place. The waitresses came and went in fishnet pit crew garb, an idea that Richard Petty was rumored to have envied, according to the local restaurant and bar tour guide. A full-sized black and purple funny car floated above the main floor, suspended by stout metal rigging. Blacklights and strobes flickered continuously from the dance floor on the second floor. Completely sealed off from the first floor by soundproofed glass, it functioned as the "high energy" fix for the many eager dancers whose tastes were a little ways removed from slam dancing. Occasionally, the upstairs PA would pipe in music from the live band on the first floor, but I sincerely doubted that would be the case tonight for Kill 'Em All.

After another round, which we drunkenly dedicated to "Breaking On Through," and some more small talk, a booth opened up in the corner of the terrace. Seizing the opportunity, we dashed like madmen over to it, seating ourselves just in time for the main act.

Just in time for the insanity, that is.

As the lights dimmed, a horrible noise screamed out from the wall of speakers. Wails of terror followed by the bleating of sheep and the snorting of pigs roared throughout the speaker enclosures, prompting some demented laughter from the gathering crowd in the pit. The sound of automatic gunfire cut quickly through the cacophony, ending Old McDonald's Greatest Hits. Then, with the blast of some wicked pyros, the band—four grunge metal-looking guys dressed in torn jeans and Saints jerseys—hit the stage, grinding and thrashing at full power. Simultaneously, the pit erupted into headbanger heaven as the kids went wild and started to mosh.

Needless to say, we laughed our asses off. This was pure catharsis, pure Loon. It was almost tempting to join in. If it weren't for the fact that Luther would probably get carried away and deck someone, that is.

"They look like the Keystone Kops!" Samantha commented, taking a swig from my beer. She was already finished with hers.

"No, they look like Saddam's boys in full retreat!" Michael said, laughing so hard that he hit the back of his head on the wall. That prudent remark brought some chuckles from the next booth. I had to admit that it *was* funny looking, too, although I didn't think Saddam's boys had been *that* chaotic. Or maybe they had been, if our PsyOps guys had been blaring Metallica or something like that at them.

"You know," I said, caught up in the crowd's wild reaction, "maybe we ought to add a few thrash songs to our repertoire, just to—"

Before I could finish, though, both Luther and Samantha were glaring at me with a "don't you dare even think about it" look. Smiling sheepishly, knowing that I was outvoted, I briefly contemplated writing a ditty entitled "Pee Wee's Sid House." But no one would ever believe it.

The broken soldiers started to pile up as we enjoyed the megadecibel onslaught. We were getting a good earful, between the music and Michael's and Luther's hooting and hollering. They were having a contest, it seemed, as to who could attract the most attention. And both of them were getting a lot. Soon enough it was getting to the point that the waitresses were afraid to come to our table. Generous tips from both Michael and Luther, however, overcame that small stumbling block.

As soon as the band took a set break, I took a break myself and hit the water closet, eager to take a break from the Loon Onslaught. While drunkenly, forgetfully, and most stupidly tidying up in front of the mirror, I noticed something that shook me. Blatantly staring into the depths of the ill-lit mirror, I noticed that my eyes had a wild, haunted look to them. Dr. Feelgood had thought, up until now, that he had dealt with those particular demons, drowning them in a veritable sea of Dr. Feelgood's own magickal potions and secret elixirs. From some dimly functional corner of my besotted brain, I hoped that it was just my own paranoid vanity that had brought about this illusion.

Or maybe it's just been my contacts this whole time?

However, as I leaned closer to check out my innocent contact lenses, I noticed a faint flicker of silver-blue light flash across my pupils, then dart to my iris, forming a pinwheel of electric blue energy. Fading softly, it arced slightly, sending a single, laser-like beam of light into the mirror. Even in my condition, the hair on the nape of my neck rose. I leaned back, away from the mirror, feeling uncomfortably numb. Strangely, no one else in the busy restroom seemed to notice what had just happened.

Starting to turn away, I stopped in my tracks, then turned slowly back around to the mirror. Something was calling me back. It was as if some force were guiding me, beckoning me to walk once more the tightrope that men call Sanity. This time, I leaned as close to the mirror as the sink would allow, until there was less than a hand's breadth between my eyes and the mirror's surface.

Clearing my throat, I reached up with my right hand and held my right eye open, a static chill coursing
through my body. Suddenly, my pupil dilated until the entire iris was black. A rush of adrenaline
washed through me, bidding me to fight or take flight. Setting my mind in stone, I faced the depths of what the mirror revealed:

Floating in the darkness of my eye was the image of a seven-pointed star—a star which broke into seven separate pieces and then realigned itself into a chilling diagram of some sort of shining, silver constellation.

In each of the seven, shining stars I saw tiny traces of light. Trying in vain to calm myself, I willed

some sort of revelation from the stars, some answer from their depths. Then, in the space of a mere

mortal heartbeat, the stars grew large, revealing the eyes within them: the eyes of my friends! I saw Sammy's, Michael's, Luther's, David's, and even Samantha's. They were shining with an intense sorrow; an intense grief, as if they were dead. My eyes, too, I saw. And I knew them in a millisecond. Knew what they held as their innermost secrets. Knew the grinning specter of Death which they held in their depths.

But the seventh pair of eyes was, by far, the strongest. Strange eyes. Purple eyes. They were *watching* me. They were *alive*. Alive with power—the Power Magick. Alive with the promise of things to come.

Then, I heard the Call: "Tatternorn, it is time!"

Nausea filled me as my mind began to realize the familiar: I *knew* that voice.

heknowsheknowsheknows...

The world went dark at that moment as I sank to my knees. I couldn't fight it. I never could. *We* never could.

"Shit! What's wrong with the lights?" Distant, behind some door.

Pitter-pat of icy cat feet. Gale force howl of wind in my soul. Banshee moan.

It was like this the day we left Zengara, the Forever City, hell-bound on our final mission.

Knees. I am on my *knees in this stupid restroom in this stupid bar.*

We died! We died. Oh, Rel help us all, we died down there in DruusDome, down there in the deepest blackened bowels of the Midnight Realm.

I *am vomiting on the floor, on* my *knees.* I *am real.* Vomit *is real.*

Tiny bugs with pointy teeth tearing at my spine. Electric tingle. Static charge at base of back, flitting there like dark moths drawn to soul's light. Pulse-throb, circulation hinged on terror. Small soul nova gone haywire. Far within myself, I listened and remembered:

Alien words. Expressions. Formulae. Magick.

With a blinding crash of glass and hissing purple sparks, the mirror shattered from within, collapsing upon itself. Excited shouts boomed from within the bathroom stalls as the lights overhead blew out in sequence, littering the restroom with debris. I bolted upright, then stood in place, my arms limp at my side. Suddenly, my mind was racing as the startled patrons raced out of the restroom, completing their respective duties on the way out. In the utter, still darkness that followed, I stood, realizing for the first time that the thin line of sanity had just been irrevocably crossed, then *spat* upon.

My own words haunted me: *Shattered mirror/broken shards. I see your eyes in every star.*

"Logan!" Michael suddenly shouted, shattering my reverie like so many shards of glass.

Pivoting on my heels, I turned to face him. Standing with his arms high on either side of the door's frame as if he were trying not to be blown back through it by some phantom wind, Michael was dimly illumined by the lights from the main floor, giving his outline an ethereal, otherworldly glow. Behind him, a worried Luther stood, trying to push his way past Michael. I could hear Samantha, Sammy, and David behind them, each one frantically calling my name.

"Everything's cool, guys," I said calmly, brushing through them then walking out past them, a glazed look on my face.

Each of them looked like the kid who just found out that Santa Claus was really the medieval patron
saint of thieves. As I walked past them, still trying valiantly to get a grip on reality, I started to laugh.

It wasn't a very sane laugh, either.

"Bullshit, Logan!" Luther roared, grabbing my arm forcefully. "Don't tell us everything's cool! You just did something totally *un*cool!" His patois vanished before his fear of the unknown. Just like my sanity.

I looked up into his wild, dark eyes. All I could see was what I had seen in those damned stars. My laughter trailed off, like the last, dying hiss of death. I looked at Michael. He was standing with his arms at his sides, an expectant look on his face. Samantha was silent, a pained look on her face as she returned my cold stare.

"What the hell do you *want* me to say?" I shouted, feeling my control slip away. I jerked my arm from Luther's grasp, which curiously required little effort on my part, then straightened my leather jacket indignantly. "That the whole world is going fucking crazy? That everything we've ever known about ourselves is a terrible fucking lie? That tonight, at long last, it's finally time to face that lie and learn the truth?"

They stared at me in utter silence. I ignored their questioning eyes. If they didn't all know by now, they never would. Judging from the gleam in their eyes, a reflection of their souls, however, I realized that they knew.

They *knew*. That was all that really mattered, in the end, wasn't it? They *knew*. I *knew*. We *all* knew.

Now, it would just be a matter of time.

CHAPTER 9: The Great Wheel Goes 'Round

"We have to get out of here," I told them in a very cold voice. In silence they complied. No remorse, no regrets. They knew, and that was that. The six of us must have made quite a scene. The crowds parted around us like the Red Sea itself as we walked out of the bar, then down the street. By the time we had crossed Bourbon Street, the paranoia had set in. I began to get the feeling that something was about to happen. It was something just at the edge of perception. That nagging feeling was crawling around in my spine again, like a nest of pissed-off ants. You would think that by now I would have had a grip on things, considering the recent turn of events. But, each time something had happened, it had faded away, as if my mind were deliberately blunting the experience, like a built in self-defense mechanism. So each time there was a new event, it was like getting doused with ice cold water. The thought of what that voice in my head had said kept ringing through my head, over and over again, just at the threshold of perception. It had called me by that familiar name: *Tatternorn*. The same name from my dreams. The same keening voice that had cried out before things went boom. Was it warning me now? Was that it?

Suddenly paranoid beyond belief, I took a quick glance up and down the street. There were easily a hundred people in my line of sight. Most of them were younger, college types, by their mien. Of the twenty or so that obviously weren't, only a few looked even remotely threatening. Hustlers and a couple of street musicians. Nothing deadly there, at least on the surface. But, then again, Ted Bundy looked like a clean-cut guy, too.

Then I remembered something concerning the art of searching. No one ever looks *up*.

They'll search the ground, the shadows in the alley, all of the conventional hidey-holes. But they'll never look *up*. You would think that would be the first place that a simian-evolved being would look, but it just wasn't the case. So, feeling very Darwinian, I stole a quick look up to the outline of the rooftops.

Much to my surprise, I saw something.

There, but for the merest fraction of a second, was the silhouette of a man's head against the skyline, peering down at the street from the roof of the building across the street from *The Dungeon*, one of our other favorite hangouts. I saw it. But it was gone so fast, that I wasn't quite positive that it had even been there. My heart skipped a beat.

What the hell is going on?

As I stood there, silently gawking at the rooftop, Samantha grabbed my arm and shook it.

"Logan!" she clipped, urging me on. "Just keep walking."

"Huh?"

I realize it wasn't much, but you had to realize that my brain had more important things to work on than verbal communication.

"C'mon, dammit!" she gritted, pulling me along like someone taking a cat for a walk.

Dazed—and still trying to figure out just what the hell was going on in my head—I let her navigate me down the street. We continued on like this until we came to Chartres, where we took a left turn and headed toward Jackson Square and the St. Louis Cathedral. We stopped in front of the Upper Pontalba building, milling about

nervously on St. Peter's cobbled stones. Even given the time of the
night, the street and the courtyard in front of the cathedral were
still going strong, as throngs of late arrivals and late departures alike
filed merrily by the six or seven different street musicians and
panhandlers.

What finally pulled me out of my trance was Sammy's singing.
The little Loon! All this sudden hell, and he was chanting the theme
to "Green Acres," but substituting the happy-go-lucky, catchy music
with that of "Purple Haze." That's what pulled me back to *reality*. No
small wonder why I was going bananas.

"So what do we do now, guys?" Sammy inquired eagerly after
a particularly moving verse. He was weaving a staggering course
through our midst. "Shall we call it a night right now and haul
ass outta here, or shall we sing an ode to insanity and seek out
some more trouble for tonight? Like some more frat boys with their
fucking knives?" he finished quite belligerently.

"Shut up, Sammy!" David urged his buddy. There was an
unpleasant edge to his voice, and it had little to do with inciting any
nearby frat boys.

While Sammy cantered about like a lost little Shetland pony,
the rest of us stood there like a group of Chicken Littles, seemingly
waiting in dazed wonder for the sky to fall on our heads. Luther's
dark eyes were narrowed as he studied the middle distance. Strangely,
his nose crinkled as he seemed to sniff the air for any sign of danger.
David and Samantha both wore an agitated-yet-confused look; the
same kind of look that you get when someone next to you yells
"snake!" then runs away without telling you where the damned thing
is. And Michael's face was set in some sort of blank-faced
concentration mode. An outsider might have mistaken his
expression for that of a stockbroker pondering tomorrow's NYSE
options. However, I knew exactly what he was doing: He was

clearing his mind and focusing his *chi*; preparing not for meditation, but for combat.

"What's up, Michael?" I asked, realizing that I probably wasn't going to like his answer.

"Nothing," he replied, giving me a wicked tiger's smile. Then he started walking over toward the front of the cathedral, his hands shoved into his flight jacket's pockets.

"What's wrong with 'im? Not enough sand for 'im here in the Quarter?" Sammy asked, his speech slurred as he went into his "Arthur" imitation.

"Shut up, Sammy! This is serious!" I blurted. "Lemme go talk to him. The rest of you had better... I don't know..."

As I walked away, Luther, who had caught my tone, nodded in silent understanding, then

diplomatically herded the others over to the locked, wrought iron fence that surrounded the square's

grassy interior. A cold, stiff breeze began to kick up, blowing in from the river, as I caught up with

Michael in the shadows of the columns outside the Cabildo Museum. He was standing with his back

to one of the columns, facing the night-black, piss-stained walls of the museum, his chin buried in his jacket. As I stood there in front of him for a silent half-minute, his green eyes never blinked. Instead, they remained focused on some hidden, silent thought.

Suddenly, without preamble, he spoke. "So, Logan. What did you see back there, on that roof?"

It was as if Michael had just reached out and slapped me. I felt the pinball machine in my head register a silent *tilt*.

"How did you—" I began, then caught myself for the fool that I was. If I had seen it with my civilian senses, then he had definitely seen it, whatever "it" had been, with his heightened, trained senses.

Michael Reese's sixth sense wasn't just a quaint, poetic expression. It was a proven fact, steeped in the fire of combat.

"I've been feeling it all night long," he said as if he were talking shop, still not looking up. "As a matter of fact, I've been feeling it ever since that dream of mine. The moment I stepped off of the plane at the airport today, I felt it: Something watching, just out of sight, shadowing every move I've made like some invisible phantom lord."

"You mean you've been trailed ever since you've been here?" I asked, still not getting the full impact of what he was saying. "Why didn't you say anything? I mean, you could have at least told me—"

"—told you what? That the boogeyman's on my ass?" Michael looked up, staring at me with a pained expression. "Do you actually think that I'd share my paranoia with you, make you think you're crazy, too?"

"You could have shared it after what you saw back at the house, Michael! It's not every fucking day you see Luther lift a two ton van, you know!"

"And it's not every day that you see blue sparks fly around the hallway, either," Michael countered, once more smiling like a tiger.

"So you *did* see it!" I exclaimed, nearly shouting. The wind kicked up again, whipping some litter into a flying fury around the base of the column.

"Yeah, I saw it," Michael said, his tone deadly in its calm. "I saw the whole damn thing, I think. Believe it or not, I was only going to see if you guys needed some help with the garbage. The fucking garbage! I just happened to get there a little late for that, though. As it was, though, I turned the corner just in time to see the air lit up with shiny, little blue things. All I could do was stand there and gawk. At some stupid fucking blue sparkles. All that training, and I gawk at blue sparkles. I just freeze, and then gawk, man!" Now *that* sounded familiar. "And then, to make matters even worse, I heard you say something that chilled my shit. You said 'We made it, Silverdancer.' And you *didn't* say it in American English, either!" Michael's hands shot out of his pockets. He began to wring them together, reflecting his doubts.

"Yeah," I murmured, "I *did* say that. In what language, though, I'm still wondering. So is Dr. Passman," I laughed hollowly.

Michael continued: "Whatever it was, it was the same tongue that was spoken in my nightmare, Logan. I'm positive about that. I just don't know how I understood it." He stopped wringing his hands together. Together, we stood facing each other like two mannequins. The wind died down suddenly, its silence followed by the distant rumble of thunder. "Great!" he sneered. "First, this weird shit happens, then Mother Nature follows suit with a cold thunderstorm. Typical Louisiana meteorology!"

I craned my neck around to take a look out into the mall area. The musicians were beginning to pack up their things in anticipation of the unheralded late night storm. Already, a light sprinkle was falling, sending the scattered cliques of partygoers to the shelter of the nearest overhang. I could see the rest of our group heading slowly over toward us, ignoring the cold, sobering drizzle. Luther led Samantha by the hand, while Sammy was bleating loudly about "Singing in the Rain," punctuating each line with a savage kick at David, who was trying his paranoid best to ignore Sammy's *Clockwork Orange* torture.

"Look," I said quickly, grabbing Michael's arm, "they have no idea what's following us, Michael! Drunk college kids are one thing, but this is a completely different ballgame. This is for keeps! We've got to get the hell out of here! Now!"

"What the hell do you mean, Logan?" he asked, too absorbed to comprehend the tone of warning in my voice. "It's just some storm. That's not our problem. Our problem is the bastards who are following us—"

"This isn't just *some storm*!" I shouted, shaking him as if he were a thick-witted child. "Don't you understand what's about to happen? Can't you feel it coming with the storm? It's coming for *you*. It's coming for *me*. It's coming for *all of us* man. *All of us!*"

Our eyes locked, and Michael suddenly realized what I was saying.

Suddenly, violently, a jagged streak of lightning tore from the sky and struck a tree on the far side of the square, sending flaming branches and bark flying down to the ground. Michael reacted as if a mortar had gone off. He spun around, hit the deck at the base of the column, and cursed like the battle veteran that he was. It took me a split-second longer to decide what to do.

"Everybody get in here, fast!" I shouted, waving to my startled friends, who were in that confused, stunned-looking state that most people assume after lightning strikes nearby.

"Cool!" Sammy shouted as he stood rooted to the spot, pointing with glee at the flaming tree. He was so far gone that he thought that it was *cool*!

"C'mon, runt!" Luther bellowed, scooping up Sammy in one arm, Samantha in the other. By the time he and David had covered the twenty yards between where they had stood and the columns of the Cabildo Museum, Michael had already risen to his feet and pulled a nasty looking combat knife from somewhere within his flight jacket.

"Get everyone over in the corner, in the shadows, with their backs to the wall!" Michael commanded, waving the evil, black anodized Rambo knife at me. How he had managed to conceal that thing on his person without anyone knowing about it was something that I *really* wanted to ask him, but he left no such time for shop talk. And because, unlike some others among us, I had actually paid attention to his lessons, I *really* wanted to ask him why he didn't draw his pistol, which I knew he had at least one of hidden on his person, instead of his blade. Some distant, buried memory, however, informed me that he was a master of the blade, and that such would always be his first choice of weapon in combat.

Michael melted around the column and disappeared into the shadows as the wind kicked up once more with a banshee howl. As Luther barreled into the shelter of the museum's alcove, he tossed Sammy none too gently onto the hard stone floor, then gently set Samantha down. David skidded to a stop right behind him, a worried look on his face.

"What's going on with Michael?" David asked as he removed his glasses and began to wipe them down.

"He couldn't stand the weather!" Sammy shouted from where he sat sprawled on the floor, air guitaring and blurting out the intro to the song. Fortunately, the crash of thunder from a double stroke of lightning nearby drowned him out. Almost. I was still touchy about any Stevie Ray Vaughan jokes, because he was the All-Time Master, and Sammy, as usual, had just committed blasphemy.

"That was a cold shot, Sammy, you—" I blurted, realizing that I had just incriminated myself with my own hypocritical words. Sammy's mocking laughter was humbling. "Shit! Look," I said, "I'll be terse, for once. Michael says we're in trouble. Someone's after us, and there's every reason to believe that—no matter how crazy this seems—that this someone or something is... is..." I couldn't continue. The pinball machine in my head kept registering a *tilt*.

"—is what?" David finished, replacing his glasses.

As he adjusted his glasses, three bolts of lightning struck in the square, one after the other, with such concussive force that windows shattered all along both sides of the square. Screams of terror from the scrambling, fleeing partygoers mingled with the jagged shock of crashing glass throughout the square, sending goosebumps up and down my arms.

"Look, dammit!" I shouted, losing my control as I backed up against the nearest column. "I *know* you've all had dreams about something wicked, something that you can't explain!"

Truth. I could see clearly now by their wild eyes that they *had*.

"And now, whatever those nightmares may have meant, they're coming true! They're *real*!"

Between flashes of lightning and the roaring, gale force squalls of freezing rain, I saw disbelief and denial bloom in their eyes. I saw the fear chiseled deeply into them. No longer could the comfort of inebriation deny their imprisoned thoughts. They were stuck in mid-breath, their bodies unmoving as their thoughts raced to the same, unforgiving conclusions that Michael and I had already reached.

"Goddammit!" I shouted, gesturing like a madman. I was trying to jolt them, to *make* them comprehend, before whatever was going to happen happened. I could feel it coming closer, like inevitable doom. "It's *real*! You saw it, Samantha! You saw that weird blue shit all over the place!" I shouted. Turning rapidly to Samantha, I grabbed her by the hands, pleading with her to

understand before it was too late. "You saw it, Samantha! You *know* you did!" I looked over at her face, which was twisted into a mask of denial. "In your fucking hallway, dammit!"

Silence, of the creepy, unforgiven type.

"You know, too, Luther!" I shouted over Samantha's shoulder, giving him a wild stare. He stared back as if I were loco. "I *know* that you *know*, or else you wouldn't have been able to lift that van like you did. And you!" I said, pointing at David, who was, just like the others, becoming more and more *familiar* with each passing second, as if some elder veil of hidden memory were being slowly lifted away. "Your beard!"

Epiphany.

"Your red beard!" I shouted. "Your red, Khazak beard! Of course!" It hit me like a ton of bricks. It whispered in my mind. His name. Not the one that I knew him by now. Not David Miller, but an older, more *appropriate* one. His Khazak name. I *knew* it. Just as I had known Samantha's, when blue sparks breathed it to me in that long, dark hallway of the soul. I stepped up to David, leaning against the driving wind, and grabbed his red, neatly clipped beard, which I knew to be but a shadow of the real, wild, hairy one that he had grown back on SenZar, the world of our *first* birth.

"Guthal Dirge! *Grog*!" I shouted deliriously, the words sounding less foreign now. "You made it!"

David Miller's face curled into a mask of horror as he choked back a scream. In the reflection of his glasses, I could see the outline of electric blue energy shimmer in my eyes, bathing him in radiant, magickal essence.

"What the hell!" Luther yelled, backing away in dread. Samantha gasped, transfixed in terror. Sammy just stood there, arms at his side, that wide-eyed look of exhilaration on his face. I released David's beard and pointed at Luther.

"Rhiannazaar!" I yelled, naming him with the haunting word that flitted on the tip of my tongue next to a more familiar one. "*Zaar*!" I remembered aloud, as Luther backed away from me as if struck between the eyes by a carnival mallet. "Where in the hell are your other arms?" I shouted with glee, a vivid memory from another life slamming into me. *He's* supposed *to have* four *arms!*

The mental tumblers were falling like dominoes, unlocking bit-by-bit a flood of memories of

another time, another place. If this was madness, then I freely embraced it, with no reservations. It

seemed, however, that I wouldn't have to embrace it alone.

Sammy, his big, brown eyes brimming with tears, suddenly grabbed me around the waist and hugged me with all of his might.

There, amidst the insanity, the impending sense of personal, lonely doom, and the chaotic storm that raged about us, Sammy Joseph looked up, met my eyes, then spoke in that tongue that I knew now to be Zengaran, the common tongue of SenZar: "Tatternorn! We made it! We're alive!"

Confirmation. At long, long last.

Luther, who had looked as if he were about to run screaming away a moment ago, suddenly smiled broadly, then scooped Samantha, David, Sammy and me into one big, bear hug, shouting triumphantly, "Tat! Mad Sam! Guthal! Silverdancer! We *did* make it!" Luther crushed us to him again, taking our breath away. Freeing us from his joyous death grip, he backed away, brushing tears from his eyes. For the first time in this world, this life, he knew who he truly was, and it was having the same effect on him, hardcore man though he was, that it was having on the rest of us. "But where's Tal'N?" he asked in afterthought, looking around the square for Michael, "Where's that crazy golden boy?"

"Michael—Tal'N, I mean!—ran off to scout around," I said, feeling extremely giddy, wondering if at any moment I might wake up. And wondering when Samantha *would*.

"For what?" David asked gruffly, fumbling with his glasses again as he wiped away some moisture from his eyes.

But, before anyone could reply, Samantha started laughing. "I can't believe this is happening!" she said, stomping her feet, holding herself tightly with her arms, as if she thought that at any moment she would disappear, or wake up. "You're all crazy! No, *we're* all crazy! This can't be happening! It *can't*!"

"It is, though," I said, hugging her to me. She didn't resist. I had to raise my voice to be heard above the howling wind.

"It's just that—things can't happen like this! We died. Oh, god, Tat, I lost you and we died!" she sobbed, her chin on my shoulder. This time, unlike the last, though, she didn't try to pull away from me. I released her, but I kept staring at her. She was Samantha Teale. Of that, there was no doubt. I had known her for more than five years, as long as I had known Luther. We had loved, been together, been apart, then been together again. Star-crossed lovers, true. But star-crossed took on an entirely new meaning now in our story. For she was also Samantha Silverdancer—of that, there was now no doubt. On SenZar, we had loved, been together, been apart, then been together again. Then we had died together. All of us had died.

And I had been the one who had killed us all, my pride our downfall.

And now, through some sort of divine providence or some devil's agency, we were together again. All of us. All of us except for one.

Sigil Talisman.

The one who had spoken to me from the depths of that mirror in the bathroom. The one who had told me that things were about to happen. Bad things. Magickal things.

He was also the one who had led us like sheep to the slaughter; the one who had gotten us all killed. It hadn't been me, at all. I had just been playing my assigned role. He was the puppeteer, Geppetto, all along, and I had always been his little malformed Pinocchio, his little puppet who had always dreamed of being a real boy, but who instead had been realized as a mere shell of a man; a host for ancient, implacable evil. He was the one who had maneuvered us from the start. And now he was calling us together again.

Thirty silver pieces for my kiss.

"We're in deep shit," I said, the smile melting from my face as the chorus of crackling lightning began to climb into a crescendo of doom. The air had an electric tingle to it. The raging storm was only the prelude to something yet to come. I knew, now, that I had once felt something akin to this very ozone tinge, but I couldn't quite place it. My dream, perhaps? I couldn't decide, but I knew that we had to get out of here. Quickly.

"C'mon," I said, looking around for any sign of trouble, "we've got to leave. Now!"

They could feel it, too. The joy of revelation that had so recently moved us all to tears now took a nosedive, crashed, and burned. Emotions, pliable things that they were, could always be relived, though. Provided, of course, that we ourselves still lived.

Still buzzing with the energy of our reunion, we forced our way into the stiff, swirling headwinds and began to work our way across the rain-slickened cobblestones of the mall area. We had to bend almost double against the freezing wind and lashing rain. The trees within the fenced off square weren't faring too well with the gale force winds, some of them already uprooted and lodged against the wrought-iron fence. We headed down St. Peter, careful to keep to the left side of the street nearest the fence of the square in order to avoid the occasional flying shop sign. Halfway down the street, a single, rapidly moving figure darted from one of the shadowed store alcoves and ran toward us, gesticulating wildly.

"Run!" Michael shouted wildly, screaming to be heard above the wind. "Fall back! Move, dammit!"

As Michael sped toward us, waving his knife and screaming, the sky seemed to heave every single erg of hateful energy that it possessed down to the ground in one mammoth, mortifying, purple bolt of lightning which struck to our left. It impacted with the center of Jackson Square, brilliantly illuminating and then slagging the statue of Ol' Andrew Jackson himself. As millions of invisible ants fought to race up and down our spines, the boom of the stroke exploded outward, shredding the few trees and shrubs that remained in the square, sending lethal wooden shards flying in all directions at tornadic velocity. Thankfully, the wrought-iron fence took the brunt of the blast, deforming in numerous spots as ruined wood crashed into it. As it was, it seemed as if we were standing on the business end of one of those tree-shredding *Asplundh* trucks. All of us, even the massive Luther, were bowled over like tenpins, or human pincushions.

By the time that we had regained our feet, the devil wind was gone, having delivered its promise of evil. At the foot of the slagged, molten statue of Jackson and his trusty steed stood a cadre of seven jet-black, demonically featured warriors. Each one of them was begarbed in sinister, strangely fashioned ornamental plate mail. They were humanoid; slender, not quite as tall as a full grown man, yet their bearing spoke of their power. They radiated the rawest, rudest aspects of pure hatred and loathing for all things mortal. As wave upon wave of *déjà-vu* roiled through my mind, a deep-rooted, racial hatred manifested itself, along with a name for their perverse, blood-drinking, evil-worshipping race: *Mokarr*. The name burnt itself into my somewhat shredded present memory, right next to such words as *Hitler, Commie,* and *Brussels sprouts.*

Their leader—a lanky, sinewy scarecrow of a demon who stood a good foot taller than his six smaller companions—strode confidently over the rubble of the statue like Darth Vader himself until he stood at front and center of his troops. His great, black dragon helm was open such that one could easily see his burning, hate-filled purple-irised eyes.

"So... these pathetic mortals are the ones spoken of in the legends?" His voice was a combination of gravel and honey. His English was strangely accented, though, with some gruff, Asian-sounding inflections.

"Who are you calling *mortal,* Mokarr?" I demanded, suddenly regretting my outburst, and wishing that we were on vacation somewhere else, like Saturn. Memories were starting to sort themselves out again, drawn out by the necessity of impending death. Mokarr were bad news: They were expert death-dealers, and they still cheated whenever they could. And, if my newfound memory were serving me properly, seven Mokarr meant a *Mokarr*

Death Squad: A specially trained team that could wipe out a small army using ninja techniques and technomagickal gimmicks. Their team resembled Michael's SEAL buddies in many different ways, except that they were a world apart in origination and a universe apart in moral fiber.

"*You*, Tatternorn!" the Mokarr leader barked, indicating me with a two inch long black talon.

He knows...

"And all of your goody-two-shoes friends, too!" he mocked, his gesture sweeping over our entire group. I fought the instinct to look away. "Yes, I know who you are. I know *all* of you. And I know that the sages who recorded your legends were gifted with imagination, and highly paid to overlook the glaring truth!" He laughed, a sound like a cat coughing up a furball. His buddies chuckled, too, careful to end their laughter when he did.

"Look, if you've got something to say, then say it, dickhead!" Sammy said, from behind Luther's leg.

"Insolent, depraved homunculus!" he shouted, foam flecking on his lips. "I am Vash Gar, first-spawned Earthborn of Lord Valthrustra!"

Heknowsheknowsheknows!

"And I, Vash Gar, have come to deliver his personal greeting of hate to you, six of the pathetic Seven Stars!"

Vash Gar's hateful eyes began to glow with a plasma of purple power as his hands traced an intricate pattern in front of him. Mesmerized like children watching a David Copperfield illusion, we stood still, minds like mush, as the energies folded in upon themselves once, twice, then thrice. From the whirling, purple cocoon of magickal force there formed a great, black blade that I instantly loathed with all of my being. As Vash Gar reached out and grabbed it from its energy cocoon, the three overlapping, alien DNA-like rows of living runes that ran along its length began to writhe. They pulsed in the pattern of an alien heartbeat, etching tracers of fluorescent light in the very air itself.

Vash Gar held the thrice-damned hell blade at arm's length, turning it slowly as he pointed it at me. The single walnut-sized purple jewel at the terminus of the blade's pommel began to throb in demonic syncopation with the triple runes. It sent an arc of interfering essence along the rampant hell-bent dragon that formed the elaborate pommel guard and tang of the hateful Shadar steel blade.

Skurge.

"Ahh... I see that he remembers you, Tatternorn!" Vash Gar leered, stroking the foul Shadar steel blade. The dam in my mind burst, flooding me with hated memories of another time, another place. I liked not at all what I recalled.

"*Skurge!*" I whispered, the very name of that hell blade choking in my throat. It throbbed in response—a silent, baleful "Howdy-do! Remember me? *I hate you too!*"

"Yes! Skurge!" Vash Gar shouted, holding the massive demon blade *en garde* with but a single hand. "And I have a message from my grim Lord, you pathetic little man-maggot: DEATH! Death to all who oppose Lord Valthrustra! DEATH! Death to this pathetic, magick-blind world! DEATH! Death to everything! For His glory, we all shall die!"

I kept thinking over and over in my head that there was no place like home. No place like *which* home, though, was the question that kept tripping me up.

CHAPTER 9: THE GREAT WHEEL GOES 'ROUND

This wasn't fair. Fighting some drunk college guys was acceptable, even if one of them did have a knife. But this was an entirely different ballgame, played in the Hell Major Leagues. For one thing, these weren't even "guys." They were Mokarr, the spawn of the Dark Earth itself. And these Mokarr had things like magickal armor—black moonlight armor, I now recalled: as light as Spandex yet as durable as thrice-steeped steel—and magickal swords named "Skurge" to back them up. Now, while it's a supposed given that we *might* have once kicked mucho ass on these guys on SenZar, it had to be noted that back then we had *probably* employed weapons of comparable magickal power to fight back with. To top it all off, while we may have once been able to actually *use* these magickal weapons on SenZar, here on Earth only Michael and I had actually ever trained with a real sword, and that was never in true life-or-death combat.

One would think that we would do the logical thing and run like hell. However, a quick sidelong glance at my friends revealed that this would never be the case. Never. Even *if* we had only been recently reintroduced to our hatred of the Mokarr, it was so powerfully entrenched in us that it was too powerful to ignore, even now.

And, as we could plainly see, that hatred burned both ways. With a horrible, hateful Mokarr death-curse on his lips, Vash Gar, brandishing Skurge, exhorted his hit team to take our souls. Like a sheer black wave of malice, the Mokarr Death Squad charged our group, their faces etched with evil rictus sneers. I barely had time to blink as they swept past my startled, paralyzed form. Vash Gar, smiling like an addled black cobra, noted my balk.

"Surprised, maggot, that my minions pass you by?" Vash Gar seared, striding forward like a stalking black tiger. "No, *you're mine!*"

For some strange reason, Skurge made an obscene fart-like noise at this point, electing to accent the out-of-place scatological sound with an equally out-of-place bright rainbow display of colors along its cruel Shadar steel length. For some strange, unknown reason, this snapped me back to my senses.

And for another strange, unknown reason, this pissed me off to no end, and hate did funny things to my Information Age-saturated mind.

Screw this! I'm a Highlander, by god! The last sound I hear should not be that of a farting sword!

So, as Vash Gar strode directly toward me, I let my hatred burn, propelling me like one of Hell's Funny Cars down the Roads to Madness. I hoped like hell that it wouldn't be my last sentient emotion. Bad karma, you know.

Instinctively, I raised both hands and shouted, *chi* flowing like quicksilver. Much to my pleasant surprise, blue energy flew from the tips of my fingers, tingling like the after effect of that lightning stroke. A single, jagged bolt of blue lightning—or some form of magickal energy that very much resembled lightning—slammed Vash Gar full in the chest, halting the force of his charge and knocking him flat on his ass, smoking and screaming.

"Damn you, mortal! You *hurt* me! You actually *hurt* me!" Vash Gar snarled as he rolled into a backflip and landed like a huge cat on his feet. Now, after having taken my measure, he held Skurge in two hands, in the *Ochs* position.

Strangely enough, it was at this point that I realized that I had no idea what I was doing.

What I did know, though, was that I had just been lucky with my little trick, and the result was that Vash Gar's pride was injured more than was his body. And the sick feeling that I had in my stomach told me that I wouldn't be shooting any more magickal blue lightning bolts from my hands until I'd gotten over this new magickal hangover.

I knew that I couldn't take my eyes off of this guy for a second. He was too fast—almost as fast as Sammy. Like I said, I was just lucky the first time. Behind me, where all of Vash Gar's buddies had gone, all I could hear was mass chaos. Luther was bellowing and Sammy was cussing up a storm. But, beyond that, I couldn't pick out anything else. *Just like Samantha's dream...*

Then, a horrible thought tiptoed in my brain: *Samantha!*

Turning, despite my resolve not to, I saw nothing but an impenetrable, smoky glaze in the air, as if a smoke grenade had gone off in the middle of the throng.

"Ahh, Frailty! Thy name is Tatternorn!" Vash Gar mocked in his gravel/honey voice.

I turned, only to see him towering in front of me, Skurge arcing toward me, death pulsing along its length. Thinking quickly, I stepped toward him, trying to intercept the arc of the blade at its pommel. But I only managed to get an armored, steel-hard elbow in the jaw, as Vash Gar modified his swing too rapidly for me to counter it. It was like running into a Mike Tyson haymaker. The impact lifted me up off of my feet and drove me into one of the mangled iron benches, one of the ones that had been bolted into the street and only partly ruined by the hurricane winds. Much to my relative relief,

I bounced off of it, and hit the cobblestones of St. Peter, derriere first. And somehow—probably quite by accident—I was still conscious.

As I tried to kick-start my brain, Vash Gar let out a wicked belly laugh and made up the distance between us in two strides. Just for fun, he smashed Skurge into the bench, slicing its wrought-iron hide neatly down the long axis in a shower of green sparks. I stared, horrified, at the impossible laser-precision cut that the wide blade of Skurge had made in the wrought-iron bench.

Noting this, Vash Gar smiled and said, most cruelly, "You're next, Tatternorn! You're next!"

Talk about bad karma.

I was prone, on my ass, in the middle of St. Peter, just about to become very dead. For a moment, I wanted to pinch myself and wake up out of this nightmare.

I have a gig to do, dammit!

Then, as Vash Gar raised that hell blade and smiled like the grinning head of Death itself, the air

behind him turned the most beautiful shade of sunset purple that I had ever seen. A tall, well-dressed man in a full-length, strangely shimmering Michael Murphy black leather trench coat stepped through the shimmering air, its essence bending around him like flowing water. His expressive, patrician features were twisted into an ironic smile as he tilted his head and cleared his throat.

"Vash Gar, old chap!" Mr. Mysterious intoned in a faintly English-sounding accent as his left hand deftly traced lines of magickal power in the air before him. "I really do not think the Marquis of

Queensberry would approve of that!"

With a crackle that rivaled the explosive bolt that brought Vash Gar and his cronies in, a polychromatic rainbow arced forth from the fingertips of the well-dressed man and struck the turning Vash Gar full in the face and upper body. The terrific blast sent the

Mokarr-thing head over heels right past me. Skurge flew out of his grasp, landing at his side with a dull *clank*. It seemed to express some sort of mute anger at this turn of events by glowing a deadly ochre along its length.

As Vash Gar sprawled there moaning, the well-dressed man walked swiftly over to where I was and extended a long hand. Hesitantly, I reached out to grasp his hand, wondering if I was going to get blasted, too. As I made contact with his hand, his "strangely shimmering" black leathers shimmered *quite* strangely, then dissolved like ripples in a tidal pool to reveal the ornately fashioned purple robes beneath the illusory veil. Cool robes, too, with lots of shiny silver-and-black Oakland Raiders-looking embroidery.

Reflected upon its multifaceted surface, as I now could see, were an infinity of staring eyes, each of which seemed to be staring right into my soul—just as the eyes in the mirror had stared. So many eyes, so many *souls*, all I could do was stare.

"Oh, come now, Mr. Logan!" Mr. Mysterious chided impatiently, grabbing my hand, and hauling me to my feet with a surprising strength. "Or, should I say, *Tatternorn*?"

It was only now that I noticed that Mr. Mysterious had pointed ears! He had ears that looked like an elf from some fantasy role-playing game, or a Vulcan from Star Trek. And his eyes, softly slanted like almonds and purple-tinged, radiant in inner magickal power. Then it dawned on me who this *had* to be.

"Sigil Talisman!" I shouted, a mixed feeling of filial love and betrayed hate washing over me. Love, hate, love.

"The very same, indeed!" Sigil Talisman admitted, bowing ever so slightly. Hesitantly, I released his hand, and his nifty robes were instantly "replaced" with his equally nifty black leathers. I gawked and Sigil talked: "We will discuss this whole sordid affair later, Tatternorn, at the Teale House. There is much to discuss, and now is not the time!"

Sigil's ironic smile faded at the sound of rapid single-shot gunfire. Instinctively, I jerked my head around to find the source of the shots, but I saw only black smoke and more black smoke. I turned to face Sigil once more, thoughts of Samantha's handgun on my mind. Sigil nodded on cue, as if he were somehow aware of my very thoughts, then walked swiftly away into the billowing, black smoke cloud, disappearing from sight.

Before I could consider what to do about Sigil Talisman's timely intervention, the sound of armor scraping on stone drew my attention. I pivoted, turning to face Vash Gar, who was hauling himself up from the ground. His face was a twisted, leering mask of hatred. His black moonlight ornamental plate armor was now ruined. The black moonlight armor dangled in sizzling, effervescing strips from its thin yet wicked looking "backing" layer of... *of obsidium! Damn! And that volcanic alchemical hyperalloy is a* helluva *lot tougher than steel.* Stunned, I noted that black, viscous blood oozed from Vash Gar's mouth and nose like hot pitch. Whatever Sigil had hit him with must have been *seriously intense.*

"Sigil Talisman, you interfering maggot!" Vas Gar spat, wiping his bloody face with one of his foul, demonic hands. "Now that you have at long last shown yourself, my lord will have your fetid soul, you Starin charlatan!"

Having delivered his typical Mokarr promise of doom, Vash Gar first looked at me, then at Skurge, which was curiously quiet on the ground between us. Then, strangely, he looked back over at me. I could feel his burning rage bore into my eyes as he silently promised me a cruel, slow, and agonizing death. More gunshots from within the cloud drew his attention for a split-second, though, and that was all the time that I needed to make my decision.

Diving onto the cobblestones, I managed to beat Vash Gar to Skurge by a fraction of a second—just enough time for me to get both of my hands beneath his on the grip of the black blade.

Clutching the grip tightly, I tried to wrest Skurge out of his iron hands as we rolled along the street. Skurge was still strangely silent, not even a single spark flying from it. Vash Gar's strength was something to be reckoned with. He was as strong as an ox. I couldn't budge him, and he was slowly but surely winning our little tug-of-war, crushing my hands in the process. Also, he was using what was left of his jagged upper-body armor to gouge flesh trenches in me; the heinous obsidium gouging them quite effortlessly through both my leather jacket and my not-quite-leathern flesh beneath. Our blood was flowing freely now, mixing together—red ants fighting black ants—staining Skurge's pommel and slickening the grip.

"I will *win*, Tatternorn!" Vash Gar hissed as he rolled over on top of me, Skurge between our faces. "The blood of the Shadar Lords flows through my veins! I am too strong for you!"

The bastard was right. His strength *was* supernatural. I don't think even Luther could take him one-on-one. But I was going about this like an idiot. Since there was no way that I was going to out-wrestle him, I decided to concentrate instead on the most important element of any life-or-death street fight: Cheating.

Pulling the blade down toward my chin with everything that I could muster, I managed to get Vash Gar to shift his center of balance forwards enough for a kick-out. With a sudden arching of my back and an equally sudden shove of the blade in the direction of his pulling, I managed to lift him off of me and flip him over onto his back.

Cool move. I was free. The only problem was that Vash Gar now had Skurge all to himself. Rolling to the side, I managed to get myself situated in a crouch before Vash Gar could completely regain his feet. As he rose with Skurge in his left hand, I shot the gap, intercepting his swing with a standing double wristlock on his sword arm. Pivoting my back into his stomach, I managed to sink a good hold on both his arm and his wrist, which I then bent as hard as I could.

"Drop it, Vash Gar, or lose your hand!" I squeezed as hard as I could. His wrist was disturbingly pliant, though I could feel his limber tendons giving way, creaking against Mr. Radius and Mrs. Ulna.

"Never!" Vash Gar screamed. He pounded my stomach with his free hand, nearly knocking the breath from me. Normally, that kind of blow would be very hard to land with the kind of wristlock that I had him in, but Vash Gar's arms were so out of proportion to the rest of his body—lanky black scarecrow thing that he was—that he could do it with little strain. That left me with little choice, as I realized that another blow like that would probably stun me just enough for him to lop my head off.

"I sure hope you don't play the piano!" I said, coming down hard in a crouch, using my momentum to mangle his left arm and snap the bones of his wrist. Much to my disgust, however, Vash Gar's *entire hand* came off at the wrist with a sickening *crunch*! I tumbled forward into a crouch, holding both his severed hand and that which it clutched, Skurge. Black blood gushed from the severed stump of his arm as he began to howl in pain. He bent over double in his agony, almost to the point of contortion, as he tried to staunch the flow.

"You will *die* for that, Vash Skurgg!" Vash Gar promised, backing away in agony.

Ahh, that name: Vash Skurgg. I suddenly recalled that the Mokarr had known me by this epithet, and had uttered it with a curious mixture of admiration and fear. Beyond that, though, I knew little more—although I sensed that, given time, I would remember everything about that most cruel name, and what it truly meant to me.

I rose to my feet and met his fierce gaze. Vash Gar blinked, gave Skurge a terrified glance, then began a scuttling retreat into the square. Prying his left hand off of Skurge's pommel, I did my best imitation of Nolan Ryan while fumbling with the blade in one hand, then threw the taloned hand at Vash Gar's backside, hard. He left a black, ichorous trail behind him like some thrice-cursed garden slug from Hell.

I couldn't help but to mock him with some harsh laughter. Then, I cleared my mind, and took the great black blade in two hands. The elemental hate of Skurge roiled into my mind like a juggernaut.

"Maggot! By the pact that binds us, I shall have thy soul 'ere this night is through!"

"Shut the hell up and let me think, you stupid black speculum!"

Skurge lit up in silent, purple fury as I gazed at it, irate that it was once more in my possession. Irate that I was once more the Master.

Right. The very first fractured memory evoked by my contact with Skurge named that statement for the lie that it truly was. *"Master" my ass. Oh, those hated and hateful memories.*

As more shards of memories of my former life with Skurge fluttered through my mind's eye—many of them half-shattered and sometimes misleading in their rapid fire fury—I realized that neither Skurge nor I was "The Master" of the other. We were and ever would be, so far as I knew, mutually sympathetic parasites of each other's soul. Forever together and One, yet forever at each other's tender, unforgiving mercies.

Or something heinous like that. In any event, now was not the time and place to take a trip down Memory Lane. It wasn't as if I were retaining any of the memories anyway. More like retaining only the impressions of them. Engrossing, true. But distracting as well. And such a maudlin distraction could very well get me—and all of my friends—damned.

So I forcefully broke the confusing mental communion with the hell blade. Until I knew exactly what was going on, I decided that Skurge would be safer in my hands than in anyone else's.

"*Fool.*"

"Don't I know it, you cretin."

Torn between pursuing Vash Gar and helping my friends, I turned my gaze back and forth between his retreating, cursing form and the oily black cloud that encompassed my friends, looking for all the world like someone watching a furious rally at a tennis match.

Decisions, decisions.

Finally figuring that Vash Gar had been properly defanged, I made up my mind and ran into the thick, smoky cloud. Acrid and somewhat sulfurous, the smoke clung to me like a veil, reducing my forward visibility to about ten feet. It also had the unquieting effect of dulling sound like some anechoic chamber. I could barely hear my own breathing. The first thing that I came to was the mangled body of one of the Mokarr warriors. His neck was twisted so badly that his head pointed almost directly behind him. Fighting the urge to purge, I tore my gaze away from the black humanoid pretzel shape and moved deeper into the noisome smoke, praying that I wouldn't find something that I'd remember to my grave.

After a few more soundless steps, I came at once to a break in the smoke field. Samantha stood facing me, her back to David and Luther in a rough defensive triangle, holding one of the Mokarr's anodized-looking katanas—more Mokarr-produced obsidium, I could see, only this time in its more potent "offensive" form—in her hands. She was employing a wicked martial stance that I had seen before only in comic books and bad martial arts movies. David was waving another captured katana at the nearest bank of smoke as if he were daring something to step a little closer, while Luther was hefting a length of tangled wrought iron fence like a baseball bat.

At their feet were the bodies of two more Mokarr warriors, broken and bloody in their armor, several gunshot wounds in the very tiny spaces that their strange armor didn't cover. Someone had been very judicious in his shot placement.

"Tatternorn!" Samantha cried out, her voice distant, though she stood only a few paces away. Her green eyes lit with a strange light as she spied Skurge in my hands.

"Yep. Back in the saddle again," I mumbled unenthusiastically as I skipped over to them, careful to avoid the fallen Mokarr. By the time I reached them, I could plainly hear David's muttered, hateful battle curses.

"C'mon, you pussies! Come on out and play!" David spat this through clenched teeth, his beard dancing on his face. At once I noted the ugly, purple blood bruise on his forehead. The wound at the center of it was dripping a fair amount of blood down his cheeks. His glasses were bent and one lens was a spiderweb of glass, but still they held.

Peering into the shadows where he stared, I noticed the faint outline of a Mokarr warrior about ten feet away. The oily smoke, only now beginning to dissipate, parted for a moment, revealing him clearly. His face, a mask of typical Mokarr hatred, transformed in an instant into a mask of fear as his eyes took in the sight of Skurge in my hands. I blinked, and he was gone, slipping away like a snake in the gas.

"Well, what do you know?" David laughed, relieved. "He ran off like a jackrabbit, all elbows and assholes at that!" David's grin melted as he turned and saw from the corner of his eye what I held in my hands.

"Don't get too confident yet," I warned, backing into the defensive formation, transforming it from a triangle into a diamond. "How many are down?" I inquired, wondering what the odds now were.

"Three that I know of. Luther got one, broke his neck like a twig," David said rapidly, quietly, as Luther rumbled an affirmative. "Michael got Samantha's gun, got a mag in, and dusted these two while I was wrestling them."

"Where is he now?" I asked, keeping my eyes peeled for any sign of movement in the smoke.

"He and Sammy ran off together, like it was old times or something," Samantha added brusquely. "I think I heard Michael say something about flanking them, or something like that."

"The square!" I blurted suddenly, realizing where they were headed. I cursed myself for an amateur, wondering how many precious seconds we'd already let them have for their escape.

"Let's go, then. Show 'em who's the Mon!" Luther said, smiling evilly.

As Luther began to lope on over toward the square, I saw that the left side of his jacket was soaked in red blood. We ran almost blindly, falling in behind Luther, who was cutting a huge path through the remnants of the Mokarr smoke field. The smoke had almost completely dissipated by the time that we found the edge of the square. The normal sounds of the night were swiftly returning, along with a steady, cool rain. Picking our way over the rubble at the edge of what used to be the fence, we sprinted the remaining distance to the slagged out statue of "Old Hickory" and his trusty steed. There, Sammy and Michael stood next to the ruined body of another Mokarr warrior.

"About time you guys showed up!" Sammy said, expertly flipping Michael's Rambo knife end over end in his hands. Michael held a pair of captured Mokarr obsidium katanas in his hands.

"We managed to off this bozo just as the other three took off in a flash of black light," Michael said grimly, tracing the outline of the fallen Mokarr's armor with one of his blades.

"You mean they just vanished?" I wondered aloud.

"That they did!" Sammy chirped, pointing his oversized knife toward the heavens. Then, breaking into a grin, he adjusted the tip of the knife toward the ground. "On second thought, maybe they went that a way."

The shrill wail of distant sirens pierced the night, beginning a Doppler wail that would soon center on this place.

"We've got to get back to the house," I said, remembering what Sigil had told me.

"Yeah, can you imagine trying to explain *this!*" Sammy laughed, pointing the tip of his blade at the body, then at the slagged statue. "Wait'll CNN gets wind of this! We're gonna be on TV! I can see the headline now: 'Old Hickory's dickory gets docked!'" He began to titter convulsively.

"Shit!" Michael blurted, scanning the square as he did so. "There are shops everywhere nearby with security cameras, and tourists with minicams. We've probably been busted."

"Sammy," I said, grabbing him with my free hand as I pointed Skurge toward the Moonwalk, "you, David and Michael go and get the van. Meet us in front of the old Mint in five."

"Why?" he asked, a petulant look on his face. "Why don't we all just—"

"Good plan. Let's do it!" Michael cut Sammy's response off with a glance. "But wipe down those blades first, then lose them!"

"Right," I agreed, realizing that, besides the blood, the blades would be the most likely giveaway that we'd been involved. Fingerprints, you know. Not to mention our spilled blood.

But as Samantha, David and Michael began the process of wiping the blades down, a voice inside my head whispered a warning about parting with Skurge. While the other blades were no doubt of superior "magickal" quality (obsidium hyperalloys and all that other good Mokarr alchemy/sorcery "technomagickal" stuff), they were but mere toys compared to Skurge. The toys we could lose. My memories, however, were slowly beginning to gel, and what they had to say on the matter bid me not to abandon Skurge on pain of death.

"I'm taking Skurge with me."

Michael shot me a heated look as he tossed his blades down on the Mokarr's body.

"You sure about that?" His tone pleaded with me to toss Skurge into the Mississippi River at the earliest opportunity.

"I have to. I have no choice in the matter." Michael accepted my news with a nod of his head, unlike anyone else.

"That thing's creepy!" Sammy said, summing up everyone else's feelings on the matter.

"So is everything else," I explained. "I just know that I've got to bring Skurge along with me. Don't ask me to explain it. I can't. I just *know*." The wail of sirens drew closer, urging us to move swiftly. "Let's move it, guys!"

Luther, Samantha, and I broke into a jog, picking our way through the ruined square, heading for Chartres. Skurge—in appearance a massive two-handed blade—was as light as a broomstick in my hands as we ran. Dimly, I realized that Skurge had always been this light in my grasp. I tried to keep it in as low a profile as possible, hoping that if someone caught a glance that they would see more body than blade. But there was really no way to hide a blade that wide and that long, short of using magick, so I silently prayed that no one noticed us. Or, if we were noticed, that the observers would chalk it all up to some Mardi Gras cosplay.

My plan was to take Chartres all the way to Ursalines, then hang a right and hit the French Market, which would give us plenty of cover until we reached the Mint. Sammy and the others would have plenty of time to get to his van and leave the parking lot, which had its terminus near the Mint. Hopefully, any eyewitnesses would report that the group of people in the square had split up and gone in two different directions, throwing off the law long enough for us to make good our escape. An encounter with the law now, after what we'd just been through, would be, at best, anticlimactic.

The natural curiosity of the remaining stragglers to look for the source of the sirens helped us out. Most of the people we jogged past didn't give us a second glance, as they were too busy looking for the source of the sirens to bother. It was probably the only time in my life that I had been thankful for rubberneckers. Still, we bit our nails, anticipating a sudden swarm of police officers to appear and arrest us. The thought that the Mokarr might be back with reinforcements didn't even cross my mind.

As we entered the French Market, which was mostly closed down for the night, we skirted its lighted expanse, sticking instead to the shadows of Decatur Street's many buildings. Slowing down to a hurried walk, we picked our way around the few merchants who were scrambling about their stalls, desperately trying to secure their goods which had become rattled by the freak storm. I noticed that the storm's freakish fury had been concentrated mostly upon the square itself, sparing the neighboring area from its full, hurricane force. The merchants—most of them living in trailers or RVs parked along the side of the streets—were, however, still cursing vehemently in several different tongues over their late night misfortune as they sorted through what remained of their wares.

Coming to the end of the French Market stalls, we stood on Barracks Street, trying our best to look nonchalant and disinterested. I stood with my back to the stone support of the pavilion, such that Luther's bulk would hide any sight of Skurge from curious eyes.

While we stood, anxiously waiting for Sammy's van to arrive, I took a closer look at Luther's bloody left side. Across his ribs, there was a six inch long gash in his jacket, soaked in red blood. Fighting my growing nausea, I peered closer, trying to see in the half light. What I saw was the slick gleam of sinew and bone of his exposed ribs.

"Luther, are you okay?" I asked, wondering how he was still on his feet. The loss of blood, together with the shock of the wound and our little run, should have been enough to at least slow him down some.

"Don't you go worryin' 'bout me, now," he said evenly, giving me a wry smile. "It's only a flesh wound, as Sammy would say."

Before either Samantha or I could respond to his macho bullshit, Sammy's van came rolling to a stop in front of us. It purred like the beast that it truly was.

"All aboard!" Sammy shouted, hanging over the edge of his window, tugging on an imaginary train whistle. David's thick, hairy arm reached from behind him and pulled him back into the van like one of those old novelty "Scary Banks," with its gruesome, coin-snatching hand. In ten seconds we were in the van and on our way, rolling safely down Barracks Street toward North Rampart. I eased into the front passenger seat, trading places with David, who gave me as wide a berth as possible, staying as far away as he could from Skurge.

"Michael," I called over my shoulder while directing Sammy to take a left on North Rampart, "take a look-see at David and Luther. Make sure they'll live."

Immediate groans of disgust issued from David and Luther.

"What about you, Logan. Uh, Tat? Whoever you are?" Sammy asked under the noise of their grumbling, not taking his eyes off the road. "You look like a water balloon with a couple of dart holes in it."

"Just a bunch of small cuts and bruises," I responded quietly, trying to play it down, cursing his all-seeing eyes. "David and Luther are a lot more banged up than I am." From the growing pain throbbing throughout my body, I knew that I'd take a look at myself later and call myself a hypocrite for thinking that Luther was the only one laying on the machismo. Feeling a bit fey, however, I realized, almost without realizing it, that this was nothing I hadn't handled before. I would heal it like I healed that cut on my chin. Quickly, too.

"All right, girls," Michael said as he made his way from the rear of the van toward David and Luther, "let's see what kind of boo boos you got."

The out of place sound of glass falling onto the floor made me turn around.

"Uh, don't worry about that," Michael said sheepishly, fiddling with his flight jacket. Thus visually cued, Mr. Perception finally noticed a small gash in the flight jacket right about where Michael's left kidney would be.

"What in the world?" I inquired as Michael unfastened the zipper of his jacket, spilling the shards of the bottle of Dom Perignon onto the van's already littered floor.

"One of those pukes got lucky and caught me with a good one," he said, turning to look at Samantha. "Fortunately, I just happened to have a little extra padding beneath my jacket," Michael smiled and dumped the rest of the shattered bottle onto the floor. "Weird, but it was Sammy who gave me the secret nod to bring it along with us after we all but drained it before we left the house. I thought he might have had some scheme or plan for later, so I just tucked it back inside my jacket. Plenty of room, if only slightly bulky. But entirely fortuitous, entirely lucky, don't you think? Thick old glass, and maybe a few remaining drops of bubbly. And a Mokarr katana, expertly wielded, turns aside. That's a big 'Hmmm...', me maties," Michael exaggerated.

Sammy pretended not to notice anything, and we all noticed that he was pretending not to notice, flicking at dials and knobs on the van's futuristic panels. More on this would surface later, of course, because Sammy had more secrets than anyone, but one could hide supernatural luck only for so long.

"Do you think your parents could ever forgive me, Samantha?" Michael inquired.

"I don't know, Michael," she began, smiling mischievously, "that stuff's pretty expensive!"

Michael, a hurt look on his face, reached into his belt and pulled out Samantha's gun. As her eyes grew wide, thinking that she had triggered some kind of delayed combat stress insanity in him, he expertly press checked it, popped the mag, then passed both gun and magazine to her. All without saying a single word. Luther and David started to laugh as Samantha lamely took the proffered gun.

"I knew you wouldn't remember that lesson, either," Michael scolded her. Then, trying to stifle his own laughter, he turned back around and began to attend to Luther and David.

Noting this, I had to ask him, "Michael? Why did you have to borrow Samantha's gun? I would have thought for sure that you would have at least one of your own."

He snorted. "You know I'm always packing, Logan. But I sent two mags of fun downrange from my own Siggy trying to burn down those three Mokarr that David and Samantha were fighting before I realized that their armor was invulnerable virtually everywhere to conventional weapons. That's when Samantha tossed me her sidearm and told me exactly where to shoot them."

"Wait a sec," I blurted. "I'm confused."

"Then I'll talk slower," Michael deadpanned. "David and Samantha were fighting three Mokarr. I burned two mags trying to shut them down. Samantha tossed me her gun—she had already taken one of the Mokarr's katana's from him, so she was still armed—and told me where to shoot them. I put two of them down then as David crunched them and kept them from moving too much. Close-in executions, basically. And only because I had forgotten, or had not yet recalled, the simple fact of Mokarr armor's weaker points. Luther and Sammy rejoined us—we had been split up for a bit—then Sammy and I headed off to scout."

"Why not just use your knife?"

"Because Sammy needed it, and I gave it to him. That last Mokarr, the one you saw on the ground by me and Sammy? Sammy did that with just a combat knife."

"But..." I stalled, then started again. "But something, some memory, told me that you were born to the blade."

"I am," Michael agreed, no ego in his voice. "But I prefer long blades over short ones. Sammy was always the best of us with the smaller blades. Better even than I or Samantha."

A pensive silence fell upon us all as the shadows of memories of another world, a world before this one, teased our minds.

Sammy was driving within reason, for once, realizing that there was no reason to haul ass and arouse anyone's suspicions. He was taking as many side roads as possible, careful to follow each and every rule of the road, even down to the point of ridiculousness. He would have failed a driving test for being too cautious! Soon, though, we had made the loop around Lee Circle and had started down St. Charles, the final leg of our journey home.

"Shit! Goat foam!" Sammy suddenly cursed, slamming his hands down on his steering wheel in his frustration. He had been fiddling with his radio, trying to pick up a station for the latest news.

"What's the matter, Sammy?" I asked.

Sammy was silent for a moment, brooding over something. Then:

"Well, besides the fact that my stupid radio is on the fritz," Sammy said, eyes fixed ahead on the thin traffic, "we just destroyed Jackson Square! I liked that place," he said with misty eyes. "We used to go there as kids and chase those spastic pigeons! Remember that, Logan? We drove everybody crazy, running around like idiots, chasing those stupid flying rats! My mom used to buy us spumoni there, and cotton candy. I even got my picture painted there once. Remember that, man?" he asked, giving me a quick glance. I could see the tears spilling from the corners of his big brown eyes. "You know, the one that I made the guy paint Godzilla in with me, too, terrorizing the square? And now, it's ruined!" Sammy sniffled, wiping his nose with his sleeve. "No, I don't mean the picture!" he added defensively. "I mean the square. It's all molten slag and wasted trees, all because of us. All because we had to go crazy all at once!"

Sammy's reverie brought an awkward silence into the van. He had just spoken for all of us. Just as a piece of us had been reborn tonight, a piece of us had died as well. The death of innocence, the rebirth of guilt. Only time—both future and past—would tell us what the final balance of that spiritual mixture would become. That was, of course, provided we lived long enough to find out for ourselves.

"Uh, this is gonna take some stitches, David," Michael announced after a while. He held a torn shirt compress to David's forehead.

"Like hell it will!" David exploded, grabbing the compress from Michael in a huff. "Nobody's gonna stick me with a needle. I'll kick 'em in the knees first!"

"Suit yourself, macho man," Michael said, moving on to Luther, who was holding an improvised bandage over his battered ribs. It had taken some time for Michael to find Sammy's medical kit, and just about as long for him to persuade Luther and David to act like good kids. "And you, big guy, " he addressed Luther, "you need about thirty or forty stitches and/or staples, not to mention some good rest for your four broken ribs. Tactical error to bull rush an opponent armed with a long blade, while you're unarmed."

"Stitches mean needles, and I don't do needles!" Luther bellowed, the strain of his wound only now beginning to show in his voice. "And, as for your martial arts tactical error bullshit, I'll bull rush anybody I damn well feel like bull rushing! I broke his fuckin' neck, in case you forgot!" he smiled wickedly.

"True enough," Michael acknowledged, always a fan of Luther's indomitable spirit. "But, for such macho, badass dudes," Michael said, exasperated with their antics, "you guys sure are whiners! Afraid of a couple of stitches, are you? Just wait until those things *try* to heal *without* stitches! Talk about pus, gangrene, and infection! Gross!"

Luther and David exchanged nervous glances. Michael's tirade seemed to have struck some nerve of common sense within them.

"He goes first!" they said in unison, pointing fingers at one another.

Sammy was about to make the turn down Samantha's street when she suddenly leaned forward and placed her hand on his shoulder.

"Make the block first, Sammy," she said, lifting her hand from his shoulder and pointing straight down St. Charles.

"Good idea, Samantha," he said, his voice still a little hoarse. Sammy urged the accelerator down, smoothly. The traffic here was dead enough for Sammy to pull back into the road without running anyone off of the road. Make that anyone else, considering his temper tantrum earlier today.

"What's wrong?" I asked her without turning around. I was too busy checking out her darkened house for myself. It wouldn't be an exaggeration to say that we were all pretty much on edge.

"Maybe nothing, maybe everything," Samantha replied mysteriously, leaning over my shoulder to take a look for herself as we cruised by the Teale House. All of the house lights were out, which was normal enough. The garage light was on, as always, for security. Robberies and rapes were common enough—even here in uptown—to merit the added dollar a month that the light cost to burn. There was nothing that I could see that was out of the ordinary, which didn't actually mean that there wasn't. But, at least, this time, I couldn't see anyone's head peeking out from the roof.

Turning off of St. Charles and rounding the block, we nearly retraced the route of our earlier joyride, which, by now, seemed almost comical in its distance in time; time having warped completely on this very long day. I couldn't even force a yawn as we pulled into Samantha's driveway, even though I'd been up for nearly twenty-four hours now. With the nightmare, the drinking, the Pee Wee thing, the drinking, rehearsal, the drinking, then the complete and utter insanity and bloodshed, you would think that I'd be the walking dead. While that point was now both theosophically and morally debatable, given what had occurred and what it might imply about the future, still I felt nothing but energy, as if something a little more potent than adrenaline had kicked in.

Stabbing a button on his futuristic, Star Trek dashboard, Sammy keyed the garage remote, opening the oversized double door. He eased into the garage as the interior lights came on, bathing the garage in bright, angry fluorescent light. Opening the door, I stepped down from the van, gingerly pulling a dead black Skurge along behind me, careful not to scratch Sammy's van.

As everyone piled out from the van, I took a good look at Skurge under the unforgiving glare of the fluorescent lights. Even in the light, it was still, as Sammy had put it, scary. Although it was no longer putting on a pyrotechnic show, it still seemed to radiate some sort of energy, some force, just on the edge of perception.

"Yuck!" Samantha said as she stared, morbidly fascinated. "I thought it wouldn't look so creepy in the light. Guess I was wrong." She moved closer to me, lightly brushing me with her hip. "Why did you bring it? Why didn't you just leave the damned thing alone?"

"I didn't really have a choice in the matter, Samantha," I told her, wishing that she of all people would let it go. "I don't think I could just toss it away now like a piece of trash. After all this time, all of these years that I'm only now beginning to comprehend, it just seems right to have it at my side—just as it seems right for all of this to be happening the way that it is. It's almost starting to make some sort of warped sense. In a very magickal sort of way."

"Well, when we all wake up from this nightmare, remind me to tell you how much fun I had!" Samantha laughed then, her voice strained, half-hitting me, half-nudging me into the house. She was ticking like a time bomb on the inside, even more than the rest of us.

By the time that Samantha and I had reached the den, Sammy had already turned on the television. He was scanning the local stations, switching maniacally back and forth between them, trying to find some late breaking news of what had just happened. All he was getting was static.

"You're not going to get anything yet, Sammy," Michael said, nursing David and Luther on the Teale's sofa. "It's still too early for them to have any sort of coverage."

"Dr. Michael's" latest snake oil medication seemed to be something that his two patients agreed wholeheartedly with: cognac—the good stuff, right from the Teale's dry bar. What neither Luther nor David knew, though, was that Michael's "medication" was his preamble for some serious poking around on their wounds. Since a hospital was out of the question right now, he was probably thinking about how he was going to anesthetize them before stitching them up. It was almost the same thing as giving a lollipop to a kid, only before the fact in this case.

Sammy still flicked through the channels, hoping to catch some glimpse of himself or his heroic actions on the screen.

"You know," he said, flicking the remote like the video game wizard that he was, "I'm really surprised that there's nothing on yet. The storm must have knocked the uplinks out, or something."

"Remember all of those lights on in the Quarter, Sammy?" I asked, watching the screen scroll like an old black and white silent film.

"Uhh..." Sammy sat back, rubbing his chin with the remote. "Ha!" he exploded gleefully, pointing the remote like a magician's wand at the screen and dialing up MTV, the twenty-four hour umbilical cord that plugs into the wall. All he got was static. Now he was really pissed. "You'd think that with all of our technology nowadays we'd at least have some sort of alternative power generation for when the power went down! Like a simple backup generator, you stupid simps!" Sammy wailed loudly. In his frustration, Sammy beaned the screen with the remote, which drew him a glare from Samantha.

"Sammy, I'm sure that if they had Jimmy Sinner here in New Orleans he'd already be on, bleating about how the end is near! So count your damn blessings!" I picked the remote up off the floor and dialed up WDSU, figuring that they'd be the first to have anything on, since they were, at last account, still stationed in the French Quarter. All I got, however, was more eye relaxing static, which did not make me happy. "Aren't they a twenty-four hour station?" I inquired of Samantha. She was taken off guard by my bumbling inquiry, and she shook her head in her haste to be rid of my questions.

"Don't ask me, I'm only the piano player!" she responded, taking a swig from Luther's cognac bottle. No one was feeling at all like laughing at the moment, even though she had just made a pretty good funny. "Why don't you try WWL?" she added after she drained away another swig of the good stuff. "They'll probably break the story first, anyway."

"They are not on the air, nor can they be at this time..."

We jumped at that ominous pronouncement, startled by the melodious power of the voice that had delivered it. The room grew silent as a tomb as Sigil Talisman stepped into the den from nowhere,

using the same sunset purple "hole-in-the-air" trick that he had used earlier tonight when he had saved my ass from Vash Gar. Grim-faced and forbidding, he stood with his arms at his sides, an aura of burning, inner magickal power about him which lit his "illusory leathers" with an awesome, eldritch glow.

"Sigil Talisman!" I cried out in not-so-eager relief, naming him for the benefit of everyone else in the room. Skurge chose this moment to crackle a neon green arc along its length, dividing the attentions of my friends between the new intruder and the baleful Shadar steel blade in my hands.

"At your service, Tatternorn," Sigil bowed, sweepingly, like some noble courtier of old. It was a slick move on Sigil's part. He had just appeared in the midst of a battle-mad group of paranoids, and he had defused the situation almost instantly. Verbally, his subservient promise had brought down the tension level in the room, and his body language had assuaged any promise of violent action on his part. Like I said, slick. Or totally contrived.

Contrived or not, however, I took this brief moment of truce to make sure that my battle-mad friends weren't about to jump him. After all, even though my friends might have thought a bit differently, I *really* wanted to hear what Sigil had to say. And I *really* wanted to ask him some very specific questions about what was happening to us, and why. Then, once the slick bastard had answered all of my questions to my complete and utter satisfaction, I could have some *really* nice words with him concerning how he had managed to get us all damned to this Terran hell.

As I glowered and fought with my emotions, both Sammy and Samantha remained silent, studying Sigil intently, as if they were trying to fix in their memory where they had seen him before. David glared at Sigil like a madman, his lips quivering as he was probably trying to calculate the quantum energies involved in Sigil's little trick. Michael shot me a quick glance, a thousand questions in his eyes which I answered with a wink and a somewhat forced "it's okay" smile. Luther, still sitting on the couch, let out a massive plume of pungent smoke, then set his dragon bong down on the glass end table with an audible *klink*.

"I am very pleased to see that you have arrived safe and somewhat sound," Sigil said, his well-featured face becoming slightly more expressive, even slightly warmer, as he glanced us over. "You have liberated Skurge, as well, I see," Sigil said, fixing the black blade with his piercing, purple-tinged eyes. Skurge remained as black as midnight and as silent as a tomb as Sigil studied it for a long, dangerous moment.

"Hello to you too, Mr. Pointy Ears!" Sammy blurted, getting to his feet. His irritated tone was a welcome reprieve from the dangerous silence. "Whaddya mean, 'they're not on the air?'"

"Very simple, Master Samuel," Sigil said, surprising us all with his obsequious "master" talk, especially where Sammy was concerned. "It is all a matter of magickal frequencies interfering with and canceling out certain technological ones. Specifically, the ones used as carrier waves."

That got everyone's attention. Everyone wanted to know *how*, not *why*. Not yet.

"In this case, the *Space Warp* which brought Vash Gar and his Mokarr Death Squad to Jackson Square *pulsed* all of the carrier waves and their mated receivers within a ten mile radius of its epicenter."

"Whaddya mean, *Space Warp*? And by 'pulsed,' do you mean 'pulse' as in 'Electromagnetic Pulse?'" Sammy asked, his tone hostile, as it always was when he was confronted by charlatans proposing wild pseudo-theories. "Who the hell do you think you are, Mr. Pointy Ears: Spock?"

If not for Luther's stifled chuckle, you could have heard the literal pin drop.

"Hardly your typical EMP, my dear little cling-on," Sigil countered, much to Sammy's surprise. "And I am not Spock, not at all. I am far, far more." A tiny crackle of purple sparks raced from his almond-shaped eyes. In that same instant, his "leathers" were replaced by his nifty Raiders robes. "I am Sigil Talisman," he intoned, drawing himself up to his full height as multicolored plumes of energy raced up his arms to his fingertips, "the Guardian of the Dragon; the Keeper of the Krystallstaff;" the energies broke from his long fingers and arced a full yard in front of him, "the Archimage of the Seven Stars!"

The lights in the den browned out—"pulsed," as Sigil would have said—as he finished his dramatic introduction. If he didn't have it before, Sigil Talisman—epithets and all—certainly had our full, undivided attention now.

"Oh, I see," Sammy said meekly, ducking behind my leg. "At least your name's not *Tim*!"

"We have much to do, and little time in which to accomplish it," Sigil said, stepping closer to us as the lights came back on. Strangely, so did his damned "leathers." "Therefore, I will need your trust—your *complete* trust—if we are to realize our goal before Lord Valthrustra realizes his: The complete, utter damnation of this world's untold billions of souls!" With that, Sigil once again fixed each of us with that piercing gaze of his. His softly slanted, almond-shaped, purple-tinged eyes implored us to believe.

"Guys," I stated, seeking out their eyes as I slowly spoke, "what he's saying is for real. Each of you has had the dreams. Each of you saw what happened out there tonight, as impossible as it might seem." I got a few nods. But they still weren't totally convinced. So I stepped it up a notch, as much as it galled me to do so. "What's more," I admitted, "Sigil came out of nowhere and saved my ass when

Vash Gar had me on the ropes." That gem raised a few eyebrows. Guess up until now they all had believed that I had bested Vash Gar all by my lonesome. "Yeah, that's right. Sigil saved my ass. And stop smiling, Sammy. This is serious. Back in the square, just when Vash Gar was about to dust me, Sigil just stepped out of nowhere like he did just now and blasted that Mokarr bastard with some sort of magickal rainbow thingie. Then, after making sure I was okay, he told me to rendezvous back here at the Teale House. After that, he just cruised off again like the Lone Ranger."

They thought about it for a minute, a brooding group introspection.

"So where's Tonto?" Michael finally asked.

"*We're* Tonto, if memory serves me right," David said, glaring at Sigil.

Ooops. Seems that someone else besides me has just caught on.

"You were the one who led us to the slaughter, you Starin bastard!" David shouted, shaking with rage. He then began to move toward Sigil, ill-intent in his eyes. Sigil, to his credit, didn't even bat an eye. David didn't quite get to exact whatever toll he was going to exact upon the "Starin bastard," however. Luther snaked a long arm out and caught him by the belt, halting him in his tracks several paces from the cool as a cucumber Sigil Talisman.

"Be cool now, mon!" Luther soothed. "There's no reason to go crazy on us before the magick mon says what he's gotta say. If he's cool, no problem. If he's a liar," he said, a wicked grin on his face, "*then* I let you go."

David, appeased by Luther's reasoning, stood his ground—glaring nonetheless.

"I feared that would be how you would perceive it, old friend," Sigil said wearily to David. "Such is the corruption of memory when one passes through the Dream Barrier."

"Dream Barrier? What the hell are you talking about?" David growled.

Sigil drew in a deep breath, then looked strangely at Samantha. "Would you happen to have some brandy, milady? This may take quite some time."

"Uh, sure," Samantha stammered. She started to walk over to the dry bar, then shot me a questioning glance, as if she were unsure of what to do next.

"You'd better bring seven glasses, Samantha," I said, wondering how much the Teales would appreciate their new guest's graces, not to mention the healthy new dent in their liquor cabinet. "No,

better make that seven *bottles*," I added with a knowing smirk. "This is gonna be *verrry* interesting."

CHAPTER 10: Transcend The Boundaries

Soon enough, we sat together in a rough circle on the floor of the den, passing bottles of Courvoisier and Kirschwasser between us like Indians passing peace pipes in a tipi. At Sigil's request, Samantha turned off the lights and lit candles and incense, giving the impression more of a seance than a reunion. Sigil sat cross-legged at the head of the circle, toying with a crystal snifter of brandy. I sat directly across from him, nearly mirroring him with Skurge placed across my lap and a hefty shot of the smooth cherry Kirschwasser in front of me. Samantha sat to my left; Sammy, to my right. David and Michael sat to Samantha's left, with David closer to her for safety's sake. Luther completed the circle, lounging nearest to Sigil, still pulling from his cognac medicine bottle.

Strangely enough, the improbable scene reminded me of one of my earliest memories of this world, when my uncle and some of his friends were having a "sit in," tripping and listening to the tunes that would later be called "Acid Rock" for want of a better name. Of course, I was far too young to indulge with them back then, but that never stopped me from wondering what they were up to. Wondering what they were seeing as that psychedelic light spun in time with those classic Iron Butterfly, Black Sabbath, Led Zep, and Jimi Hendrix tunes.

Now, as that absurd wheel had gone round, full-circle, I think I knew.

"The sun is about to rise on this new day," Sigil began, tracing the intricacies of the crystal snifter with his fingers. "Before the dawn, however, each of you will realize what you are, what you were, and what you have become. This *Weird* that I place upon you will force you to recall some piece of your past; to relive some distant, telling memory which will unlock the hidden doors of your past lives on SenZar."

The mention of the place, SenZar, sent a chill through the room.

"How do we know that you're not just gonna pull some hocus pocus on us, hypnotize us or something?" David asked, his anger not quite so livid as before.

"Because, Guthal Dirge, we are going to do this one at a time, yet together," Sigil explained patiently. "Each one of you," he continued, taking a brief sniff of the brandy, "will witness the others' *Weird*. You will live as they lived, through their eyes. You will learn not only of your companion, but also of yourself. It is that which shall multiply the effect of the magick, making it both extremely efficient and effective. There are other, easier ways, of course." Sigil took a long pull from his glass before continuing. "But we simply do not have the time." A wistful half-smile played across his face as he continued. "*The Weird* is a highly personal affair, my friends. It is sometimes painfully revealing. But it is nothing that you do not already know of one another, or of yourself. Or of *yourselves*."

"Isn't what you're doing sort of like mental rape, Sigil?" I asked, exploring his eyes for any sort of hidden motive that he might have. He *did* save my life back there, but, so far as I knew—or remembered like David—he had also *taken* it back on SenZar, leading us into an impossible situation that only death could resolve.

"Rape is an affair of unconsenting partners, Tatternorn," Sigil said, placing his glass down on the floor. "If you choose not to participate, then you—and the world—will have to live with those particular consequences."

"So it's our choice whether or not to bend over, huh?" David growled as he passed his bottle over to Michael.

"If you choose to use that analogy," Sigil said stiffly.

"Well, you can count me out!" David snorted.

Before David could remove himself from the circle, however, Sigil raised his left hand, long fingers extended, and placed them on Luther's right leg, much to Luther's dismay. As Luther's eyes grew wide with surprise, Sigil's hand began to glow warmly, a golden light weaving its way from his palm to Luther's leg. The golden glow spread at once, enveloping Luther's upper body like warm, springtime sunshine, concentrating specifically upon his wounded side. His eyes dilated under the influence of Sigil's touch, almost as if he had just taken a big hit from one of his many bongs. He stiffened, then relaxed, as the glow persisted for a full three seconds. Then, as suddenly as it had begun, the golden glow faded away, leaving a smiling Luther in its wake. After Sigil removed his hand from his leg, Luther started to examine his wound. His happy grin left no doubt as to what had happened.

"No way, now!" Luther said joyously, removing the bandage and displaying his scarless, unbruised ribs for a startled David to see. "Damn, I feel good! David, mon, he ain't playin' around! This is for real!"

"*That*," Sigil calmly said, as we stared, unbelieving, "is rape. I did not ask his consent; therefore, I raped him of his freedom of choice. You should consider carefully, Guthal Dirge, what you have just seen. It used to be a common sight around our campfire, you know."

"What? Rape?" Sammy giggled to himself.

Sigil, to his credit, completely ignored him. "Once, Guthal, I even reattached your hand after that axe-wielding Akir maniac, Hammarsvold, cleaved it from you. Do you remember that?"

David sat there, engrossed in some painful memory. He raised his left hand and stared at it, flexing it slowly. Fuzzy cobwebs were parting in my memory. I, too, was getting fragments of some other place; some cold place with lots of snow. To my right, Sammy started laughing.

"I think I remember that Akir creep," Sammy said slowly. "Oh, yeah! Now I do!" He started laughing like a little imp as he brushed away those cobwebs. "We were up in Hammarshold, and the weather was shitty. No, make that really shitty! And cold, too! Anyway, we were up there on some kind of mission, something like... uhh... to find something in those ice caverns, wasn't it?"

"...and that crazy, pirating sonuvabitch tried to kill us all for violating his so-called 'territory!'" David interjected, still looking at his left hand. "I lost my friggin' hand when that asshole and his gang of half-breed trolls jumped us in our camp in the crevasse. Damn near lost my other hand trying to pry my axe out of his skull!" David laughed heartily at this, reliving that insane time in the Ice Caves of Hammarshold.

"Yeah, Dave," Michael said, lightly laughing, "I think I remember playing rearguard for you when you charged into them like an idiot, waving your axe in your one good hand and spreading troll brains like herpes."

Now, perhaps cued by that sexual reference, Samantha started laughing, too, her face blushing. As I was beginning to recall, we were literally caught with our pants down during their surprise attack. If it wouldn't have been for sheer luck, we might have ended our careers there as nude ice sculptures. Herpes-free ice sculptures, of course. There was no such thing as "herpes" on SenZar. Not per se, at least. There *were* things like "The Dark Crawlies," though.

"Excellent!" Sigil said, a slight smile tugging at the corner of his mouth. "You are beginning to remember." He let that sink in. "With each passing moment, you begin to see more and more of your former selves. You begin, with each passing moment, to rediscover your true potentials. Believe me, if there were time," he said, his thoughts a million miles away on some other world. "Ahh, if only there *were* more time. This would be the only way that I would reintegrate you with your former selves. We would sit and drink and remember in our tight-knit circle of peace, gently recalling every iota of *what was*. Such a course would be wonderful: to gently reacquaint you with yourselves in such an easy way." Sigil's gentle voice trailed off for a second. "But such a thing would take weeks, months. Perhaps even years. As I said before, though, time is of the essence. Every minute is precious now, for every precious minute brings us one step closer to Armageddon. And each one of you needs to be in complete grasp of your special powers and abilities before we leave this circle."

"Well, what do we do?" I asked him, feeling the adrenaline in the room start to flow.

"You must first relax your thoughts, Tatternorn," Sigil replied, his eyes growing a deep purple as he gathered more focus for what was to come. "You must free yourself of your inhibitions. You must free yourself of the patterns and things of this modern world and immerse yourself in the waters of another time, another place."

Sigil's voice began to take on a droning, measured cadence, drawing us into its power. "Luther Gates—*Rhiannazaar*—you will be first."

Luther gave me an expectant look, then smiled as I gave him a good luck thumbs-up.

"Break on through, Luther," I told him in words of Jim.

Luther's smirk was the most telling facial expression that I'd ever witnessed in my life. As ever, Luther Gates would be the first guy on the block to try the new "Good-Good." Lucky bastard.

?

The shadows of the burning candles throbbed and pulsed in a wicked, hypnotic pattern, providing a visual counterpoint to Sigil's vocal rhythm. A whirring wind kicked up from nowhere, like the roar of a fighter jet—yet the candles weren't extinguished. I forced my heavy eyelids open, only to see a kaleidoscope of images projected on the walls and the ceiling: images of a vast, Paleozoic jungle in which great, colorfully feathered pterodactyls soared on volcanic thermals. Images of a wide, slowly flowing river, its banks lined with thirsty herds of brightly feathered giant saurischians and ornithiscians, and steaming, sulfurous fumaroles.

Then, suddenly, as if a movie director had just called for a zoom-in, the vision focused tightly upon a grove of mammoth, towering black-wooded and azure-foliaged trees which would have put any redwood forest on Earth to shame. As the vision zoomed in closer, panning its way through the

canopy of the upper level of the trees, a strange, bustling community of vast wooden huts took form.

They were built into and around the tops of the giant trees, using the natural form of the trees in a highly efficient, ecologically sound way. Moving closer still, I could discern the forms of the many

fascinatingly multicolored people—*Azaar?*—moving about their daily business. Their four-armed

figures moved animatedly about as they exchanged pleasantries with one another in the singsong,

flowing tongue of the People of the Trees.

The vision moved along, a ghostly voyeur, into the walls of the great central hut. Some sort of council was in session, an important meeting in which the younger males were standing before the older ones. The vision settled upon one of the younger warriors, the biggest by far of his brethren, then rammed directly into the back of his white mohawked head, merging with his thoughts.

That's when we began the Magickal Mystery Tour of Luther Gates' mind.

No, I thought, correcting myself, *Rhiannazaar's mind.*

CHAPTER 11: See Ya In The Next World, And Don't Be Late

"The young ones have gathered here today," boomed the stentorian voice of the Spokesman. "Strong and brave, as hard as the very rock of the Great Walls themselves, to prove without doubt before the Great Spirit's all-seeing eyes that they are ready to become true Azaar warriors. That they stand ready to win the right to bear the mighty blade of our people, the mojo-mazumba!"

The crowd, hushed until now, exploded into excited hoots and proud yells. Their individual skin pigmentation mirrored their emotions in a kaleidoscopic rainbow festival of brilliant pulsating hues and bizarre flashing patterns. The still-silent young warriors, however, stood at attention, their emotions focused, their skin still, and their jet eyes fixed dead ahead.

"Now, warriors-to-be," the Spokesman continued, striding before the line of young warriors like a drill instructor on inspection, "do you think yourselves worthy of *Talashar*?"

The line of young Azaar warriors growled as one, slamming their upper pair of arms heavily into their chests in some sort of salute. Or challenge.

The Spokesman stopped in front of one of the warriors to Rhiannazaar's right, eyeing him intently. "You, Alazaar, son of Alrazaar the Weaver. Do you truly believe that your time has come to become a man?"

"Yes, wise one!" Alazaar spoke with no hesitation. "I will myself slay a mated pair of shellbacks and craft them into washtubs for the children to play in!"

The crowd erupted into another round of hoots and shouts, drowning out the chuckles of Alazaar's fellow warriors-in-waiting. The Spokesman wasted no time. He smiled once, tightly, at Alazaar, then resumed his pacing as the crowd wore itself out. He came to a stop at the end of the line, four men down from Rhiannazaar.

Now, as Rhiannazaar turned his head slightly, I could see all of the young braves gathered here in the Great Hall of the People of the Trees. Besides Rhiannazaar, there were eight others, each of varying stature, mien, and pigmentation. Their names rolled into my consciousness, as if I had known them all of my life. There was Manak, the youngest of them. He was skilled beyond his years with the mojolo-mazumba, the Azaar's great four-handed bow. There was Nilatar, who was good with his ironwood spear. There were the twins, Annar and Annat. They were friends who had shared more than jokes and shroom with me...

...me?

Sigil's spell was becoming stronger, destroying the barriers of thought, merging my—*our*—

consciousnesses together into one big uni-mind. It was more than an illusion. It was *real*. We were

actually there with Luther in that otherworldly experience, a group trip, if you will. So, rather than

ruin the experience, I gave in completely, reining in my own natural mental barriers. Why only go

half-assed on what could be the very best trip of all time?

...there was also Razaar, who was skilled with the many-bladed gwanga—though he could fight better with it in-close than he could throw the treacherous thing. There were Lutar and Kelden, who were friends only when it came to raiding the nests of the spear-beaks.

Finally, there was the boastful Alazaar, who stood at my side, my second in this quest—my rival in more than just *Talashar.*

Alazaar was my nemesis. He was strong, brave, and quick with his mind—and he was always ready with some bragging remark about how much better he was at something or the other than anyone else. It was he who had driven the nail into my dearest Shaleeta's heart, causing her to forego her choice of mate until one of us had proven himself in *Talashar*, the Rite of Passage.

For all that anyone knew—though all seemed to freely whisper the tale—he was the very one who had planted my spear outside her house for all to see, that last festival night. Alazaar was the snake—sharp fangs and all!

But now, the Spokesman had stopped his course in front of me, glaring at me with his night-black eyes.

"And you, Rhiannazaar, son of Thannar the Hunter, who has rejoined the earth! Do you think yourself worthy to walk in your father's mighty footsteps?"

"Yes, wise one!" I said proudly. "I will bring back what no one has made trophy of since my father did it in his Rite of Passage: I will wear the teeth of the mighty gor-gar as my mark of passage!"

The Spokesman's eyes narrowed as he considered this. Alazaar jerked his head around, staring at me as if I had just made a great, empty lie. The crowd was hushed, shocked by this greatest of boasts.

"To win your sword, you would dare this?" The Spokesman whispered.

"I dare, wise one," I said, meeting his stern gaze. "And what is more, I will succeed!"

The crowd went wild at this. Even the Spokesman joined in the celebration, raising an arm in salute to the brave warriors who stood before the elders of the tribe. I looked into the crowd, hoping to catch some glimpse of my darling Shaleeta's face. When I finally caught sight of her, though, her eyes were brimming with hot tears as a sad azure hue flushed throughout her. She could only shake her head and mouth the words, "you fool, you fool..."

She did *not* understand. I *had* to win her from Alazaar, and only the teeth of the gor-gar, the terrible tooth-lizard, could be her price. A simple claw-lizard or even a fin-back wouldn't be enough to win her heart. There had to be no doubt in her mind as to who the bravest warrior was. And Alazaar was in her heart now, taking my rightful place! The strutting bastard! Let him bring back his stupid mated shell-back bathtubs for the children. When they saw the teeth of the gor-gar around my neck, they would be too busy following me around, begging me to notice them, than to play in his stupid tubs.

As a group, we received the blessing of the Spokesman, who spoke for the entire tribe in this matter. Then we filed out of the Great Hall of the People of the Trees, walking in single file, passing through the crowd as fathers cheered their sons and mothers wept for them. They threw flowers, azure garlands gathered from the boughs of the towering ironwood trees, in which our homes were built by the grace of the Great Spirit. The children ran up to touch us, hoping that our bravery would rub off on them. We set our faces into masks of determination. Our forms became the colors of the shadows and glades. Now, we were ready for our sojourn into the jungles of the Great Rift, the Land of the Trees Between the Great Walls.

Before we left the walkways of the tribe, the maidens came forward to give their blessings to their favored ones. Shaleeta came through the crowd, dressed in the soft skins that I had won for her. Her white hair fell softly down to her waist. She held a single, polished agate bound with a leather thong in her outstretched hand.

"Wait, brave one," Shaleeta cried as she moved forward toward me. Her other hands were busy trying to wipe away her tears. I stopped where I stood, wondering if she had finally seen things from my eyes.

"Yes, my heart's fire," I said hopefully, meeting her eyes.

"She doesn't mean *you*, Rhiannazaar!" Alazaar said coldly as he stepped forward to meet Shaleeta halfway. Her eyes met mine for a fleeting, guilty moment. Then she turned stiffly toward Alazaar, like a dancer caught in indecision.

"Take this as a reminder of my... love," she said, brushing away her welling tears as my heart grew cold. "Let it guide you. Let it bring you home victorious."

"I accept your love, dearest Shaleeta," Alazaar said warmly, masking his words in the tongue of the snake. "And I will return with it, along with my shell-back trophies, and I shall pin it over your heart on our day of union."

Shaleeta stood there, in Alazaar's cold embrace, her eyes locked with mine. She gave him her heart then, taking mine in its place. My arms fell to my sides. I tried to say something, but the words just wouldn't come. So, alone before my people, I turned away, her eyes in my mind, and walked to join my brothers. They were already making their way through the trees.

We made camp that first night along the rocky banks of the Gisshagumm, the Waters From Below, under the light of the full moons. There were three days of *Talashar*. Our first day had been fruitless. We had followed the spoor of several fin-backs for quite some time, only to find them later, holed-up in a massive box canyon for the night, trying to mate. Since none of us really had it in our hearts to rile a fin-back in rut, we had decided to call it a day and hole-up ourselves in the safety of the riverbank. Of course, the treetops would have been much safer, but they were off-limits for shelter during *Talashar*. A true warrior would make the elements bend to his will, to serve him, not the other way around.

So, it was at first camp that Alazaar broke his snaky silence. "Brother Rhiannazaar," he said as we sat, cold and shivering, before the feeble warmth of a hot spring, "why do you wear a long face? The hunt still has two more days. We will all make warriors of ourselves before the moons lose their shiny faces."

"You talk as if you already have your trophy, brother Alazaar," I replied, not giving him the honor of my eyes. "We saw nothing today, save for a few love-mad fin-backs. It would hardly be worth the effort to fill them with arrows. No one would be able to bear the stench of their love-soaked fins long enough to call you a brave warrior!"

Muted chuckles rung out from our companions. They weren't quite certain as to what to do when it came to laughing at one of my or Alazaar's jokes, especially if one of us were the butt of it. The invisible lines of command weren't clearly defined, yet. Yet.

"Manak said that he saw what may have been the tracks of a thunder-beast," Alazaar said, ignoring my jibe. "Right, Manak?"

Young Manak was visibly distressed at having been put on the spot by his superior in the chain of dominance. His face flushed several random patterns of various dim and dull hues as he struggled within himself for the proper answer, any answer. He wrung his hands and toyed with his bow before he responded in his slow, measured way.

"Well, I *might* have seen the tracks, brother Alazaar," Manak temporized, "but there was really too much undergrowth to tell for sure. We were walking with our arms at the time, you know!"

"Nonetheless," Alazaar said, "where go the thunder-beasts, goes the gor-gar, as the old women are so fond of saying to the gullible children. What do you think about that, brother Rhiannazaar?" he asked, the corners of his eyes briefly flashing a deep crimson as he set the bait. "Do you believe in that old woman's tale?"

"You know as well as I do that there is some merit to that belief, brother Alazaar," I replied, eager to meet his words. "The gor-gar likes nothing better than to feast upon the ponderous thunder beast, save to feast upon the Azaar who is too slow to find a tree!"

There was more subdued laughter. Alazaar, irritated that his baiting was getting nowhere fast, got up from his place and walked over to the shore of the river to plot some more mischief. After Alazaar disappeared from sight, young Manak got up from where he sat with his great bow and walked over to where I sat against a large boulder.

"You know, brother Rhiannazaar," Manak said softly, such that only I would hear his words, "Alazaar would like nothing better than to see you fail in this rite. This is his third and final time, you know. You, the twins, and I, this is our first time. We are not expected to succeed. He *has* to, or he will never win his mojo-mazumba. His bravery will become suspect, not to mention his... betrothal."

Manak leaned against his bow, embarrassed at having stated the obvious.

"I am the youngest of us all," he continued. "I have but recently passed my fifteenth ZoZo. Yet my skill with the mojolo-mazumba, as my father has taught me, has allowed me the chance to prove myself. You have only a year on me, Rhiannazaar—and only through your *own* heart have you learned the skills of the hunt, for your father has rejoined the earth—yet your great strength has spoken for you with words of truth that even the old ones can hear! You are *already* as strong as Zannar the Hunter, who is one of the strongest of us, *ever*. With each passing day you grow stronger still. *You will succeed*," he told me, nodding his head knowingly. "I know this to be true. But Alazaar, for all of his vaunted skill, has failed in his previous two times. There is more to it than unluck. I will not say what I *think* it is. He is nervous now, wondering if he will return home emptyhanded his third and final time, and he seeks to make you doubt yourself so that you will share his fears."

"You are wise beyond your years, brother Manak," I said, studying his bright eyes. "Yes, there is something about him, something that fuels a fire within him. I have noticed it gnawing at him like a hungry flea, and he channels his feelings into evil thoughts for me. But," I said, placing an arm on his, "I am a big boy now. I think I can live with it."

Manak laughed softly, leaning into his mighty mojolo-mazumba, as if the massive ironwood bow could shush his laughter. I smiled at him, reassuring him that I would keep his words in confidence.

Just then, Annar, who had been foraging near the camp, came walking through the brush, a broad smile on his face as he picked his way through the slippery rocks of the riverbank.

"Look what I found!" Annar said excitedly, holding up a small, resinous black-leafed plant—roots and all. "Good-Good! Anyone care to celebrate our first night of *Talashar*?"

We sat in a circle and smoked like the true warriors did after a successful hunt.

The next day, however, was a series of misleads and near-misses. Only once did we spot any shell-backs, and that was from a long distance. It was almost as if the Great Spirit were deliberately herding the great beasts away from us. That night, we camped without fire in the pavilion-like roots of a mighty mud tree. We were exhausted, covered with muck and mire, and sorely in need of female companionship. The jungle would do things like that to the young warrior. There was more than one way to prove one's manhood, and when one of those ways wasn't working, then the other ones had a nasty way of surfacing to annoy the living hell out of a young warrior-to-be.

So, from within the confines of our mud-hovel, I began to hum a song, "Last Tear From the Sky," a song which dealt with the loss of a lover, sorrowful rain and other such things. My brethren, even snaky old Alazaar, joined in, for such is the way of the Azaar. Noble warriors that we were, we all prayed that the noise of a nearby fumarole would drown out any emotions, any nervous clearing of throats; that the darkness would obscure any reflecting glint from rainy eyes and hide the true

sight of our sad azure-blue skin.

It was near dawn, when we were once more ready to hunt, when Alazaar approached me, a strange look on his face. "Brother Rhiannazaar," he said, stumbling on the words, "I have something that must be said." Alazaar motioned that we should be alone, so we walked a short distance from the camp, out

of earshot of the others. Once we were secure, he stopped, turned around to make certain that no one

was near, then began to speak.

"What I have to say pains me more than you can know, old friend," Alazaar began. I did not have to tell him that we were neither old, nor friends. If he could be polite, then so could I. "I... Shaleeta, that is," his face began to blush uncontrollably, darkening to a deep shade of purple. My eyes darted to the stone that he wore around his neck, the one that she had given to him instead of to me.

"What do you have to say, brother Alazaar?" I asked of him impatiently. He was wasting away time that we did not have. "Speak, for the sun rises soon, and the hunt must go on without us. We would not want to return empty-handed."

Alazaar smiled a smile rich in irony then, thinking that I had purposefully insulted him. I had only meant to speak the truth.

"Nevermind, brother Rhiannazaar," Alazaar said, waving off whatever it had been. "It will keep until we return. Until *I* return, that is. With *my* trophy." He turned, and walked back to camp without another word.

Later in the day, as we stalked a group of fin-backs, which we were going to have to settle for or go home dishonored, we came upon a perfect site for an ambush of the herd. A small grove of ferns, perfect for camouflage, hid our approach as we closed with the noisy, munching monsters. This time they were not in rut. I saw the anticipation written in everyone's eyes. If the Great Spirit were with us, we would all come home as heroes, for these great, stupid beasts were standing ready to be slaughtered.

We had spread out in a rough crescent, about ten strides apart. We signaled by hand our intended targets. No one would interfere in someone else's kill. To do so would be dishonorable, not to mention foolhardy, as an Azaar in bloodlust would likely go for anything around him as a potential target. I signed to Alazaar that I intended the large male fin-back at the center of the herd.

He smiled and indicated the large, fern-munching female next to it. All the way down the crescent, the targets were selected. Making sure that my daggers were loose at my waist, I readied my ironwood spear in my right hands, drawing a bead on the fin-back's heart.

Suddenly, the big fin-back raised his head, sniffing the air. His fin flapped up into a defensive posture, stiffening like a membranous sail catching a breeze. But it was too late. With an Azaar war cry on my lips, I charged into the glade along with my brethren, gaining momentum for a mighty hurl. Dodging past one slow-moving beast, I hurled my spear, a prayer to the Great Spirit on my lips. The great spear caught the creature a foot below the fin and a foot above its front leg. With a sound like the ripping of cloth, the spear sank deeply into the fin-back, sending rivulets of brackish blood spraying about the glade. It roared in pain and disbelief, if such it could reason, and reared up on its hind legs awkwardly, turning a half-circle as it did so. Then, it turned its wickedly toothed maw around to worry the spear, which, I now saw, protruded through its other side. Hunks of bloody meat and ripped sinew dangled awkwardly from its magma-tempered ironwood point.

The fin-back was already mortally wounded. It just hadn't realized it yet. So I obliged to help it along its way. Not checking my forward speed, I drew my daggers, one in each lower hand, and vaulted onto its side. I landed behind its front leg, far enough back to avoid that gaping, toothy maw that could snap a warrior's back in twain. Clutching its rough, scaly hide with my free hands, I plunged the daggers over and over again into its steely hide. I carved it like some monstrous side of meat as the blood and bile rained down on me, covering me with its sticky, salty heat. It was like breaking in a maddened, saurian steed. Yet I rode it out until there was nothing but a faint twitch and a dying hiss from its oversized mouth.

At last, I tore myself loose from it, an exhilaration building within my heart. Seized with an irresistible urge, I placed my foot on its ruined side and howled. I was the Beast-Slayer! I was a warrior! My first great kill as a warrior, a great thing to be treasured and talked about by a roaring fire, a jug of fresh wine, and a great feast before me!

After what seemed like hours of glory, I turned to regard the carnage that we had wrought. There were nine carcasses strewn about. It looked like a butcher's shop, stocked overflowing with spears, arrows, blood, and offal. And standing, dazed and elated, over the fallen bodies, were nine newly-initiated Azaar warriors. This would certainly be the first time in recent memory that all of the warriors had returned home as men!

We stared at one another, some ancient, warrior kinship blossoming as we did. We had hunted together, killed together. These were bonds that could never be broken. Then, in awed silence, we fell to stripping our grisly mementos from the fallen fin-backs.

On our long march home, our bloody trophies on our shoulders, I began to think of Shaleeta. And of Alazaar. And of Alazaar *and* Shaleeta. As my brethren began a happy, joyous song of celebration, I fought back hot, stinging tears. We would all be heroes. Of that, there could be no doubt.

But *he* would have *her*, and *I* would not.

I would silently witness their betrothal, there amidst the tall branches, and their Song of

Union would live to haunt me forever.

But, I would not get by that easily, as the Great Spirit had a mysterious way of changing the rules of both love and war.

As we hit a small plain of scrub and waist-high grass no more than a half-day's walk from our home, a terrible roar came from behind us, cutting off our song of celebration in midverse. We turned as one, a cold fear gripping us as we saw the mighty, three-horned monster charging toward us. Its titanic form covered forty feet with every leaping stride that it took. Its daggerlike teeth gnashed its own cavernous mouth in its bloodlust.

"Spirit protect us!" Alazaar shouted. He nearly dropped his fin-trophy from his numbed hands as he regarded the gor-gar that charged us, death in its evil little eyes.

"It smells the blood! It's after the fins!" I shouted, making myself heard over the chaos. "Drop them and we have a chance to make it to the trees!" I hurled mine as far as I could toward the side, hoping that the gor-gar would pursue it before us. Manak and the twins took this as truth, and proceeded to pitch their blood-caked trophies. The others, seeming to weigh the choice of coming home empty-handed and becoming lizard food, stood confused, rooted to the spot.

"No!" Alazaar shouted, throwing his bloody fin to the ground. He hefted his spear and stood his ground as the murderous beast advanced.

"Alazaar, damn you!" I shouted, running over to him, shaking him. "We've got to make a run for it, or we will all die!"

"Coward!" he spat, his eyes crazed. "Where are your boasts now, Rhiannazaar? Here comes your gor-gar! Why don't you just *ask* him for a couple of his teeth? Maybe then dearest Shaleeta would give you a second glance!"

My first thought was to kill him for what he had said. My second was that even though he spoke like the snake that he was, he might have spoken some grain of truth.

"She'd much rather see us alive than dead, Alazaar," I snarled. "Consider *that*, you pompous ass!" I turned, resolved in my course, then started to move hastily away from the path of the saurian death machine.

Unfortunately, Alazaar remained where he stood, his spear poised defiantly as he waited for the gor-gar to close. And, at his side, Nilatar, Razaar, Kelden and Lutar stood at the ready, spears and great bows ready to let fly.

"Hurry, Rhiannazaar!" Manak called from up ahead. Now, I could see that the twins were already out in front of Manak, making a beeline for the nearest clump of trees. Now, I was torn inside.

Alazaar was going to die, along with the other fools that he'd influenced with his glory talk. Yes, I had boasted that I was going to return with gor-gar teeth. But that was expected of any young warrior: Brag like hell, because you'll probably never get the chance to tell such bald-faced lies in front of anyone else again and get away with it.

But, the thought nagged me, *could I let my friends die without sharing my blood with theirs?*

I stopped running. My father had done it. I could do it.

Never mind the fact that it was my father's second attempt at *Talashar*, and he was an expert by then with the mojolo-mazumba.

To the horror of Manak, Annar, and Annat, I loosened my spear and daggers, then turned back toward the hell-beast and began to run. The gor-gar was already a pincushion by the time that I reached it. There were six arrows sticking out of its scaly, armored chest along with two spears lodged in its horrible maw.

"Ha!" Alazaar shouted over the din. "The mighty hunter returns!"

Alazaar had to dodge a lunging snap of the thing's jaws as he taunted me. The gor-gar wasn't even slowed by the tiny, pointy things that stuck it. I watched, in horror, as it feinted a lunge with its massive jaws, then swung around with its log-like spiked tail and smashed poor Razaar into a bloody pulp. It paused a split-second to snatch up his lifeless body with a snake-like strike of its upper body, gulping him down whole. Red curtains of rage descended over my eyes, blinding me to retreat. I would die now, going to Warrior's Hell in my rage, but I would take along this damned thing with me, kicking and screaming if necessary.

Screaming, I raised my spear high and charged the gor-gar as it lunged for Lutar. I was only half-aware of poor Lutar's death scream as my spear pierced the gor-gar's armored hide, sinking half of its length into its gut. As steaming bile and half-digested meat rained down on my face and arms, I pulled down on the haft of the spear, tearing a gaping wound in its gut all the way down to its groin.

Suddenly, the world went dark for a second as it raised up its leg and booted me away from it as if I were an annoying gnat.

When the sun once more shined, I was on my back, about five strides away from the gor-gar's mad death dance as it engaged both Kelden, who was down to a single dagger, and Alazaar, who was gouging it repeatedly with what remained of his broken spear. I got up, cursing the blood that kept trickling into my eyes. I howled, caught in the hellish, hateful rapture of true Azaar bloodlust, then raised all of my arms—saluting the gor-gar a final death salute. It completely ignored me, so intent was it on killing Alazaar and Kelden. I took this as a sign, and began to circle it, trying to make its rear.

Taking a dagger in each lower hand, I made a running leap for its flank as it stooped to snatch Kelden's head from his body, and I managed to latch onto it at the base of its neck. As the gor-gar gulped down Kelden's essence, I reached forward and sank both of my daggers into its eye sockets, twisting them and turning them with every ounce of hatred that I could muster; Manak's earlier words of my strength fueling my fire. The gor-gar's eyes popped like eggshells, splattering red gore and thin, hot liquid down the lengths of my arms. The gor-gar roared, head pointed at the sun that it would never see again, then swayed from side to side, its feeble forelimbs desperately trying to reach and remove the daggers. It bucked and raged like a mad saurian steed. I lost my grip on my daggers as I desperately tried to hang on.

Below me, Alazaar yelled an oath and charged into its body, mad with bloodlust. He pulled my spear out from its ruined belly and jammed it back into its chest—a true blow, well struck—seeking its deeply buried heart. Instead of finding glory, Alazaar found a two foot swath of his side removed as the gor-gar, reacting blindly to its new pain, snapped its head downwards and clamped its massive jaws shut on his upper torso. It shook him like a ragdoll, to and fro, then hurled him down to the ground, broken and unmoving. Reason fled at that point.

Shaleeta!

Reaching forward, I managed to grab one of my daggers, which was still deeply lodged within its eye socket. Seeing only the bloody dagger in my hand, I began to pull it toward me with all of my strength. It was a strength tempered by the loss of my friends, my brethren. Not even the horny, iron hide of the gor-gar could withstand the strength of my madness—the strength of the *mightiest ever born* of the Azaar.

With a sickening, stomach-turning wrench, the dagger slid through the bony ridge of the gor-gar's eye socket and made a deep incision in its horny skull. Clear, foul-smelling fluid began to spurt from the widening gap of flesh. The gor-gar roared once, then twice, then staggered to its knees as I forced my hands into the gap and pulped a double-handful of its brain. Finally, it rocked forward, then fell on its face like a drunkard. Its spiked tail continued to swish back and forth like an angry snake for some time, plowing up the bloodied earth around it. I pulled myself from its back and sank to the ground, knee-deep in a foul mixture of blood and offal. It took some time for Alazaar's voice to register.

"Rhiannazaar..." he gurgled, drowning in his own blood.

I forced myself up to my feet and stumbled over to where he was in the trampled grass. As I did so, I noticed Manak and the twins running toward us, great bows dangling from their hands. They were perhaps a hundred paces or so away, shouting something that I couldn't make out. Still, my main concern was Alazaar. I drew close to him, ignoring his exposed, half-devoured ribs glistening in the sunlight. He took my hands in his good ones and gripped them with the grip of a dead man.

"There's something that I... have to tell," Alazaar gurgled, coughing up a mouthful of blood and clear fluid. He was growing pale, almost white, the color of death for our people. I helped him prop up his head, to allow his final breaths to come more easily. "It's Shaleeta. She's..." Alazaar, my nemesis, gasped. With the grip of the dead, he pulled me closer to him just as the others came running up, breathless.

"What about Shaleeta?"

"The reason that she... cannot... go to you, Rhiannazaar. It is not that she holds no love for you. She does!" Alazaar's eyes lit with damning truth. "It's just that... she's..." Alazaar, the snake, gurgled a final, bloody gasp as he drew in his final breath. "She's with child, Rhiannazaar. My child."

I set Alazaar's lifeless, chalk-white body gently back down on the grass. The red, filthy grass in which he died, fighting for... something. I didn't understand.

I really didn't want to, now.

Shaleeta... How could you?

"...and we sank a dozen arrows into it, but it still kept going until you pulled out its brain!"

Manak was rambling uncontrollably, gesturing wildly with all four of his arms. His voice was all wrong for this moment of mourning.

"Be still, Manak," I said heavily. "By our brothers' fallen spirits, which have now rejoined the earth, this cannot be a day for joy."

My words left no say in the matter.

The others looked upon our fallen, mangled brothers, and sorrow filled their hearts. Slowly, I stood up, tears streaking down my face like molten lava. Like a blind man, I felt my way over to the gor-gar and retched all over its ruined carcass. Then, like a dead thing, I pried out its best teeth with my dagger, claiming my hell-bought trophy.

Those who greeted us upon our return were disappointed in our silence. Their disappointment turned to grief when they realized that no more warriors walked behind the four of us. We walked through the majestic avenues of the trees, along the wide pathways hewn from the great ironwood trees themselves until, like zombies, we came at last to the Great Hall of the People of the Trees.

Those gathered there to greet us were shocked by our silent, grim bearing. I walked past the grim-faced Spokesman, ignoring his pleading eyes.

I wore the teeth of the gor-gar on my chest. He could no more stop me than stop the rain.

I walked up to the waiting Shaleeta, who already wore the colors of mourning, pale azure and phthalo blue, for she had already lost a loved one in either event, no matter what the results of *Talashar*. Her bright eyes were brimming with tears as she stood bravely to receive the news of Alazaar. I stood before her, burning her image over and over again into my mind, at a loss as to what to say to her.

What was there *to* say?

Then, I reached down and pinned Alazaar's agate over her heart. Shaleeta stood there, crying, as I turned to face the assembled throng, my bloody badge of courage in place along with hers.

"See you in the next world," I whispered, my voice carrying through the silence of the throng, "and don't be late."

I locked the colors of mourning into my mind, for I would wear them and nothing else forevermore. Then I simply walked away, passing like a forgotten hero through the gathered ranks of the mourners before me, leaving behind forever Shaleeta and the People of the Trees.

?

Return.

The scene faded to black, returning us once more to the world. The only sounds that I heard were those of people trying to pretend that they weren't crying. It was an emotional hellride that we had just gone through in Luther's mind. I never realized the depth of emotion, the pain that someone *else* was capable of feeling until I had felt it *myself*.

I never knew. How could I?

Rhiannazaar—or Zaar, as we knew him—had never told us that story before back on SenZar, not even when he was totally shit-faced on Foaming Death. Sure, he'd hinted at how he had left his people in a tiff, and why he had chosen to habitually wear the deeper and darker hues of his people. But he never went into it in much depth, not even with me or Sammy. And we were *tight*. Now, looking back, I could see why: It hurt like hell.

But I'm not sure what hurt more: The fact that Zaar had never shared this with me, or the fact that I'd just experienced it to the *extreme*.

Looking back, of course, I'd have to say that both hurt equally, if only for different reasons: the latter, for the sharing of loss; the former, for the loss of sharing.

I glanced over at Zaar. What my bleary eyes saw didn't so much surprise me as relieve me. He was truly an Azaar once more. He had four massive arms poking out from the remnants of his frayed jacket, arms that Arnold would *die* for. His overall pigmentation was as I had always known it to be: pale azure and deep phthalo blue, the hues competing for dominance, each according to subtle changes in his mood. His ears were high on his head, slender and gently pointed, like Sigil's, but a bit more pronounced. His mohawk had grown. Now it was bristly yet wavy; full of spiky life—yet still as white as if bleached. Now, though, it was quite real. Nonetheless—even though he looked a lot bigger than before; *ripped* and *freaky*, mind you—he was still recognizable as the once and former Luther Gates. Even though he was now and forevermore Rhiannazaar, the Azaar warrior who had just spilled his soul for all to see. Zaar was busy examining his new/old self, looking with unabashed awe at his four ripped arms, noting his reflection in the bottle of cognac before him.

Sammy blew his nose, cleared his throat, then spoke: "So, like, I have a question, Sigil," he asked, raising his hand like he was in some high school class. Sigil nodded his head, like the foreboding schoolmaster that he was. "I was wondering a few things. First, how come Luther—I mean, Zaar—wasn't talking in his patois? I'm starting to get a few things back so far as memory goes, and I seem to remember that even back on SenZar he spoke in a mishmash patois. I mean, at least when using Zengaran, our old *lingua franca*. And second, how did he know those Jimi Hendrix lyrics? I know it wasn't more than a paraphrase, but still! Is that some sort of bleed over effect from his present life merging with his former life on SenZar? Or did his Azaar culture have some sort of analogous saying?"

"First, Master Samuel," Sigil said, smiling faintly, "you need not raise your hand to ask me a question. I will not bite your head off, although you might say that is due to the fact that I have grown accustomed to your—shall we just say—your 'outbursts' in the past. Prior conditioning, as it were." He steepled his long fingers, as if in prayer. "Now, as to your questions, the reason that you heard no patois—or, in this case, an *accent*—in his speech is simple: You experienced the events exactly as if you were there yourself, as *he* was, with his own perceptions. There is no accent in one's native tongue, Master Samuel, especially if one is perceiving the events as that native did."

"But—"

"Second—and yes, before you even ask, I *am* familiar with the Hendrix lyrics—"

Well la-dee-da! Score one for Mr. Hip.

"I would hazard to suggest that, while the Azaar culture and the cultures of several peoples on Earth are very similar, there is nothing which could directly, logically, lead him to have some sort of 'bleed over' effect, as Luther Gates was born here on Earth a Jamaican."

"Uh, wait a minute, Sigil," Sammy interrupted, his curiosity rearing again. "How did you know Luther was born in Jamaica? I mean, sure, he's got the 'island patois'—at least when he wants it—but there are a dozen or more islands in the Caribbean that could qualify a native as a speaker. And not all of them are Jamaica, if you get my drift. So how did you know where he was born?"

I set my glass down on the floor in front of me as I considered Sammy's damn sharp observation.

"I have been watching him, Samuel," Sigil said, his slanted eyes narrowing slightly, "as I have been watching all of you. I have, more or less, been keeping tabs on each of you for almost a decade now; always there in the shadows; watching, waiting for some sign that it was time."

Samantha and I exchanged glances, each of us probably wondering if we had been chasing Sigil's elusive shadow all those long ago nights in the Quarter instead of those forever-hidden New Orleans

vampires. She smiled a tight smile as she seemed to read my mind, giving my hand a squeeze to let me know that, yes, she *was* reading my mind.

"Alas," Sigil said, noting our exchange, "lest we become sidetracked by trivialities, let us continue, for our time is short."

"But I wanna know *why* you've been—" Sammy began petulantly, waving his arm to get Sigil's attention.

"There is another possibility, however," Sigil continued, ignoring Sammy's glare, "that we may be overlooking, my Master Rogue. And that is not a bleed over effect so much as it is a *bleed-through*

effect. It is called the Anshadar Effect, and it is the Stuff of Dreams."

A bell went off in my head as he said that word: *Anshadar*. I seemed to remember something from my studies back on SenZar with...

Cobwebs.

Then, miraculously, cobwebs swept aside.

Kiril Spellsinger: Master Bard and originator of the magickal profession which bore his name: Spellsinger. Yes, that *was* his name. And Kiril Spellsinger, my mentor and dear friend, had instructed me on that forbidden word, *Anshadar*. He had revealed many a dark secret on those brilliant, starlit nights back in the Krystallmyst Forest, oh so many worlds ago.

Ahh, Kiril, my good old Starin friend.

With but a bottle, a lute, and a song our common bonds, we had shared many good times. Many bizarre, dangerous, and potentially Loon times, too, if my slowly crystallizing memories were to be believed.

But this *Anshadar* business.

It was not something that you were supposed to mention in casual conversation, provided that you even knew something about it in the first place. Such things were in the same realm as Old Wives' Tales and ghost stories to frighten the children. There was more than this, I realized. Much more. But the cobwebs were deeply set in place around that particular memory, either by necessity or design.

I immediately got a bad feeling about that name: *Anshadar*.

It seemed to haunt me in some inexplicable way, like Sigil had said about it being "The Stuff of Dreams," and all that. More like nightmares, not good dreams. Nightmares, like the ones that I'd—no, that *we'd*—been having. My memories were slowly starting to piece themselves back together, like some massive mental jigsaw puzzle. I just wished that things would hurry on along, though, because I knew that something was on the edge of my mind, ready to explode. The only question now was time, as Sigil had been insisting. It, like everything else in the whole damned world, had become just a question of time. Skurge, which had been strangely silent until now, chose that particular moment to growl softly, like some black tiger about to pounce.

"We must continue, now," Sigil implored, softly. He patted Zaar once on the leg, as if to tell him that everything was all right now. Zaar smiled dangerously at him, then raised his four arms above his head and... yawned—thank god—flexing his monstrous blue biceps. I was too damned paranoid for my own good at the moment. That *Anshadar* crap had me on edge. "Now, as we delve deeper into our collective psyches," Sigil droned, his voice level and deep, "we move into the Kingdom of the Khazak, the realm of those who live beneath the mountains, beneath the very world itself in the Midnight Realm. Now," Sigil said, his eyes fixed upon David, "we enter into the hidden past of Guthal Dirge, heir to the throne of Kaza Ka."

Even as Sigil spoke, the world seemed to do a perfect pirouette, drawing all of us along with it in its twisted revolution. When the world outside settled, we were transported body and mind into the soul of Guthal Dirge, who had once been known to us as David Miller.

CHAPTER 12: For All Eternity

I am shamed.

The thought echoed over and over in my mind, driving me closer and closer to the realm of insanity that my people called "The Forever Dark." In chains I writhed, in the deepest levels of the Dungeons of the Forsaken, left here to rot while my people fight amongst themselves like idiot sycophants for the glory of the newly crowned Ka: Kozar Dred, the Lord of the Khazaks.

We *are shamed.*

I had fought the good fight for the honor of my clan. I had shed blood for the honor of Kaza Dirge. I had fought with every ounce of my strength for the honor of my fallen father, only to be cut down by Kozar's treachery and Mokarr tricks. I had walked the Dark Path for the honor of my clan, only to have the prize snatched from me at the last moment by my enemy, Kozar Dred. The usurper. The Mokarr sympathizer who had spoken with black sorcery on behalf of the clan of Kaza Dred.

It was nothing more than the absolution of an ancient debt, paid for with the blood of the kin. And now, I sat in chains, awaiting my final sentence—to rot here for all eternity. I would never be given leave to die an honorable death—a death by the sword or by axe in some glorious, all-avenging, final battle. Nor would the mercy of my death ever be granted me by secret execution, this shameful act carried out by Kozar's own blasphemous Mokarr henchmen. At their merciless black hands, I would win my release either by a single obsidium crossbow bolt to the back of the head, or die in an entirely more agonizing manner—death by inverted crucifixion, with venom-laced nails, here in my own filth-choked cell. The quick release of death, however—by whatever means—would never be granted me. No, my failure—and Kozar's own blood-oath—had ensured that there was but one recourse for me: I would rot down here. Alone. Shamed. For all eternity.

How had it come to this?

I sat, heavy black chains binding me to the walls of the Dungeons of the Forsaken, and I remembered.

?

"So, Guthal, heir to the throne of Kaza Ka," said Kozar Dred, a mocking tone to his voice, "would you seek to right your father's shame by the strength of your axe arm? Would you brave the test of the Dark Path for his vindication?" Kozar sat back in his high-backed oaken chair, safe in his diplomatic refuge—in my hall, at that, the bastard! He had the bad sense to insult me in my own hall, the hall that had once stood first in line to the throne of Kaza Ka, before his Mokarr-loving kin had set recent events into motion.

My kindred wanted his blood for the words that he had spoken. They leaned forward in their chairs, waiting for the order that could never come—the price of my father's folly.

"Yes, far-cousin," I said, blowing triple rings of firemoss smoke from my obsidian pipe, "I seek, as *you* have chosen to say." I leaned forward in my chair, meeting his beady-eyed coward's gaze. "And I shall vindicate the name of my clan, and my father—who may not be named—even if it means my death."

I fixed Kozar's eyes with mine, daring him to give me the honor of a blood-insult, now that I had spoken of my willingness to die. He sat back in the chair, smiling, his prissy black beard quivering in mute rage. Still, he ignored my challenge.

"You do realize, far-cousin Guthal," Kozar said, his tone still flippant, "that to set foot upon the Dark Path means that you *willfully* accept the shame of your clan, along with the price that is implied with it. Twenty-four hours will seem like an eternity in that realm of the Forever Dark, where nameless horrors slither and hop, chop and rend!" He allowed himself a small, evil smile.

"Of course I understand the price of the path, and still I seek it, far-cousin Kozar," I blew a trail of thick smoke rings from my lips, giving him a small gap of time for my words to sink in. "And, perhaps you realize, far-cousin, that when I return, absolved, *your* blood will stain the double blades of my clan's axe of honor!"

Kozar's eyes narrowed, but his voice was still. His six bodyguards shifted in their chairs, their black-deviced Khazak battle armor scraping on the oak, yet they did nothing. Kozar Dred gripped the arms of the chair until the veins stood out in his arms, but still he said nothing. He was far too cagey to allow me the satisfaction of splitting his fat head before I undertook my quest. Finally, without a brave reply, he stood, bowed stiffly, and made his way from the table, his six nervous bodyguards falling in behind him.

As he made the door of the hall, Kozar turned to face me and spoke as the coward that he

truly was: "When—and *if*—you return, far-cousin Guthal."

Kozar Dred spun on his booted heels and walked through the doors of the hall, gone along with his hollow threats.

Golek, my cousin, spoke as the great oaken doors slammed shut. "He is not going to forget your words, Guthal," he said, setting his clay pipe down on the table. "You gave him considerable discomfort with your *truthful* words," he added, nodding toward the others seated at the table.

From my kin rose murmurs of approval. What Golek had just said was as much a pep talk as anything else. Each of us knew the danger to come; the blood that was yet to be spilled in these dangerous times.

"Kozar knows, Golek, whereof I speak. And thus he knows fear," I said, tamping my obsidian pipe with the tip of my dagger. "The stench of fear was upon him like the stench of death. And fear makes men do dangerous things. Everyone here knows that he will try everything in his power to thwart me, even if his means his own dishonor before the throne!"

There were grunts of agreement from around the table as my kinsmen nodded their heads.

"Kozar Dred is that kind of coward. He would rather have the throne for himself—not for his clan. And what is more, if he were unable to seat himself upon the throne, I tell you that he would rather see it fall!" I slammed my hand down upon the table, upsetting a goblet of stout ale and Golek's clay pipe, which spilled its smoldering contents upon the scarred oaken tabletop.

"Are you saying, Guthal, that Kozar Dred would betray the faith of the throne itself if he were to fail in his cause? Could even *his* heart be that black?"

The speaker was my uncle, Galen, the elder of our clan, now that my father was gone. Galen's authority—judged by the power of his axe-arm—was second only to my own in the clan. His wisdom, however, was second to none. Galen stroked his hoary silver beard as he awaited my response, his one good eye still crystal blue and crystal sharp.

"Kozar's heart is as black as the Pit, Uncle Galen." I shook my head as I said this, for what I had to say next would be extremely unpleasant to speak of before my family and friends. "And, what is more, my brethren, Kozar's heart is as black as the jet-black hides of those that pull his strings. For it is more than hushed rumor that Kozar Dred is in league with the Dark Earth, and its maggot-eating legions, the Mokarr."

There were murmurs, hushed whispers, and muted curses from around the table as this blasphemy of blasphemies sank in. In my kindred's eyes were expressions ranging from shock, to disbelief, to smelting-hot rage.

"Those were my father's words, spoken to me the night before he was falsely accused and hauled away to die!" My tone told them that this was truth. My eyes silenced the whispers going around the table. "My father spoke to me in confidence the night before his betrayal, bidding me avenge him should his enemies succeed in their task." Galen watched me intently, his wise eye measuring my expression. "And it is only now, after the casting of the gauntlet, that I may tell you of this. He named Kozar as his enemy. He named Kozar as the enemy of the Khazak. He set out that final night to gain his proof, proof of Kozar's involvement with the Mokarr. He mentioned that it may prove to be his end, such were the forces against him. But he said that the stakes for our people were too high to ignore, as they involved not only the Kaza Dred, but also the elders of several other clans." The silence was measured in heartbeats.

"Did he name the others?" Galen asked momentarily, breaking the silence of the table.

"No, he did not, for the reason that he could have incriminated the innocent," I replied.

"Did he mention what this proof was to have been?" Golek asked, to the murmured approval of several around the table.

"He did not name it. But he did hint that whatever it might be was heavily guarded within Kozar Dred's own hall. Whatever it might have been—might *still* be, I say!—is no doubt hidden now beyond our measure to find it. There is only one way now for our clan to be vindicated. And that is for one of our blood to walk the Dark Path. And to return."

Each of the men gathered round the table, each of the proud Khazak warriors who had proven his courage countless times and more in defense of our proud throne, bowed his head in silent acquiescence. They knew without asking that the honor would be mine. There was simply no other way.

After a moment of silent prayer to the gods, who were by now casting their lots upon the floors of heaven, I left the table and walked swiftly to my quarters. The servants of Dirgehall were quick to bow, to avoid my eyes as I passed, lest they see Death itself in my countenance. I took the stairs two at a time, disdaining the damp, slickened granite. Let the gods cast their lots as they would—I'd be damned if I'd slip down on my very own stairs for their amusement!

When at last I reached my chambers, I quickly shut the oaken double doors behind me and barred them with a heavy slat of iron. I knew that it really wouldn't stop anyone who was determined enough from getting in, as a good axe would take down any door given time. It was more for the feeling of isolation, the distance, that I had to place between myself and my kin as I reflected upon my father, Garnet Dirge. He had died in chains at the foot of the throne, protesting his innocence before the Ka himself.

Father, I prayed, my heart deep in sorrow, *grant me the strength, the conviction, the heart to walk this path. The chance to fulfill my blood-oath, even if the price be my death.*

That night I fasted. That night I prayed for vengeance. I prayed to the Grim Gods who didn't give a damn whether or not we lived or died, so long as we kept their names alive. I prayed, bowing over my great axe, until the breakfast chime sounded. Only then did I buckle on my well-worn silversteel battle armor, which had served me well against both fang and steel. Only then did I remove the chamois from my equally-worn silversteel spiked shield and heft it on my arm. Only then did I strip away the leather case from the head of my silversteel-gilt great axe, Thrumble, the honor axe of Kaza Dirge. Not even the pronouncement of my father's dishonor could remove the sheen of glory from about its battle-scarred double blades. No falsehood ever could.

Hefting the honor axe of my clan, I bowed my head and said my father's name aloud, in spite of the decree of the Ka, swearing vengeance by it. Then, a knock sounded at the door, jolting me despite my warrior's resolve.

"Guthal," Galen asked, speaking as if in ritual, "are you prepared?"

I quickly knocked the iron slat from its place on the doors with Thrumble, sending it clattering across the granite floor of my chamber until it came to rest at the far wall. Galen pushed open the doors, his blue eye glittering in appraisal.

"I am ready."

Then I strode forth, axe and shield at the ready, more for ceremony than function. Galen fell in place behind me, my second in this ceremony of mistruth, and together we walked down the granite stairs of the Dirgehall. As we made the open doors of the hall, the warriors gathered there in their finest fell in behind us, a grim, determined procession. Fifty-two strong, we wound our way down the wide streets of Kaza Ka which our forefathers had carved out of the living rock itself, countless centuries before, a war chant measuring our step. Some that we passed averted their gaze, marking themselves as the cowards that they were. But, more often than not, those whom we passed raised their right hands above their heads in salute to those who were about to die.

Soon, our parade stood in review before the steel-reinforced, heavily barricaded granite plug that guarded the entrance to the Dark Path. We stood in battle formation there in the Great Circle of Honor, oblivious to the gathered throngs of the curious; ignoring the cold stares of the warriors of Kaza Dred, who wished nothing but ill will to all but themselves. The Ka himself was not present, as was his station, nor were any of his servitors, save for a single, hourglass-bearing scribe whose job it was to time and record the passage of those who opened the great doors and set foot upon the Dark Path. The royal honor could not be soiled by connection to a quest of the dishonored. At last, I turned to face the gathered throng.

"I, Guthal Dirge, of the Kaza Dirge, do swear to brave the Dark Path for the honor of my father. The honor of my kin! The honor of my people!" I raised my axe high in salute to the hushed crowd and my equally silent kinsmen.

Kozar, who stood at the front of his gathered clan, smiled frostily at the silence of the crowd. Such was the Way of the Dark Path: No one would show any emotion whatsoever, no matter how strong his personal feelings. Not even to raise a salute.

But the time for matters of state were past. Let the scribe write what he would. Let him measure the time with his false glass filled with sand. All that mattered was what we felt in our hearts, a multitude of voices without words.

With a nod, Galen directed the men to form up at the plug. They did so, splitting into two groups of twenty-five each, each group laying to a thick cable of wound silversteel which joined with a pair of mighty iron rungs at the edge of its right face. Galen raised his right hand into the air, then lowered it down sharply. The men fell to with a collective heave-ho, straining in unison as they pitted their strength against the massive multiton plug. The cables pulled taut with a grinding sound, a sound like a slow motion earthquake. The great iron rungs complained, but held, as the sinews of my kin levied against them. Ponderously, the massive plug began to work its way outward from the wall, causing many of those present in the crowd to put their hands to their ears and grit their teeth, as if some dragon were clawing a slate board in evil spite.

Slowly, inch by inch, the plug moved. Despite its massiveness, its well-kept state was testament to the craft of the Khazak who had built it aeons before. Back during the Dark Years, when the Shadar

Lords had ruled the land. Back when their emasculated minions, the Mokarr, had prowled freely the shadows of our lighted cities for suitable sacrifice to their demon gods.

The great plug came to an abrupt halt as it reached its critical zenith of forty-five degrees from the wall's face, leaving a few good paces of space for use. Experience had taught us that was all that we could ever allow, for such were the huge things that dwelled in the blackened bowels of the Dark Path. Such things were not meant to exit. For that matter, I was not expected to exit, either. During the many years that the path had served as our test—our elusive Rellian Golden Grail, if you will—fewer than a handful had ever returned. Of those handful, fewer still had returned sane. Of course, it had always been common knowledge that those who set foot upon the Dark Path had to be, from the onset, a bit touched to begin with.

With that in mind, I strode into the darkness of the Dark Path, a slight nod and a sidelong glance to Uncle Galen my farewell.

By fifty paces, the way had become jet-black, save for a faint silver tracing along the path itself. It was as if someone had walked the path a very long time ago with luminescent paint on his boots, paint which had never fully dried. The faint illumination would be enough, though, for one with the gloom sight of the Khazak, the heritage of my deep-dwelling ancestors. I tested the weight of my shield, finding that it was more comfortable at my side than when raised in front, in defense. I kept Thrumble propped up on my right shoulder as I walked, knowing that I could just as easily attack with it from that position rather than from a position of guard. It would also help to ease the eventual fatigue that I would be sure to feel after some hours of walking. And down here, every bit of energy would count.

I considered the test. The various statistics were not on my side. I had roughly a full day to find the Silver Key and return with it to the plug before the mighty barricade was sealed once more. From whispers and snatches of rumors that had made their way into the folklore of my people, the Silver Key was suspended from a strand of silversteel over a vast, incalculable abyss that led, according to legend,

straight to the bowels of the Pit. There were numerous crawling, slithering, hopping horrors that guarded the path, eager to play their role as spoilers. From what was whispered, the silver trail led to

the key, a clear beacon in an otherwise dreary, gloomy expanse of subterranean real estate. I knew there to be many side tunnels, not to mention pitfalls and other such geomorphical maliciousness, but

that came with the territory down here. I had a gut feeling that things on the path would be intensified

and exaggerated to an extreme, not at all your leisurely cruise in the Midnight Realm. I began to hum a chant of war, careful to keep it subdued, if such were actually possible, in the event that something would be trying to strain an ear or some other auditory appendage to listen for prey.

What the hell, I rationalized, *it's next to impossible to sneak around in steel-shod boots anyway.*

I walked on, my boots striking a measured, practiced cadence. After about an hour, I came to a striking grotto, as large as the main hall of Dirgehall, resplendent in its fungi-lit stalactite/stalagmite opulence. A narrow, lazy stream of slightly glowing mineral water bordered the Dark Path, coming within arm's reach at several spots, then winding away to the far wall of the grotto, apparently flowing right into the sheer rock face. Although I didn't stop to admire it properly, as a true son of the mountain should have, I did notice as I walked through that the walls of the grotto were rich in silver, with exposed veins as wide as my shield. I made a promise to myself that I would investigate this further upon my return, provided I had the time.

As I made the far end of the grotto, I heard a faint *sploosh* behind me. Wheeling around, I raised my shield and axe, adrenaline surging.

All I could see, though, were ripples in the small stream, where some eyeless thingie had breached a second before. Mighty hunter let out a short, nervous chuckle, then backed out of the grotto like a crab, safe in his awesome silversteel battle armor from the hideous, sightless carp.

I moved on, pace a little quicker now. During the next three hours, I had to carefully find my way around three gaping pits that had opened without warning beneath my feet in the darkness. If not for my earlier years as a trailblazing deep engineer in the forces of the Ka, my life would have ended there. But with every suddenly opening pit, there is an equally sudden, preceding tremor that can be felt by one knowledgeable in the art, even through steel-shod boots. I was thankful for the engulfing darkness, for I had to rely more upon my sense of feeling rather than my sense of sight. I could still see, of course; the faint, silver paint flecks of the path were more than enough for that for a Khazak's gloom-bred eyes. Yet, it was still more like trying to see in the woods on a night with heavy cloud cover and no moons, so I relied more on instinct than on visual perception. Fortunately, it was enough. For now.

On the sixth hour, I stopped for a snack of sourdough and a sip of ale from my flask. I was careful to keep my back to the wall, senses keen, as I took this short breather. In two minutes, I was once more traveling. And, judging from the strata, I was about two miles beneath the city, relatively speaking. Two miles down, and roughly twelve miles straight away. I calculated the triangle, arriving at approximately twelve miles and some spare change. Or, to be precise, which was both rote and rigor for a deep engineer, 12.16553 miles, which rounded to approximately 12.17 miles. Some calculation for someone who knew the Great Tables of Jhed by rote.

Nerves. Just nerves. *All that really matters is the objective distance, not the abstract hypotenuse,* I reminded myself.

Having no idea if I were on schedule or not, I filed my calculation away with all of my countless others, silently hoping that the Silver Key would be gleaming somewhere along mile number twenty-four, or sooner. The sooner the better, of course. The sooner that I could get home and split Kozar's overripe head with my axe, the sooner I could exonerate my father's name.

By the tenth hour, I had cultivated the notion that this was going too well. The only beasties that I had seen were of the "pet" variety, fit for children and old men: small, pale rock-lizards with bulging, lidless eyes; translucent, segmented worms nesting at the base of stalagmites; fist-sized, chitin-armored spiders and scorpions scurrying about seeking their hidden prey. Only once had I detected the spoor of a dangerous beast—a kvortha, a battle tank-sized slime-crawler—but its hour-old trail led down a side passage, off of the Dark Path. I was nearly tempted, maddeningly enough, to pursue it and stain my axe with its dross-like blood, just to get in the right spirit. But good sense, for once, stayed my hand.

Thus far, to tell the truth, the Dark Path had been a letdown. A pessimist to the end, however, and perhaps too much a realist to let down my guard, I set my mind for what *had* to lurk ahead. Slightly after the eleventh hour, poetically enough, I found what lurked ahead. The path had narrowed considerably during the course of the past hundred paces, down to a little more than wagon-sized width. The silver had all but died away, leaving what faint light there was coming from the terminus of the passageway ahead. Suffused and ambient it was, like a beacon in the blackness, stabbing through the corrupt bleakness like the light of the pre-dawn sun struggling to make its presence known through the grand peaks of the Khojor Mountains. I forced myself to slow my pace, to put caution before valor. I knew that the Silver Key was before me, beyond the jagged cleft. I could feel it there, feel its purity. But there was something else there, too. That, I also knew. Whatever it might be, though, be it demon or dragon, I would face it with axe in hand, for the honor of Kaza Dirge. I muttered a prayer and followed it with a string of nervous curses as I approached the cleft, axe and shield at the ready. Then, I took the corner.

My war cry died in my throat as I beheld what stood before me.

There, upon the narrow, jutting peninsula of bedrock that stretched across a yawning, gaping stygian abyss of night stood a grinning Kozar Dred—the Silver Key in his left hand, his axe in his right. In front of him stood three slender, ink-skinned warriors in wicked black moonlight ornamental plate mail. Each Mokarr was smiling grimly; slight, sharp fangs glistening in the magickal light of the cavern. Each of the Mokarr warriors bore a straight, short, obsidium blade which plainly dripped with caustic green venom. I stood my ground, mouth gaping at this blasphemy, some ten paces from them as Kozar extended the key toward me, tantalizingly, mockingly.

"Looking for something, far-cousin?" Kozar inquired most evilly, scratching his strawberry nose with the tip of the Silver Key.

"You traitor!" I screamed, red rage blinding me. "My father was *right*! You are in league with *them*!" I shook Thrumble at the three Mokarr, who seemed unmoved by my accusation.

Realizing what sort of deep shit I was in, considering the distinctive Mokarr brand of sneaky treachery, I tried to make myself aware of my surroundings—especially as to what might be stalking up behind me—while not taking my eyes off of them for a second.

"I believe I smell sour ale, dear far-cousin," Kozar continued, his voice mocking to the core. "You're upset because I've won the Silver Key first, as you've every right to be. For it means that your fallacious claims have been buried once and for all, dear cousin. As you yourself shall soon be."

"Kozar," I said, trying to buy some thinking time, "how the hell did you get here before me? I saw no one else on the trail. No one could have passed me by without my knowing it."

"I transported here, dear Guthal, using my magicks," he admitted casually, damning himself for using forbidden sorcery. "It sure beats the hell out of walking the Dark Path, like one idiot that I know!" Kozar laughed, a high-pitched titter, as he saw my beard quiver in barely suppressed rage.

"Why have you betrayed your people, Kozar Dred?" I asked, still stalling for time. "What evil has driven you mad?"

The Mokarr were starting to get antsy. Their weasel eyes betrayed their intent. They were eager for the kill. But then again, so was I. Still, something drove me to hear more. I wanted to know Kozar's price. What had driven him to this perfidy? Kozar responded immediately, waving the Silver Key like a wand to emphasize his ranting.

"No evil has driven me *mad*!" he raved. "I have betrayed no one! I have, instead, ensured the continued prosperous existence of our people. Now, as soon as I have won the throne, which is only a matter of eventuality," he said, waving the key in front of him, "we will have a tacit understanding with our deep-dwelling friends, the Mokarr. In the past, our peoples were too obsessed with ancient vendettas to make any sort of decent mutual progress. Both sides suffered as a result of this. But now," he continued, his voice rising, "we have come to an understanding! It is a very simple one, dearest Guthal: The Mokarr assist me with my usurpation of the addle-brained Ka, then I resolve a gradually enacted treaty which paves the way for the resolution of our prior grievances. Mutual gains for both sides, and both sides win in the end! There will be an exchange of cultures, of ideas, which have only been dreamed of before! When I assume the throne, I will usher in a new era, one in which *knowledge* is power! With the power of the sorcery of the Mokarr—to which I have been indoctrinated as a token of their good faith— we will forge an empire that will, in turn, reforge the world!"

"So all you have to do is sacrifice a few babies to the Dark Earth once in a while to pacify your Mokarr string-pullers, right?"

"You simple-minded idiot!" Kozar ranted, pointing the Silver Key at me, "You can't herald in a new era without a few sacrifices, can you? And who cares what blood spills and for whom it spills, so long as the goal is obtained! Besides, Guthal, I've already taken care of that end of the pact. The only blood that will be shed to the Dark Earth will be the blood of the blind, the slow, and the lame. We will weed out the undesirable even as we strengthen ourselves. The net result will be a superior race of Khazak, able to employ both science and sorcery to the fullest possible potential! We will prosper as never before!" Kozar's eyes blazed with his conviction.

Even though what he said repulsed me to the depths of my being, I still had a strange compulsion to listen to him—to *hear* his words and to *believe* in them. My head swam, taking laps inside my war helm. I was drowning inside my own mind! Kozar was trying to charm me, the cretin! I bit my lip until the blood ran down my chin, trying my best to resist his sorcerous will. I filled my head with the images that I knew were to come should he achieve his wicked way: Dark towers, bodies hanging from the battlements; banners writ in living fire, slogans of death and war; columns of dark Mokarr warriors leading the hopeless into chambers of sacrifice, heavy black chains fixed upon their dragging legs.

"Never!" I screamed, shaking with rage as I broke his spell. "I'll see your life's blood first, you son of a bitch, before I sell out my people!" I advanced toward the grinning Mokarr, white knuckles gripping my axe.

"You never were one to appreciate the sublime, Guthal," Kozar mocked. "But perhaps you will appreciate this!" With that, Kozar Dred held the Silver Key high above his head, its mirrored surface glittering in the ambient chaotic light of the chamber. Then, with a flick of his wrist, he tossed it over the side of the jutting peninsula into the void below. "Fare thee well, Old Way! We welcome now the New Age!"

As the Silver Key plunged into the dark abyss, voiding forever the mystery of the Dark Path, Kozar cackled like a mad banshee as gusting hot winds flew up from the darkness below.

"I'll have your goddamn head for that, Kozar!" I broke into a mad run, trying my best to hit the first Mokarr with a full head of steam. If we all went over the edge, then so be it! I'd be damned if I'd go to the Pit alone!

But such would never be.

The first Mokarr sprang into the air and somersaulted over my head, blade flashing, leaping as if he had springs in his legs. Somehow, he managed to catch me on the back of the helm, clanging my head like a gong. I felt a dull red heat begin to spread from the back of my head, as if I were slowly lowering my skull backwards into warm water. But hate kept me moving forward, along with the initial momentum from my charge, until I was within range of Kozar's other two flunkies. Momentum spent, I stumbled into the raised obsidium blades of the two Mokarr who stood before Kozar, sweeping a hellish arc with Thrumble, the axe of honor of Kaza Dirge, ignoring the burning sensation which threatened to set my brain on fire.

Kozar raised his puny single bladed axe into a defensive posture, retreating a few steps behind them, his mouth smiling, but not his eyes. The Mokarr weren't smiling now, either, faced with the prospect of close combat with a battle-mad Khazak warrior, even though they were three, plus Kozar, to my one. The Mokarr on my right tried a lunging slash at my midriff, an obvious feint to set up his friend on my left, who was squatting so low in some strange martial stance that it looked as if he were doing a split. I figured that convention wouldn't work here, given the circumstances, so I ignored the two in front of me, gambling that the one behind me was moving in for the death stroke.

So I stepped into the feint, praying that my armor would hold, and pivoted rapidly to my left, swinging blindly behind me with all of my might. The gods, fickle beings that they were, must have been napping, for my battle-worn armor held and Thrumble caught the Mokarr behind me as he was in

midair, halting him in place for a split-second, rupturing his insides even as his dark armor held. Though the black moonlight outer layer hissed and effervesced away from the cut of my silversteel axe, the underlying obsidium layer stood only slightly dented from the telling blow.

Even as the Mokarr's ruined body hit the stone, I was turning to intercept a head cut from the squatting Mokarr, who was now moving along the ground like some sort of demonic mallard, bobbing

and slashing, slashing and bobbing. I caught the head cut between Thrumble's heavy double blades, twisted my wrists violently, and snapped his obsidium blade in twain. Then, of course, I immediately launched a lusty kick to his groin. The bladeless bastard got a leg up just in time to deflect it, but he still fell back from the shock of the steel-toed impact. His friend, the one who had feinted earlier, was wasting no more time. He came in from my flank, sword flashing as he took a swipe at my side. I got my shield between us a second too late. The envenomed obsidium blade bit deeply into my left side, easily passing through my well-worn armor this time—the difference between a feint and a true strike—tickling my ribs with its numbing, caustic coldness.

In the heartbeat that it took for me to register the pain, my left side froze, paralyzed, as if a giant's hand had suddenly grasped me and rooted me in place. I cursed, fighting the growing stiffness that was spreading over the left side of my body, and I nearly lost my balance as I tried to move. The Mokarr, confident in the potency of their venoms, retreated a step, moving back into their original positions in front of Kozar, blades at the ready. I stood rooted in place, feebly cursing the gods as I tried to raise my axe up with my rapidly numbing right arm.

"Does it... does it *hurt*, Guthal?" Kozar asked from behind his Mokarr bodyguards, his eyes gleaming with genuine curiosity. "I've always wanted to find out if the vaga venom caused the victim any discomfort as it worked its paralysis, and I've never had the chance to inquire as to its effects before. The other victims were always led away before I had the chance to, you know?"

Kozar let out an evil chuckle, then advanced until he was between the two remaining Mokarr.

"Come closer you bastard. See if it hurts," I managed to say through clenched teeth. The cold had spread down to my toes and was slowly causing my chest to contract. It took a tremendous effort to breathe, let alone hawk some spittle in his direction, which landed, much to my chagrin, at his feet.

"Impressive, Guthal," Kozar said, taking a step closer. "With some practice, you might one day be the King of Spit."

The Mokarr to Kozar's right suddenly raised his slender arm, barring Kozar's path. "Lord Kozar," the Mokarr whispered sibilantly in his sharply accented attempt to replicate my native tongue, "give the vaga venom time to work its course, or you may yet regret this day. Guthal Dirge is *very* sturdy, even by the high standards of your race."

"Yes, of course you are right, Luthad," Kozar calmly spoke, backing away. "We never know what old stamina-minded Guthal might be planning with his last ounce of free energy."

Kozar Dred studied my face for some reaction, saw nothing, then smiled anyway.

As I was trying to raise Thrumble once more, which amounted only to a slight tremor of movement from my numbed arm, he began to speak again. "Mark well this moment, Guthal, for it will be the last moment of freedom that you will ever know. By now, you must have made the connection, far-cousin. I do *not* intend your death. No," he said, leering, "*that* would be far too simple, far too final. I will not grant you that quick release, for my vengeance is the vengeance of the inspired! You will not die... yet. Instead, you will live out the span of your life in the deepest depths of the Dungeons of the Forsaken, in the darkest of the dark pits of the insane, relegated to the bowels of the Forever Dark. There, you will dwell in darkness and misery, forevermore contemplating your pathetic, futile, dishonored existence. There, you will ask yourself over and over why it is that you suffer in silence, forgotten and wasting away. It will take quite some time for you to waste away, too, for your will is strong, Guthal. But, eventually, even *that* will waste away until you are doddering and drooling, wallowing in your own excrement while I rule as the new Ka! Consider that, far-cousin, and remember how you have failed your traitorous father—and failed yourself—*while you rot for all eternity.*"

Kozar Dred's laughter boomed throughout the hot, windy chamber of the Silver Key as he advanced toward me, his eyes glowing with sorcerous energies. With a flourish of his hands, the world faded away, leaving me in darkness. I silently screamed, cursing Kozar, the gods, and myself for the blind men that we all were.

I am shamed.

?

Once again, the movie set in our minds wound down, spluttering its flickering, damning images; leaving us to evaluate for ourselves to whom the credits belonged.

The first thing that I did was to take a look at Guthal Dirge, the former David Miller. He was the *same* as before, but *different*, although not quite so different as Luther had been after his "Now I'm Zaar!" mind trip. His trip through *The Weird* had totally healed his earlier wounds. His shirt was ripped at the chest and the shoulders, revealing a shaggy carpet of bristly, coarse red hair. He looked as if he had just added about fifty pounds of gristle and muscle to his upper body. His biceps looked almost as large as his thighs, which were themselves now about twice the size of mine. Even though he was still sitting down, I could instinctively tell that he had lost about a half-foot in height. As usual, though, I was missing the most important visual clue that he had transformed: his wild, bushy, tongue-of-flame red beard! His beard, once neatly clipped and manicured, was now the same sort of wild, shaggy thing that one would expect from one of the denizens of "Grimm's Fairy Tales." Or, maybe, Yosemite Sam. I could only imagine the insanity that Sammy would cause once he made the connection, if he hadn't already.

Guthal, one step ahead of me, pulled his massive legs up in front of him, resting his thewed, hairy arms on his knees as he gave Sammy a nasty glance that *dared* the little runt to open his mouth. The silence, however, was consuming.

Guthal sat still, seething inside while the rest of us pretended not to notice, while we pretended to forget what we had just experienced in his mind. The pain of shame. The bitter silence of betrayal.

First Zaar, then Guthal: humiliated, ripped raw, and dissected before our prying eyes.

"Sigil!" I shouted, startling everyone except him. "Enough of this bullshit! Why don't you just snap your fingers and splice us all back together? Why are you trying to fuck us out of our minds before we even have them back?"

"Yeah, Sigil," Sammy added, "shouldn't we leave Pandora and her hot little box alone?"

"They're right, Sigil," Samantha said, her eyes on Guthal, who slowly nodded his head, "we're getting too close, too fast. Maybe this time we should quit while we're ahead. I'm already remembering a lot of horrible things myself. I'm sure everyone else is, too."

Everyone except for me nodded in agreement. For some telling reason I was still stuck on that Anshadar crap.

"Only yesterday," Samantha continued, her voice rich in feeling, "we were content in our mortal ignorance. And now you want us to forget everything we've ever done, felt and been? To embrace this madness with no regrets and go on merrily from there? It's *too much*, Sigil! *Too much!*"

"I feel your words, milady," Sigil spoke slowly. "I feel them and they sting me. Yes," he said for Sammy's staring, unbelieving benefit, "I *feel* them! Do you truly believe that my heart cannot be touched? Do you truly believe that emotion cannot endure in my heart? Do you believe me *that* far removed from humanity?"

Sigil paused to consider *his own* words for a long, awkward moment. "Forgive me, my friends," Sigil apologized, wearily shaking his head. "The strain of time is hard upon me. My energies are not what they should be, nor are my manners. Forgive me."

"Fuck you!" Guthal growled, jolting the room. "Fuck your fairy put-on emotions! Fuck your pre-planned, patronizing words! You just made me break a Khazak blood-oath, you Starin bastard!"

"Chill out, Guthal!" Sammy warned, noting Sigil's purple irised eyes flicker with dangerous magickal energies.

"Piss off, Sammy!" Guthal replied, not even looking at Sammy. His eyes were boring into Sigil's. "You Starin bastard," he said dangerously, his voice like the warning growl of a mad Pit Bull, "you just revealed a Khazak soul secret for everyone to see. Your goddamned magick just signed the death warrants of my friends; just gave them a one-way ticket to their graves! Damn you, Sigil Talisman!" Guthal exploded, rising slowly to menace Sigil. "I made a blood-oath! I swore *never* to reveal to *anyone* what you just made everyone see! A Khazak blood-oath, sworn on my father's *soul*! Such a thing follows a warrior to his grave! Or to the graves of those who hear it revealed."

Before any of us could move to intercept Guthal's warpath, Sigil fixed him with a glass-cutting
glare that froze him in his tracks. Lips quivering, Guthal fought it with all of his will, yet still he did not advance. Then, like a fading rain, his face grew calm as his anger died away, flowing into the inner depths of his soul, to be reclaimed for some future, unforgiven foe. With a shuffle of his boots, he walked back to his place in the circle and sat back down, a calculating expression on his face.

"You... you're right, Sigil," Guthal grumbled quietly, removing his now unnecessary glasses with one of his craggy hands, placing them by habit in his ruined shirt pocket. Shaking his head methodically—as David Miller always did when in Monster of Math mode of thought—he said, "You're abso-fuckin'-lutley right, you bastard."

"So you comprehend, Guthal?" Sigil asked him, leaving the rest of us in the dark.

"Perfectly," Guthal responded. "Your logic is, as ever, Sigil Talisman, cold and cutting-pure."

"See what? See *what*?" Sammy asked Guthal impatiently. He hated to be left out of any logic discussion.

"That a dead man carries his blood-oath to his grave, Sammy," Guthal said, turning to face Sigil again as the import of his words burned the room. "And that, because we're all *dead*, my blood-oath has been fulfilled. I carried my secret to my grave," he said as full comprehension dawned upon him, "and I never told *anyone*. Not once. Not ever. Not when you first met me and I lied and told you my name was 'Grog'. Not even when we shared those long, lonely, soul-sharing campfire nights together, whispering our innermost secrets to each other over bottles of Bor's Mead. Not even when we were falling-down drunk in *The Guppy*. Not even when we were blasted as blasted can be in the *Whore'N'Brew*. Not even then."

He spoke truth, this forgotten heir to the throne of Kaza Ka; this Guthal Dirge—my friend, David Miller.

There were no holes in Sigil's logic, as devastating as it was to comprehend for some of us. By all accounts, we *were* dead. We had died in that final, soul-damning battle with Lord Valthrustra back on SenZar oh so many years ago. How else could we have been reborn here on Earth? We *were* dead. But, for some strange reason, we were just too stupid to *stay* that way.

And now we'd probably have to die all over again!

"Now that you comprehend your uniqueness, my friends," Sigil said, noting the various looks of desperate resolve etched upon our faces, "it is time for us to continue *The Weird*. This time," he said, seemingly from a speaker in the back of my head, "we enter the soul of Sammy Joseph, who was once known in another time and another place as Mad Sam Sprunge: joker, mischief-maker, free rogue, and one-time apprentice to the Master Rogue of the Forever City, Zengara."

CHAPTER 13: Diary Of A Madman

"**W**ell now, Samuel! You bear more toys for the attic, I see!" Felix Gildergloves, the Master Rogue—not to mention the coolest guy, too—of Zengara called merrily through the steel-slatted peephole in the thick iron-bound tower door.

"Of c-cc-course I did!" I merrily chattered back, giving the peephole a quick, friendly poke with my fingertip. Felix, amused, I think, cursed heartily at this. "Now let me the hell in there bb-bbefore I ff-f-ff-freezetodeathFelix!"

Puffing on one of his nappy smelling hand-rolled cigarettes, Felix slid back the iron bolt on the door and opened it about a foot, plenty enough room for me to scoot on by him into the smoky confines of our decrepit Old Guards Tower hidey-hole—the very same Old Guards Tower hidey-hole that we had *snifed*—it rhymes with "rife" but more or less means "steal", for all of you normies—from Eddie the Hatchet and his band of Morons. And all *that* simple little exercise in skullduggery had taken was a couple of buckets of "liquid smoke" from the local black market alchemist, and a bit of good luck.

As it just so had happened, Eddie the Hatchet and his Morons had been utterly predictable and had vacated the Old Guards Tower hidey-hole premises at once—the vomit-brains had actually thought that the place was on fire! See? Good luck! At least for us, not for them.

And good luck, of course, came with the territory so far as I, Samuel Sprunge, Master Rogue-in-the-making and all-around fun kinda guy, was concerned.

"Did you get all of the goodies this time, Samuel?" Felix inquired mirthfully as he bolted back the heavy iron-bound tower door. As if in afterthought, he tugged at his greying whiskers, his yellowed talons plucking a stray ash from one of them.

"You know I did! I got it all!" I danced around the floor a bit, just to let him know how I felt.

Felix, never one to let a good jig go to waste, joined in, and we cut a merry rug, arm in arm. Once we

finished, I jumped up onto the knife-scarred table—too many hands of sailor's poker from Eddie and

his boys—and dangled the loot bag in front of me like a master hypnotist, trying my best to tantalize

Felix, who was staring at it with all of the feral wile reserved for his feline namesake. The silly

cigarette hanging from his lower lip, not to mention the silly hoard-it-all look that had just crossed

his eyes, made Felix Gildergloves look just like the silly gangster that he truly was. It was good to be home!

"Well, my little felon-to-be! Why don't you deliver the goods to Old Felix! There's a good chap!" Felix snatched at the bag, but, as always, he caught air in his hands. Nobody—*nobody*—was *that* fast. Not even Felix Gildergloves, who had the blood of the tiger people, the Tygor, within him.

"Uh-uh-uh!" I teased, holding the bag back behind my back. "What's the magick word?"

"Puh... puh... puh-leeeze?" Felix stammered, the words choking out of his smiling face. "May I *please* investigate the contents of your magick bag, O Master of Malfeasance?"

"Certainly, Old Molester of Young Waifs! I deem thee worthy to look upon my works and despair, for I have been *busy*!" I held the leather bag out to him, leering in my impetuosity.

"Now, let's see!" Felix said, snatching the bag from my hands and dumping its contents onto the tabletop in one smooth, practiced motion. Five distinct objects smacked down, like the winning hand of a dockside gambler. Gold, silver, and gemstone-studded jewelry shone in the feeble light of our cozy little Old Guards Tower loft, glistening like reflected wild things' eyes. The first hoard item was a solid gold ankh, the holy symbol of Rel, which was, fittingly, the least of the haul. True, it was solid gold. But it was only an ankh, and even pigs could make that kinda noise! The clunky old pig-noise thing looked out of place sitting beside the rest of the haul, though, for the remainder were almost demonic in demeanor, ranging from the silver-plated skull goblet to the emerald-encrusted phallus. Sadly, the other two thingies were mere baubles, with only enough shiny things to make them hoardable. Cool-looking, mind you. But not worth mentioning. Unless one was really into deranged farm animal figurines.

"You've outdone yourself, Samuel," Felix said after a moment of appraising the goods. He particularly found the emerald phallus interesting, studying it with an arched brow for almost a full ten seconds. "I would say that some noble lady will be most upset before the day is done, her best friend and companion gone now." He *heh-heh*'d a bit, then tossed the items back into the bag before giving them back to me.

"Uhh... I got that from Duke Vasagio's nightstand, Felix, after I gave his war hounds some raw meat doped with sleeping dust," I disclosed, hoping not to spoil his good humor. "And, as we both know, he's *not* a married man. Who could be, with dogs like hell hounds? Imagine if he had a fight with honey pie: 'Zounds, wench, be that way! Sic 'em, Fido!'" I thought it was funny, so I laughed.

Felix, though, who loathed most canines—except for the very pointed ones in his mouth—seemed thoughtful. "I would say that the rumors were true, then."

"What rumors? I haven't heard any rumors." At once, I began to file through the hidden stores of Maelstromm knowledge in the cobwebs of my more often than not perfect memory. "The current gossip going around the courts is that Duke Vasagio has had, uh, not the best of times adjusting to his, uh, *loss*," Felix continued for my benefit. A wry grin spread across Felix's man-tiger face.

"You mean when he caught the arrow with his groin in the Battle of the Rook?" I inquired, finding the knowledge that I sought. I was late, but I was *right*. And that was all that really mattered, after all.

"The very same, Samuel!" Felix laughed. "And I fear that since the poor Duke has been emasculated, he has been, well... emasculated, if you can forgive my redundancy of speech."

"You mean he's *sandy*?" I asked, disgust in my eyes.

"Not exactly, Samuel," Felix responded, a look of patience on his dark, slender-boned feline face.

"Then what *do* you mean? Is he sandy, or just kinky, or both?" I windmilled my arms in exasperation. Inquiring mimes *had* to know!

"I think the word 'self-serving' would be most appropriate," he said quickly, embarrassed with my insistence. "Now," he added before I could ask anything else, "why don't we have a nice toddy of rum and discuss tomorrow night's artistry!"

Needless to say, I jumped at the chance to drink some of Felix's spiced rum and talk shop. After all, that's what I was apprenticed to him for: to talk shop. Felix had taken me in from the cold and lonely path of free agency, a dangerous thing here in Zengara, and had taught me his art these past three years with a passion that only a master and a most-apt pupil could enjoy. The Master Rogue of Zengara had taken a "jewel in the rough," as he had called me when we first met, and had polished it with precision into what was now surely a flawless gem.

Felix had never quite gotten around to *telling* me the latter, mind you, but I'm certain that that's how he felt about things.

After a few sips of Felix's cider-tainted rum, I felt the night's exertion fade from my mind. The earlier night's danger faded away from my mind, too, along with the earlier night's extreme fun, and I felt myself relax, ready for what Felix had to say.

"Well, now, my felonious friend," he began, his habitual preamble for laying the foundation of his artwork, "it seems that I've got a good, nay, *excellent* one this time!"

"Speak more, O Illustrator of Woe," I implored, stirring my toddy with a sprig of mint. Then I eased onto a more comfortable section of the tabletop, one more suited to catching the warmth of the feeble fireplace that served the ancient chamber.

"I shall, I shall!" Felix set his toddy down and leaned forward in his chair, his green cat's eyes gleaming with the revelation to come. "It has recently come to my attention that a certain priceless treasure has found its way into the heart of our noble city. My fellow artists tell me that a treasure no less than the Sphere of Kadar-Noth lies within the gates of a certain noble lord's manor! Here, within the venerable walls of the Forever City itself!"

I searched my mental stores for any and all information pertaining to the Sphere of Kadar-Noth. Maelstromm, the mad alchemist who had breathed life into me, had given me many secrets, many cubbyholes of data. The trick, though, was finding them amongst the silvery cobwebs that made up my memories—a result of the fractured mistake that had cost Maelstromm the perfect man and had instead given him a less than perfect example of humanity.

I *should* have been *perfect*, mind you! Instead, due to some celestial error that only Maelstromm the Mad could have cooked up, I had been born a bit... prematurely. Four foot, one inch tall would be pushing it, not to mention a few jokers short of a full deck, as Felix would tease. But let's leave it at that, okay?

Tearing through the silvery mists of my mind, I categorized and cross-categorized Kadar-Noth, jumping from Zengaran to Mokarran to Rotathian histories, separating the wheat from the chaff in the space of a few seconds. False leads, dead ends. Then, suddenly, as I brushed aside a silvery strand of thought, I found what I had been looking for, mentioned in a compendium of magickal artifacts from the Sixth Age, one written by a committee of wizards from Tornharm, Zengara's far-western sister city. I seized it, then cross-referenced it once more, just to make sure that it was a *true fact*.

"That's an interesting one, all right, Felix," I said, wishing I had more to go on—like the Sphere's rap sheet, for instance.

"Tell me about it, Samuel."

"Well, I don't know as much as I'd like to about it, Felix. But from what I'm remembering, it seems that the Sphere of Kadar-Noth was once used as the focal point of a summoning spell, one that took at least three Master Wizards to perform. That alone would make it priceless, on any black market."

"Ahh, then it's a magickal *focus*!"

"That's not all, Felix. It was mentioned in a text from the Sixth Age, so that makes it at least a thousand years old. And, perhaps most interesting of all, the wizards who spoke of it described it as an 'eye of the demon,' which, if you knew Mokarr, means that it was associated with the summoning and control of demons!" I took a gulp from my cup, careful not to poke my eye out with my sprig of mint.

"Then the wheel goes 'round, Samuel," Felix said gravely, "for the nature of the dreadful thing reveals the heart of the one who possesses it." He finished off his rum, then set his cup down carefully. He was, of course, going to make me ask him.

"Okay. I'll bite. Who has it? Who's the potential demon summoner?"

"One who sits high on the council of the Overlord, Samuel. One who deceives the good people of Zengara with his sugarcoated approach to Law and Order. I speak of none other than His Eminence, Lord Tannan Thant, Chief Justice of the Council of Law!"

You could have pushed me over with a feather, but I would have seen you coming and stolen it.

Lord Tannan Thant! The hypocrite! And he had the gall to call *me* an outlaw! And, all the while, he had been collecting evil, nasty, horrible, putrid artifacts of obviously dark nature. What an ass! Well, he had just put the noose around his own neck, for once, instead of some poor food-snifing street urchin's. I *still* hadn't forgotten what had happened to my good friend Lars, and I *never* would. Death by hanging, for stealing a loaf of bread.

"Let's nail 'im, Felix. Now!" I said, nodding my head thoughtfully, swearing to Lars that tonight he'd finally rest in peace.

?

The Thieves' Highway—a highway in name only, for it was nothing more than a collection of routes across the treacherous rooftops of Zengara's notorious Thieves' Quarters—served us well, for Felix and I knew *all* of the shortcuts, not to mention all of the Guild-patrolled outposts. The Thin Man's various assassins, thieves, and assorted goons were good, but only so far as you could throw 'em. In less than the space of an hour, we had bypassed three goon-held outposts and traversed the slick, icy dangers of Marnia's Hellhold, which was four city blocks of dangerous switchbacks and hairpin turns, none of which was less than four stories above the muck-filled alleyways of the city's cobbled streets.

I led the way, Felix trusting my enhanced senses even over his animal-sharp own. Felix could tell you if a pin had dropped behind him, his tall, keen ears so much like the tiger that he resembled. I could tell you its mass, its composition, and the vector identity of where it had landed, not to mention... well, you get the point. I may have been half-baked in some areas, thanks to inopportune fate, but there were some facets of my being that *were* perfect. Maelstromm may have been mad, but he got a few things right!

Soon enough, we sat on our haunches, braced against a bitter wind that had blown in from across the bay; our backs against a third floor chimney overlooking the pristinely manicured—not to mention pristinely guarded—estate of His Eminence, Lord Tannan Thant.

"It's a little too cold for one of my blood," Felix muttered, lying again, as usual. His grizzled fur was more than enough to keep him warm, even in the freezing cold Deepwinter weather.

"Yeah, right," I whispered back to him. "Keep on bitching about the cold, Felix. I know you have to have *some* excuse, just in case your arthritic hands bungle some latch tonight."

Felix chuckled, a sound that was more a deep purr than a laugh. Then, with a barely perceptible sound, he had his sailor's spyglass out of his backpack, scanning Lord Tannan's compound for any sign of activity.

"I've got two guards in the high tower, and one walking patrol on the grounds," he said after a moment's study.

"Yeah, I know," I whispered, careful to keep my voice still. "And the one on the left in the tower is playing with his rusty ol' dagger, showing the other deadhead how daft—I mean *deft*—he is." Was it really showing off if I *could* see better than his spyglass?

"My, my, my, how your eagle's eyes are sharp tonight, My Treasured Concubine!" Felix hissed, replacing his once-maligned spyglass in his backpack.

"The better to see *you* with, O Purveyor of Fine Filth," I whispered, careful that my words carried not over the wind. I scrambled over to the edge of the rooftop for a better view. The guard who was walking patrol had already disappeared behind a clump of chandelier trees, a testament to Thant's wealth and influence. The chandeliers were not only notoriously difficult to keep up in the city, but they were also illegal to import for cultivation as of about three months ago, when Mir Kestral, the new Overlord of Zengara, in a fit of conservational fury, had decreed that the sacred trees of the Starin be barred from the city proper. It was the result of some sort of political pressure from the Starin Council, a powerful lobbying force of witches and wizards of the Good Earth, who had threatened to boycott their eternal support of the city unless he put an end to the "pagan's misuse" of the sacred trees. Some misuse. The chandeliers were beautiful, with their upswept, cone-bearing evergreen branches—a sight that would still even an Azaar warrior in full bloodlust. Not even the most villainous of cretins would intentionally think of harming one of them, but still Mir Kestral bowed to political pressures to keep them scarce and sacred, the wimp.

I smothered my contempt and strained my eyes to pick out the ground-roving guard, who might prove to be a thorn in our sides once we penetrated the outer defenses of the compound. Roving guards were always tricky, as paranoid as they usually were. More than once one of them had been the undoing of an otherwise successful snifing.

I saw him stop in front of the tree nearest the wall of the compound, look around a couple of times, then turn his back to me, his hands going around in front of him to his waist. He fiddled around a moment, then stiffened his back as he began to water the tree. Seizing the opportunity, I waved Felix on, and we quickly made our way down to the street. We sprinted to the wall of Thant's compound, where Felix launched me up to the top of the wall without missing a stride. I was already in the bushes, my eyes on the still-pissing guard, by the time that Felix had his feet on the compound's turf.

As Felix stalked silently over to where I had hidden in the bushes, he shook his head in silent appraisal of the guard's bladder capacity. Felix signed in Silent Speech that our target was the second floor balcony, the one nearest us. From there, he continued, we would go inside—*with our hands to ourselves*, he emphasized.

I nodded my understanding, then sat still, waiting for the guard to button himself back up. Soon enough, Ol' Iron Bladder obliged, then walked quickly away from the scene, as if he were guilty of something besides being a guard.

We waited until he was ten paces away, then we skulked out of the bushes, mirroring his footsteps until we were close enough to the wall of the manor to slip into the shadow of the balcony. The bottom of the eaves' supports came within a paltry ten feet of the ground, so Felix tossed me up to them, and I scaled them easily enough. Felix followed closely behind me, the leap to the eaves' supports not much for one of his ability. He waited at the underhang until I leaned over the railing and gave the "all's clear" signal, then he hefted himself over the rail and landed softly on the pads of his *tabi*, those weird two-toed boots that he always used for missions like this one. Felix said that he had learned of them during his travels in Mao Yen, but I never could tell if he was telling the truth. I think he really used them because his feet had claws on them, and they just wouldn't fit in normal boots.

Soon enough, after carefully listening for signs of activity within the darkened room, we moved within the spacious suite, silently padding across the marble floor. I kept my hands to myself, for once, as there wasn't much of value in the room that could be easily heisted. Pausing at the threshold of the room, we both perked our ears up and gave it a silent one-to-ten count.

Nothing. Nary a peep.

So, moving as one in silence, we made the hallway, and, at Felix's urging, took a left and headed for the stairs, which, of course, had banisters of purest Rotathian black onyx. As we took the stairs, I hopped up onto the banister rail, leaning forward to counter the slope of the slick onyx. Felix gave me a sidelong glance, then stifled a smirk on his face. Continuing along, with me on the rail and Felix tightly against the wall, we came at once to the third floor landing. From here, we had the option of going either left or right. Neither looked too appealing, as the path to the right led to a single oaken door and the path to the left mirrored it exactly, even down to the ten paces it took to get there. I had a feeling that Thant was behind one of them. But the Sphere of Kadar-Noth came first. He'd get his, in time.

I was just about to take my lucky silversteel Eagle coin out and flip it for celestial guidance when Felix suddenly crouched down and stiffened, his whiskers moving like the tendrils of a sea anemone as he sniffed the air for something. He moved gingerly into the hallway, first turning left, then right, on the track of something fascinating. Finally, he straightened his back and pointed at the wall directly in front of us, making the sign for "door" and smiling as he did so.

This I could not believe.

I slithered down from the rail and loped over to the wall, bending close to the marble floor, close enough to get an ant's-eye view of any architectural inconsistency. Finding none, I signed my disbelief to Felix. He shook his head slowly, then plucked a small feather from his ridiculous piper's cap, holding it at arm's length before the wall. As he released it, it wafted to-and-fro, moving away from the wall on a slight current of air as it fell to the floor. Felix, of course, snatched it up before it hit the floor and stuck it back into his cap, flashing me an "I told ya so!" look as he did it.

It was the old "Illusory Wall" trick, one that I'd seen a couple of times before, only not so good as this particular one. It only figured that Ol' Thant would have the resources to hire the best spell-slingers to do his hidey-work. It only followed, logically, that his hoard must be behind the wall, too—protected just as well, if not better, than the entrance. And that was so much the better for me, because once I helped Felix get that Sphere-thingie, I was gonna pay a visit to Ol' Thant himself in his nice, comfy bedroom, and whisper him a secret I'd been keeping for a long time.

Felix gave the sign that he was going to go in first, with me following on a silent three. Without a sound, Felix walked into the wall, passing through it with a barely perceptible shimmering of the illusory veil. On three, I followed, a tingle of ants crawling all over me as I stepped through the veil into total, all-encompassing darkness.

At once, I dropped into a defensive crouch, my slimsword quickdrawn and raised in front of my face. Fighting down the tremors that raced up and down my spine, I willed myself to be calm, to listen.

I hated the dark. And it certainly hated me back.

Normally, thanks to the some of the stuff that *did* go right with my creation, I could see almost as well in the dark as I could in light. But that was only if I were outside and a couple of stars were shining away, dancing in ultraviolet, or if there were a candle in a cave shedding its feeble, philosophical light. Gloom was fine for me. Even normal darkness, as most people—most humans, that is—know it.

But not *this*. This was magick, and I hated it!

Fighting an urge to run away, I stood my ground, senses keened for any sign of normalcy. For an instant, I thought I felt Felix off to my left. But the feeling was gone as quickly as it had come. He was here, but he wasn't. He was playing that little Mao Yenese hidey-trick of his, a trick which made him invisible—invisible even in darkness—as paradoxical as that sounded. Well, at least I knew now that we hadn't been separated, or disintegrated. Still, the ants wouldn't stop crawling over me.

Magick did that to me. Ants.

So, realizing that this was getting nowhere fast, I made a decision to get out of the dark and into the light. Setting off at a forty-five degree angle to my right, I moved quickly across the slick floor—it had to be more marble—using my slimsword as a blind man's stick. After five paces, my sword encountered a wall, one that made a dull, resonant thud when I tapped it, even up to the limits of my reach. Heart sinking, I jerked my sword forward and lunged. That, too, caused a dull thud, which confirmed a horrible suspicion of mine, answering the ants that still crawled all over my naughty bits.

As the Maelstromm knowledge hit me like a heavy weight, I realized, with finality, that we were both trapped within a *Sorcerous Sphere*. It was a fiendish trap from which there was no escape, save by more powerful magick.

"Felix!" I whispered, panic giving way to common sense.

"Yes, I know!" Felix whispered from off to my left, closing the distance between us before the words died away. Suddenly, he leaned close to my ear, causing another tremor of fear to wash down the back of my neck, dislodging some ants. "Be quick, now, my friend, and fetch forth your vial of *Quickfire*."

"But what's that go to do with—"

"Quickly!" Felix hissed, his fine-tuned control fading rapidly away as he, too, felt the pangs of the unknown bite deeply. As I moved numbed hands to obey, I heard him rummaging rapidly through his own pack, cursing softly under his breath. After a moment of finger-reading the raised labels of the vials in my side pouch, I selected the one labeled *QF* and pressed it into his waiting grasp.

"What are you gonna do?" I asked, already close to the alchemical answer.

"I am going to get us out of here, if Bel is with us," Felix whispered. "If not, then I'll save Ol' Thant the trouble of hanging us." With that, I heard him begin to strike the vial fiercely against another vial, one of his own; which, if memory served—and it always did—contained a similar dose of *Quickfire*; which, if agitated just right, would heat up hot enough to melt steel. Or, in this case, marble. I smiled, despite the fear, as I considered the other explosive possibilities.

Just then, though, the lights came back on.

"That will be enough, animal!" Lord Tannan Thant, Chief Justice of the Council of Law, boomed from the far side of the once-darkened chamber. Thant's normally ponderous voice was strangely distorted by the still-shimmering sphere of force that held us. "That will be *quite* enough," he reiterated, his fat hands stroking the chestnut-sized purple gem set in an onyx pendant about his neck. Felix ceased his frantic vial-bashing and stared hard at Thant, whose bald head, bulging eyes, and hanging jowls made him look like a gloating toad.

Thant was only twenty feet away, but he might as well have been on the other side of the Zone of Destruction with that sphere still between us. He was grinning like a fat bullfrog sizing up an even

fatter bug, swaying back and forth on his heels. Behind him there was an obscene tapestry that stretched across the entire far wall, depicting a madman's version of the Pit, complete with flames,

demons, and a host of black crucifixes that held limbs and torsos, but not complete bodies. Weird, that. Anyway, the remainder of the chamber was bare, save for a small dais to Thant's left, which bore a large iron-bound book. It was opened to some place near its midsection, a tatter of a vellum bookmark hanging from it.

"Well, well, well," Thant taunted, his voice even thicker and chunkier from the sphere's effect, "look what's dragged itself in: an alley cat and its little mouse." He chuckled to himself, pleased with his bad pun, fat fingers still stroking his little purple bauble. "To what kind fate do I owe this pleasant house call?"

"Well," I leered, "we felt the city leaning a little bit in this direction—"

"Shut up, half-man!" Thant cried, his face shooting beet red. "You came here to assassinate me, didn't you?" He raised a beefy finger and shook it at us. "I know who you are, you villains! Felix Gildergloves and his little partner in crime, Samuel Sprunge! Pawns of the Thin Man, Master of Assassins! Did you think that it would be *that* easy? Did you think that you could just walk in here and get your kicks? I am the law here in Zengara! The law!"

"You are a hypocrite, Thant," Felix said evenly as he moved his hands behind his back, still holding the vials. "And you are wrong on all counts. We do not serve the Thin Man. We never shall, for his soul is as black as yours. You are the Chief Justice, the paragon of Law and Order here in the Forever City, yet you employ dark sorcery like a... Mokarr. At least you could do everyone a favor and be consistent like the Thin Man, who holds no such illusions as to where he stands, no?"

Thant's eyes narrowed, and his breathing began to grow heavy as he stroked his amulet with his sweaty hands.

"I don't have the time to bandy semantics with an illiterate cutpurse, cat-man," Thant replied, his eyes growing crafty as he spoke. "However, I do have time not only to rid myself once and for all of you and your puny companion's feeble attempts at pilfering and assassination, but also to save Mir Kestral the cost of a grand hanging!"

With that, Thant held forth his purple-stoned amulet and cried out, "Behold! The Sphere of Kadar-Noth, Master of Demons!" A noise like the shredding of fabric pitched throughout the room as the purple stone began to glow, then pulse, then writhe, forming a perfect sphere of pitch-black arcane energy about it, almost a hand in diameter. "With this, I remember the ancient Unspoken Ones, I sign their seal, I speak their words. Come forth, O Elder Nightmares, and remember the words, signed in..." then, he pointed his index finger at us, and, finishing his incantation, said, "soul's blood!"

Instantly, the floor began to shake as a plume of green, sulfurous smoke issued from the floor in front of us. Demon summoning wasn't something that I had ever witnessed personally, especially not while standing on the wrong side of the summoning circle. Or, in this case, summoning sphere. So, naturally, I screamed bloody murder.

Felix, however, began to work feverishly with the vials. He banged them together so hard that the metal began to heat up in his hands, sending the acrid stench of burning hair to meet with the stench of the infernal within the confines of the sphere.

"Come, Eternal Night!" Thant bellowed, his voice amplified by the magick of the summoning. "Take their souls unto the Dark, but leave their shells here for a public display! Teach them the Lesson of the Dark! Take them screaming to the Pit!"

Foam flecked Thant's billowing cheeks as substance formed from the chaos in front of us. Flashes of horn, sinew, scale, and tentacle flickered within the noisome smoke. Deep, scary bleats and howling blended into a cacophony of madness. All the while, the mass of smoke continued to grow, reaching man-height and more as the boundary 'twixt Here and There was torn asunder.

"Thant! Wait!" I shouted, remembering what I had told Felix about Kadar-Noth's silly sphere. "It takes *three* people to pull this off! You're gonna call up a wild demon!"

Thant's eyes never blinked, so intent was he in his focus. I looked over to Felix, who appeared to be on fire, such was the smoke around him. He was growling in pain as he held the white-hot vials to the floor, directing their seething flame into the marble, cutting into it like a lathe. He looked up at me. His eyes filled with tears. Then, staggering back, he dropped the white-hot vials onto the molten, slagged marble. The pool was slightly over a foot in diameter, still smoldering, when it suddenly gave way and fell flaming to the floor below.

"Go, Samuel," Felix commanded. He drew his longsword with his maimed hands and turned to face the shambling horror of the fully formed demon.

"You can forget about *that*!" I screamed hysterically as I sank a hurled stiletto into the demon's bulging, insect-like central eye. Ignoring the addition to its optic nerves, the demon swung an outsized chitinous claw at Felix. He barely managed to dodge aside, still keeping himself between its total insanity and the hole.

"Get out of here, dung head!" Felix screamed as he hacked off one of the demon's slimy thoracic tentacles. "I'll be right behind you! Now go!" Charging, his blade a blur, Felix managed to drive the thing back to the edge of the sphere, shaving off bits and pieces of it as he pressed it.

"I'll be back for you later fatso!" I yelled at Thant as I took Felix's advice and dove headfirst into the pit. Flipping in midair, I managed a pretty good landing on the floor below, which was now smoldering fairly well. The molten marble had landed on a rug in the center of a sitting room. Soon, this whole room would be on fire. Patting out a small fire on my generic old non-fireproof cloak, I looked up anxiously, hoping to catch some glimpse of Felix.

"Felix!" I shouted, not caring if the guards heard now. I was certain that they were already on their way now, if they were worth their pay.

But humans, as predictable as they always are, weren't my concern at the moment. Dodging a plummeting piece of slag, I tried to peer through the smoky haze of the hole, but all I saw were shadows and flashes of fire. Outside the room, guards were already banging on the heavy oaken door.

Predictable, like I said. I backed against the wall and readied my blade, wiping the soot from my eyes.

Suddenly, a grim silence filled the air as the shadows above ceased to move. A sloshing, chewing sound came from the other side of the smoky hole as a green nimbus of eldritch fire loomed from within, moving closer. Then, as a chasm yawned wide in my stomach and my senses left me, the bulbous eye of the demon leered through the hole in the ceiling while it regurgitated the entrails

of my friend, Felix Gildergloves, onto the flaming rug of the sitting room. The demon clacked its

mandibles twice, then began to chuckle vilely as it set to the task of digging through the marble. Above it all, I could hear Thant's insane,   gibbering   laughter;   taunting,   goading, condemning—naming me as mad as He Who Had Created Me.

In that soul-etched moment, the door before me burst inward, followed by three guards in full chain mail. One held an axe; the others, short swords and shields. I stood, fixed in place, glaring at the demon, wishing Death and Pain on all of them. As one, the guards saw the smoldering fire, then

me; then the leering, nameless demon. Two of them screamed in terror and fled while the third stood

his ground, petrified. Like an automaton detached from its own existence, I withdrew another stiletto

from my sleeve and buried it in the doomed guard's left eye before he could blink.

I stood for a moment, lost in somewhere else, as a horrible thought crossed my mind.

Reaching into my belt pouch, I numbly pulled out every vial, every bag of noxious poison, every secret dirty trick that was in my extradimensional bag, and dumped them on top of the flaming rug. I knew fully well that I was signing my own execution sentence—I knew my inventory by rote, and I knew what using it all at once would do. But... I really didn't give one cold damn. It would burn everything locally to the ground, and then some. It would destroy everything. And, yes, there was a small probability that, once started, it would consume the entire city. And, yes, I couldn't care less if a million souls joined us on our way to the Pit tonight.

Felix was a father to me. Thant and his pet demon took him from me. Now they would die.

Felix.

"I'm sorry, Samuel," the image of Maelstromm the Mad consoled, his ethereal hand tousling my hair, sending an epileptic tingle over my body. "I meant to make you the perfect man, but I failed. You aren't perfect. You're broken. Broken. Broken forever."

Someone else guided my legs to the sill of the window.

Someone else turned on his perch, and, before leaping to the ground below, witnessed the growing column of acidic black flames eat into the floor and spread across it like a plague of black angels.

Someone else watched the flames engulf the compound like so much drought-dry tinder.

Someone else heard the demon howls and death cries of those trapped within the flaming hell of the estate.

Someone else watched the precious chandelier trees burn to the ground, their sacred boughs wreathed in black fire.

Someone else heard the wails of the banshee wind and knew what it was that had birthed Pain and her brother Madness.

Someone else watched from afar until the chill rains of the morning shed their tears of steam upon the ruins of Hate.

?

This time there were no tears.

There was only shock. The shock that roils within the mind in that perfect, brief sunset of the soul that hearkens the first fatal footstep down that long, bitter path that men call Madness.

Sammy.

My heart was torn. Sammy sat so still, there within our circle, in a purgatory of silence. He looked catatonic, distant; lost back in the past, where he was reliving that horrible, mind-wrenching event. I fought the urge to clinically analyze him, to transform his essence into some nameless, uncaring number. I knew that I would only wind up analyzing myself, anyway, so I let it go, the echoes of Sammy's *Weird* pounding in my brain.

Someone else heard the wails of the banshee wind, Sammy had thought in that terrible moment, *and knew what it was that had birthed Pain and her brother Madness.*

Knowing Sammy as well as I did—growing up with him in that simple-valued small town, moving with him to Baton Rouge to attend LSU, then rooming with him for our entire collegiate careers and more; each of us the brother that the other never had—only served to bolster my growing pain. I knew Sammy as I knew myself. Yet, this hidden thing from the soul of the SenZar Sammy smashed my preconceptions of his life and times here on Earth. I—Christopher Logan—knew Sammy Joseph's life as if it were my own, even down to the most humbling, intimate details. We were *that* close.

But our lives on SenZar?

There were things that we had *never* discussed, *never* brought up, not even in the most shared of times. It was exactly what Guthal had emphasized: We were comrades in arms, brought together by the necessity of self-preservation—not by the all-consuming, all-revealing necessity of true friendship. And, as such, with the ever-present threat of the hangman's noose on our necks, there were some things that we had *never* shared with one another.

And now, the secrets of another lifetime were peeling away like so many layers of onion skin, revealing deep, dark soul secrets that were best left—like well enough—alone.

"C'mon, Sammy," I whispered, my voice near cracking, "come home! We need you in the here and now, not back in the past." Sammy remained motionless, not batting an eyelash.

"Thant received no less that he deserved, Sammy," Sigil reassured. Still, Sammy did not respond.

"C'mon, Sammy!" I pleaded, grabbing him by the arm. "Pry those fucking coins out of your eye sockets! You're not dead. You're alive! Alive! So come back home, please?"

Just as the moment stretched too long for the comfort of sanity, Sammy blinked his eyes once, slowly.

"Yeah," Sammy said distantly, blinking his eyes again, "no place like home, Tat. Even if you don't know where the hell *home* is."

Bitter smiles, nods of agreement.

Leaning over, I crushed him to me like a brother, letting him know that we would never have secrets between us. No matter which life we currently lived.

"We're gonna *win* this one, man," I promised him.

"Right," Sammy replied despondently, separating himself from my embarrassing grasp. "Tell me that *after* we've won, and maybe I'll believe you, Tat... uh..." he looked at me sheepishly, his voice faltering, "...I mean, Logan?"

Sharing Sammy's sense of temporal displacement, I smiled at him and said: "Logan *or* Tat, I'm still the same guy who's had to put up with your bullshit on *two* worlds."

Laughter, remembrance.

"Sam-I-Am!" Zaar bellowed, rolling the words around on his tongue as only an Azaar/Jamaican could, laughing as he regarded Sammy's indignant look. "You're *still* the same, mon! Sammy Joseph *or* Mad Sam Sprunge—New Orleans *or* Zengara—you're *still* a little shit with the same name! Not even the big black sleep could change that!"

"Aww, shaddup, you big blue banana!" Sammy retorted, feeling his oats return.

"Screw you, lil' mon!" Zaar countered, egging Sammy on with a pair of low-flying blue birds.

"No," Sammy shouted defiantly, flying the bird right back, "*screw you!*"

More laughter defused the situation as we recalled that this was vintage Sammy behavior. Both of those two Loons would *perpetually* be at each other's throats, no matter which world or which life they shared. Such was their way. Such was *our* way: The Way of the Seven Stars, champions of the Cause, heroes of Zengara, the Forever City. Idiot psychopaths, all.

"Now we continue *The Weird*, my friends," Sigil interrupted solemnly, an age-old cadence to his voice. "This time, we see through the mind's eye of LT Michael Reese, USN, who was once known to his fellow Stars as Tal'N: Silestion, Shy'R Warrior, and Prince of Petra."

As we faded away, I noted that Sammy was *still* flying the finger at Zaar.

The more that things change.

CHAPTER 14: Sad But True

From the One Sea we sail, to the clouds and far
    Beyond the Sun, beyond the Veil
Warriors of the stars

We sang together, my brother and I, "The Song of the Sun." We cast our cares on the clouds to fly away, as we scaled the granite slopes of Mt. Silar, eager to reach its snowcapped summit before nightfall.

It was only our second day of freedom—freedom from the daily grind of training that only the best and brightest of our Silestion people received: The Way of the Warrior, the Path of the Sun.

Royal blood notwithstanding, my brother and I were as everyone else in our discipline. Neither rod nor rule was spared, as to learn the Way was to learn Self. Even the Malakon's sons were not above the rule of the Warhall, as we had learned early on, much to our regret. Shy'R'a, our dearest mother and equally dearest Malakon of our people, would laugh herself silly at our escapades, managing her bright, knowing golden smile when the instructors' straps would fall upon the royal rear ends, raising dark golden welts with each pass. She would say without saying, her eyes still smiling, that she herself once had to endure the very same torture when she had sought the Way.

Neither my brother nor myself could imagine such a thing, though, as she was now One with the Phoenix. It was the paradox of the child not seeing the parent as a child.

Nevertheless, we were determined to do some skiing—a rare treat indeed for our people, considering the tropical climate around Petra—and, quite possibly, to get some spelunking in during our week of leave. Our packs were loaded, prepared for any eventuality: skis, canteen, a chord of silk rope for climbing, and a glow stick apiece. The single "weapon" that each of us carried was a Shy'R punch-dagger—a foot of sun-forged solara blade bound with another forearm's worth of solara support—which rested for now in thigh-scabbards on both my brother and myself. As blossoming, self-reliant Shy'R Warriors, we carried more than enough for any climb or exploration of the depths.

It was thus, as we paused atop a flat, wind-blown outcrop at high sun for water, that I asked my older brother, Shy'R—named for our mother's tenth grandfather, the Master of the Way of combat which bore his name—the Question.

"So, dear brother," I began, leaning against the warm granite, "where do you plan to go once you graduate from Warhall?"

It was the same question that every young candidate found himself asked by everyone else when graduation time grew near. Where? There were, of course, many different responses. All were based upon the merit and rank of the student. Only the best *chose* where they were to go. The others were assigned; the assignments, once again, according to their merit.

I was shocked by his response.

"I'm *not* going to graduate, Tal'N," Shy'R replied, his heart not in his words. Turning, he regarded the expanse beyond the edge of the boulder. After an awkward moment of silence, he turned back to face me. He took another swig from his canteen, pretending not to see my face. Then, seeking my eyes, he continued: "Why are you so surprised, brother? You know my class rank. I am not even in the top ten in my class."

"So? Every seventh-year student has a slump before the final crunch," I said, capping my canteen and returning it to my pack.

"*You* won't!" Shy'R replied, raising an auburn eyebrow.

I laughed. Two years was a long time from now.

"But that is *certainly* the case with most," Shy'R continued, swishing the water in his canteen to emphasize his coming point. "Yet, that is not the case with *me*. I have reached the point of diminishing returns, little brother. Witness: We are now, only as seventh-year seniors, learning the art of the Silent Strike. Did *we* not learn this from Commander Tel'R in our early youth? Did he not also teach us the finer points of the sword before our classmates had taken their first lessons? I am learning only by regression, not by progression. The same may be said of you, as well."

"I can see your point, but I do not agree with it completely," I replied, wondering where this was leading. "Yes, Commander Tel'R taught us a whole hell of a lot way back when. Maybe more than he *should* have. But the most important thing that he taught us was that we learn something new from every experience. We learn something new even from something old, provided that we—"

"Listen to you!" Shy'R interrupted. "You sound just like the rest of them, ranting and raving about 'The Way,' pontificating like one of the Seekers at High Mass. Maybe you're still too young, little brother, to look beyond your own horizons and see the other shore."

I couldn't believe what I was hearing. This was no longer a simple matter. It was now an affair of state, as the firstborn prince's destiny reflected upon the people, just as it did upon the Malakon. And, right now, my older brother was not acting like the firstborn Prince of Petra.

My temper got the better of me. "Then what in the hell *are* you planning to do, Shy'R? Abdicate?" I shouted, hoping that my voice wouldn't carry through the several leagues of thin mountain air back to the base camp, where our retainers nervously awaited.

"Not exactly, dear brother," Shy'R said coolly, his head, as ever, level. "I am going to fake my own death, here on this mount, then I am going far, far away to begin my studies of the mystic way. I am going to become an initiate of the Order of the Dark Moon. How do you like that?"

I blinked. His jest actually caught me with my shield down. I laughed, a trickle at first. Then, as my

brother began to laugh, too, I let fly with gales of laughter, happy that he was only shining my sword

about running off and joining the Dark. My brother, the jester.

"I'm not joking, Tal'N!" Shy'R suddenly blurted, still laughing.

My laughter died away, even as his grew more mocking. I looked into my brother's eyes: orbs of solid blue, just like mother's, a steel-set determination in them. Suddenly, the import of his words struck me. The precision of his craftsmanship put me at a distinct disadvantage. Here we were, the two heirs to the royal throne of Petra, alone on the slope of a mountain which could, given half a chance, claim the lives of the two young princes. There would be no one around to help. The usual bodyguards were vacant as befitted the wishes of the older brother, who had dismissed them with a wave of his hand. He had claimed that he had wanted some quality "relaxation time" with his younger brother before he graduated and went off to see the world. Of course, death would be the ultimate relaxation time for anyone who experienced it.

A chill ran down the small of my back. Our people, the People of the Sun, were not casual partners to plots of regicide. Or plots of fratricide.

"Why?"

The one question that no one really addresses. I had to know *why*, not "how" or "when." I wanted to know *why* my brother had decided this horrible, foreign course of action. As ever, though, I was the naive little brother, too trusting of my own blood bonds, to consider the other unspoken elements of Shy'R's plan.

"Because it suits me to do so, dearest brother!" Shy'R explained, staring hard at me, his blue eyes stabbing at my heart. "Unlike the rest of our royal family, I was born an old soul, a conquering one, in the spirit of our greatest Malakon, Warhawk, who now rules from Beyond the Sun as Supreme God of War. I am not complacent to simply sit on an old, worn out throne when my time comes, say, a hundred years from now. In case you *have not* noticed, mother hasn't exactly *aged* since she became One with the Phoenix. She's at *least* as old as Seeker Shal'R, who is an old man by the standards of our people, yet she remains as if she were thirty! Do you understand how long *you'll* have to wait before *your* time comes? We could be well into the Eighth Age by then! Don't you see the cruel pattern of stagnation emerging, Tal'N? Or are you such a royal stick in the mud that you'll gladly wait your turn, like a good little soldier, even if it should not occur until a hundred years from now?"

"I'll—"

"But fret not, young brother!" Shy'R continued, his lithely muscled arms gleaming as he slowly flexed them, palms down before him. "*I* have the ambition, the talent, and, most importantly, the *balls* to rekindle the true spirit of our people: the spirit of war! We will fan the flames which have not stirred in an aeon! We will set sail in our great golden ships and conquer all those who oppose us, uniting this sphere under the one, true, Sun King—me!" he growled, his hands clenching.

Shy'R's eyes burned with the fire of his convictions. My own blood was racing, stirred by his warrior's words. Such was ever the way of our people. Duty, destiny, and war—our *true* gods—always fired our souls with the dark sunlight of utter madness.

"And what do you plan to say to mother when you return to rekindle these flames?" I asked, eager to counter the effect of his maddening words. "*Stand down?*" I growled back, taking a single step forward.

"Ahh, alas, Tal'N," my brother mocked, "you hit the nail on the head the very first time." Shy'R rose to his feet, smiling. "Remember what that philosopher from Zengara said about choices? 'How can one *make* a choice that has *already been made?*' Dearest mother will have but one choice in this matter, decided for her by the people of Petra, who long to walk once more the path of ancient glory." He paused to build the tension of the moment, just as any good commander would. "*I* will not abdicate, Tal'N. *She* will!"

In his passion, Shy'R was flexing his muscles, posing like a battlefield orator. Or a champion gladiator. This only served to remind me that the two years that he had on me were the ones most important for developing the physique. It was slowly beginning to dawn on me, as that youthful, filial trust began to erode irrevocably away, that I would be the one to stand in the way of his plans. He had already informed me of his plan to fake his death here on the mountain. How could I be allowed to return with the knowledge that this was so? How could he allow me to return at all, knowing that I would do everything in my power to see that he failed in his usurpation?

I had become a liability. In the space of a hundred heartbeats, I had come to realize my own

mortality.

The cold wash of the knowledge was enough to get the blood flowing. I suddenly watched as the face of my brother, the beloved companion of my life, became an alien, hateful thing. In visage he did not change. Yet, the effect was still there. I looked into his blue, distant eyes, and saw chaos. Shy'R was not mad, though. No, not at all. Madness would have been the sole key to clemency for him, for our Seekers knew how to deal with such diseases of the soul. No, Shy'R knew *exactly* what he was doing. And he *liked* it.

"Why tell me all of this?" I bade him, quickly scanning the surrounding area for any sign of further treachery. "Why not just do your dirty work without my ever knowing?" I asked, backing up to the face of the rock, my left hand searching my thigh for my punch-dagger. My temples were beginning to throb.

"Because, dearest brother," Shy'R replied, his voice calm, "there was always the possibility that you would see things my way and join me." His earlier mania was now gone, replaced with smug satisfaction. "Pray tell, Tal'N: Do you see the Light?" Shy'R's tone was the same as one of our holy Seeker's, speaking the words of the conclusion of the Confession Before the Light. This time, though, unlike all of those others, there was only one answer that I could give him. And it was, unfortunately, a final, fatal one.

"Shy'R, reconsider your words," I desperately implored, finding the strap of my scabbard and drawing my punch-dagger as I spoke. "We may *yet* walk down this slope together, as brothers. No one need ever know the words you spoke. I love you enough to keep my peace, provided that you do the same." I held my punch-dagger out, its gleaming golden point directed toward his heart. My eyes blazed with a determination no less formidable than his own.

Or so I hoped. My head was pounding as if I were one hundred fathoms beneath the sea.

"Now, what do *you* say?" I asked, easing into the first formation of the *Dragon Dance*.

Shy'R shook his head. "I'd say that you made the only choice that you knew how to make, little brother," he replied. "Admirable. But typical. Typical." He did not draw his punch-dagger, or advance. My head kept on pounding, though, and I prayed that he would not notice the tremors in my blade arm.

"Then what do you plan to do next, brother?" I asked, my voice sounding hollow in my ears. "Do we shed blood here before the Sun; commit fratricide, here and now? Or do we... do we—"

I felt my knees give way as vertigo claimed me. I fell hard, breaking my fall only by reflex. Slowly, ever so slowly, I distantly felt Shy'R pry the punch-dagger from my strangely numb grasp, then rummage through my pack. Then, my brother's strong hands turned me over so that I might face the Sun before everything faded away. Shy'R's face was a groggy blur outlined by the pulsing, life-giving rays of the great, golden Sun, Silestion. In his hands he held my canteen, a smirk on his face, as he poured its contents out on the hard, unforgiving rock. Next, he poured the contents of his own into mine, sloshing it around, finally pouring that out, too. Then, he tossed both of them down the side of the cliff.

"*Waters of Amnesia*," Shy'R said, still smirking. "Colorless. Odorless. With the temporary side-effect of paralysis, too. But very effective, dearest brother. Very effective. The vertigo sensation was the easier of the two to employ, though," he explained as he held out my punch-dagger by its gleaming blade, avoiding the arm-binding support as he did so. This, too, he tossed over the edge of the precipice. "I knew that you had already made your choice," he continued, "so I doctored both your canteen and the binding support of your blade this morning before we set out. Insurance, as it were. We were fortunate that you waited until high sun to drink, just like a good soldier would. If you would have stolen a sip from it a little earlier in the morning, it would have taken a *lot* of explaining to persuade our retainers that you were just tired of hiking and needed some rest!" Shy'R laughed at his insulting statement. "It's rather ironic, though, Tal'N. They *did* teach us how to doctor things with poisons and venoms in Warhall," he said, smiling wickedly. "Too bad they waited until seventh-year to do so."

I tried to say something, but only managed to gurgle a thin stream of drool out of the corner of my mouth. Things were fading fast. I had to do something.

"But fear not, my brother," Shy'R said as he bent down close to my face, "for I will *not* seal my fate in your blood. The avalanche that will 'claim' me will leave you with only a minor head wound. You will mourn my loss, like a good brother would, even though you will bear the blame of my loss. Your guilt will *mask* my departure," he said as he closed my paralyzed eyelids with the side of his hand, sealing them from the fury of the Sun. "No one will dare question your righteous, personal blame, for fear that you will take arms against them in their *ignorance*. Forever will you blame yourself for my loss, for you believe that you *could* have saved me! You will wear the *mask* of my loss, along with the Honor Crest that you will one day bear. And no one will ever know!" Shy'R chuckled, damning me for all time with his words. "But beware in your dreams, little brother. Beware. For I will return one day to claim what is mine, like a phoenix from the ashes."

Shy'R—named for our mother's tenth grandfather and Master of the Way which bore his name—kissed his little brother farewell, as a true brother would, leaving the dark things for the nightmares to come.

?

"I never knew," Michael Reese—Tal'N, Prince of Petra—said, his voice becoming the focal nexus of our return to "reality."

A simple scene. A vignette of all of our inner soul scars. And even though it had been a short scene, still its impact had hit home with train cars full of slamming bricks.

"Sigil!" Tal'N erupted, his eyes wild. *Solid* green eyes, too—no readily apparent pupil or iris. No whites, either. Just green, and more green. Wild. "How many years have passed? I mean, how many years have passed since we left SenZar?"

Tal'N paused, his palms upturned, his face a mask of wild inquiry. Through the magick of *The Weird*, his skin was now a deep shade of gold; nearly bronze, at that. His hair had become long, curly, and rich with the color of the sunset—the same as he had chosen to wear it back on SenZar. And his Honor Crest seemed to blaze with some strange, inner fire; seemingly transcending its "hawk" state unto that of the legendary Phoenix of the Silestion pantheon. With some specific Silestion differences, he now resembled an old hero of mine: Doc Savage, the champion of the pulp heroes of the roaring thirties.

Fantastic! Now we had parodies of the Grape Ape, Yosemite Sam, Bilbo Baggins, and Doc Savage in our little group. I was fully The Foole, and I'm sure that would be the case in both lives. And who knew what Samantha would be? Jesus. And let's not forget about Mr. Spock as Master of Ceremonies.

Now, having assimilated and labeled just about everyone, I could only consider my own bias and hypocrisy! The constant need to assimilate our conditions, mark them, tag them, then try to comprehend them was wearing me down. It was—as Samantha had pointed out a seeming eternity ago—a sure sign that too much was happening too fast.

"The span of time has been a constant, fixed between the two spheres," Sigil stated, his voice too melodious and full of rich inflection to ever be truthfully compared to any mythical Vulcan's. "Such is not always the way. But, in these strange times, the two have vibrated much the same." He did not smile as he said this.

"Roughly a quarter-century, then?" Tal'N muttered.

"Not to mention those months in Mommy Dearest," Samantha added, shaking her head in disbelief. "And whatever time we may have spent in Limbo, between the worlds. Right, Sigil?"

Sigil nodded once.

"But that doesn't quite add up," Sammy said, counting on his fingers. "We all weren't born on the same day, or even in the same month. Close, but no cigar, Sigil! So you better cancel my subscription to *your* resurrection, baby!"

"That's right," I added, giving a mental nod to Jim, whom Sammy had just paraphrased. "And that leads us to another interesting question: When were *you* reborn, Sigil?"

For a moment, Sigil was silent, his face stony and distant as the rest of us stared at him, waiting for some mystic revelation. Then he looked straight at me. Or straight through me. "The Dragon works myriad mysteries, without benefit of explanation," Sigil responded. "There are times, my friends, when I must do so as well."

"Don't give us any more of that Mr. Mysterious bullshit, Sigil!" Guthal growled. "We've already had our fill."

"Yeah! Fair is fair, Mr. Pointy Ears," Sammy said, his tone more mocking than menacing. "Are you gonna join us in this *Weird* thing, or are you gonna sit this one out, too?"

"I cannot join you, Samuel," Sigil replied, a knowing half-smile on his face, "nor can I spare the time to give you my personal history. Suffice to say, for now, that I passed through the same hell that each of you did. My magick, however, allowed me some semblance of control over my fate. As it was, I was not born again here on Earth. Although, due to the trauma of our uncontrolled, soul-blasting passage through the Dream Barrier, I did manage to wander around for nearly a decade, totally unaware of my own potential, as a transient."

"You mean, you were a *hobo*?" Sammy asked, his voice like a curious child's.

"That is *one* way of appraising the situation, Samuel," Sigil said, his expression a bit warmer. I would swear that he was almost blushing, at least by the straight-laced Starin standards.

"But what about my traitorous brother, Shy'R?" Tal'N interjected, his mind at once on the fate of his SenZar homeland, Petra. "We've got to get back there and find out what happened. We've got to get back *now*!"

Sigil raised a long hand, silencing his passionate outburst.

"You have lived a lifetime away from your home, Tal'N," Sigil reminded. "Whatever has happened, has happened. And there is nothing that you can do now to change the past."

"I have a responsibility to my people, Sigil," Tal'N said, "one that comes before any other. Even this."

Even as Tal'N's solid green eyes lit dangerously, his Honor Crest seemed to effuse a faint, polychromatic play of light, almost like the sheen of oil on water. Upon witnessing this most unusual display, I suddenly realized that perhaps he *had* transcended unto the Phoenix, dying and being reborn and all that mystic kinda stuff. Which would serve, if my newly hatching memory were correct, to make him "One With the Phoenix."

Maybe, but a fat lot of good it would do him if he chose to freak out on Sigil right now. "Archimage of Krystallmyst" carries a hell of a lot more weight than "One With the Phoenix" does—even though comparing the two is like comparing "H-Bombs" with "A-Bombs."

"Then allow me to enlighten you, Prince Tal'N," Sigil explained evenly, "on matters of magick. Do you recall how those Mokarr blasted into Jackson Square?" We all nodded, somehow included in this lesson from the Archimage. "That was a *minor* version of a *Space Warp*. What we need to return to SenZar is the grandfather of that spell, the *Master Warp*. However, I can assure you that the seven of us together could not manage such a feat, even if we clicked our heels together three times and wished for it, for Valthrustra would intercept us in mid-transit and annihilate us. Here, on this magick-blind world, he would note such a vulgar display of the Power Magick in a millisecond and act accordingly, instantly, dooming us all to destruction. These magicks," he said, indicating the seven of us with an inclusive gesture, "I can cloak from his perceptions, though it costs me dearly to do so. The *Master Warp*, however, is impossible to cloak, for it touches all things at once. For so long as Valthrustra exists to thwart us, the warp is foolhardy at best, and suicidal at worst."

"Then we're stuck here, right?" Tal'N asked, disgusted.

"Precisely," Sigil said, steepling his long fingers. "After we retrieve the Krystallstaff and the remainder of our possessions, then destroy Lord Valthrustra, then—and only then—may we safely return to SenZar."

"So you just quested us?" I asked, knowing better. That simply *wasn't* the way that those kinds of things worked, but I had to do it after my earlier braggadocio. Besides, I was as pissed off as everyone else after learning that twenty-five years or so of my SenZar life had passed me by like a foul breeze.

"No," Sigil replied simply. "And you know better than that, Tatternorn," he reminded me, a sly tug of his lips betraying his annoyance. Now I remembered why he would be so peeved about my immature statement. He was reacting as any Starin would, insulted by my impertinent insult. He was supposed to be *above* such mundane things as "questing" someone, which was a ploy for those spellcasters who were very evil, or who were just too damned lazy to do things for themselves. Even though *one* of those things kept cropping up in my mind, I gave him a shrug and let it go.

"If I have to spell it out for all of you, then I will," Sigil continued, his blush replaced by a tightly drawn expression. "We must finish *The Weird*. I will need your awareness of the capabilities of your former selves in order for us to have a fighting chance. Next, we must retrieve more than Skurge to have a fighting chance. Several of your more important artifacts managed to survive the transition. Then we must find Lord Valthrustra and destroy him, his minions, and his twisted schemes. After that, if we are fortunate enough to still be alive, we will return to SenZar, if such we decide."

He hooked us with that one, I'd give him that. Mention loot, especially artifacts, and you'd have any of us foaming at the mouth.

Yes, we were that greedy sometimes, and it had certainly gotten us into tons of trouble back on SenZar.

"I have the information that we need to obtain them," Sigil said, noting that we were staring at him like hungry piranhas. "For this, I need more than your warm bodies. I need the Seven Stars, whole and entire. This world needs us. All of us, fighting at our full SenZar capabilities, with our full powers intact. Not just pale, powerless, Terran shadows of our former selves. On SenZar, we were the best on a world filled with incredibly powerful entities. We saved our own world many times, fighting both mortal and immortal madmen, demons, and even self-styled gods. We never lost. No, not even at the end, in our final battle with Valthrustra. Had we lost, then, indeed, our souls would have been forfeit. The Dragon had other designs, other fates, for us, than those which Valthrustra had sought. The fact that we are all alive now is testament to that fact. So, now, we have the chance to make things right. To avenge ourselves upon Valthrustra, for his blasphemy before the Dragon," he said, staring hard at me, "and save this world, and SenZar itself, in the process. For surely that is Valthrustra's true target, as it has always been. That's what I need you for. Vengeance. Salvation. To save two worlds this time, not just one. I ask only the impossible: the destruction of the most powerful Shadar Lord of all. Are you up for such a challenge? To fight a living god? Even should your own souls be forfeit?"

Momentary silence, then I noticed that everyone was staring at me, waiting for me to say something. Then, it finally sank in. I had been the nominal "leader" of the Stars. Now, they were simply falling back into old form, which was great, for it meant that we were actualizing and manifesting our former SenZar souls. Yet, it also was not that great at all, and somewhat slightly embarrassing, because I still felt mostly like Christopher Logan, confused mortal musician, and not some otherworldly SenZar hero. So, temporizing, I just made a harsh wolf-face and growled deeply, feeling that "Tat" probably would have done the same thing. And it worked, as my nodding, agreeing companions silently confirmed.

"And now," Sigil said, his monotone filling our ears with honey, "we delve into the deeper secrets of Samantha Teale's past life, when she was Samantha Silverdancer, daughter of Fredrech Silverdagger, the self-styled Thin Man, Master of Assassins."

"Ha!" Sammy giggled, giving Zaar the old "moose-horns-behind-the-head" treatment. "See? She kept *her* name, too!" Then his hand flew to his mouth as he recalled something embarrassing from his *Weird*. "Ooops! Sorry about that, babe," he rapidly apologized to Samantha. "Guess I shoulda kept my thoughts about the Thin Man and his goons to myself."

We would have laughed, but we were already there.

CHAPTER 15: Love, Hate, Love

I ncense.

Clouds of it filled my father's Chamber of Contemplation like a dismal purple fog. It was always like this when father came to think of things. Special things.

I passed between the hanging strings of chrysoberyl that hung from the chamber's mouth, careful not to let my passage stir them. The delicate strands of chrysoberyl beads were like so many gleaming cats' eyes, each reflecting a rivulet of feeble light from the single black candle on the tiny shrine of the Black Wyrm at the far side of the chamber.

Pausing, I regarded the figure of my father, who was known to some, and then only by hushed whispers and conjecture, as the Thin Man.

Not that my father was thin. He was well-proportioned, far taller than average; far more intelligent, too. A Master Artist. His title of Thin Man was merely an ancient label of power, handed down from Master to Master for many an age. And he wore the mantle well.

Deep in meditation, the Thin Man floated in the lotus position a foot above the mandala rug, the perfect axis of its many wheels. His concentration was electrifying his hair, causing the long white braids to float on a pillar of crackling blue energy. He had already been in here for twelve hours, purifying himself for what was to come. Such was his way before commissioning an artist. Whosoever would receive his favor would be highly honored. His many agents—from the blind beggars of the grimy ill-lit backstreets to the noble lords of the brightly polished inner council chambers—would, in fact, duel amongst themselves for the honor. If such were permitted.

Troubled by another dream of the Wolf, I sought the Thin Man's wisdom.

I reached out with my mind as he had taught me long ago, careful to be polite in my inquiry. Although he knew that I was here, it would be very rude, even for his only daughter, to intrude upon his contemplation without some measure of tact.

"*Father?*"

"Yes, Silverdancer?" He spoke over his shoulder, not turning around.

"I dreamed of him again."

The black candle flickered on in silence.

"It was more powerful this time, more vivid than the others. This time I saw his eyes, father," I said, willing him to see what my mind held. The image that I held in my mind of the Wolf was the one that best revealed his searing blue eyes. "They shone with the Power Magick. Blue, haunted; hunted and hunter. This time, father, I saw his blade." I fixed the image of that damning black blade—the Wolf's soul companion, part of him even in the Dreamworld—in my mind's eye and held it, painfully, for my father to see.

Father raised his head at this, then slowly pivoted in midair, turning until he faced me. His ice blue eyes were gentle, reassuring. "And what *was* this blade, Samantha?" he asked, his voice bidding me describe it.

"It was a thing of black, of hatred and... of long-forgotten evil," I responded, willing the image away from my mind. The Wolf's hell blade was frightening even for one of my station. Dealing with such hellish fiends as Mokarr and demons was commonplace. "Yet, I could tell that it was unable to sway the will of the one who bore it.

It *lusted* to possess him—this black hell blade did—but his mind was too strong."

"How strong?"

"When I tried to touch him, father, he looked right at me and growled, like a wolf. Like a wolf, father. Even in my dream, he was formidable, for he *knew* it for what it was—a dream."

Father blinked his eyes, which was something that he rarely did, for it was a sign of indecision. For a flicker of the black candle, he was away in thought, his soul with the wind.

Then: "Do you love him, Samantha?"

What? I thought, astonished. *Love could never abide in the heart of a Silverdancer...*

"No, father!" I hissed, wishing such things as "love" to the Pit, where they truly belonged. "How could I love someone that I've never even met? Hate, yes; for hatred burns with purity! But not love! Never, father, for I do not believe in such petty, pathetic, weak-minded human emotions. Besides, there is no room for such a thing as 'love' in the heart of a Silverdancer."

"*But what stirs within, daughter?*" father asked with his mind.

"*Nothing. How can I know* any *love save for the love of my art?*"

"Then we shall see, daughter," father said, reverting back to the speech of man. "We shall see."

With that, he floated back around to face the brazier. But still did not dismiss me, a sign that he did not believe fully my words. The air in the chamber seemed to stir, currents of blue crackles dancing this way and that as the Thin Man gazed into a place only he could see.

The candle burned for another hour, its black wax spilling over onto the shrine, forming an elaborate pattern of still thought. I stood as father had taught me: empty, but aware. What could a mere human hold for a daughter of the Sidhe? Was not my mother of the blood of the Sidhe? Did not her spirit burn within me?

But did not my father win her heart, and was not he then yet a mortal? I was not quite so empty as I wished to be.

At last, my father spoke, his back to me: "Daughter, it has been decided. You will ride the night. You will seek out this *wolf*, as you name him, and you will paint him a canvas of black. Then, with great care, you will bring me his black blade. Go, and do not return until your masterpiece is complete."

Candle extinguished, the chamber grew dark with my heart.

?

Zengara, the Forever City, was torpid in the heat of the Midsummer night. The backways of Thieves' Quarters, though, were thriving despite the steamy, sticky breeze which blew in from the polluted harbor. The maggot men and their worms were engrossed in treachery, prostitution, and deceit, their bland fare for the night. Every black pleasure was for sale to the highest bidder. Every disease had its price, paid for in coin or blood. They were sheep, led to the slaughter by nameless black shepherds. Crawling or slithering through the muck and mud of the last torrential thunderstorm, they meandered on, faceless and pathetic.

Humans! Their brief lives were less than the wax of my father's black candle, melting away into slag, into the Void.

Among the gargoyles high atop the fire-condemned Bright Temple of Rel (an ironic name, considering it was now neither bright nor a temple), I watched with disdain as my quarry approached *The Guppy*, that dismal boil of a bar, striding as if he were the Overlord himself. The wolfpack which he led was mildly interesting in its diversity, composed of a mightily thewed, half-naked Azaar and his passenger—a bellowing, drunken midget riding upon his broad blue shoulders. The latter drew my attention immediately. He was a crafty little man by the unlikely name of Mad Sam Sprunge, an insane little renegade rogue who presumed to operate outside of father's influence.

Excellent. An added attraction at this Feast of Fools.

Obnoxious and uncaring, they entered *The Guppy*, the big blue Azaar shouldering aside those who gawked too long. A glance overhead to the Lovers' Moons—the humans' pathetic appellation for those two dead rocks of the firmament—confirmed that midnight had long ago passed. More than ample time for my composition to reach fruition.

The *artiste* attended her tools of the trade: Silver vials which contained many nasty alchemical tricks were in place in garter-bandolier. Obsidium stilettos were secured in Mokarr-crafted black leather boots, both boots and blades mystically enchanted to total silence. Silver belt held collapsible grappling hook, lockpicks, and a long, unbreakable chord of witch's hair. Silver crescent moon pendant was in place, to ward off any ill-magick. Skin-tight armor of black moonlight was secure, as soft as silk yet nearly as durable as Khazak-forged silversteel. And, finally, there was my katana, the Soulsword: three feet of Soulforged tears—tears of betrayal—curved like the crescent moon itself. As unbreakable and as unbroken as she who would bear it. The Soulsword was the brush with which I painted my master works. Tonight it would paint in soul's blood.

Death stalked this night, a dance of doom.

From the shadows of Newt Alley I made entrance into *The Guppy*, my place of calling, a padlocked cellar door pathetically easy to pick. After dancing over the tripwire at the foot of the stairs, I stood still—empty, but aware. No one near, save the rats, my Sidhe senses informed me.

The dark, smelly wine cellar was easy to pick through, its ill-conceived tricks and traps no match for one who had been taught by Silverdagger himself. In a trice, I stood before the stairs, ready to ascend, to corner the Wolf in his own lair.

At once, light and sound flooded the room, and I became one with the shadows beneath the stairs. A young barmaid plodded gracelessly down the rickety stairs with a rusty old lantern in one hand, and her nose in the other. The reek was too much for one of her "refined" upbringing. Pausing before a large hogshead at the foot of the stairs, the ignorant little sow held the lantern up to her face, which I could see was young, yet hard. She then pretended to read the "Bor's Mead" emblem on the barrel. Snorting to herself, the barmaid called out loudly to some distant companion that, yes, there yet remained another barrel of mead; that, yes, it looked to be a bit too heavy to move without help; that, yes, she really hated such dark creepy places filled with rats; and that, yes, she was coming right back up to the kitchen at once before the vermin spirited her away. Then, she took the creaky, rotten stairs whence she came one at a time, moving like some crass parody of bipedal swine. Passing within an inch of her grave, she walked on by me, ignorant of Fate's taloned hand, muttering some more banalities about the rats. Obviously, she was totally unaware of how subtle a difference in scent truly separated them.

With a silent bound, I was at the top of the stairs and through the door before it lazily closed shut behind her. Cursing the well-lit kitchen, I bypassed the still-babbling barmaid, several slaving cooks, and a small garrison of servants. They all seemed much too concerned with preparing their greasy seafood and keeping their sorry customers satisfied than to bat an eye in my direction. Then, as the noise of the common hall grew nearer, I took to the wide oaken beams which zigzagged a nightmarish path beneath the ceiling of the hall, a veritable Thieves' Highway in miniature.

Safe in the shadows of the poorly lit house of sin, I silently made my way to the common hall of *The Guppy*, where a junction of several man-thick beams made a perfect stand for my observations of the Wolf and his pack.

From here, a mere ten paces from their corner booth, I could easily pick out their conversation. The savage Azaar spoke first as he sharpened his monstrous four-hander with a whetstone, his massacre of Zengaran amusing in its peculiar inflections.

"Say, Sam-Sam, my boy! Why you not happy?"

"I'm just thinking about what we were talking about earlier tonight," the rebel Mad Sam Sprunge said, his voice rising like that of a petulant child's. "You know, turning things around and all that drivel? With our unique... uhh... talents," he giggled, "we could really make a difference in how things are done in this city. We might even win a regency, or at least a *pardon*!" Mad Sam laughed like a slow child at his own joke.

The Wolf flashed a lazy smile at his small companion, then placed his great hell blade on the table in front of him. It was bound by a scabbard of... *black moonlight? How did he get that?*

"You really *are* considering that offer of amnesty, aren't you, Sammy?" He sat back in the booth, a cocky smile on his face as his fingers gently brushed the pommel of his hellish black blade. I made careful note to treat the handling of that dark, baneful thing with the utmost care.

"Well, it's not every day that the Overlord *himself* bothers to put out the feelers for a personal audience to discuss such matters," Mad Sam said as he hefted a tankard of ale to his greedy lips.

"C'mon, Sammy," the Wolf said, "you know Mir Kestral! Don't you smell a rat somewhere? Like maybe..." he paused, his power obvious as he conjured, "...in your cloak?"

With a flourish of his right hand, the Wolf reached into Mad Sam's cloak and produced a small brown dock rat, which he dangled with glee in front of the laughing little half-man.

"Maybe we oughta just run away and join the circus!" Mad Sam tittered, accepting the rat from the Wolf with a look of sheer exhilaration blooming on his face.

"Sure, now!" the Azaar spoke, looking up from his blade. "We got the strong man, the charlatan, and the lil' jester!"

Mad Sam held out the squiggling rat to the face of the Azaar, who immediately wrinkled his broad blue nose in disgust. "Take the lil' thing away, Sammy-boy, before Zaar cook him up with you in the same pot!"

The Azaar—Zaar, I now knew—shook a massive, troll-sized fist at Mad Sam to emphasize his point. Yet the little man did naught but snicker with glee at his gigantic friend's consternation. Surely, the Azaar must have been enchanted in some fashion, not to have pulverized the little villain right on the spot!

Suddenly, before the Azaar could break his charm-trance and slip into the legendary Azaar state of bloodlust (and solve at least *one* of my problems for me), the Wolf reached out and snatched the rat from Mad Sam's twitching hand. Then, quite gently, he placed it on the tabletop, stroking its fur as a huntsman might stroke his faithful hound.

"I'm afraid I couldn't let you do that, Big Blue," the Wolf laughed, the rat preening before the touch of his conjuration-master. "Ol' Fido here is gonna do Tatternorn a favor, then I'm gonna let him go home."

With that, the Wolf—*Tatternorn,* I now knew his name, and with such comes power—leaned forward and whispered something to the rat. The rat eagerly bobbed his head as if in approval, then scurried off beneath the table.

"Cool, Tat!" Mad Sam cheered, craning his neck to follow the hastily scuttling rat. "Really cool! Do you think you could get him to bring us back a couple of tankards of brew?"

The little simpleton was already so sauced that his words were slurring. He certainly needed no more ale tonight. *But so much the better if he did, for ale-dulled reflexes would prove to be his undoing should I choose to add his head to my bounty tonight.*

"Maybe, if you're a good little boy," Tatternorn—the name fit him now, somehow—said as he busied himself with a pouch at his side, which was out of sight beneath the table. His face—lean and powerful with its high cheekbones; etched with the tanned lines of the trail—was a constant study of reflection as he seemed to wrestle with some inner dilemma.

After but a moment or two of relative quiet, the easily distracted Mad Sam pulled out a deck of dog-eared cards and began to cheat himself a game of *Cutthroat*. Zaar kept at his blade sharpening, an occasional perk of his tall ears his only participation in the silent conversation. I began to get the disconcerting feeling that this was going to be too easy an affair, something altogether unworthy of the true talents of the sole daughter of the Thin Man. They acted like novices—even the infamous rebel rogue, Mad Sam Sprunge. Novices or not, they would be dead before the night was out, unaware of who had danced the final dance with them.

Bored with the utter predictability of the occasion, I forced myself to reexamine what I had heard them say, to search it for any exploitable factor.

The offer of amnesty was a total falsehood, of course. Mir Kestral did not forgive and forget. He was tough, yet fair-handed. He would just as readily grant a pardon as carry out an execution, provided that those pardoned immediately compose some spontaneous poetry, art, or music in honor of Zengara, commit themselves to some act of community service for the betterment of public life, or otherwise perform some widely noted act, deed, or quest which exalted the glory of the Forever City. Despite his many eccentricities, or perhaps because of them, the people of the Forever City loved him. That was the sole reason that my father had allowed him to live thus far. The morale of the people must always be at the forefront of any decision made by the Thin Man, with no exceptions.

I was not one to question the motives of my father, who was guided by forces beyond mortal ken in his decisions. Yet something had been gnawing away at my heart since he had given me my commission. It was a feeling of doubt, which had never stirred my heart before, not at any time during my previous, innumerable, commissions. Not until the dreams. Not until the Sight of the Sidhe had spoken its inscrutable wisdom to me in my dreams.

Not until the Wolf. Not until Tatternorn.

Returning my attention to him—*Tatternorn? What's so naggingly familiar about that name?*—I noticed that he held a purple shard cupped in his hands beneath the edge of the table, something which cast an eerie, purple glow on his face. Fascinated at this display of krystallomancy—the only thing that it possibly could be, a purple shard glowing like that—I adjusted my crouch, so as to lean farther forward. I was careful to keep my movements precise, slow, and cloaked in the shadows. As I did, my peripheral vision picked up a small flicker of light which the topmost beam had hidden from me until now.

Not more than two paces away, nestled there on the "V" of the neighboring beam where it joined the ceiling, was a small brown rat, its eyes glowing a soft purple! A cold wave splashed over me as, at that moment, all three of the villains at the table turned their gaze toward me, smiled happily, then waved as one.

Stunned, caught in the act, busted—all of this hit me at once! Distantly, I noted the thrice-cursed rat move away, its head bobbing up and down again in mocking, animal laughter. The blood welling in my brain threatened to burst out of my eyes.

Never before. Never!

Tricked! Tricked by the most lowly magicks! It really pissed me off! How could I ever look father in the eye again?

I was considering a sloppy, all-consuming way of salvaging my dignity—of completing my masterpiece. But the moment before I could curl my numbed fingers around the *Oil of Hellish Fires*

that rested in my garter-bandolier and hurl it down upon the lot of them, Tatternorn, wearing that unforgiving, heart-stabbing smile of his, waved me down to... to *join* them?

The nerve.

He was laughing at me! The... *human bastard!*... was mocking the Sidhe-born daughter of Fredrech Silverdagger, the Thin Man himself! How ignorant was this *human* of how close he and his companions were to true oblivion! The gall of that *human!*

Still.

The germ of a sinister thought entered my mind, a germ which flourished under the mocking, smiling manure-faces of the three soon to be no more fools who stood between me and my greatest masterpiece.

There were always craftier ways of finishing a dance. After all, the chaotic blood of the Sidhe flowed through my veins. And was not my mother a *nymph*?

?

Laughing.

We were actually *laughing*!

I felt Samantha's—*Samantha Silverdancer's?*—head hit my shoulder as she rocked with belly-wrenching, no-holds-barred laughter. Considering this something bigger than a Hallmark Moment, I pulled her toward me and planted one on her, no-holds-barred style. And she met me more than halfway.

"We made it, milady! My Silverdancer," I whispered to her in the lofty, romantic-sounding High Speech of Zengara, the Forever City. For this particular moment, the "common" speech just wouldn't do.

"Silverdancer, huh?" she whispered back in good ol' American English, her nose to my ear. "I kinda like that."

"So next time I look into your eyes, my dear," I asked, "and blue sparks come shooting out of my eyes, what are you going to do?" I gave her a stare, and I felt the power start to trickle out of my eyes in the form of dancing, blue sparks. They danced between us, floating here and there, teasing and tickling our noses. Her telling expression proved beyond any lingering shadow of doubt that such minor league glamours were now no more than a commonplace, easily accepted thing. Now, at long last.

"You'd better hope that we're alone when you do that, love," Silverdancer teased, pulling me closer to her and wrapping a warm thigh over my lap. This close to her, I could just make out the hint of her softly pointed ears hiding beneath her long white hair. I was just beginning to recall the other less noticeable but quite erotic subtle differences in her Sidhe physiognomy, too, and Mr. Libido was just beginning to scream for release.

Just as I was considering how to weasel out of my *Weird* and fulfill about twenty-five years of pent-up former life lust, though, the sudden laughter of my friends brought me back to the here-and-now. Much to my regret, I might add.

She was *absolutely* right about mommy being a nymph.

"So how in the hell did you catch her?" Tal'N asked. Both he and Guthal were casting curious eyes at me, Sammy, and Zaar.

"Was it the rat, or what?" Guthal asked, his cheeks flushed almost to the same color as his beard.

"Well, you know she was as sneaky as sneaky could be, bearding us in our own lair, *The Guppy*," I said, reluctantly breaking away from her grasp. "In that old shadowy hellhole there was no way for us to get a bead on her. Hell, as I remember things, anyone in the place could have had—and probably *did have*—a bead on us! And we owned the damn place!"

"Yeah," Sammy added, grinning as some bizarre, drunken memories flitted by, "lots of respect there. Anyway, you know what kind of hardware she had on us with all of that Mokarr stuff she was wearing, so it was no small wonder how she managed to get as far as she did. That, and her obviously superior Thin Man-trained expertise," he added for brownie points.

Smiling, Sammy looked over at Zaar, who was busy on another bottle of Good-Good. Zaar just shook his head in besotted agreement. Obviously, he remembered everything about that adventure quite well. He just wasn't about to waste any words on it while he was drinking.

"So what about it, you big blue banana?" Tal'N demanded, exasperated. "What did you do—smell her?"

Half a bottle of "Good-Good" later (most of which shot out of his nose), Zaar began to double over in laughter, all four of his arms clutching his sides. Samantha shot Tal'N a nasty glare, then pouted for a second, waiting for me to come to her defense.

Just as she was about to finish her long-awaited masterpiece, I stabbed a finger down at Skurge.

"The goddamn thing *told* me I was being watched! Really!" I added hastily, seeing the stony stares of disbelief. "Skurge pulsed me a good ol' dial tone of warning, something it only did when there were Sidhe—you know, *faeries*—around." I had to shrug my shoulders at Samantha's indignation. In both incarnations, she *hated* to be associated with such saccharin, mindless things as faeries. She hailed of the Fae, of course, but she was Sidhe, not some lowly Tinkerbell faerie. "I learned that little trick when I spent some time out in the woods with Kiril Spellsinger, my old teacher. Sorry, Sigil," I added, suddenly remembering how he loathed Kiril's roguish, none-too-Starin ways.

"Let us all hope that *he* does not appear in *your Weird*, Tatternorn," Sigil said under his breath, his eyes narrowing somewhat.

"So you sent the rat to go take a look while you looked through its eyes, right?" Guthal postulated, ignoring Sigil and looking expectantly over at Sammy. The War of the Big Brains would never end between those two.

"Yep. That's it!" I said merrily, tapping Skurge for emphasis. Instantly, Skurge sent a warning pulse along its frame, like some malignant, idiot watchdog; seeming to warn me that there were faeries all around. "Shut up, you!" I laughed, my friends wondering why I was talking to my sword.

"And when I found out that Daddy Dearest had put out a contract on *me* for 'failing' my mission," Samantha said, snapping me out of my good-humored sword-taunting, "I decided to start a new career path. You guys just happened to be in the right place at the right time."

"More like out of the frying pan and into the fire!" Tal'N exclaimed, rapping his leg in convulsions of delirious laughter.

"Yeah," she added, casting accusing glances around the room, "you guys *really* helped me along the path of righteousness! After daddy retired, I got into more trouble with *you* bozos than I *ever* got into when I was *his* right-hand girl! Thanks a lot. Thanks a whole goddamn million!"

Samantha's voice had only the slightest edge to it, but it was enough. The laughter died away as we remembered how things really happened. It hadn't been all fun and games. It never had been, no matter how much we tried to make it so. Ol' Silverdagger had "retired" all right—but only after he had thought long and hard about what he had almost done to his daughter in his wrath. The fact that the bastard had hassled us into wrecking most of his organization might have had something to do with it. The fact that Silverdancer had held her Soulsword to his throat and threatened to take his soul might have had something to do with it, too.

Eventually, after calling off his vendetta against us, Silverdagger had wished her the best, like the "good" father that he was, had left her a considerable dowry of secret properties, and then had disappeared into anonymity. Or into "forced retirement," as it were. Then Sigil had come along just as we were getting out of control again and sinking into our worldly ways. He had offered us a way out (basically, "join me, or Mir Kestral will *crucify* you!"), then he had linked us up with Tal'N, who had grown tired of his princely wanderlust. Then, as a group of six on a mission for Mir (as it turned out, he and Sigil just "happened" to be dear old chums), we hit a rather nasty part of the Midnight Realm known as "The Dungeons of the Forsaken" (we were searching for a rather nasty Mokarr Sorcerer by the name of Alth Dreg Nor, whom we never found) where we stumbled onto a rather disheveled, definitely imprisoned "Grog" (who had lied about his name to protect his Kaza from the shame of his "failure," I now knew). And this "Grog" decided in his bearded wisdom to hitch a melancholy ride to freedom with the biggest bunch of idiots that he had ever seen. So, of course, "Grog," or "Guthal Dirge" as we later knew him (like *much* later), chose to travel with us to Zengara, probably with the idea to fetch up a merc force to reclaim his empire from the dark clutches of the cruel Kozar Dred.

That never happened, though not for lack of trying. We were constantly sidetracked by "missions" for our new patron, Mir Kestral, who had decided by then that "if you can't crucify 'em, then hire 'em!"

And that's how the Overlord "coined" our name: The Seven Stars.

That's right. We were named after the basic monetary unit of Zengara. A stupid piece of silver, at that! We could've been named "The Seven Samurai," or "The Seven Psychos," or even "The Seven Shitheads From Hell!" But you get the point. Nevermind that the Gospels of Rel spoke of "The Seven Stars" as the avenging angels of the Cause, and Mir was always trying to get on the good side of the Church of Rel. We chose to ignore that obvious connotation, each in his/her own pagan fashion.

And thus, the Seven Stars were born. The Seven Stars: Champions of the Cause; heroes of the world; righters of wrongs and avengers of injustice. And all that other silly stuff.

Suddenly, I had the urge to get back there, to see Zengara, to snag a drink and some greasy seafood at *The Guppy*. To walk the sandy shores of the Sea of Stars. To get really, really, stupidly drunk with my best friends and rescue some poor village from the plundering claws of a ravaging dragon. To have Mir throw some stupid, eccentric party at his palace and parade us around as the heroes of Zengara, showing us off like so many prized Akir draft horses for his fawning retinue of dukes and duchesses.

Well, except for the last part, I was perfectly happy to get back home, wherever and whenever "home" might be. The more I began to remember, the stronger the feeling became. It would only get worse, wouldn't it?

I thought about it. I was eventually going to get homesick no matter which world I was on, right? Talk about bad karma.

Sigil spoke again, his voice showing signs of the strain of the spell that now was drawing to a close. "Now, as the darkness outside gives way to the light, we conclude our voyage. This time, we see through the eyes of Christopher Logan, who was—once upon a time—Tatternorn. And more..."

CHAPTER 16: Most Of This Is Memory Now

My head hurt! There was only so much stuff that would fit into it before it burst. And Father Merrin was always trying his best to see that such would happen.

Or so it seemed. On top of my daily chores, I was studying hard, trying my best to grasp the subtleties of the Starin High Speech before our annual spring pilgrimage to the Grove—the very spot from which Rel had ascended unto the stars two millennia ago—and the Grove was nestled deep in the Krystallmyst Forest, which was as Starin as Starin could be. And this time, I wanted to be able to understand every word they were saying, especially when they were smiling.

It wouldn't have been so difficult except that the Starin had a different word for *everything*! The only thing that drove me, though, was the beauty of their tongue—rooted as it was in sound and music, two of my favorite things. This time I was going to bring my lute.

Looking out my window, I watched the sun begin its rapid winter sunset. The street below was beginning to get crowded, the many laborers winding their ways home, finding some peace of mind in the unseasonably fair winter weather. I had an hour or so before dinner, so I did what any student would do—I took a break.

Replacing the moth-eaten scrolls back into their ivory cases, I stood up from my desk, closed my shutters to keep out most of the noises of the early evening traffic, and stretched my aching back. Then, I plopped down face first onto my cot, eyes shut tight before I landed.

Suddenly—or so it seemed—Father Merrin's thespian baritone wrenched me from my nap, mental feet dragging, back into the world of the aware.

"Awaken, sleepy-head!" Merrin called playfully, tussling my hair with his coarse, callused hands.

"Huh?" was all I could manage as I rolled onto my side, wishing someone would send me back to the fair maidens of my dreams. Not that I had enough time to dream, but that's what I *wanted* to dream about. Oh, cruel puberty.

"You slept through dinner, Tat. Not to mention choir practice," Merrin said as his eyes darted over to my desk, where the scrolls were, of course, looking quite unstudied in their cases. At least my lute wasn't sitting in bed with me, like it had been found many times before. I rubbed my eyes, then swung my feet over the edge of the cot. The floor was cold beneath my bare feet. I didn't remember taking my shoes off.

Merrin seized this moment to seat himself in my chair, scooting it across the floor until he sat directly in front of me. There would be no escape from him. He was going to *quiz* me.

"Well, young lad," he began, his dockworker hands searching the leather apron over his robes for his pipe, "let us find out if your Starin studies have been fruitful. We'll begin with the past tense of the verbs of being. Now, what is the first person, singular?"

"*In sentence shall I use it, O great bear of the woods?*" I asked in decent Starin, the musical language playing tricks with my still-changing voice. Although it was far from flawless in its inflection, it did the trick.

Merrin smiled as he lit his pipe with a gesture of his index finger, a minor manipulation of the Power Magick that I had seen him perform before on numerous occasions. "So you *did* study well, eh?" Merrin chuckled, the tobacco glowing hotly as he puffed it into life. "At least you have the good sense to return the scrolls to their cases when you're through with them. Young Barad down the hall," he smiled, nodding toward the door, "he had the bad sense to leave a copy of 'Sindal's Treatise on Modern Thought' on his desk overnight. Come morning, much to his chagrin, there remained naught but the smallest remainder of the rat-chewed old thing!"

We both laughed at that. Sure, it was a loss to the mission, as scrolls were expensive and we never really had much support from the church. But it was funny in a way, because of whom it happened to. I guess you'd have to know "studious" Barad to appreciate the humor.

"Wait a minute!" I barked, looking over at the shuttered window. Its edges were illuminated with the grey of a new winter storm. I could hear a coach passing by beneath the window, its wheels splashing through mud puddles. "What time *is* it?" I asked, confused.

"Did I forget to mention that we missed you at breakfast, too?" Merrin asked, amusement in his eyes.

"But... it was almost time for dinner, wasn't it?" I rubbed my chin, wondering what could have possessed me to sleep away the night. I couldn't have been *that* tired.

"I see a young lad who's driving himself a bit too hard," Merrin said, his eyes glinting with some inner secret. "And I know why you're putting in the late hours, my lad!" he said, hooking a thumb over his shoulder toward where my lute hung from a peg on the wall. "You're just like I was when I was your age. Always trying to impress the young ladies, pointed ears or not!"

"C'mon Merrin, you know that's a load of horse-stuff!" I replied, indignant because he was right. "I just want to be able to talk to one of those guys in his own tongue. I want to see their weird purple eyes light up when this mortal kid holds his own in a conversation with them. I want to ask them to teach me a song. Is that so wrong?"

"No, of course it isn't, Tat," Merrin deferred, leaning back in the chair. He sat there, his knowledgeable old blue eyes still holding some secret joy, as they always had since I was old enough to remember.

Father Merrin. Father by proxy, more like it. He was the one who had taken me into his fold of young orphans, street waifs, and other such abandoned souls. Here, in the heart of Thieves' Quarters, he ran his little rag-tag mission, financed by the odd donation or two from his squalid flock and a meager yearly stipend from the Church of Rel. Merrin had taken me in as a child and raised me like one of his own. That's how he treated each and every one of his children—like one of his own. We didn't have much, but what we had we earned with the toil of our hearts. Our mission produced some of the finest young artisans to come out of this poor part of our city, and that was quite often their only ticket out of the slime and mud.

I had been here for nine years, taken in when I was roughly five or six. I had to take Merrin's word for it, though. Everything before that was a blank slate. It didn't matter how hard I tried to remember things from before; I just couldn't do it. No knowledge of how I got here; no one recalling my presence in the streets before then. Just a scared looking little boy with the strangest blue eyes. Old eyes. Haunted eyes, as if something had so terrified him that he had shut down rather than shut off.

The closest rationalization along those lines was that the night before I was found, there had been a terrible fire that had burned a large swath of the Garden District to the ground. Several hundred people had been killed before the fire was contained, most of them foreigners and adventurers staying in the many inns that lined the wooded boulevards.

No one ever claimed me. And, over the years, even when the wealthy did come to adopt one of us, I always managed to make myself scarce, or, when cornered, act is if I were slow or touched. Finally, Merrin, comprehending his new burden in life, laid it on the line, telling me to hit the street or face facts and decide upon a future.

I told him that I wanted to grow up to be like him. From then on, we were Father and son.

"Can I get up now, Merrin?" I asked.

"What for?"

"I've got to use the privy, okay?" I said, trying not to laugh at how fast he got up and moved his chair aside.

"Then by all means, go!" he bade me in his deepest pulpit-tones, waving toward the door. "Let it never be said that I was so mean-hearted as to keep my flock from that most sacred of calls!"

With a laugh on my lips, I bounded up, crossed the room, and opened the door. Then, remembering how cold the floor was, I turned around and began to rummage about for my shoes. As I was fighting "that most sacred of calls" and searching the floor desperately for my shoes, which were nowhere in sight, Merrin, laughing, pointed toward the small bench that sat beneath my lute. There, beneath my tattered cloak, the tips of my shoes jutted out, streaked with newly dried, green-flecked mud. Without thinking, I began to pull them on, stumbling around in my hurry, then ran off down the long hallway, pursued by Merrin's jolly laughter.

The day was without incident. The night, however, was an entirely different matter.

Taking Merrin's advice to heart, I was able to wrangle up a pass to take myself and my lute and hit the streets—the public squares and other such places my supposed destination. Normally, I wouldn't have had a snowball's chance in the Pit of going out unescorted at night. But, after some arm-twisting on my part, Merrin, who really thought that the night air might do me some good, gave in and bade me good fortune. He knew that I was going to bring back a handful of coins, so that made things easier. What he didn't know was that, in addition to my lute, I had taken along my knife, hiding it in a crisscrossed strap of soft leather that I had stitched into the lining of my cloak. It was within easy reach, should things get a little too rough at the taverns—my true, truant destination.

With a jolly fare-thee-well to Merrin and a flourish of my cloak, I was out the bleak wooden door of the mission and well on my way to fame and fortune, those two elusive prostitutes of the ego. The cobbles of Market Street were slick with the accumulated mud and slime of the day's storm. A lot of the faces of the street that I knew were absent from their normal haunts, content to stay at home, warming themselves before whatever feeble flame they could manage. I realized that was the reason why so many fires were started here in the poorest part of the city. It also made me wonder how that all-important fire started way back when, the one that might have taken my parents from me.

A passing coachman, his team of nags restless, called out a hearty "Make way!" His ramshackle black buggy slid through a slippery corner and around the way, sparks shooting from the iron-shod wheels as it scrubbed the curb. I stopped and stared as shutters flew open a few seconds behind the coach's passage; grouchy shouts, curses, and fingers an ill-conducted choir of discontent. Typical.

For the next few blocks, though, I walked with eyes peeled for wild coachmen.

Pausing on a curb to adjust my lute's strap—I wasn't really used to slinging it over my shoulder like that—I suddenly noticed a peculiar thing that struck me at once as being both fantastic and absurd. There, walking on the other side of street, was a tall, raven-tressed beauty with... *with pointed ears!*... who was flowing her way through the pedestrians as if they were moving under the sea. I stood, jaw agape, as she paused a moment at the intersection, then, with a swift upward glance and a sweep of her soft grey cloak, took a left onto Western Way and darted off like a flushed doe.

"Shit!" I exclaimed, startling a passing lady of the evening, who looked at me like I was horse-stuff or something worse. Having no time to offer an apology, I started off at once after the mystery woman with the pointed ears and raven tresses without so much as a thought as to what I was doing. The only thing that mattered to me was getting a chance to talk to her, or play her a song. Hell, a second glance would do me just fine. The thrill of my fanciful chase would at least get the juices flowing for the later evening, should I not catch another glimpse of her.

As I ran along, dodging people and puddles alike, trying my youthful best to keep her in sight, I could hear Merrin's secret laughter rolling around inside my head. He was right and I knew it. So what if I was being foolish, trying to follow and impress a woman who was probably older than Merrin? At least I was having a good time while I could.

After eight breathless blocks of jogging along behind her, I realized that I wasn't going to catch up to her unless I poured it on. The fact that she was heading toward the wicked heart of Thieves' Quarters did little to dissuade me. Here, in the still of the night, not even the Overlord's guards dared go. Here, the rules were different from the rest of the city. Here, the sharks ate the little fish, and the scum-suckers cleaned up the rest.

Much to my relief, she broke her league-consuming stride but several blocks later. She came at last to a halt before an abandoned, fire-gutted warehouse which seemed in danger of immediate collapse, so blackened were its stones. I stopped in my tracks a half-block behind her, sucking in cold, lung-searing gulps of smelly air to get my breath back. Remembering what I had heard of the Starin's acute senses, I ducked into the shadow of the building in front of me, willing my rasping lungs to silence. She hadn't looked back the entire time that I had been following her, but I had the nagging feeling that she might have had eyes in the back of her head. After all, idiot that I was, I had dogged her the entire way, not even considering stealth.

As I berated myself, she walked up to the front of the burnt-out warehouse, glanced up at the sky, then melted into the shadows of the far side of the building. Not wanting to lose sight of her for long, I jogged up to the far side of the warehouse, eager for any sign of her. There was none.

In front of me there was a narrow, misty alley, which ran the full length of the warehouse and came out some one hundred feet later on the next street. Rubbish was stacked knee-high along the side nearest the warehouse, coming to a four foot tall peak about a third of the way down. Snake-shaped puddles settled along the opposite wall, brackish water reflecting the dim streetlight. My mind raced back to what I had been learning about the Starin. They could do this kind of disappearing act at will in their native woods, the very elements bending to their will. But in an *alley*?

Suddenly, I didn't very much like the rules of this game.

"*Hello?*" I said softly in my best Starin, discretion getting the better of me. I could always explain my lunacy, I hoped.

Nothing. *Shit.*

I stood poised on a razor of indecision. *Oh well,* I reasoned, stepping into the alley, *at least I can see the other side.*

Stepping clear of the puddles, I walked slowly on through the misty alley, an eye on the piles of rubbish. I was ready to bolt should some bony, rotting hand erupt from within. Nearing the peak of the trash, I noticed a glint of metal behind the pile where it leaned against the wall. Drawing closer, I saw the clear outline of a rust-eaten steel door, one which could not have been more than three feet in height. This demanded attention. A three foot high door, bound with steel, was more than unusual here in the squalor of the Quarter, where even rusty steel commanded a premium that few could

afford. And highly unusual again considering the fact that most folks were considerably more than

three feet tall.

Curiosity had me in its steel vice. Detecting no other signs of life in the alley, I began to shift aside the debris, lowering what I could gently to the ground. Wiping the grime off on my cloak, I studied the rusty door. There appeared to be a fine tracing under the film of the rust, but in the dim light, I could make out little of its detail. Much to my delight, there was no padlock, nor keyhole, for that matter. Just a rusty old steel door set flush into a charred old stone wall.

I fished out my knife and gave the door an exploratory prodding. It sounded solid enough, giving a dull response to my tapping. I traced the outline, scraping my blade along the stone. There wasn't so much as an eyelash of a crack between them, which was beginning to undermine the door theory. *Then how?*

I considered things: Had the Starin maiden somehow been able to gain entrance in those few seconds that she was out of sight? Or had she simply pulled a fast one and bolted away without my seeing it? I was sure that, if pressed, she could have gotten away unseen and unknown if we would have been locked together in the same room. Hitting that inevitable wall of frustration, I shrugged off any more notions of stalking a Starin, sheathed my knife, then turned around and walked out of the alley the same way I had come in.

If it wouldn't have been for my dejected mood, I would have never seen it. Head bowed, I was walking down the street, heading back toward more familiar territory, when I saw it. There, on the tips of my shoes, was a fresh layer of glistening green slime. I took another three steps, each one slower than the one before, until I had ground to a halt there in the middle of the street.

Mysterious sleeping spells. No dreams. Weird, because, up until recently, I always had dreams. Shoes flying off in my sleep, winding up covered in goo. And now this grimy green slime all over my shoes (again!), except this time I was awake! It had to be more than a coincidence that tonight, out of the blue, Madame Mystery Starin leads me on a wild goose chase to a mystery door in a burnt warehouse.

Pieces of a grand puzzle, one which I was only beginning to put together.

The breeze picked up slightly, whipping my cloak against my legs. The street was unusually quiet. There were no normal sounds of the night, no distant voices, or rumbles of carriages. Suddenly, I felt very alone, here in the midst of buildings, standing in the middle of the street.

"I don't like this," I whispered to myself. Imagination running amok, my skin began to crawl, all the way down to the small of my back, as I suddenly felt a presence stirring behind me.

Then, every bad dream I ever had reared its head and screamed as I heard the Voice: "Turn and face me, Star-Eyes!" the Voice declared in sharply accented Zengaran, aging my very soul to hear.

Shutting my eyes tight, I turned slowly, ever so slowly around, not wanting to face the source of that hollow voice. Despite my best effort not to do so, my eyes flickered open, revealing a mind-numbing sight.

On a carpet of green mist she stood, resplendent in her jet-black, form-revealing leathers. Her right arm was raised in front of her, guiding the edges of the mist toward my feet like Rel's divine parting of the waters. Her hair was wild, her face, circumspect. Both were as inky black as her leathers. Her sepia eyes held the promise of something to come—something I instinctively knew I didn't particularly want to be a part of. She was no longer Starin, not by the farthest stretch of the imagination. She was of the blood of the Dark

Ones. She was Mokarr, the Spawn of the Dark Earth, of that I had no doubt.

For some reason beyond my ken, though, I was no longer afraid.

"What do you seek, Mokarr?" I asked boldly, my voice deeper than it should have been. Something about this was familiar to me, like the preamble of some arcane ritual. But I couldn't put my finger on it.

"Your other side is in ascendance tonight," she stated flatly. "That is good. You will need every ounce of your strength tonight, Lost One, for this night is the third and final night for you to prove your soul before the Void."

She lost me with that one.

"What do you mean, Mokarr?" I asked, my voice still, for some unknown reason to me, rich and strong.

"Do you not recall your previous failures? You play your game well, Lost One," she said, her softly slanted eyes finally blinking.

"Why do you name me thus?"

"You are He."

"He *who*?"

"He Who Was Lost."

"Okay, supposing I am?" I asked, my senses nearly in control of my voice once more. I actually had to *think* of what to say, though, as if someone else were using my voice to talk. "What do you wanna do about it?" My voice still sounded funny, as hard as I was concentrating, like someone else was talking through me.

"Complete the pact," she replied, her eyes calculating and suddenly dangerous. "Our pact, Tatternorn."

I felt hollow inside despite my newfound voice trick. *Tatternorn? My name is* Tat!

"I don't want to," I said, a crazed idea in my head. "So why don't you crawl back to where you came from like a good Mokarr, and give my best to Ol' Eighteyes!" With that, I turned around and ran like a fiend possessed, lute banging like a paddle on my rear.

I got about half a block before she materialized in front of me. She blocked my path, her arms outstretched like a menacing black widow. I considered trying to dodge her, but thought better of it considering her Mokarr reflexes. I lowered my shoulder and tried to bull right over her, trusting my adolescent human mass to cancel her lighter, more fragile Mokarr mass.

She smiled, her face a serene mask. Sidestepping at the last possible moment, she caught my right arm with a snake-swift, gripping hand and, with a twist of her arm, flipped me in midair, entirely checking my momentum. The cold street met my back, kicking the breath out of me as a numb sensation spread down my ribcage. As I struggled to catch my breath, she suddenly appeared above me, hovering over me like a black raven. With a swift, fluid movement, she straddled my chest, her hands pinning my shoulders to the street. She was smaller, lighter, less muscled than I, yet she held me fast, as if I were a child. I tried to kick out, using a move that Merrin had taught me from his sailor's days, but she just smiled tightly and applied a terrific pressure to my shoulders.

"Do not force me to hurt you, my prize," she whispered through clenched teeth, her breath a pleasing, seductive heat on my face. Sensing that she would carry out her threat, I stopped my bucking, much to the relief of my shoulders.

But that's when she started *hers*. Slowly, she moved herself down my frame, still pinning me down. She paused a moment as her thighs brushed mine. Then, she began to grind. It was slow at first, a teasing, glancing touch with her thighs on mine. Then, her gyrations grew in intensity and quickly fixed themselves upon my nether regions. This stirred in me the mixed-up feeling that although this felt *really* good, that it was, in reality, something far more deadly and dangerous than I could *ever* imagine.

"Do you remember me, my lord?" she asked as her thighs tightened around my waist. She then bent down and stroked my eyebrows with her molten tongue, drowning me in the scent of musky, mind-consuming... femaleness? I had never been this far before, not even with those pretty, painted women who strutted their stuff at the pubs. Close, but not *this* close!

"I wish I *could*!" I whispered, wishing that I were someone else who could *willingly* sleep with a Mokarr woman. Someone who wasn't scared to death of dying at the hands of a manhood-devouring demon-sorceress.

"Ahh, but you *shall*, my lord!" she whispered through clenched fangs, pushing me down hard to the street with her vast, uncanny strength. She began to pound my groin with hers. Staring—since there wasn't much else I could do, considering her position on my groin—I noted a hauntingly familiar mark curling from the outer edge of her left eyelid. It was the mark of one of the Dark: a finger's breadth of flowing, curving lines that formed the darker-than-dark image of Ol' Eighteyes himself—Ohmm, the Mokarr's foul spider-god. Eyes roving, I noted that deep within her sepia eyes there were blue sparks dancing around, flitting back and forth across her iris. Familiar blue sparks.

And I saw:

Waves of another self washed over me, drowning me in long-forgotten Time. My body was on the street, pinned under her lithe form. But my mind was some*when* else, flying along alien corridors of consciousness, racing headlong into madness. I was displaced, lost somewhere in Time.

Vertigo. Twisting, turning into the Void.

I am Skurge.

I am a god, worshipped by those of the Dark, an age before the rise of the puny Rel and his mindless minions! The glories of the Fourth Age are mine once more! From the black spires of the

Four Towers, we rule the world, rainbows in our eyes. We are the Shadar—the first-spawned of Chthon herself, masters of the world—and there are none to oppose us in our ways.

I am Skurge... Hate/Pain/Death-Brother!

The towers stand in black fire, spires aglow with damned souls' light. A thousand years of the Void; the Age of the Screaming Skulls. The taste of flesh; the stench of the blasted bodies stacked like cordwood about the base of the Four Towers. The dark brightness of the invisible sun; the Void Moon flaring in ultraviolet, searing the eyes of those who behold. The Weirding, its darkling wonders, and its Nine Evils. The Forever-Silence of the Void!

I am Death incarnate!

The Voice, in tongue of Death: "Do you see?"

Yes, I snarl. *I see everything.*

"Do you comprehend your current state?"

I am a god, and you are my slave, Mokarr.

"No. That I am no longer, Dark One. That is the past."

I hate, therefore I am.

"Yes. And hate is what makes you strong, my lord. Stronger even than death."

What is this place?

"You are in the city of Zengara, beneath the shadow of the South Tower, Dark One. The Seventh Age is upon us."

Silence.

I am yet a god.

"No. You are a shadow in the Void. And I have brought you forth from its Forever-Silent grasp in order to task you, Dark One, in the Pact of the Impossible Blade!"

You have no such power, whore!

Electric rage tingles... anticipation?

"Perhaps not, yet this boy does. For he is of the Bane of the Shadar. His power is the Stuff of Dreams. He is *Anshadar!*"

Electric shock, black fury. Black eyes on heart, piercing.

He is not yet realized, whore. His soul may yet be claimed.

"That is truth, but not *your* truth, Dark One. Not yet. Still your eternal hate, Dark One, and hear me out: I hold the key to your cell. I hold it for a price. Heed my words, Dark One, for they are potent in this place."

Lights, dark dancing. Nausea, vertigo, assault me as space is bent and time is stilled. Cold cobbles yield to colder steel. Ant dance on spine, static in air. Weightless floating, spinning in Void. Dark portal in burning, brilliant green.

Three moons shine, idiot stares from beyond.

"I have spirited the boy—your essence's focus—unto the Chamber of the Void. Do you know this place, Dark One?"

Yes. From within, I ruled my quarter of this sphere.

"Shared between you and your brothers, correct?"

Yes. My brothers.

"Skayth, Skythe, and Skurge! The brothers three, sharing one-fourth of SenZar between them. Do you remember them?"

Yes.

"And do you remember He who conquered these mortals, crushing all before him? Do you remember He who divided the lands of the world amongst his dark progeny? Do you remember He who was *your* lord?"

Fear, a reverence of hate.

Valthrustra.

Heknowsheknowsheknows...

"Yes, Valthrustra, the Deathlord! For His glory we all shall die! Does this not stir your immortal soul, Dark One? Do you not know His call when He beckons from beyond the Veil, beyond the Void, where He was banished these long ages past by the forces of the Light? Do you not know His hand when it guides you? Do you not feel His hate?"

Open door, yawning abyss. Dark Hate Lord. Death Kiss.

Yesss... Command me in Thy task, my lord! Command me to die, and in so dying, bind! Skurge awaits with thoughts black—to seek, to hunt, to slay, to hate!

Pride, Rel's fiery plunge from the stars.

"Then I bind thee, Skurge, as was bound the Word, when the stillborn of the Void were cast down unto this darkness, down from the stars, unto these Towers black! With my sacrifice, with my soul's own blood, with the seed and with the soul of this Anshadar, I seal the Pact of the Impossible Blade! The Key to the Void, which shall birth again the Deathlord, such that He may reign once more in His Undying Hatred!"

Primal scream, exploding pain. A green hell of pain. Giving birth to a cancer, a parasite. Immaculate deception. Hate by example. Death by Shadar steel. Soul rape.

My screams fused with the Mokarr woman's, obliterating the thick, murky tethers of thought which had held me in thrall. In my hands—held white-knuckled in my fearful, uncomprehending grasp—was a black blade, silently promising Hate and Pain. A bastard in more than form and function. Its triple rows of blade-spanning purple-green runes were buried deep within the bare, still-heaving breast of the Mokarr. Her black blood sizzled where it ran down the length of the seething Shadar steel. Her once-sepia eyes were white; her soul, extinguished, in satisfaction of the Pact of the Impossible Blade. Her body, once lithe and comely but now naked and shriveled up horribly like the form of some desiccated mummy, contorted into a grim caricature of her former exotic beauty.

Resolved unto the silence of fear, I watched as the blasted corpse fell from the blade to the floor of
this darkened tower, where it crumbled into dancing, dark dust. Eyes wide, I once more watched mutely as the black sword turned in

my grasp, turned until the center of the tracings along the blade was facing me.

A loathsome, hateful *Mindtouch*: *At last... The Dragon's Game begins anew!*

My hands felt as if they were going to catch on fire, such was Skurge's power! I tried to let go of it, to hurl it away, but I could no more control my own actions than I could this blade. I looked around, ignoring my nakedness and the throbbing in my midsection, searching for some way to get out of this foul place. The chamber was monstrous; black and twisted in its ancient, alien architecture. The ceiling was like that of a cathedral, spiraling upwards to a single intersection of gnarled, twisted Shadar steel girders. A single, open skylight about thirty feet above my head revealed what I had seen earlier in my... *possession*. I was in the top of the South Tower. The two... *lovers'...* moons were out. The sky, clear. But the light from the moons was somehow *wrong*. The third moon I had earlier caught a fleeting glance of abruptly rose from behind the moons, now in conjunction, shining in hateful ultraviolet light.

It was the Void Moon!

With my own mortal eyes I could see it plainly revealed for the hateful thing that it was! I could *feel* its baleful glare! It was as if some invisible, draining hand were passing between the sky and my eyes, clutching at my very soul! It... it was *looking* at me! They all were looking at me! The stars were looking at me! Those eyes, within the stars, staring at me! Who—

"TATTERNORN..."

The Dragon itself speaks my name! All That All Which Is, All That All Which Binds! It knows my name! It... it has always known my name.

I have always known my name.

CHAPTER 17: I Remember Now

Silence. Bitter, biting absence of decibel influence.

Then: "I remember now," I whispered, more to myself than anyone else.

I *did* remember. The scents, the smells, the pangs of victory and defeat. That awesome epiphany of being, I now understood. Until I had met *myself*, I had no idea of the emptiness of my soul.

The things that were me were mine once more.

Tatternorn: Spellsinger, Bard, Nomad, and Wanderer; cursed living embodiment of the Pact of the Impossible Blade; forever searching for that missing piece of being, that quintessence of knowledge.

Power was mine once more—the Power Magick—the power to make a difference in this world. Magick was my voice; my voice, magick. The gift of tongues, the gift of melancholy. I was a more than capable warrior, at ease with more than sword and bow. My friends had seen to that. And while I could never hope to attain the level of combat perfection that Tal'N or Silverdancer had attained, I had both my spellsinging and the unholy power of Skurge to back me up. With Mad Sam Sprunge and Rhiannazaar I had taught the noble lords of Zengara to fear the shadows of the night. With the Seven Stars I had made a difference for the world, ostensibly serving the Cause—that ancient code of heroes. And although at first we had served only ourselves, in time that sterling code became our own as we found our true calling.

We had become more than thieves, assassins, princely heirs, and outcasts. We had risen above the plane of aspiring musicians, soldiers, and engineers. We were the Seven Stars, once again, now and forever.

God help us all.

"So what happened to you after that, man?" Tal'N asked me. "Reality" glared suddenly, hatefully, back to life. "I mean, how did you, a kid, get out of that damned South Tower?"

"Ask *him*," I said, nodding toward Sigil, who allowed himself a slight, tired grin. *The Weird* had taken a lot out of him. Now that I had some idea of the power level, or Order, of that spell—not to mention the balance of his performance earlier tonight—I had a deeper comprehension of what "Archimage" truly meant. And it wasn't just H-bombs and A-bombs, either. For every secret charm and magick spell that your typical "high level" wizard was supposed to know—and they were, as rule, supposed to know a whole *helluva* lot of them—Sigil Talisman, the Archimage of Krystallmyst, knew *at least* ten more. Considering that the histories of SenZar mention him as far back as the histories go—some seven "Ages," or some seven thousand or so years removed, relatively speaking—you get an idea of the time with which he's had to learn things. And some small idea as to the amount of time with which he's had to spin his little Dragon-serving webs of deceit, too.

Tal'N gave Sigil an inquisitive stare. "Well?"

"Suffice to say, I felt the gross disturbance of the balance of power that the Mokarr woman's magicks caused," Sigil said as he took a small white cloth from one of his robe's sleeves and dabbed the perspiration from his face, "and I immediately sought out the nature of this blasphemy of good will. From the Krystallkeep I made my way to Zengara, where I came upon young Tat in the South

Tower. Poor Tat was near to the point of madness. Skurge was...
cruel to him. Calming the frightened youth, I bade him reach within
himself and fight Skurge's influence, to cast off the yoke of that
Shadar fiend. Much to my joy, he did, and he forced the weakened
spirit of Skurge into submission."

"You helped me, Sigil," I admitted, wondering why my vision was
suddenly, steadily growing blurry. "There was no way that I was going
to mentally outduel that thing *there*, in its place of power!" I had to
stop myself from wondering aloud if they had somehow managed to
forget to mention the fact that Tatternorn must have had cataracts.

"I only helped you realize your own reserve of magick power,
Tatternorn," Sigil replied, "which, until that moment in time, had
only begun to be tapped. *You* were the one to fight that fight, not I."

"Why didn't you just kill me then and there, Sigil?" I asked him
as I began to rub my aching eyes. "As long as I lived, connected with
that blade, Lord Valthrustra and his Shadar Loons were free to roam!
Maybe you could have saved the world a whole lot of grief if you
would have just stopped it before it started."

"How did Samuel's Vulcan interpretation of me put it?" Sigil
retorted, one of his eyebrows arched high above his eye. "*The needs
of the many outweigh the needs of the few, or the one...* These were his
words, were they not?"

"Then, logically, you should have offed him right then and
there!" Sammy the Trekkie shouted, triumphantly, his finger
wagging at Sigil. "Tat was *the one*, and we were *the many*, right?"

Hiding his head in his craggy hands, Guthal began to moan in
disbelief. I think he knew what was coming.

"No," Sigil said, shaking his head, "you were *the few*, Samuel. The
souls of the world—the souls of all of the infinite worlds—were *the
many*. I could no more murder him than murder the world. There
was no guarantee that the Shadar would return from the Void, even
if the Pact of the Impossible Blade *were* enforced. I would not have

the blood of an innocent youth on my conscience merely for the sake of possibility."

Sigil got a few disbelieving smirks from that one.

"Moreover," he continued, ignoring our bad attitudes, "I sensed that *something* had been put into motion, catalyzed by this turn of events. There was every indication that great good could come of this blasphemy, if such could be wrested from fate. You might say that this one event more than any other set the course for the Seven Stars to come together. And, despite the fact that the Shadar *were* eventually set free, we certainly changed the course of events of the world for the better. Together,

we made a difference that may have, even now, changed SenZar for the better."

"Or for the worse!" I exclaimed, still battling with my bleary eyes.

"Yo, mon," Zaar said, his four arms waving animatedly, "how do we know *what* happened while we were dead? You gambled with our souls!"

"So we were scapegoats the whole time, huh?" Sammy leered, his face a near-perfect imitation of Jack Nicholson's Joker.

"We have had this discussion before," Sigil said, his eyes roving us. "And, as before, I must say that we follow the dictates of our own hearts. No force compels you to act as you do. Each one of you follows his own higher calling. It is that simple in its complexity. Nothing more, nothing less."

"*Sure* it is!" Guthal spat.

"Why don't you get off your high horse and say it like a man, Sigil?" Tal'N urged. "Just give us your Dragon-dictated orders and spare us the sympathy. We don't have to like *it*, or *you*. We just have to do what we do best: kill in the name of the Cause!"

Looking over at Tal'N, who now was a golden blur to me, I had the feeling that he may have said the same thing before. Perhaps to some higher-up in the Navy while he was Michael Reese, or to some instructor in the Shy'R Warhall while he was a budding Shy'R Warrior, with perhaps the same conviction. Sigil, whose form flickered and grew vague, sat there and took it on the chin. Not like a

man at all, but like the Starin that he was—in total control of his emotions.

"Shit!" I cursed myself for the fool that I was. My contacts! Something so damned *obvious* that I had forgotten completely about it. They must have dried out without my realizing it, causing my eyesight to blur as if I had gone snowblind. Hastily, I started to get to my feet so that I could change them before they could glue my eyes shut.

Then, without warning, Sigil spoke: "You do not need to change them," he said, his voice connected to a blurry, purple-tinged form. I stopped my question before I could get it past my twice-dumb lips, remembering Sigil's supernatural perception. He smiled in acknowledgment. I think. "As Guthal Dirge no longer needs the corrective lenses of David Miller, thus does Tatternorn no longer need the contact lenses of Christopher Logan," Sigil pronounced most profoundly to a chorus of stifled giggles.

"Hey, Sigil," Sammy noted impishly, "you sound just like Leonard Nimoy narrating an episode of *In Search Of...*"

That did the trick. The room temperature fell from "boil" to "simmer," thanks to Sammy's irreverent jest. I mean, to insult Leonard Nimoy like *that* was terrible!

Never one to look the proverbial gift-equus in the maw, though, I seized the opportunity to fish out my now useless contacts and flick the hateful little eye-damagers over my shoulder and onto the floor, where I'd never have to endure them again.

"So now what in the hell do we do?" I asked, overjoyed to see the world in natural 20/20 again for the first time in many years. Cool.

"We get the hell out of Dodge and go to the Bahamas," Sammy jeered, much to Zaar's delight.

"Screw that, you little shit!" Tal'N argued, looking at Sammy as if he were a total asshole. "We stick it all the way up Valthrustra's big black Shadar ass before he wrecks this world like he did SenZar!"

"You think I don't know that, Tal'N?" Sammy whined, returning his hard stare. "Don't think for a minute, buddy, that I'm not gonna whip his ass good for what he did to us back on SenZar!"

"Not to mention here on Earth, man," Guthal added grimly. "He just waltzed on into our lives and shit all over us, in case you've forgotten. I mean, don't you think it's gonna be little more than difficult to explain this transformation to our friends?"

"Or to our families?" Samantha added. "Or to mom and dad?"

She looked at me, a pained expression on her face. Her face spoke a thousand words of loss. She didn't have to say another word, for everyone in the room felt it together: the pain of death, the agony of rebirth, the loss of something more precious than life itself.

Now, we were dead. To our loved ones both here on Earth and back on SenZar we were no more. We were shadows now, quested to perform in silence our noble/ignoble deeds. From the looks on my friends' faces, I realized that they, too, comprehended the gravity of our unique situation. And it was hitting them just as hard as it was hitting me.

"Yes," Sigil explained gravely, his words hammering into our souls, "things will never be the same. They *cannot* be. You have broken through the Dream Barrier. You have culled life from death. And more. Neither your SenZar-selves nor your Earth-selves exist as before. They have now been permanently synthesized into a greater whole; a new, unique entirety of being. And with such a transformation comes a new order of being, one of power. And that power is the Power Magick of the *Anshadar*, and it is the Stuff of Dreams!"

Silence filled the room, punctuated only by the occasional sound of the soft drizzle of rain outside, as each of us considered the implications of Sigil's soul-numbing soliloquy.

"Sigil," I began, measuring my words as I worked on his logic, "death is a difficult concept to accept, let alone comprehend—*even if one has experienced it firsthand*. What you have said, or what your logic dictates, is that all of our former bets are off because we have seen the Reaper and called him Grim. And now, like Christ reborn on the third day, we become something greater than ever before, something with the power of a demigod? Anshadar? Get real, Sigil!" I accused, my temper growing as that final cobweb of memory snapped. "You know as well as I do that Anshadar are *made*, not *born*!"

Nodding his head slowly, Sigil granted me the confirmation that I had been seeking for two lifetimes. The sparkle in his slanted eyes named him for the Master Schemer that he truly was. The smug bastard had known all along what he was doing when he had led us into Lord Valthrustra's black lair. He *knew* what the stakes were, back on SenZar. He had known them since that night of mental damnation and soul rape in the South Tower when that Mokarr bitch had set the cosmic wheel in motion once more: the Great Wheel of Fate, which dictated that no Shadar could exist without a balance of Anshadar to counter them. And he had known *exactly* what he was doing when he had rescued me on that long ago night. He had known *exactly* what he was doing when he had bound us all together under the banner of the Seven Stars. He had known *exactly* what he was doing when he had led us like sheep to the slaughter in Lord Valthrustra's domain. He had even known *exactly* how to interfere with Lord Valthrustra's casting of *The Dragon's Breath*, in order for us to break through the Dream Barrier and, if the gods were willing, damn us into another life on another world. All so that we could one day have that *too* ripped from us as we transformed from the chrysalis of human existence into "The Stuff of Dreams."

Dreams. Hell. More like nightmares.

"You cold, calculating bastard," I said to Sigil as I comprehended his mad handiwork. Apparently, I was the first one to reach the correct conclusion, for my companions looked at me as if had gone daft. They soon *would* reach it, though, I promised myself.

"I see that you realize the cup from which you drink, Tatternorn," Sigil said, still staring at me and nodding his head. In his ineffably Starin way he was asking me for my acceptance, for me to tell him that everything was all peachy-keen and cool now. Silly Starin.

"Then, Abba, O Father, let this cup pass from me, 'cause it leaves a fucking *bitter* taste in my mouth!" I rolled the *Kirschwasser* bottle across the floor toward Sigil, staining the floor with the thick, syrupy cherry brandy. The bottle came to a rest in front of him, clinking to a halt against his crossed legs. For a long moment, Sigil looked down at the bottle of cherry brandy, a sad look etched upon his somber features. Then he reached down, picked up the bottle and held it before him in his long hands, studying it carefully.

"Pasternak," he whispered softly, his eyes far away. "How subtle," he said mysteriously before setting the bottle down before him, this time upright. "As well you know, Tatternorn, the Christians believe that Jesus had no choice but to obey the will of His father. His fate was predestined, ordained before Time itself, set down by the Higher Power as a player in the mysterious Passion Play of Jehovah. He had no choice. But *you* do." Sigil spoke calmly, explaining The Word as if he were a teacher explaining to a truant that it was wrong to skip class.

"Spare us the Calvinist argument and its abrogation of free will, Sigil," I said impatiently, "and get on with it."

"As you wish," Sigil replied, a slight nod of agreement from him. "Each one of you can return to *normal* life here if you wish, for you have that *choice*. I will not seek to stop you. That is not my way. However, you will forevermore wonder what it was that you missed, what magnificent destiny it was that you denied yourself. Here, you will have the power that this world has granted only to its mythological heroes—power enough to make your life an easy thing, a comfortable thing. Perhaps you will even have the power to make a difference in this world, power enough to shape or reshape the lives of those around you for the betterment of all."

Sigil's eyes flared with purple fury.

"But you will *never* see this fairy tale to its pleasant, idyllic end! Lord Valthrustra will make that a *certainty*! He will begin with those whom you love and he will slowly, painfully damn them to a soulless existence as powerslaves for his planet-consuming soul batteries. He will make you live with the knowledge that you were powerless to save them. He will *make* you know. He will invade your every waking and dreaming thought with the knowledge that you have *failed* those you love. He will play the cat to your helpless mouse while he rapes this world of its essence—its very life force—and perverts it to his own twisted ends. Yes," Sigil said, his voice choked with a rare display of emotion, "you will *live*, certainly enough, just long enough to *die* forever. *That* is your choice, my friends. *That* will be your fate if you choose the easy way. This world that you have come to love will burn in black flames, its multitude of souls screaming out in soul-pain forever in the hellish throes of the Void!"

Sigil sat back then, his face flushed with deep blush lines of purple as the import of his fiery words burned into our minds. He had us and he knew it. The bastard. He had waited until the draining effect of *The Weird* had worked its numbing magick upon us, transformed us into whatever we had become. And then, while we were dazed and confused, had delivered his *coup-de-grace* with the finality that only an Archimage could deliver. Or a revivalist preacher. Sigil had chosen his scapegoats well, I'd grant him that. Not one of us would pass up the opportunity to "save the world," good little heroes that we were, especially since our families and friends *lived* here. And our roles were, according to Sigil, already written in fire, etched in stone, and all that other good stuff. Even the Blind Man could see how obvious a no-win situation this had become. But, speaking for all of us, I was damn sure that we would try our best to improvise and end up with a standing ovation before we exited stage left from the Stage of the Damned.

"You make one hell of a point, Sigil," I said, speaking for my friends, who, by their expressions had already reached the same damning conclusion. "We've got about as much of a choice of roles as He did. Still, what good is power without responsibility? What good is the martyr without the Cause? Yes, Sigil," I said, staring hard at him, "we'll *gladly* go along with *your* plan. But—and I mean *but*—if I see it going sour like it did those oh so many years ago on SenZar, I swear to you—*we swear to you!*—that we'll go riding on a witch hunt that will set this world on fire, and we'll fuck up as much as we can before this shithouse goes up in flames!"

There was a grim, silent pact between us then, sealed with a shared nod and a tightened fist. It was a soul covenant, like Guthal's blood-oath, which bound us together tighter than any contract or quest ever could. Sigil nodded his understanding, conceding the point.

We had grown in our exile. Grown powerful, according to Sigil. Grown hateful, according to ourselves.

Death could do that to a soul. Now he knew our Price. Now it was time for business.

CHAPTER 18: A'Hoarding We Will Go

"What the hell," I said, diffusing the tension. "Let's get on with it. Whatever *it* is. This *Weird* shit is starting to make us all a bit weird."

I didn't expect the laughs that I got. In any event, I got up from the floor, unkinked my legs, and helped Samantha up. Not that she needed it. I was only being considerate. Now that she was once more Samantha Silverdancer, the Mystic Assassin, she could have flipped up and stuck to the ceiling like a ninja from *Shogun Assassin* if she would have wanted to, I'm sure.

Anyway, as a group we all got off our duffs and shook out the bats from our belfries. Then, of course, we all stood around like newly animated mannequins, looking over ourselves with unabashed awe, checking out how things worked now. Once we were all standing up and ogling each other, I suddenly knew why my "weird" remark had set them all to laughter.

Hell, we *were* weird. I guess I now was the most "normal" looking person in the room, barring my "Star-Eyes," as the Mokarr bitch had so succinctly put it, and my long black hair. Normal. Right. Anyway, Samantha's long white hair, her height, and her Fae features made her very distinctly *interesting*. Guthal looked a helluva lot like Yosemite Sam on steroids; short and stocky at about five feet and some change, but massing out at some two hundred sixty-pounds of pure gristled muscle. Sammy—a third of Guthal's mass and a good foot or so shorter—resembled, eerily enough, a well-proportioned Bilbo Baggins with shoulder-length brown hair, sans the hairy feet and pot belly. But the only "Hobbit" that Mad Sam truly resembled was, perhaps, one in the vein of the sharpened toenails variety, straight out of the classic spoof, "Bored of the Rings." Tal'N was the Man of Bronze reincarnated with wild hair and Shy'R Honor Crest. Now that he was standing, I could see that he had grown an extra inch or so in height, yet had managed to keep his same chiseled proportions as before. So that made him about three inches taller than me now, as well as some forty or so pounds heavier than me now, too, considering his formidable upper-body development. Zaar was, well, Big, Blue, and Scary; a white mohawked four-armed genie with a seven-one, five hundred fifty pound "gangsta" attitude.

And Sigil was the freak of all freaks, or at least that's what I told him he was.

Anyway, we looked first at ourselves, then one another, then checked things out. Things like gravity, for instance.

Sammy, feeling his newfound oats, suddenly let out a "*Wee!*" and proceeded to cartwheel across the room, spinning like a madman, out of control and into the wall, where he promptly dislodged a reproduction of Van Gogh's *Starry Night*, which promptly came down on his head with a heavy thud of its mahogany frame.

Guthal was the first one to his side, but Sammy waved him off, a disgusted look on his face.

"Sheep shit!" he cursed, rubbing his head with both hands as he rose to his feet.

"You *meant* to do that, huh?" Zaar teased.

"Aww, go eat yourself, you big blue banana head!" Sammy blurted, flying the finger the whole while to any and all who were looking at him. "I just got a little bit out of control, that's all. I'm not used to being this, uhh, this potent."

"Sammy's always been *im*-potent before, you know!" Zaar said, shaking with laughter. This prompted more laughter from us. And more disdain from Sammy.

Suddenly, Guthal got a strange light in his eyes. You could almost see the light bulb flash on above his head. Snapping his fingers, he suddenly ran out the room. I looked over at Samantha, who just shrugged, still concerned about the painting, which she probably valued more highly than Sammy's rock hard head. In less than a minute, he returned, a fireplace poker in his hands, along with a couple of those other strange iron things that always accompany the one nameable thing in the fire-tending arsenal.

We looked at him as if he had gone mad.

Guthal stood there, grinning like an idiot, while he waited for us to board his train of thought.

"No thanks, man," Tal'N said, ending the drought as he pulled his combat knife out, "I've already got something."

"Hey!" Sammy shouted. "I thought *I* had that!" he exclaimed, exaggerating his "pretend-to-search-for-something" movements.

"I was lying about your dagger skills," Tal'N mocked him, wrist-rolling the dagger up and down both arms. "And you're not half the 'rogue' you pretend to be. I could have stolen your own ovaries from you."

"No, you big golden idjit!" an exasperated Guthal said, rattling the fire tending implements. He had to pause a moment, however, to properly pile on and mock a distraught Sammy. "Tal'N, you fuck. That was funny. Stealing from the Master Rogue himself, then dissing his dagger skills! However, now, it's time for a test! A test of strength, get it?"

"All right, then," Sammy said, his eyes mischievous, "you go first, Guthal. Breathe on 'em, and see if they bend."

"Asshole!" Guthal swore, taking a swipe at Sammy's head with the poker. He missed, of course, but the effect was impressive nonetheless. The poker, continuing on in a vicious arc, whacked the once-maligned Van Gogh painting, splintering the near side of its hardwood frame and slashing a good six inches of its canvas.

"Slowpoke!" Sammy taunted, his hands making moose horns on his head.

"Stop it, you goons!" Samantha yelled, moving between the two of them. "Don't you two have any brains? You could have taken Sammy's head off, Guthal! Look what you did to that frame! That could have been his head, you know."

"I-I'm sorry, Samantha," Guthal stammered, the impact of his swing dawning on him. "I don't know what came over me. I just reacted. It was just instinct, like we'd done this a thousand times before, always with the same result."

"That was a nasty strike, Guthal," Tal'N said, stooping to examine the trashed frame. With a smooth motion of his right hand, he reached over and relieved Guthal of the bent poker, his expert eyes at once combing it for data. "Let's see. This is wrought pig iron with a heat cast coating of brass. You put more than a good dent in it, too. Look," he said, holding it out for Guthal to see, "you compromised its integrity!" With a quick pass of his hand over the end of the poker, Tal'N snapped it off with a *thuk* and handed it back to the unbelieving Khazak.

"What kind of stress dynamics were *those*?" Sammy asked, sauntering up to Guthal and taking a scientist's view of the poker.

"Damn serious ones, Sammy," Guthal responded in an awed monotone.

"NFL offensive lineman, maybe?" Sammy posited, scratching his head. "Budding, mutant superhero maybe—like spider strength or something?"

"Well, mon," Zaar said, walking over with a smirk on his genie face, "then let's see what Poppa Luther can do with the lil' things!"

At a speed that belied his massive form, he took the iron fire tools from Guthal and went to work on them with his howitzer biceps. As we stood there gaping, Zaar *wasted* them, twisting them into a demented new wave sculpture as easily as if he were twisting taffy. Expletives weren't deleted.

The van trick earlier tonight had just been an appetizer. We knew without saying that we had

seen things even more ludicrous from him before, back on SenZar. But here, on Earth, the picture

was somehow incomplete. What was missing?

"Didn't you use to have some sort of magick to do that with, Zaar?" I asked, trying hard to remember what it had been. As much as I did remember now, I was aware of a telling gap or two in my memory. I chalked it up to the trauma of death, that ultimate amnesia.

"That he did, Tatternorn!" Sigil announced, a soft hum of magick power emanating from his person as he drew a strange dark cloth resembling a handkerchief from his left sleeve. Holding the weird handkerchief out with his right hand, he passed his left hand over it once, muttering something in a language that I couldn't make out clearly over the hum. Then, with a flourish of prestidigitation, Sigil pulled forth from the cloth a giant-sized golden girdle and its accompanying armor plated spiked suspenders. By girdle, I mean, of course, the macho variety, like the kind worn by the Roman centurions. And by spikes (jutting from the armored suspender supports, which extended to cover the exteriors of the bearer's upper arms and his legs; with "upper arms" of course indicating our favorite Azaar) I mean the kind worn by a foam-flecked mad dog.

The whole conjuration reminded me of a Bullwinkle routine, though, despite its obvious *Yellow Submarine* portable hole connotation. I half expected Sigil to say "Hey Rocky! Watch me pull a war harness out of my hat!"

"Ahh, yes, mon!" Zaar yelled, beaming with pride. "The war harness! Now that's something I never expected to see again!"

Upon saying that, Zaar strode over to Sigil and accepted his old war harness, the War Harness of Gor-Gar (not to be confused with the mutant dinosaur thing from Zaar's *Weird*) Bloodbath, a Sauran warlord whom he had bested in personal combat—in one of the bloodiest, most violent ones I have ever witnessed—about a year after we had begun adventuring together as the Seven Stars. He had claimed it as a trophy along with the Sauran fiend's head. Its magickal properties were impressive. Among other lesser ones, it made him extremely resistant to the element of fire, much like the dragon lord who supposedly had enchanted it in the Sixth Age. Its most impressive asset, however, was its strength-enhancing ability, amplifying its wearer's natural physical strength by some tenfold. For a normal person this would be enough to be intimidating. For Zaar, the strongest Azaar who had ever lived, it was heinous.

"Where'd you find this, Sigil?" Zaar asked as he strapped the huge girdle and accompanying spiked plates on, taking his time so as not to poke himself with the suspender spikes, which were, as I recalled, sharp enough to scratch diamonds. Something that he had frequently used them for to weed out the paste gems from the real jewels after many an adventure.

"An interesting query, that," Sigil responded, signaling with his eyes that we were to listen to him. Not that we weren't, mind you. He *was* talking about *loot*. "Back in the final battle—the one of your dreams—we, along with our personal effects, were blasted through a rather mean-minded spacetime warp which shredded most of what we possessed—including your physical bodies, I might add; the effects much akin to the effects of an interrupted *Master Warp*—into entropied junk. Many of our things did not survive the trip. However, some of our things did."

Hoard lights shined in six pairs of eyes.

"The ones which did survive were the most powerful items—items which were enchanted to the highest possible level of power by the most powerful of artificers. Even then, there was a factor of chance to consider, one for which there is no magickal precaution."

"Then god does play dice with the universe!" I exclaimed. That Einstein quote had always bothered me for some strange reason.

"Yes and no, Tatternorn," Sigil replied, an uncharacteristic smirk on his face, "but the cast of the die depends upon the nature of the game. In this particular game, we have yet to know those governing rules. Now," he continued, "some things were lost while others were not. Of those latter things, you see two here before you: Skurge and the War Harness of Gor-Gar Bloodbath. And, as I am certain that you are remembering even as we speak, we had many more things of the latter category; the gains of heroes, as it were. One of them—the final item that I have managed to obtain through my own weakened personal energies—is one that Master Samuel, in his ever-hoarding ways, might find interesting."

As Sammy's eyes lit up with hoard-glee, Sigil produced from his illusory Michael Murphy black leather trench coat a small purple tobacco pouch, which was tied with an intricately braided knot of dragon beard. Sammy, recognizing it at once, started to jump around spastically, waving his arms like a castaway who had just seen his ship sail in.

"My pouch! My hidey-pouch! Oboy! Now I can hoard anything I want!" He cartwheeled over to Sigil and made a courtly bow, then snatched the pouch from Sigil's hands so fast that it looked as if it had suddenly materialized in Sammy's hands.

Sammy's hoard-glee was quite easy to rationalize considering the nifty little item that he had just regained. His "hidey-pouch," or his Ultimate X-Bag, as it was known to those who wished they could possess it themselves, was an extradimensional (hence the "X") storage space of insane, warehouse-sized dimensions. It took very little perception to realize that, very soon indeed, the Snifer Supreme would renew his old snifin' ways, and all Terran computer stores and comic book shops would know fear. If the damned thing weren't already stuffed to the brim with SenZar goodies, that is.

As Sammy ran off to a secluded corner of the room to set to work on sorting out his long-lost hoard inventory, I asked Sigil the obvious question:

"So where's the Krystallstaff?"

Even as I asked my question, I could see what was coming. We were going to have to track down the rest of our things, to equip ourselves as best as possible for the battle yet to come. As powerful as we were now—even with Skurge in our clutches—we had to have every hidden ace in our hands to win. That, and some serious ass kicking luck on our sides, because Lord Valthrustra was the dealer, and he was a notorious cheat.

"Ahh, yes, the first item on our agenda," Sigil said, exhaling sharply. "The Krystallstaff—which is, as you know, my focus of power—is in Los Alamos, New Mexico."

"Where?" I asked, wondering if I had heard him correctly.

"Los Alamos, New Mexico," Sigil repeated, a little more slowly for my benefit. "That is where we must first go."

"What in the hell is it doing there? Sightseeing in the desert, or whacking tarantulas?" Samantha asked cynically. Guthal and Tal'N exchanged glances, wondering who was going to explain it first. Tal'N hunched his shoulders and smiled at Samantha.

"New Mexico isn't all desert and tarantulas, Samantha," he said, still smiling.

"It just so happens that there's a pretty high tech installation there," Guthal added quickly. "One—a government one—that deals with high energy experiments and all that good quantum physics stuff. If you remember your American history, you'll remember something called 'The Manhattan Project,' the code name for the research during WWII that led to the atomic bomb. A lot of it was done there in Los Alamos. The bomb itself was detonated on or around July 16, 1945, near Alamogordo, which is a little to the south of Albuquerque."

"Enough on the history lesson, Guthal," I said, cutting him off before he could really get going. He could be just as annoying as Sammy when he went off. "Why is Los Alamos so important? Why would Sigil's staff be there?"

"Because that's where the Los Alamos National Laboratory is! You know, 'The Hill?'" Guthal said breathlessly, his eyes wide in his exasperation with my devoid-of-science Liberal Arts background. "It makes perfect sense if you consider the channels the government works through. I guess it would depend on how, when, and where they found it, but I can tell you that something like the Krystallstaff would rate an eleven on a scale of one to ten in R&D priority! Chances are, they have it in the High Energy Lab, or H.E.L., as they not so jokingly call it. It's kind of like Hangar 18, but underground; guarded by all sorts of 'hell' from high tech static defenses to active, highly trained human defenses. SAP security clearance just to get in the doors."

Sigil eyed Guthal carefully for a moment.

"Then it will be more than difficult to secure?"

"You'd have a better chance of playing the Lotto without using your clairvoyance, Sigil."

"Then that explains why Lord Valthrustra hasn't gotten his hands on it yet," I said.

"Perfectly, though not for lack of trying, I'm sure," Sigil said, lowering his head.

"Maybe we can get something else first, then go pick it up?" Tal'N said, making it sound all the more like some easy shopping mall list.

"No," Sigil said, still not looking up, "that is out of the question. Without the staff's power to aid us, we will never acquire the other items in time."

"Well, if time is the most important factor," I said, "then why don't you just snap your fingers and transport us to it? You can scry it first, then you can transport us to it, just like in the old days, right?"

"I'm afraid it's not quite so simple, Tatternorn," Sigil admitted, finally looking at me. "If such were the case, I would already possess your items, along with Lord Valthrustra's head. Alas, his power is the stronger here. He has had more time to consolidate it, while we were in the daze of unbeing. His power is such that without the staff to back us up, he will trace our transport and annihilate us in transit. That is why I have had to push myself so hard to mask my own transits—to cover my tracks with more energy, a very draining thing, I can assure you. To mask a group transport is in the realm of impossible given my current status. And to attempt to retrieve the other items—we need every one of them, too!—is foolhardy to the extreme without the staff's power. It simply must be the first thing that we retrieve, or everything falls out of joint, the pieces of the chessboard lost before the board is set."

"I don't like this chess shit," Zaar growled, staring hard at Sigil. I had to admit that I didn't like it, either. "Chess has pawns. Pawns are like slaves. We aren't your slaves, Sigil."

"Are you sure that you just don't want *your* toys first?" Sammy quickly asked from the corner, trying to cover for Zaar, who looked like he was about to pounce on Sigil.

"As you well know, Samuel," Sigil said, his voice for the first time cracking, "a spellcaster must draw upon many sources of power to employ his arts. The Krystallstaff is an extension of my own soul. Without it, I am less than I am. With it, I am more. With it, we will be able to move faster, perhaps fast enough to arm ourselves to the teeth and achieve our goal before the allotted time."

"Which is?" I asked, sensing that I wasn't going to like the answer.

"Ash Wednesday."

Well wasn't that fitting. The irony did not escape me, considering the Shadar penchant for raining on parades. So much for making it big in the world of music. See ya, Mardi Gras! See ya, MTV! I have to go save the world!

"SHIT!" I yelled, not caring if I shredded my vocal chords now.

I got a few stares.

"Well," I asked, regaining my composure, "why don't you at least tell us what we're missing out on, Sigil? What else is on our cosmic shopping list?"

"Yes, of course," he said wearily. "Some incentive for my pawns, as you would put it." He looked at Zaar, then at me, then shook his head. "Forgive me, Zaar; Tatternorn. I am feeling all too human at this moment. The stress of the past few days has been unbearable."

"Yeah, sure," I said, looking away, "for all of us."

"As for the other items," he began, "I know what I have heard whispered by the wind, spoken by the rain. There is yet Samuel's Shadowcloak—near to us, yet hidden completely from my eyes. The staff will make its location clear to me, of that I am certain. There is yet Guthal's battle axe, the mighty Axe of Thrumble, and his silversteel battle armor. There is Silverdancer's Soulsword. There are Tal'N's twin blades, Warhawk's Avenging Talons. And then there is Tark, Rhiannazaar's Asperim demon blade. Many of these artifacts we won on SenZar while adventuring as the Seven Stars. And we shall win them again, here on Earth, as the Seven Stars."

More hoard lights shined. It looked like even Zaar was reconsidering his "slave" remark. Slaves don't usually get artifacts.

"There is every possibility that other items may have survived, hidden from my perception," Sigil continued, suddenly breathing heavily. "The Krystallstaff will illuminate this darkened path once we have found it. But find it we must. And soon."

With that ominous pronouncement, Sigil swooned and fell forwards, eyes fluttering. Without thinking, I intercepted his fall, catching him in my left arm, then gently lowered him to the floor. He was nothing but sinew and steel in my grasp, even though he was a lot lighter than I would have imagined.

As a group we gathered around Sigil, all of our earlier aggression toward him melting away like the most fickle of snowfalls. Almost immediately he began to speak.

"Do not concern yourself with me," Sigil said, his voice little more than a hoarse whisper. "My strength shall return, provided I rest." He turned his head up to me and smiled faintly, reassuringly, in the same Sigil way that I had seen him do before back on SenZar when he had been on his last legs. It dawned on me that he must be drawing upon his own personal reserves and more—like his own life force—to do what he had been doing tonight, as weak as he was in this world that had tipped its balance of power toward the Dark One. He needed the staff, as much as a sun-bleached man needed a drink of water.

And that, despite anything that he had said, suddenly made the Krystallstaff Priority Numero Uno.

"Tal'N?" I asked, still looking at Sigil.

"Yes?"

"Didn't you say that you were watched at the airport?"

"Yep. It was probably one of those Mokarr goons."

"Then flying there is out of the question. Valthrustra would probably nuke the plane. Sammy?"

"Yeah, yeah I know!" he hooted, "I know what you're gonna say next: How long will it take to drive there? Then you'll ask me, Is your van gassed up? Tell me I'm wrong!"

I shook my head and smiled like the Big Bad Wolf.

Continued in *The Roads to Madness - Book II of The SenZar Evolution*

THE SEVEN STARS – BOOK I OF THE SENZAR EVOLUTION

Published by Anshadar, LLC. 3645 South Truckee Way, Aurora CO 80013

mobi ISBN: 978-1-7329802-6-6

epub ISBN: 978-1-7329802-7-3

DAVE NEWTON AND TODD KING

Dave Newton & Todd King

Dave and Todd met at NASA, and bonded over shared experiences – as in roleplaying game design, gaming, and MMOs. When Todd brought up the idea of writing again, Dave mentioned that he had some ideas percolating. These ideas meshed well with the ideas Todd had, and the two decided it had to happen. There was a story to be told, and the more they worked on it, the bigger it became, until the scope was cosmic. The two of them formed

Anshadar, LLC to create the new world of EarthZero, wherein they and others will explore the boundaries of magick, morphogenetics, hekatek, and Simulation Theory.

Dave lives in Colorado with his wife and two daughters. He's discovered he doesn't hate the snow. He listens to music, is a DJ for a pirate radio station in his spare time, and is a prolific reader. He has written and co-written a variety of roleplaying games and fiction, including The Mythus FRPG, Rapture: the Second Coming, Twisted Bedtime Stories and Quest! Roleplaying for Kids.

Todd has served as a contractor for various federal agencies, including DoD, MDA, and NASA, producing multiple intellectual properties in disparate realms, including Chaotic Systems, Cryptography, Logistics, and Nanotechnology. Previously, he mutated from lead guitarist to vocalist, playing in several bands, including Zaemon Blaiz, in the southern heavy metal scene, opening for acts as diverse as Lynyrd Skynyrd and Pantera. He created the SenZar role-playing game, which sold in 14 countries, and has virally influenced certain Void themes in both the current tabletop and computer genres.

TODD KING

Dedication

From Todd: To my awesome wife, Renee, the better angel of my soul. To my two SenZar co-creators, The Brüne & Joseph Giacone, for the game. To Roland Paris, David Catoire, Faith Newton, and our whole SenZar and Anshadar crew for the awesome art. To Gary Gygax and Dave Newton for the FRPG inspiration. To Stan Lee and countless Marvel, DC, and other creators for the superhero inspiration. To H. P. Lovecraft, Robert E. Howard, Boris Pasternak,

Lester Dent, Kahlil Gibran, Tom Clancy, Stephen King, Gregory Widen, Anne Rice, Dr. Seuss, Dave Barry, Looney Tunes, Gene Roddenberry, George Lucas, Robin Williams, Richard Pryor, Sam Kinison, Jim Starlin, and Alan Moore for their words and art. To Niccolò Paganini, Yngwie J. Malmsteen, Stevie Ray Vaughan, Steve Vai, Van Halen, Iron Butterfly, Jimi Hendrix, Shawn Lane, Queensrÿche, Fear, Zebra, NWA, Crimson Glory, Kiss, Lillian Axe, Lynyrd Skynyrd, Pantera, Metallica, Megadeth, Iron Maiden, Black Sabbath, Ozzy Osbourne, Prince, Earth, Rush, Billy Sheehan, Paul David Harbour, Philip Anselmo, Sting, J.S. Bach, Wind & Fire, Adrian Belew, Led Zeppelin, The Doors, Stevie Wonder, Soundgarden, Trent Reznor, Tom Jones, and Zaemon Blaiz for their music. To Big J for all the great gigs; we miss you, Jim. To all of my SenZar players for the fun. To all of my music fans for sharing some fun times.

Anshadar, LLC is pleased to present the first novel in the series: *The Seven Stars - Book I of The SenZar Evolution.* Stay tuned as we give you more science fiction, fantasy, and horror.

Quest! Roleplaying for Kids by Dave & Christi Newton

The Lightbringer's Sigil - Book I of The EarthZero Evolution by Dave Newton and Todd King

The Anshadar Effect - Book II of The EarthZero Evolution by Dave Newton and Todd King

The Death Horde- Book III of The EarthZero Evolution by Dave Newton and Todd King (coming soon)

Bloody Kudzu by Dave Newton (coming soon)

The Seven Stars - Book I of The SenZar Evolution by Todd King

The Roads to Madness - Book II of The SenZar Evolution by Todd King (coming soon)

The End of All Things - Book III of The SenZar Evolution by Todd King (coming soon)

VoidSpawn - Book IV of The SenZar Evolution by Todd King (coming soon)

The Far Side of Shadow - Book V of The SenZar Evolution by Todd King (coming soon)

The Eye of Chaos - Book VI of The SenZar Evolution by Todd King (coming soon)

The God Wars - Book VII of The SenZar Evolution by Todd King (coming soon)